Tuesday, September 1

City of Saviors

CITY OF SAVIORS

SAVIORS

Rachel Howzell Hall

A TOM DOHERTY ASSOCIATES BOOK

NEW YORK

CITY OF SAVIORS

Copyright © 2017 by Rachel Howzell Hall

All rights reserved.

A Forge Book
Published by Tom Doherty Associates
175 Fifth Avenue
New York, NY 10010

www.tor-forge.com

Forge® is a registered trademark of Macmillan Publishing Group, LLC.

The Library of Congress Cataloging-in-Publication Data is available upon request.

ISBN 978-0-7653-8119-4 (hardcover)
ISBN 978-1-4668-7804-4 (ebook)

Our books may be purchased in bulk for promotional, educational, or business use. Please contact your local bookseller or the Macmillan Corporate and Premium Sales Department at 1-800-221-7945, extension 5442, or by email at MacmillanSpecialMarkets@macmillan.com.

First Edition: August 2017

Printed in the United States of America

0 9 8 7 6 5 4 3 2 1

For Jill

Acknowledgments

Five years ago, all I knew was this: I wanted to create a heroine who would help rewrite the story of mysteries set in a city that I loved. I wanted to create a heroine with a big heart, a quick quip, and the desire to live her best life. I've wanted many things before and have been told "no" a lot. But this time, I was told "yes," and Detective Lou Norton got her chance.

Thank you, Jill Marsal, for being an extraordinary agent—I've benefited greatly from your tenacity and wisdom, from your belief in this character and her LA story. Thank you, Kristin Sevick, for championing this series, for your "Attagirl" for both Lou and me and rallying the good folks at Forge on my behalf.

City of Saviors required that I learn some things, and I'd like to thank retired detective lieutenant (and Forge label-mate) Neal Griffin and retired "Deputy Dave" Putnam for answering my many questions. Thanks to my childhood friend Lori Nelson, M.D., for helping me make Lou sick. D.P. Lyle, M.D., you are a national treasure to crime writers everywhere, and I thank you for your expertise. My siblings Gretchen, Jason, and Terry, thanks for answering random questions that always come up when I'm writing a story. My parents Nate and Jackie, I'm forever grateful for your love and support. David and Maya, you are my rocks, my fellow adventurers, my loves. Thank you for your patience and enthusiasm and understanding and acceptance. It means so much to me.

I was as hollow and empty as the spaces between the stars.

RAYMOND CHANDLER, *The Long Goodbye*

1

The three off-duty, red-faced cops seated in brown vinyl chairs had been broken—by guns, by fists, by life. And at eight o'clock in the morning, I sat across from them, in the sun-brightened waiting room of Matthew Popov, M.D. I harbored fractures, too—mine were as fine as cracks in a china cup that still held tea. But the trio didn't see me or my cracks after their T&A check. Just their casts, their bandages, their bruised balls.

"Them kids just don't get it," crew-cut Darren complained. "It ain't always about color. You look suspicious? I'm gonna stop you."

The nerve beneath my left eye twitched, and the stress headache spilled across my forehead like warm milk. I snatched the month-old issue of *People* from the coffee table. One glance at the cover—BABY DRAMA FOR KIM—and I tossed the rag back into the swamp of "Divorce Looms for Jon!" and "Charlie's Drunken Night!"

With my God-given tan, camel-colored pantsuit, and delicate ankles, I'm sure crew-cut Darren assumed that a computer keyboard had caused my job injury. Carpal tunnel syndrome from typing some true detective's paperwork. What would he say if he knew that I was *that* Elouise Norton who had rammed a Toyota Rav4 into a Parks and Rec truck high above Los Angeles? That I'd fractured my left arm, cracked two ribs, and concussed my head in the process? That the monster who had killed Chanita Lords and other girls from my old neighborhood had flown through the windshield and chopped into pieces all because he hadn't worn a seat belt on the way to the place he wanted to kill me? What would Darren say if he knew that I was *that* Elouise Norton?

Good job, Lou.

Why'd you do something stupid like that?

You got a death wish?

My phone vibrated from my bag—a text message. *How was your appointment? Don't forget we're bringing breakfast on Saturday morning. See you then. Love u, Mom.* She'd discovered emoticons, and now there were sixty pink hearts trailing "Mom."

Haven't gone in yet, I texted back. *I'll call later. Love u, too.* Then, I tapped the Scrabble app.

Darren was now rubbing his tattooed left calf as he told Brad and Tony about chasing some banger-trash down Hoover Avenue. "Then, that summabitch hopped over the fuckin' fence like Hussein Bolt."

Tony laughed. "Usain Holt, dumb ass."

Usain Bolt and you both are dumb asses.

"What the fuck ever," Darren said. "I jumped over, too—that's my point—and tore my ACL. Can you believe it?"

Out in the parking lot, a gardener wielded a leaf blower. Dead foliage and grit swirled around him like confetti. A garden party.

My phone vibrated again. *Get felt up yet? Call me later. I have a proposition.* My best friend, Lena Meadows, had also used emoticons—ones that my mother hadn't discovered yet. A lipstick print, a martini glass, and a smiling purple devil.

I texted Lena back. *A proposition? Doesn't sound healthy nor wholesome. I rebuke you.*

No message from Syeeda McKay, my other best friend. Or former best friend. Or . . . Relationship status: *it's complicated.*

The door that led to the exam rooms opened. A doe-eyed blonde nurse called out. "Elouise Norton?"

In the vitals alcove, the nurse took my blood pressure (138/90), my weight (120 pounds), and my temperature (99.3). She cocked an eyebrow as she recorded the results in my chart. Then, she led me to the bathroom.

After peeing in a plastic cup, I followed her into exam room 8. I placed my bag in the chair, undressed, then pulled on a blue gown with thousands of ties. With nothing else to do but sit, I studied the posters on the walls.

DID YOU GET A FLU SHOT?

Nope.

LEARN THE TRUTH ABOUT HEART DISEASE.

Okay.

DO YOU HAVE POST-TRAUMATIC STRESS DISORDER?

I gulped, then clamped my jaw before sending my gaze back to flu shots and clogged arteries. And I kept them there until Dr. Popov's gray eyes bore into mine.

His wintergreen breath had almost covered the smell of coffee. "Your blood pressure's up," he said. "Has your pressure been high lately?"

I futzed with one of the ties on the gown. "No."

His large soft hands tilted my head this way and that. "Have you been charting it with the machine I gave you?"

"Yes."

"Are you in pain right now?"

My cheeks warmed. "No."

Three lies told in less than twenty seconds. The Hussein Holt of Lying.

Dr. Popov consulted my chart. "You taking anything for the pain you're *not* having?"

"Ibuprofen every now and then." My nose ached from growing so much and so quickly. "I've been taking allergy meds. A lot of fires burning right now."

"Your elevated BP is a little worrisome. Hasn't been this high since I cleared you three weeks ago for normal duty." The doctor squinted at me. "You smoke?"

"No."

"You drinking?"

I cracked a smile. "What do you have?"

"Seriously. Are you drinking?"

We held each other's eyes. My underarms prickled with sweat, and my upper lip twitched.

Dr. Popov sighed, then examined the last scars high above my right eye, my right ear, and behind my hairline. He pressed on the scalp wound, then held up his fingers. Blood. "You have to stop scratching that. It starts to scab, but then . . ."

"I keep forgetting it's there," I said. "I'll stop. Promise."

"Does it still hurt?"

My eyes watered as though his fingers were still pressing the wound. "No."

"You sure? I see tears."

"Allergies because of all the fires."

"You didn't take anything this morning?" he asked.

I shook my head. "Didn't want to compromise my urine test."

"We can tell Claritin from Percocet. The miracle of science." Then, he lifted my left arm.

A dull twang spun in my shoulder like a pinwheel.

"You winced," he said.

"Sore from physical therapy." I smiled. "And I'm back in Krav Maga for strength training."

True, and true.

My phone *caw-cawed* from the inside of my bag—the eagle ringtone for my partner, Colin Taggert.

"When you're sore like this," Dr. Popov was saying, "what do you do?"

"Heating pad and Icy Hot," I replied. "Long baths and hot showers."

After promising to lower my numbers through clean living and exercise, and after receiving a flu shot, I trudged to the scheduling desk where the doe-eyed blonde nurse pulled up a calendar to schedule my next visit.

The eagle *caw-cawed* from my bag again. This time, I answered. "Happy Tuesday."

"It's not even nine o'clock yet," Colin complained, "and it's already eighty-six degrees."

A heat wave now roasted Los Angeles—yesterday, we hit 103 degrees in the Valley, 94 degrees downtown, and enjoyed 80 percent humidity, courtesy of a hurricane currently destroying Baja California. Fires to the north of us, fires to the south of us, fires to the east of us. All we needed was an earthquake and a Sig Alert on the 405 freeway to complete the "Seasons of LA" bingo card.

I stepped away from the scheduling desk and wandered to a corner. "What's up?"

"All these fires are making my eyes itch," Colin whined.

"You use the drops I gave you?"

"No."

"Then stop complaining."

"We're on deck," he announced.

"Just when I was about to go out on the yacht."

"So, you're driving to 8711 Victoria Avenue, off Crenshaw and Vernon."

"What's today's special?"

"A suspicious death. An old guy dead in his old house."

"Dead, you say?"

"Seniors are droppin' from the heat. It's like we're standing on hell's patio."

I gave the doe-eyed blonde nurse the "one minute, please" finger, then said to Colin, "Old guy, old house, no A/C probably. Nothing suspicious about that. This shouldn't take long."

"You'll get to go out on the yacht after all," he said.

I scheduled my next appointment for October 2nd, then left the medical office of Matthew Popov, M.D., with a bloody wound in my hair, sparks shooting in my shoulders, and sparks shooting at the base of my skull.

I was *healed*.

At the lobby gift shop, I purchased a bottled water and a morning bag of Doritos (*baked* Doritos: my first step toward clean living). By the time the elevator stopped at P2, I'd already popped four Advil and a Claritin. I stepped out of the air-conditioned car and into the muggy underground parking garage. My eyes flitted from dark corner to darker corner. Shadows. Weird echoes.

A man stood . . . by the . . . ? *What is he . . . ? He looks like . . .* him. *But's he dead. Right?*

That's what I'd been told. That's what I'd read. But those seconds before the crash . . . couldn't remember.

I darted to my Porsche Cayenne with my heart pounding, my nerves frayed, my lungs pinched so hard I could barely breathe.

The same state I'd been in when I first arrived.

That shadow moved . . . The man, his shadow . . .

No. Don't go there. Just the wind. Dr. Bernie Shankman's soothing baritone filled my head. *Just the wind blowing, Elouise. Just the wind. Take a breath. Take a breath.*

I reached my car, panting as though I'd run a mile in a minute. Knees weak, I leaned against the car door with my eyes squeezed shut.

Your pounding heart? That's the wind. The scent of a man's cologne— but it smelled like *his* cologne—*that's the wind, too. Just the wind, Elouise. Breathe. Breathe.*

Second time in an hour that I'd employed visualization to coax me off the ledge.

And now, in my mind's eye, I reclined in a chaise surrounded by palm trees. I was relaxing on my favorite Big Island beach. The breeze lifted my hair and ferried the aroma of Lava Lava Club's sticky-sweet drinks and pineapple-fried rice. Waves. Fluffy white clouds. Blue sky. Quiet. So quiet.

"Open your eyes," I whispered.

I was still hunkered in the dark parking garage. But there were no ghosts now. No shadowy man in the corner. No Zach Fletcher.

Yet.

2

Dr. Shankman's relaxation technique worked. Even after a three-minute conversation with my mother, Georgia—*how'd it go, what did he give you, do you need to take it easy, do you still like bagels?*—my breathing had slowed, and my hands had lost some of their clamminess. But then that clamminess could've been caused by the weather.

It was ninety-six degrees at nine thirty, and Colin was still complaining to me over the radio about the heat. "The end times are upon us," he said, "but no one cares except for the boy from Colorado Springs." He was right—Angelenos had no fucks to give.

The city was up and at 'em. Cars and buses swooped up and down Crenshaw Boulevard. Old ladies pushed rickety carts to the Laundromats. Pods of day workers loitered at the U-Haul store. Just a few years ago, the space shuttle *Endeavor* had traveled on this wide, tree-lined street. Smiling people of all shades of brown had waved at astronauts, the mayor, and other VIPs. Crenshaw High School's marching band had jammed for us as we tucked into Styrofoam containers of Dulan's smothered chicken and black-eyed peas.

"Happy black people and rocket ships," I said, remembering that afternoon.

Colin chuckled. "God bless America."

"That's all about to change," I said.

He shouted, "The white folks are coming! The white folks are coming!"

And they were. Paler faces now cruised the aisles of Ladera Heights supermarkets, the mall in Culver City, and the hiking trails off Stocker Avenue. The new subway line would rumble beneath Crenshaw Boulevard to the airport. The Santa Barbara Plaza, where my sister Victoria was last seen alive, was now home to heavy equipment bulldozing dilapidated hair salons, night clubs, and art galleries. Replacing it: a new 8.6-acre medical facility.

"And why wouldn't we come?" Colin asked. "Rent's too damned high where I'm supposed to live. Just think: hundreds of coffee shops and benches everywhere. A Trader Joe's. Yoga studios. All kinds of white-people shit."

"Hooray. Bringing with them more ways to stay broke." I turned right at the 7-Eleven, then made another left onto Victoria Avenue.

The street had been blocked by cop cars with swirling lights, fire trucks with swirling lights, an empty ambulance that had turned off its swirling lights—never a good thing for folks who had called EMTs.

"You go in yet?" I asked Colin.

"Nope," he said. "Wanna share those first moments with you."

A firefighter in dingy yellow pants and galoshes vomited on the sidewalk. Seeing that made me sit a little longer in the car.

Colin, tanned and big-eared, weaved past the parked emergency vehicles to approach my SUV. He wore the too-small blue shirt with the stubborn taco-sauce stain on the cuff—a shirt he refused to toss because a cute assistant district attorney said the color brought out his eyes. And now he saluted me, then clicked his heels. "What's up, Sarge?"

My promotion to detective sergeant wouldn't make the dead man inside 8711 Victoria less dead or more alive. I rolled down the driver's-side window and stared at the sick hero. "Umm . . ."

"What'cha waiting for?" Colin's gaze followed mine. "Oh yeah. That."

"Why is he doing that? Vomiting?"

Colin shrugged, but the vein in his neck jumped. *Liar.* He knew something.

With ice in my belly, I climbed out of the car.

"The heat," I said. "That's probably why he's throwing up."

"A fireman not used to dead people in the summer?" Colin asked. "Sure: I'll take that answer."

Fifties-era California bungalows with square angles and wide lawns lined the block. A McMansion had been shoved into every fifth lot—an elephant crammed into a zone designed for zebras. Sunlight glinted off glass, chrome, and the badges of patrol cops gathered on the sidewalk and made Victoria Avenue disco-ball bright.

"I used the eye drops," Colin said.

"Better?"

"Yep, but looking at this place, it's not gonna matter much."

This place. A dingy yellow Craftsman with wide eaves, a raised porch, big windows . . . and a junk pile beneath the colossal magnolia tree. Another pile of junk blocked that raised porch. Another heap almost hid the rusted gray Chrysler Le Baron. Old toilets. Broken who-knows-what. Flashes of fluffy pink this and plastic black that. A breeze thick with the stink of dead things and animal urine. Weeds and large yellow dandelions sprouted between the occasional gaps of trash. Some of the junk within the piles . . . *moved.*

"Cats," Colin explained. "Cats and their enemies."

I slipped off my blazer. "Enemies—you mean mice?"

"Rats. And then, the raccoons come. They mostly come at night . . . mostly."

I swallowed. "Tetanus and rabies and . . . Aliens would be cleaner and . . . My lord, what are we about to see?"

The four uniforms gold-bricking beneath the magnolia tree glanced in our direction. Then, they whispered to each other.

My ears burned—the side eyes and gossip involved me.

"Fitzgerald, one of the jerk-wads over there," Colin said, nodding toward the klatch, "he's the R/O."

I grabbed my leather binder from the passenger seat. "He's doing the best he can with that tiny brain of his."

Tavaris Fitzgerald turtled toward us, passing a rusted toolbox, a tangled nest of wires, and an abandoned air-conditioning unit. He wiped his sweaty brown face with his wrist, then gave Colin the "what-up" nod. He regarded me as though I'd eaten the apple fritter he'd been saving all day.

"Who's our special guest this morning?" I asked him.

Fitzgerald flipped open his steno pad. "Eugene Washington. Lives here alone. A Bernice Parrish"—he pointed to the closest radio squad car, where a pair of thin brown calves ended in feet clad in dusty gladiator sandals—"found him in the den around seven fifty this morning.

She claims to be his girlfriend. Has a key to the place. Anyway, EMT got here about ten minutes later, pronounced him dead, and they've been throwing up ever since."

The now-recovered fireman was patting the back of another vomiting hero.

"And we're here because . . . ?" I asked.

"The EMTs found a gun near the body. No obvious bullet wounds, but . . ." He shrugged. "It was there and we can't ignore it." Suspicious death? Sure.

"You talk to anybody other than Bernice Parrish?" I asked Fitzgerald.

"Nope."

"Anybody other than you and the EMTs enter the house?"

The patrol cop smirked. "You don't have to worry about lookie-loos going off in there." He eyed my silk blouse, my slacks, and loafers. "Must be nice."

My face flushed and I cocked an eyebrow. "It *is* nice, thank you. Anything else?" Would he dare speak those words he had whispered behind my back today, and many days before? *Crazy bitch. Suicide queen. Ass kisser. Dick sucker.* Would he? Fitzgerald had never liked me—to him, I thought I was "all that" with my B.A. and J.D., my Porsche and silk blouses. To him, I wanted attention so much that I'd hurled myself and a small SUV into a parked truck. I had used my boobs and color to be promoted from patrol to detective and, now, detective sergeant. Overrated. Underserving. Two full scoops of cray-sins. And he was not only a member of the Screw Lou fan club—he was also the president.

Please do it. Please say something. A bead of sweat slipped across the scar above my eyebrow. The sting made me grimace and pissed me off just a little bit more.

But Fitzgerald knew better than to insult a woman packing two guns on a hot day. He said, "Vic's in the den," then turtled back past the toolbox, past the wires and past the air-conditioning unit to reach his posse beneath the tree.

"All that sexual tension," Colin said as he doused two handkerchiefs with Aqua Velva. "Thought you were gonna take him behind the house and make him a star for three minutes."

I took a hankie from him. "Well, I'm glad you stayed. If we'd been alone, I would've straddled him on top of the rotten mattress over by that hill of cat poop."

Colin and I zigzagged through metal tubes and broken Igloos, very dead felines and moldy cardboard boxes. We bounded up the porch's rickety stairs, passing four very alive cats now chillin' on banisters as though visits from homicide detectives occurred every Tuesday at nine thirty. After signing in with a round female officer who obviously had no sense of smell, I pressed the cologne-soaked hankie against my nose and stepped across the threshold and right into the living room.

Two grubby, mustard-colored armchairs faced a cold fireplace and an entertainment center holding a thirty-inch television and a VCR. Dusty paintings of lighthouses, countryscapes, and sad clowns hung lopsided on the walls. Dark crown molding, natural light, and hardwood floors in a moderately clean house would've made the cottage-cheese ceilings tolerable. But the worrisome . . . *everything else*—from the rotten carpet and the moldy walls to the vermin—was nowhere in the realm of tolerable.

"Wow," Colin said.

With the handkerchief to my face, I used my other hand to work my mini-Maglite around the room. "I spy, with my little eye . . ."

"Tetanus," Colin said.

"You said tetanus outside."

"Fine. Hantavirus. My turn. I spy, with my little eye . . ."

Atop the stack of boxes near the fireplace, a gray momma cat licked two skinny kittens nestled in her paws. "I spy feline HIV."

We moved down a dim hallway crowded with sagging boxes of vinyl record albums, mildewed stacks of *Reader's Digest*, clothes on and off hangers, beer bottles, and plates and bowls in various states of dirty, filthy, and broken. Something crunched beneath my loafer—and it wasn't dirt.

My calm was starting to flake off like old paint. With a shaky hand, I pushed the hankie harder against my nose. "Glad I had Doritos for breakfast."

The funk of bad meat, abandoned fruit, and forgotten eggs intensified with each step. In the kitchen, dishes piled high beside thousands of empty tins of cat food, plastic milk containers, and food wrappers.

Cats and clutter filled every drawer and cabinet. Two cats perched atop the fridge—the orange one had no right eye, and the gray one was just a bag of bones.

In the den, the heavy green curtains had remained closed since John Lennon's murder, and the folds in the fabric had petrified. None of this bothered Eugene Washington. Dressed in green and gray flannel pajama bottoms and a gray wifebeater, he sat in a stained plaid armchair surrounded by old newspapers, fast-food bags, soiled boxers—and a Smith and Wesson revolver. He no longer watched the *Judge Mathis* episode now playing on the ancient floor-console television—his eyelids had swollen shut.

The TV's shoebox-size remote control sat on the old man's right thigh. His right hand, covered in red welts, had clenched into a tight fist. Froth had dried on his swollen tongue now stuck between swollen blue lips, and blue splotches now colored his freckled butterscotch complexion. No blood anywhere from a gunshot wound. And a gun that big would've left its mark all over the place. Blowflies darted around his gray hair and beard. A silver cat sat atop the television, waiting.

Gee. And Dr. Matthew Popov had thought that red wine played a major role in my high-blood-pressure woes.

"At least we got here before the cats started nibbling," Colin said. "Cats don't care about *jack* when it's time to eat."

I aimed the flashlight's beam at the man's swollen blue face. His tongue, also enlarged, stuck out from between his crusted lips. "No maggots yet. No decay. Did he eat something?"

On a rusty tray beside the armchair, I spotted a half-empty forty-ounce bottle of Schlitz and a white casserole dish with blue flowers around the rim. Inside the dish was something goopy—and delicious to the roaches now stuck there. Other roaches sprinted in and out of the malt-liquor bottle and swarmed over their dying compatriots trapped in the casserole dish.

And the flies. Oh, the flies. Their buzz competed against the TV plaintiff named Cinnamon now yelling at Judge Mathis about the money being a loan and not a gift.

"I can't . . ." Colin stumbled backward, bumping against plastic milk jugs filled with worrisome yellow liquid.

The fumes of cat urine, dust and dander, and dead things made my eyes tear. Made it damn-near impossible to study the dead man before me.

There was no inhaler, no EpiPen, and no medic alert bracelet on Washington's wrist—objects often found near those with asthma or known food allergies.

I aimed the light at the man's left bicep.

The blue-black ink of a tattoo. TO HELL AND BACK 66–69 VIETNAM.

The cologne's atoms gave up and the protective power of the handkerchief disappeared. My gag reflex awakened, making me back away from Eugene Washington. With my stomach roiling, and knees threatening to dump me into a mound of fur and bones, I stumbled through the maze of trash and back out into the hot, still air.

To hell and back.

3

You will not vomit.

I tripped to the front porch. Found stability by crouching against the rotted wood banister. Willed myself to swallow spit and bile.

You will not vomit. Not now. Not in front of them.

I hid my face in the crack of my arm, and whispered, "Just the wind. Just the wind."

"I damn-near endoed off the porch." Colin's gravelly voice scraped against my tender nerves. "But almost breaking my neck kept me from hurlin' all over the—you okay, partner?"

Still flustered but less gaggy, I forced myself to stand. "I'm good."

It was hot and mean out here, but there were no crummy ceilings or dead men. At least.

Fitzgerald had slicked yellow POLICE LINE—DO NOT CROSS tape through the property's white picket fence. His partner, Monty Montez, doubled up with bloodred CAUTION BIOHAZARD tape to drive the point home. Here there be monsters and dragons and roaches and all kinds of bloody bogeymen that you can't get off your shoe soles or out of your mind.

Neighbors stood behind the tape with their arms crossed and their faces wet with sweat. Most held phones to take pictures and video. No one cried—a strange thing. Typical crime scenes came with their own soundtracks: wails to the heavens, curses at cops, *why oh why lord* and *that's my momma in there.*

This scene's soundtrack featured the gags of men, the splatters of vomit, and the purrs of cats. Tetanus and mesothelioma were silent killers.

"Being inside that house . . . that was simply remarkable." I blew my nose into the handkerchief, clearing it of insect eggs and vaporized cat poop.

"So?" Colin asked.

I rested against the banister. The urge to puke warmed my ears again. "So, what?"

"No dead people speaking to you, telling you who done it? No shining? No ghost-whispering?"

"The gun's odd, but I see no blood. Plus, he's old, it's a hundred and thirty-eight degrees today, and there's cat shit and asbestos and jugs of pee everywhere. He's *supposed* to be dead. *We're* supposed to be dead, goin' off in there unprotected."

Colin gaped at me. "But . . ."

"I get it: You want me to point to the mold on the wallpaper and say, 'Aha! Those spores originate in the mountains of Bolivia, so, someone must've planted them there two years ago to slowly kill him.' That's what you want?"

Colin's mouth moved, but no words came. Finally, he said, "Yeah. That's what I want."

"Give me a minute, then, all right? It's a hundred and thirty-eight degrees today."

A moment later, Fitzgerald and the other uniforms huddled with Colin and me on the porch. "No one goes back in there yet," I instructed. "We still need to figure out what happened. Let's put up a tarp, though, to shield the door. And from now on until forever, we'll wear full protective gear, top to bottom."

Break!

"Call the M.E.," I told Colin, "and call Zucca, too, if you could. I'll go chat with the girlfriend."

"So, you think this is murder?"

"Good question," I said, walking away from him. "Call Zucca, okay?"

Did someone kill this man? *Had* he been shot and we just couldn't see the fatal wound from our vantage point? Did he die from the heat like most of the other old people around the city and the gun just happened to be there—like the other countless pieces of crap near that armchair? Or had his lungs simply filled to capacity with dust and decided not to work anymore?

Even though my head said, "natural death," my gut said "murder." Because I knew Death—we were homies. Closer than close. Heart attacks, strokes, hypothermia—not my domain. Strangulation, gunshots, decapitations, stabbings? That was me, all day.

Once a medical examiner arrived and took possession of the body, I'd get to find out which part of me—brain or gut—would reign supreme until the next case.

Bernice Parrish sat in the front seat of Fitzgerald's squad car. Her bloodshot eyes flicked between the badge on my hip, her dead boy-friend's house, and the screen on a cell phone that matched her Pepto-pink shorts set.

I introduced myself, remembering to say "sergeant" now instead of "detective."

"I ain't done nothing," Bernice Parrish snapped.

"I ain't said that you did," I snapped back.

This woman knew her way around a rat-tail comb, edge-control gel, and curly Remi hair extensions. Her hard brown eyes suggested that she was just twenty-seven years old, but her calloused and scarred hands told the truth: mid-to-late fifties. She rocked in the car seat and fanned at her face with those middle-aged hands. Beads of sweat pebbled on her hair like morning dew on vines. "Lord Jesus Father God," she whispered. "Be with me, be with me, Lord. It's too damn hot today."

"I totally agree. It *is* too damn hot today." I opened my binder. "Your full name, ma'am?"

"Bernice Parrish. That's with two *R*s." She lived in Inglewood, across the street from the Forum, and owned a hair salon over on Market Street. "Who Do Yo Hair," she said.

I blinked. "Umm . . . Her name's Herschelle, and she's over on—"

Bernice Parrish sucked her teeth and rolled her eyes. "No, sweetie. That's the name of my salon. Who Do Yo Hair."

I smiled. "Oh. Got it."

She squinted at my ponytail and fringed bangs. "Sweetie, I ain't mean to be rude, but you needs a trim."

I flushed, and millions of pins pricked my warm cheeks. "I know. It's been a while."

"You on some drugs?"

"Excuse me?"

"I can tell." She pointed at my head with one copper-polished fingernail, then used that finger to flick at my bangs.

I tensed and came *thisclose* to breaking her hand. "Ma'am, you need to remove your—"

"Drugs always come out in the hair. Makes it dull and brittle. Tell her to give you a protein pack after your next relaxer. Then, she need to follow it with a clear cellophane. And *then*, she gotta give you a good trim. You gotta get that stuff off before you go bald."

"I'll tell her next week when I see her. Thank you."

She frowned, shook her head. "A man put his hand up in there, he likely to cut his finger off."

This morning, a man *did* have his hands up in my hair. But the blood on Dr. Popov's fingers had been mine.

"Cuz you look nice with that suit," she was saying, giving me the up and down. "I saw something just like it at the Walmart over in Torrance. Is that where you got it? At the Walmart?"

I forced a smile. "How did you know Mr. Washington?"

"He was my boyfriend."

"How long were you dating?"

"Six months or so."

"He lives here alone?"

She snorted. "He did, if you don't count all them cats."

"How old was he?"

"He just turned seventy-three yesterday." She craned her neck to look at the house. The sweat pooling in the scoop of her clavicle trickled down her breastbone. "When y'all gon' let me go in? Gene left me something."

I lifted an eyebrow. *Too soon, Bernice. Too soon.*

"It'll be a moment, ma'am," I said. "Tell me how you came to find him today."

"Every Tuesday," she said, "I help him straighten up a bit. And today is Tuesday."

I paused before saying, "Straighten up . . . what?"

She cocked her head. "The *house*. What you think?"

I pointed at the yellow house behind me. "*That* house?"

"Yes, *that* house." She narrowed her eyes as Fitzgerald and Montez unfurled a blue tarp at the foot of Washington's porch. "Folks from church gon' be coming by soon, takin' stuff when Gene told me—"

"No one's going in, okay? Now: you got here at what time?"

"Around seven fifty. I used my key to get in." She fished around her stained suede bag. Pulled out a key ring that held a crucifix the size of a freeway sign, an I HEART JESUS fob, and a mini bottle opener. "I stepped in and shouted, 'Gene—,'" she yelled.

I startled and almost dropped my pen and binder.

"'Gene,'" she shouted again, "'where you at?' And then I smelt it." She sprang up out of the passenger seat and pinched her nose. Standing, she wasn't that much taller. "It usually stank off in there, especially with all them cats. But this stink was different. Extra cheesy smelling. And sweet. Like . . . old sticky cherries mixed with Parmesan cheese. You know what I'm sayin'?"

Impressed, I nodded. "Did you touch him?"

"Oh, *hell* no. Not with all them bugs crawling everywhere. Gene said I could officially have his—he called 'em his 'soup pennies.'"

"What's a soup penny?"

"You know, bullion coins? Bouillon is soup, ain't it? And pennies are bullion coins. Soup. Penny." She laughed. "He had a way of naming things interesting. But he said that they're mine. He wrote all that down somewhere. Officially."

"In a will?" I asked.

"That's right," she said with a cocked chin. "Back in July, our church, Blessed Mission over on La Brea, had a will-making seminar and we was all required to go."

"*We?*"

"Anybody over fifty-five. See: white folks do their wills and be-hests and all that, but we black people, we wanna bury our money in the ground with funerals and don't take care of our family. But with a *will*, everybody know they been taken care of."

With numb fingers, I was writing all of this into my notepad.

Bernice Parrish had just uttered one of the most magical words in a possible homicide investigation: *WILLS*.

"This required seminar," I said, "is that where you saw Mr. Washington making his will?"

The proprietor of Who Do Yo Hair grinned like a dwarf who'd just discovered a mine. "Uh huh. He got all kinds of stuff off in there, just sittin'. And most of it officially belongs to me now. He told me so. I just need to find where he put his will at."

"When was the last time you saw him alive?" I asked.

She sat back down in the squad car. "Our church picnic on Sunday evening, over at Bonner Park."

Bonner Park. Tiny razors cut up and down my spine. Even though I had no memory of it happening, I knew that I'd been rolled away on a gurney after my last visit there.

"Sister Elliott drove the church van," Bernice Parrish was saying, "so she picked him up and brought him since Gene don't drive no more. The picnic was really nice this year. We had a lovely time. Played dominoes, spades—you know how we do. People made potato salad and chicken, ham and lemonade. We ate a little bit of everything. Best thing was, way up in the park, you didn't feel all scratchy-eyed from the fires over in the mountains."

Mention the gun? Nope—I'd keep it in my pocket just in case Bernice had used it and hadn't realized that she'd left it behind.

"You cook for him recently?" I asked.

"You askin' if I made that cobbler he was eating?"

"Is that what that was?"

She pushed moist strands of hair from her face. "Uh huh. Peach cobbler. But no, I ain't made that."

"You said . . . *peach?*"

"That's what it look like to *me.*"

"You know if anyone else who went to the picnic got sick?"

"I ain't heard nothing about people getting sick."

"Does he have a food allergy?"

She closed one eye as she thought. "He eat nuts all the time."

"What about shellfish or mangoes or milk? Wheat, maybe?"

She shrugged. "To be honest, I don't pay much attention to what Gene eat and don't eat." She jiggled her knee, then glanced past me to look at the house again. "How did he die?"

"We're not sure," I said. "Could've been the heat. Where did he get the peach cobbler?"

She shrugged. "Gene freezes a lot of stuff. That cobbler coulda been made back at Easter. I coulda made it. Sister Green coulda made it. Don't look like my dish, though, with them blue flowers."

"You touch that dish?"

"No."

"I'll still need your fingerprints." For the dish *and* the gun.

"My fingerprints are gonna be all over that house."

"Right. That's why I need them." I shrugged and smiled. "So did you hear from him at all yesterday?"

"No," she said, fanning her face again. "He usually shut himself in on Mondays, especially after being in church and then going to the picnic on Sunday. He get cranky, and so I leave him alone until Tuesdays. He ready to see me on Tuesdays. I give him a trim and a shave, fix him some lunch and dinner for the week, straighten up a bit, do our thang, you know?"

"Did he have health problems?" I asked.

"Gene just had his physical last week for his new insurance policy—he hadn't been to the doctor in ages." A far-off look filled the woman's eyes. "The doctor said he had high blood pressure. That's about it. He was supposed to get some blood work done but never got around to it. But he ain't ever complained about feeling bad. He was in high spirits on Sunday, sayin' that he was about to come into some money, and he wanted to take me to Fiji to celebrate his birthday." Her wet eyes glimmered with joy, and a smile softened her hard face. "And I kissed him, and I told him, 'Gene, just tell me when to pack,' see, cuz I always dreamed of—"

A sob burst from her mouth. She flung her head back and threw her hands in the air. "I can't believe he's gone. He's gone, Lord. That ol' buzzard . . . He left me. Why he leave me, Lord?"

She flapped her face as she dropped back into the passenger seat of the patrol car. Finally, she took a deep breath and slowly released it.

"You okay?" I asked. "You need a paramedic?"

She shook her head. "I'm fine." She dried her cheeks with the heel of her hands, then said, "So, Officer, when y'all gon' let me in?"

4

Alive on Sunday evening. Dead by Tuesday morning. No decay. No maggots. Peach cobbler and Schlitz malt liquor for a last supper. A fortune-hunter girlfriend.

"So, what?" Bernice Parrish asked me. "Two, three hours before y'all let me in to get what's mine?" Her voice sounded flat. Her tear ducts were drier than all of California.

Not a good look, especially to murder police.

"Not sure yet when I'll be able to let you in," I said. "Stick around a bit, though, just in case. And give me your address and phone number. Someone's gonna take your fingerprints so that we have them on file. You've been inside Mr. Washington's home—you know what we're dealing with, what we're up against."

She snickered. "Sweetie, you ain't gotta tell me." Then she recited her address again, and corrected me twice on the proper pronunciation of 'Arbor Vitae,' her street's name.

"I know you have a key," I said, "but you cannot go in until I say you can. Understand?"

She sucked her teeth, then nodded. "I got it, Officer."

I thanked my first person of interest, then trudged back to the front yard.

Cats darted, crept, and skirted around the towers of trash. High in the sky, that white ball of death, now in its ten o'clock position, pounded the city, and the ibuprofen I'd taken in Dr. Popov's elevator had quit me—every vulnerable nerve burned, from the wound hidden in my hair to the small callus on my left pinky toe. I needed to pop another Advil, but there was no popping-pill privacy. And Tavaris Fitzgerald hunkered beneath the giant magnolia with his eyes pecking at me like a backyard chicken. He'd sound the alarm if I popped a Luden's.

"Keep an eye on Miss Parrish over there," I told him. "Make sure that she stays."

"She'll be pissed off," he said.

"Yeah, well, we're all frustrated."

"She under arrest, though?"

I squinted at him. "No, she's not under arrest, but the day's still young."

Colin and I reunited to walk the perimeter. As we climbed over stereo speakers and televisions and hopped over bricks and wooden beams, I recounted my conversation with Bernice Parrish.

"Soup pennies?" Colin said.

"What the hell does *that* mean?"

"Soup is to bouillon and bullion is to gold. Penny is to coin and—the struggle is real with the heat, all right, so just go with it, damn."

"Fine. So gold coins—that's why we're looking for clues in a junk pile?"

"For that, for his will, and to be sure that no one hid a bottle with a skull and crossbones label on it."

"Coulda been regular old food poisoning," he said. "Back in the Springs, when I was twelve, thirteen years old, there was a church picnic and the entire congregation got sick from Sister Perry's ambrosia salad. For real: puke and shit *everywhere*. I got sick. My mom got sick. The pastor and his wife got sick. After that, Dad put the kibosh on us eating other people's food. Fly, fight, win—you can't do that if you're crappin' and hurlin' everywhere."

"We didn't do church much after Tori disappeared," I said. "We went a few times asking for their help, but we stopped. Mom said that she'd rather be a miserable failure in private. And all those special prayers and laying on hands just got to be embarrassing. Not that any of it worked in the end." Sadness had lodged in my throat next to the buildup of asbestos and cat hair.

But forensics would make it all better. Maybe.

Lead criminalist Arturo Zucca looked far too relaxed. His black hair touched the tops of his ears; his shoulders sloped and rested in their natural position. The side effects from three weeks of vacationing in Turin. Zucca had witnessed countless strange things around this city, and I had stood beside him on many of these occasions. No shocks. No surprises. But now this veteran of horrors gawked at the mess before him as though Ed Gein, Leona Helmsley, and the Blob were all bathing together in a rusted tub of raw eggs and ground pork.

"Today, you become a man," Colin announced.

"And if you need help during the journey," I said, "you'll probably find a pair of dusty balls somewhere in that pile of rusty nails near the tower of beer cans."

Eyes wide, Zucca turned to me. "You're . . . kidding about this. I'm . . . ?"

"Excited?" Colin asked.

"Challenged?" I suggested.

Zucca sighed. "I wanna go back to Italy."

"Brooks is on his way," I said. "In the meantime, let me give you a personal tour of the premises."

Assistant criminalist Krishna Houzanian hadn't torpedoed a crime scene in six days. But ability now took a day of rest as the blue-eyed bottle blonde half-assed stapled plastic sheets to the beams of Washington's front porch. "What?" she snapped at me. "I'm setting up a staging area."

I whipped my head around to glare at Zucca. "Dude. Really?"

"Sorry," Zucca said to me, red-faced. "Krishna, get a real tent and set it up on the side of the house, along with a covered plastic path leading to the front door. Thank you."

Krishna rolled her eyes, yanked off the plastic, then smartly got the hell out of my way.

Colin pat my shoulder. "You didn't Ike Turner her. Guess therapy's working."

I grinned. "Today, I choose to embody our core values, partner. Krishna's trying to force me to disrespect her. Nope. Not this time."

It took Krishna only ten minutes to set up the staging tent. In the realm of homicide investigations, ten minutes equated ten hours—and a year from now, a defense attorney would make hay of the time span during cross-examinations. And I planned to blame it on her being born a Leo and a general-purpose basic bitch. The judge and jury would certainly understand.

At most crime scenes, homicide detectives didn't slip into bunny suits. On this occasion, though, because of the miserable conditions inside the Washington house and the rapidly deteriorating state of its owner, I decided that I'd given enough of myself to the job. Bunny suits for everyone!

The staging tent offered enough space for three people but no space for any air or privacy. Quiet and dark, it was still a nicer retreat from the sun.

Colin stepped into a white Tyvek suit. "Bet when you rolled out of your empty twin bed this morning, you didn't think you'd be doing *this* today." He tugged at the zipper. "I need a suit with a bigger crotch."

"A bigger crotch and a bungee cord to yank you from the pit of your delusions." I stuck one of my loafers into the suit's built-in booties, then eased my hands through the armholes.

"So, Sherlock," Colin said, "how did Miss Bernice kill Eugene Washington?"

"She slipped something into his beer and/or his peach cobbler. Notice how she can't wait to get off in this piece of crap house?"

Colin handed me a full-face respirator. "Why would a woman date an old man who lives in a filthy house?"

"Hidden treasure has led many women to do the unthinkable. Consider Anna Nicole Smith, Rupert Murdoch's wives, et cetera. Shall I continue?"

Colin breathed heavily through his respirator, then said, "Luke, I *am* your father."

"Low hanging fruit, Taggert. How about this?" I took a deep breath from the respirator, then said, "Shut up! It's Daddy, you shithead! Where's my bourbon?"

Colin blinked at me.

"Dennis Hopper, *Blue Velvet*?"

Colin shrugged, shook his head.

"One of David Lynch's best films?" When he shrugged again, I shouted, "Get off my lawn."

Zucca stepped into the tent and grabbed a suit from the box. "What did young Mr. Taggert do this time?"

"Claims he's never heard of David Lynch," I said.

"Is he, like, some famous actor?" Colin asked.

We stepped out from the tent and walked the plastic corridor to the blue-tarped front porch. A few bug-eyed neighbors backed away from the barrier tape. Tyvek suits meant Ebola, contamination, and danger.

Over near my car, Luke and Pepe were climbing out of a dusty silver Impala. Pepe had recently interviewed for an open position with Internal Affairs, the cops that policed the police. I didn't know how I felt about that. Okay, I did—I didn't want him to leave my team and Southwest Division for a bunch of rules-spouting cubicle dwellers down at Parker Center.

"I'm still not sure why I'm here," Zucca said. "It's hot, and an old man died in his filthy house. It's been happening all summer."

"There's a gun near him," Colin said, "and money may be involved."

"Hence, suspicious death," I added.

Zucca pointed at Colin. "You said 'may.'"

"And if his death were natural," I said, "there should never be a 'may.'" I nodded in Bernice Parrish's direction. "*She's* why you're here."

The woman now paced behind the yellow tape with the pink cell phone to her ear.

Colin smiled. "Thank her when you get a chance."

"And if it's natural," I said, "and this ends up being a wasted trip for you, I'll buy everybody an ice-cream sandwich. How's that?"

"Exciting. This isn't the best scene," Zucca warned. "It's gonna be hard to get good prints with all the dust and cats and dead things everywhere. I spray Luminol, everything's gonna glow. And I can't really set up a proper field lab cuz everything's contaminated."

I nodded. "There will be little yellow tents everywhere. Understood. Let's just do our best, all right?"

Minutes later, we congregated at the front door. Everyone on Zucca's team held fancy equipment: cameras, brushes, light meters, whizzy-wigs, and dumbledores. My crew wielded pens and pads, as though we were working at a simpler crime scene.

"So you thought the Chatman fire was bad," I told the small team. "But this? We haven't worked a hoarder scene quite like this."

"Mr. Maghami," Pepe said. "Over on Denker."

"He hoarded dogs," I pointed out. "Today, we have cats, trash, kitchen sinks, the yeti, and a Bermuda Triangle forming off the back porch. If you think it, it's there, so please be careful and focus on solving this case. And wear protective everything at all times."

"What are we looking for?" Luke asked.

"All official-looking legal papers," I said, "especially a will and insurance papers. Also, look for medications, household poisons . . . I want everything around him—the Smith and Wesson, the goopy stuff, the dish that it's in, the beer bottle, remote control, all of it. The coroner should be here soon to claim our victim. Once Mr. Washington's gone, I want anything that had been beneath him, so use your fancy Dustbusters. There may also be valuables scattered throughout the property. Gold coins, jewelry, cash. Take pictures, log it, tag it, and bag it. Be thorough cuz who wants to come back into this house again?"

Luke raised his hand. Some people laughed.

Before disappearing behind the tarp and trekking back into the house, I glanced at Victoria Avenue.

People were taking selfies with the hoarded house behind them. And Bernice, phone still to her face, waved her free arm at someone down the block.

Zucca's photographers wasted no time capturing on film the inside of the filthy Craftsman. Their cameras clicked and whirred as they murmured, "See that?" "Oh my gosh!" and "What the *hell*?"

Camera and sketchpad ready, I stepped into a well-lit room with built-in shelves and piles of clothes in bags, clothes out of bags, and clothes hanging on a clothesline that crossed from wall to window. I spotted the edge of a mattress—this was a bedroom. A wicker basket was filled with pens, pill vials, and wires. There were towers of shoe boxes, empty and full suitcases. Golf clubs stuck out of piles like tarnished silver gophers. Cobwebs heavier than lace tablecloths draped from each corner of the room.

Somewhere else in the house, Colin shouted, "Oh *shit*."

Pistachio shells cracked beneath my feet. *Yeah. Sure. Pistachio shells.* I glared at the golf clubs, at the dirt and webs and all of the mess. *If you'd taken more time off, perhaps you wouldn't be here right now. Leave, Elouise. Just leave.*

Eugene Washington had issues. A man couldn't live in this house with a mob of cats and a multitude of roaches without having issues.

I pushed aside a hip-high pile of clothes to open the mirrored closet. Boxes, dresses, men's suits, a fluff of gray fur . . . A small skull had been crushed beneath a stack of Del Monte crates. A chill zigzagged up my spine and broke apart at my shoulders. My heart dropped to my feet, and I groaned.

After snapping pictures of the closet and that poor flat cat, I lugged each crate to the porch.

Colin stumbled out of the front door, nearly crashing against the blue tarp. "Freakin' unbelievable. It's just . . . just . . . It's like . . ."

"Like your place but in a better zip code."

"It's all crushed and re-formed and cat skeletons and dirty underwear and old food with . . . with . . ."

"Cheese and bread, Taggert," I said. "Take a knee. You're stressin' me out." I pulled a petrified towel off the first crate.

Medals, clean and glistening, sat in the clutter of batteries, business cards, and paper clips. I tugged at a purple ribbon—with it came a heart-shaped fob imprinted with George Washington's profile. "Is this a Purple Heart?"

"Yeah. Wow." Colin pulled from the crate a red, gold, and white ribbon. The medallion on the end was star-shaped and stamped with a bald eagle and sword. "My dad's got this one. A National Defense Service Medal."

Hot tears stung my eyes and fogged my face mask. I pointed to my left bicep. "He has a Vietnam tat . . ." My words spun in my mind like a gyroscope. A vet dying like this . . . So wrong.

"In the bathroom off the den," Colin said, "one of Zucca's crew found stacks of *Life* magazines that almost reached the ceiling." He paused, then asked, "Who's gonna clean all this up?"

"You are." I started to paw inside the next crate. Receipts, catalogs, old bills, and . . . sheaths of legal-size papers neatly clipped together.

"Order in the bedlam," I said, pulling out the bound documents. "Light in the darkness. Let's see . . ."

> *I, EUGENE JOSEPH WASHINGTON, of 8711 Victoria Avenue, Los Angeles, California, declare that this is my last Will and Testament.*

"Yahtzee," I whispered.

Colin peeked over my shoulder. "You see Miss Bernice's name anywhere?"

I scanned the typed document. *No living children . . . no wife . . . I give my entire interest in the real property to Oswald Little . . . personal automobile . . . collection of gold bullion coins to my friend Bernice T. Parrish.* "There she is. And she gets the soup pennies."

Colin took pictures of the crates and the will. "You find 'em yet?"

"Nope. You?"

"Nope."

I continued to search the rest of the Del Monte crates and found bank statements and contracts, an expired U.S. passport, and a birth certificate—*Eugene Joseph Washington born August 31, 1941 in Little Rock, Arkansas.*

But: no gold coins.

"She still out there?" Colin asked.

I snooped past the blue tarp.

Bernice now huddled with a tall, bald black man wearing wraparound shades and a Pistons jersey.

"You may be right about motive," Colin said.

Anger flickered inside me—and I didn't push it away. I needed anger like Titan missiles needed rocket fuel. "Let's go back in the house and keep looking."

In the hallway closet, we found three more Smith and Wesson pistols, four shotguns, and two high-powered rifles. In a bedroom closet, we found twenty-seven English-language King James Bibles, one Korean language, one French, three Spanish.

"Why so many guns?" Colin wondered.

"Same reason for the thirty-two Bibles," I said. "He was a hoarder, dude."

We had avoided the kitchen but couldn't any longer. I failed to distinguish one thing from the other. My brain tripped over the trash and piles and cats and cans of spoiled food. There were spray bottles of 409 and Tilex on the window sills.

In the kitchen, wearing respirators was as useful as reading a Bible at a strip club. The smells blitzed the filters in our masks, rendering them useless. Only death trumped the sulfur of rotten eggs, the corpsy stink of rotten meat, and the clumpy sourness of spoiled milk.

With knees as saggy as the boxes all around me, I stumbled into the dining room. Even though Brooks wouldn't perform surgery here, the dining room table was still the cleanest spot in the house. Beside the yellow tents—now at '66'—sat a pile of envelopes, a key ring, a Bible with a Sunday service program for Blessed Mission Ministries, and a battered brown wallet. Inside the wallet was a driver's license, a certified mail receipt, one bank card, and seventeen hundred dollars in cash.

"Bernice said he was about to come into some money," I said. "Wonder if this is it."

The church bulletin contained a Sick and Shut-In announcement and listed ailing members of the congregation. *Sidney Alexander, Paula Todd, Karina Mandrell* . . . Thirty more names, but none of them were Eugene Washington.

Back in the den, the air now buzzed thick with thousands of flies. Myerson, the forensic entomologist, swished around his butterfly net to capture a few. But which flies had come as a result of Eugene Washington's death? Really: roaches and beetles, disturbed from their nooks and hamlets by human feet, skittered over every place skitterable.

A criminalist snapped pictures of Eugene Washington seated in his stained armchair. Zucca had already tagged and bagged the dish, the gun, the remote control, and the beer bottle.

My throat locked and nausea flitted around my belly like the room's flies. *You can leave right now, Lou, before it's too—*

"Anything else before the coroner takes him?" Zucca asked.

I focused on objects that weren't moving—not much available. "That."

I stepped over the pile of ancient *TV Guides*, empty beer bottles, and jugs of pee to stand before the giant television console covered in a foot of dust and cat hair. "I want this." I pointed at the framed picture of Eugene Washington with his arm around another old black man. They stood on a red fishing boat and held four large fish. Big smiles to go along with their big catch.

"Bass fishing with a best friend?" Colin asked.

"He looks happy here. Normal, even." I couldn't stop staring at the picture. My eyes saw something that my brain hadn't identified yet.

"Maybe this fishing buddy can tell us about Miss Bernice," Colin said. "I haven't seen one picture of *her* anywhere."

"Bros before hos," I quipped, my attention still focused on the photograph.

Especially gold-digging dwarf hos in search of soup pennies.

5

Speaking of gold-digging dwarves . . .

Bernice Parrish called my cell phone twice. Both times, I let the calls roll to voice mail.

Message 1: *It's hot out here. Y'all almost done?*

Message 2: *How long I got to stay? I need me some lunch cuz my blood sugar's gettin' low.*

Then, there was a last message. *It's me. Just calling to say "hi," so . . . Hi.* Sam Seward's voice made my breath catch and butterflies flutter around my belly.

I saw straight any time the tall, green-eyed assistant district attorney shared my space. Alas, we only shared space now to prepare for Max Crase's murder trial—a trial Sam was prying himself from because of our friendship. We had already muddied the waters with a kiss here, a hug there. More friend than lover. Explainable offenses. But an obvious affair with sexting, weekend getaways, and matching tattoos? Crase's defense attorney could certainly argue that the case had been compromised, that the prosecuting attorney had a conflict of interest.

Max Crase: screwing up my life since 1985.

At half past one o'clock, it was time to wrap up. The crowd had lost some mass—it was damned hot at ninety-eight degrees, and one could watch that blue tarp for only so long. The hose draggers had finished clearing a path for the gurney that would ferry Eugene Washington to the coroner's van parked in the driveway. No camera crews recorded shots of me standing near that white-and-blue wagon. No camera crews took B reel of cats sitting on a Chrysler Le Baron already covered in rust and bird poop or the United Nations army of naked Barbies caught between the tangle of phone cords and twine. If it were October, and if there'd been a Freddy Krueger mask atop the stack of boxes, 8711 Victoria would have been the perfect haunted house.

Spencer Brooks, M.D., deputy medical examiner, wouldn't meet my gaze as I described the scene. His brown eyes skipped from the porch's wooden slats and the Barbie army to Colin or the magnolia tree. "Did the cats get to him yet?" he asked.

"No," I said, "but they would've eventually. There weren't any bowls of food or fresh water around."

"Insects?"

"Other than the native population? Don't know. When we got here a little before nine, there were blowflies, but no maggots."

Eyes closed, Brooks leaned against the banister with his cinnamon-colored arms crossed. "And now?"

"*Now*," Colin said, "everybody's having babies."

"Zucca took the temp inside the house," I said. "Eighty-eight degrees."

"Mr. Washington have any family around today?" Brooks asked, squinting at my shoulder.

"No," I said, "but his girlfriend is at the tape. Says he turned seventy-three yesterday. They'd even talked about a trip to Fiji. She's also looking for the gold he left her."

Brooks cocked an eyebrow. "Real gold or . . . ?"

"Real. He mentions it in his will."

Now, both of his eyebrows lifted. "She shoot him?"

"Don't think so," I said.

Colin added, "We're thinking poison."

"Oh," I said, "let's remember to find those insurance papers to see if—"

"If Bernice Parrish is a beneficiary?" Colin jotted in his pad. "Maybe there's a policy in one of those crates you found."

Brooks stalked over to the staging tent to change into a Tyvek suit. It didn't take long for him to reemerge fully suited and march into the house without saying another word to us.

"He's in a mood," Colin said.

I shrugged, then dropped into a chair that faced the overgrown backyard. Beads of perspiration dripped into my eye. As I unzipped the Tyvek suit, cool air chilled my wet silk blouse. I reached into the cooler and grabbed a bottled water. Guzzled half. *Too much.* I clamped my hand across my mouth as water spurted between my fingers. Dizzy now, I leaned over and spat into the dirt, staying in that position with my eyes closed.

Just the wind. Just the—Nausea found me again, and I lunged out of my chair and over to the rusted, chain-link fence.

"She okay?" Pepe asked Colin.

"Yeah. All the shit around here."

The bad air, with its fine particles and carcinogens, had thickened—we were all playing Russian roulette every time we took a breath.

I wobbled back to my chair and wiped my face with the collar of my blouse.

Colin crouched before me. His eyes were bloodshot from dust and exhaustion, and his face creased from wearing the tight respirator. He placed his hand on my shoulder. "If this is too much for you—the heat, the junk—and you need to get off the ride . . ."

My guts twisted around my lungs, but I still managed to fake a smile. "Thanks, Dad. I'm fine." I rinsed my mouth with water, spat it into the dirt, then toddled to my feet. "Let's go see which tool Brooks is sticking in one of poor Mr. Washington's organs."

A thermometer. His liver.

Brooks read the gauge. "Eighty degrees. So he's been gone about twelve or so hours."

Colin counted backward on his fingers. "One, two o'clock this morning, then."

Brooks shone a light on Eugene Washington's swollen face—the blue splotches had turned bluer and had spread to his ears. There was the dried froth on his lips but also down his chin and the front of his crusty wife beater. "Looks like he vomited," Brooks said. "Food and . . ." He moved the flashlight's beam down Washington's pajama pants. A pool of vomit had dried on the dead man's thighs.

"Poison?" I asked.

Brooks clicked off the flashlight. "Possibly, but which poison? Lividity's usually reddish pink with arsenic. Or this could be an allergic reaction to food—the swollen face and tongue." He slipped off the respirator, sniffed, then grimaced. "Yikes."

I snickered. "The girlfriend said that she smelled cherries and Parmesan cheese when she got in this morning."

"That's just two in millions of smells." Brooks replaced the mask over his face again. "Myerson take bugs?"

"Yep."

"I'll do standard tox screens for narcotics and carbon monoxide. But I'll throw in screens for arsenic, cyanide, and a few other poisons. Guess I'll take him now."

"When should we come down for the autopsy?" Colin asked.

"I know you have a lot of bodies from the heat wave," I said, "but if he's been poisoned, this is obviously a priority."

"Obviously," Brooks said. "Tomorrow morning should be fine."

I waved a hand at the body. "We'll get out of the way and let you do your—"

Brooks had already pivoted away from me.

"Okay, then." My face burned as I stomped back through the mess to the front door.

Fires surrounding the city had tinged the sky red and gray. Pieces of it swirled down upon us, and even the junk smelled as though it was burning.

In the tent, I shimmied out of the bunny suit and stumbled outside with my hands clenched and with my eyes open but not seeing junk that spread out to infinity. Everything and nothing glistened. Everything and nothing stood out to me. Had the murderer hid the poison in the tire well of the Le Baron or in the bowels of that dead Siamese cat?

"Who the hell knows, Lou," I muttered.

Ninety-eight degrees may have been too hot for lookie-loos, but not too hot for Bernice Parrish. She now pointed at the house as she shouted at Officer Fitzgerald. Her bald Pistons-jersey-wearing friend had disappeared.

Colin now sat on a milk crate beneath the big magnolia tree. "You plannin' to keep Miss Bernice here all day?" he asked. "I know she's waiting for her soup pennies."

I found another crate and sat. "Misery, company, hit dog, holler, et cetera." I plucked my phone from my pocket and turned off DO NOT DISTURB. Notifications immediately scrolled down the screen.

Dominic can't wait to see you! And don't call him that to his face! Lena's text included a picture of a man with a mischievous, "hide your panties" smile, skin the color of pralines, and a chin strong enough to anchor a small barge.

Dominic Campbell was single at thirty-three years old. A hose dragger (excuse me, *firefighter*), he had no felonies, no arrests, a house in View Park, and a late-model Suburban.

Voir dire to start three weeks from today. Sam about the Max Crase murder trial.

Please call my mother. Her house got broken into. Thx! Greg Norton, my ex-husband.

The squeaky wheels of the gurney made me look up. Both Colin and I stood as the coroner's team pushed Eugene Washington, covered now by a LACCO blue blanket, out of the house and down the walkway. Brooks, following behind his team, tossed me a glare.

Fire burst in my gut. My feet were moving to confront him before my brain realized that I'd already acted. "What did I do to you?" I demanded. "Why are you pissed off at me?"

"I'm not pissed off," he snapped, frowning at me. His nostrils flared. His shoulders were hunched. In America, that meant *pissed off*. He shook his head as he watched his crew slide the body and gurney into the back of the van.

"You don't return my calls," I said. "You can't even *look* at me—"

"You're such a . . ." He closed his eyes, took a deep breath, then slowly exhaled.

"*What?*" I screeched. "I'm such a *what?*"

He squinted at me. "Was that the only solution? Of all the solutions in the world?"

I blinked at him. "What are you talking about? I saw the gun on the ground, the blue splotches on his face, then listened to his girlfriend talk about—"

"I'm not talking about this case. All of life ain't about *work*, Elouise."

"I'm . . . lost."

Brooks chuckled without humor. "Yeah. You are." For the second time in too many months, he looked directly at me. His eyes softened the way they did every time he met the dead. "I'll get to Mr. Washington tomorrow morning."

Ninety-eight degrees out here. Cold gripped me, though, as I watched the van inch north and away from me.

6

Greg had been many things throughout our twelve years together—friend, lover, protector, liar, adulterer—but he'd been a fastidious homeowner. Our small lawn had never browned. Circulars and phone books never sat in our driveway for more than six hours. No paint flaked from the eaves. Ours had been a shining Shangri-La.

Too bad he treated our marriage like Eugene Washington treated his house.

After the swirling orange lights of the coroner's van had disappeared around the corner, I spotted my Porsche still parked at the barrier tape. It would be quiet in there, and there was a big tub of Advil in the glove compartment. I thought of munching a big shaved ice while chasing it with a frosted glass of fruit punch. I thought of smearing Icy Hot all over my body, then disappearing beneath a down comforter with a remote control in my hand and *The Poseidon Adventure* on the television screen. Then, I thought of my reality.

The last thing I wanted to do was look up at that death star in the sky and point to a home security camera that didn't work because home security cameras *never* worked.

Before that day in Bonner Park with Zach Fletcher, the man who had killed teenage girls from my old neighborhood, the old Lou would've walked in two-hundred-degree weather, stood on the sun's surface. Before Zach Fletcher had also tried to kill me in that park high above Los Angeles, the old Lou would have given that death star in the sky the finger, then used her other finger to point at a home security camera that didn't work. And she'd be cool with that nonworking camera. Cuz those were the breaks. Now, though? Nuh uh.

Colin squeezed my shoulder. "You okay? Need a minute?"

"Nope. I'm good." I longed to climb into the Porsche so badly that beads of sweat pebbled on top of other beads of sweat that had already bubbled across my face and neck. "Really. I'm cool."

He leaned closer to me. "Take a moment, all right? Don't worry, I got it. Zucca's inside collecting and—"

"Why are you trying to push me off my case?" I blurted.

Colin's eyes widened, and he stuttered, "I . . . I . . . It's not, I'm not . . . pushing you out. It's just . . . Sorry."

Muscles tense, I said, "Let's see if Mr. Washington had any late-night visitors."

Colin hesitated, and his lips thinned before he said, "So, camera checks?"

"But first, we'll stop and chat with our bestie Bernice again and her friend."

The big man in the wraparound shades and Pistons jersey now towered over Bernice Parrish. His name was Joe. He didn't say if it was short for Joseph or John, and he sure as hell didn't give me his last name.

"Then, you need to move over there." Colin pointed toward the end of the block.

Joe sucked his teeth, then spat, "Joseph Rice. Satisfied?"

"Thrilled," I cracked. "Why are you here today?"

"Bernie called and asked me to come." He sounded scratchy and slurpy, like he held runny grits and gravel in his mouth.

Bernice scratched her scalp. "Joe ain't got nothin' to do with this. He's my emotional support."

Shifty-eyed Bernice. In the movie, she'd be "Crackhead Number Two." *Been clean for three whole days now*, she'd boast, chest puffed out, chin high.

"When can I get my stuff?" she asked me again.

My mouth opened, but no words came—spiking past the stink of dead and old were the aromas of sandalwood, vanilla, and soap. *Zach Fletcher.* Bile burned up my throat, and I swallowed to force the acid back to my stomach. I turned away from Bernice and her friend to search for those puppy-brown eyes, that flawless smile, those bloodstained scrubs.

"Soon," Colin said, since I'd been rendered speechless. "We're still looking. As you know, it's a bit of a challenge finding anything in there."

She waggled her head. "Oh yeah, but if y'all need my help—"

"Glad you said that." He handed her a business card. "Did Officer Fitzgerald take your fingerprints yet?"

She shook her head. "I don't trust him."

"You trust me?" I asked, coming out of my trance.

She nodded. "You don't look like I'm gon' see you on YouTube next week."

"Thank you, Ms. Parrish," I said with a smile. "Can you come to the station tomorrow so that we can cross it off our to-do list?"

"Tomorrow sounds good." Her eyes shifted to the space between my shoulder and Eugene Washington's house.

"You'll have to come down anyway," I said, "once we find—"

"I said that tomorrow's good." Her eyes widened and she gave a slight head shake.

"Once you find what?" Joe asked her.

Bernice waved a dismissive hand. "Just something Gene left me."

Joe cracked a grin. "What he leave?"

Colin pointed to Joe. "So do you know Eugene Washington?"

"Met him a coupla times," the man said. "That fool need to clean up some, but he cool."

"You see him recently?" Colin asked.

Joe's Adam's apple bobbed behind his razor-bumped skin. "Naw. Ain't no reason I need to see him."

He had just lied, but I let it slide. My scalp was tightening, and the colors around me had paled, then glinted mirror-bright. My mouth filled with thick, prevomit saliva. I needed to move. "Bernice, we'll see you tomorrow." Then, I hurried toward the dusty pink bungalow on the right side of Washington's property.

Colin said something else to Bernice and Joe, and then he hustled to join me. "That's it? 'See you tomorrow'? You didn't wanna—?"

"Right now, in this heat, no. I didn't wanna. You must be tired from talking so damned much." A vise clenched my lungs, making me take shallow breaths. I searched the eaves of the pink house. "No camera." I pivoted in the opposite direction, passing the Washington house again and stopping at the white-and-blue Spanish-style.

"No cameras here, either," Colin said, his eyes on the eaves. "Think the houses across the street have anything?"

The houses across the street included a McMansion in its last stages of construction and a deserted-looking 1950s-era cracker box with a weedy lawn, peeling paint, and a year's worth of supermarket circulars stuck into the iron security door.

"No, don't think so." I didn't want to walk over there, not with my need to upchuck intensifying with each step I took.

Bernice Parrish, her eyes as wild as a spooked horse's, hustled in our direction. "Hey, detectives. I'm gonna get on out of here."

"Somethin' wrong?" Colin asked.

She pointed at an ancient gray Astrovan now parking near the barrier tape.

The van's back passenger door slid open, and a young black woman wearing BluBlockers and a vibrant yellow-and-blue dashiki dress climbed from the backseat. An older woman wearing a pearl-gray skirt set and clutching a lacy hankie as big as a sail climbed from behind the van's steering wheel. A third woman, chubby and sporting the prettiest gray dreadlocks I've ever seen, left the front passenger seat. She held a tambourine and joined the others on the sidewalk.

"Them fortune tellers is here," Bernice Parrish whispered. "Some people at church say they're prophetesses, but I ain't about all that. Neither is the bishop, and he kicked 'em to the curb."

Colin chortled. "Like, they tell the future and see the future?"

But Bernice had already scurried toward a blue Saturn, soup pennies be damned.

"Maybe Mr. Washington promised them a toaster oven," Colin said.

I cocked my head. "They don't look like witches to me. Kinda remind me of the vendors at farmer's markets on the weekends. The ladies selling homemade bath oils and aloe vera plants."

The three women smiled at us. "Are you the officers in charge?" Lace Hankie shouted.

Colin and I considered each other, grinned, shrugged—*here we go*—

then sauntered over to the trio. As we came closer, BluBlockers said, "The detective and the chief join us today."

Someone smelled of maple syrup. Another woman smelled of cinnamon and cloves. Grand Slam at Denny's instead of hair of troll, eye of newt.

I introduced Colin and myself, then said, "And you are . . . ?"

"Dorothea Tennyson," Lace Hankie responded. Her gold eye shadow shimmered in the sunlight.

"I'm Idell Messere," Gray Dreads said. "So pleased to meet you."

BluBlockers didn't speak. Instead, she cocked her head.

"May I have your name, ma'am?" I asked her.

"Ssh," Dorothea Tennyson said to me, finger to her lips.

"She's . . ." Idell Messere studied the young woman.

"She's, what?" Colin asked. "Mute or deaf or . . . ?"

"She's receiving a word from the Lord," Lace Hankie explained.

Colin eyed me. I waggled my eyebrows and waited.

"What is it, sister?" Gray Dreads asked, lightly tapping the face of the tambourine.

I glanced at my wristwatch. "If you all would like us to come back—"

"Then the king promoted Daniel," BluBlockers said.

"And gave him many great gifts," Dorothea Tennyson said.

"And he made him ruler over the whole province of Babylon and chief prefect over all the wise men of Babylon," Idell Messere completed, still tapping that tambourine.

And then, the trio sang, *"If I can help somebody as I travel along, if I can help somebody with a word or song . . ."* A joyous song, one that made onlookers standing on the sidewalks smile.

What a wretched day. A day of dirt and death, and now, Mahalia Jackson gospel songs. Damn it all to hell.

After the two-minute song ended, after everyone listening clapped, Colin said, "We still need her name."

"Ebony Quinn," the young woman said.

I grit my teeth, then scribbled her name alongside the others. "You ladies knew Eugene Washington, I'm guessing."

"Yes," Dorothea Tennyson said as she twisted the tail of the hankie around her wrist. "And we've come—"

"To bless the body." Idell Messere pulled out a bottle of amber-colored liquid from the pocket of her caftan and handed it to Dorothea Tennyson.

"You're a little late," I said. "The coroner took him about twenty minutes ago."

All three women smiled.

"Did he now?" Dorothea Tennyson said. Then, she turned away from me. She lifted her arms, the bottle in one hand and the lace hankie in the other.

I squinted at her, but said to the other two, "Is there something we should know about Mr. Washington? Or about . . . anyone? Anything *hard* and not . . . prediction."

Idell and Ebony smiled at each other. "Someone's told you about us," the older woman said.

Dorothea sang, *"Soon as my feet strike Zion, lay down my heavy burden—"*

"We are not witches," Idell said with a warm smile. "Men like Solomon Tate want to control us—"

"And he cannot control us," Ebony said. "He cannot control his young wife—"

"He cannot control himself," Dorothea said. "Never could. And what do all men do—?"

"To women they cannot control?" Ebony asked.

Dorothea continued to sing. *"And we gonna live on forever, we gonna live on forever—"*

Idell started pounding the tambourine. Ebony regarded me from behind sunglasses suited for older people. "You'd be seen as a witch," she said to me. "You *are* seen as a witch when you only seek the truth."

My face burned. "Is there—?"

"Will you let them control you?" Ebony asked me.

What the hell is going on here? "No one's controlling—"

"May we bless the house?" the young woman asked.

"Something is wrong here," Dorothea said, now finished with her song.

"Something has been wrong here for a very long time," Idell said.

"May we bless the house?" Ebony asked again.

I glimpsed my tiny reflection in the young woman's glasses. "No. It's a crime scene. Can't let anyone on the property."

None of the women were sweating even while wearing caftans, long skirts, and dashikis. Ebony held out her hand in my direction, then whispered, "Do not fear those who kill the body but cannot kill the soul. Rather fear him who can destroy both soul and body in hell."

My kidneys pressed against my lower back, and I had the sudden urge to pee.

"He trusted when he shouldn't have trusted," Ebony said.

"Others trusted when they shouldn't have trusted," Idell said.

Dorothea pointed at me with her lace hankie. "You trust when you shouldn't trust."

The three women now held up hands, and together they said, "Do not trust anyone except for Him."

"They will bury you in the ground," Idell said.

"And reap your reward," Dorothea said.

And then the women smiled at Colin.

He said, "What about me?"

"We have nothing *for* you," Dorothea said.

He said, "Great. If you have anything . . . *solid* to add to this investigation . . ." He offered them his business card. "Unless you know my phone number already."

Dorothea took the card. "The young man laughs because he's young." Then, she and her sisters moved past us. Once they took up staggered positions along the yellow tape, Dorothea sprinkled oil into her hankie and dabbed at the fence. She and Ebony sang as Idell played tambourine. *How I got over, my soul looks back and wonders . . .*

Onlookers—patrol cops, firemen, neighbors—snickered at the women and took pictures.

Colin slipped on his aviators. "I love this fuckin' city."

My head felt like it would soon have a heart attack. "*Who* trusted when he shouldn't have trusted?"

"She's talkin' about Eugene Washington trusting Bernice." Colin found his Tic Tacs container in his pants pocket, then dumped candies into his mouth. "Hocus pocus."

"They're right about something being wrong here," I said.

"It don't take three prophets to tell you that."
You trust when you shouldn't trust.
Whom should I not trust, I wanted to ask.
What do men do to women they can't control?
Call them witches and burn them at the stake.

7

The sun hung low as we prepared to abandon the yellow Craftsman in the middle of the block. Long shadows slanted from trees, cars, and pyramids of junk that sparkled like treasure. The three prophetesses trundled back to the Astrovan. Officer Fitzgerald blocked the front door with crime scene tape, then handed off the watch to a new pair of patrol cops. Without Washington's mess, the neighborhood seemed pleasant enough. Big lawns, lots of impatiens and rosebushes, portable basketball hoops, and tricked-out RVs. So close to the chaos of Crenshaw Boulevard, and yet incredibly homey and hopeful.

I sat in the front seat of my Porsche with the air turned to MAX COOL. Four ibuprofen were now breaking down in my blood. Good times. I lifted the Motorola to my mouth and toggled the switch. "Wouldn't be surprised if one of the neighbors killed him."

Colin laughed. "He *did* screw up their property values with his towers of trash." He sighed, then said, "We have to come back, don't we?"

"Yeah, but not today."

We had other things to do today. Like shower.

But the Bible verse Ebony Quinn had zapped me with—*Do not fear those who kill the body but cannot kill the soul*—would not wash off me and disappear down the drain in the women's locker room shower. No matter how hard my loofah gloves scrubbed, those words stuck to me like tar, staying with me as I trudged toward my desk.

The detective's bureau of the Southwest Community Division reeked of sweat and sour bodies. Millions of foam cups and bottles of water and Gatorade littered every flat surface. The overworked air conditioner had quit on us back in July, and now, seated at my desk, ten fans droned from strategic spots at breezeways and windowsills.

Colin and I had combined our resources to purchase one of those high-fallutin' fans that resembled a knife blade and made air so cold you longed to drink it. A bicycle lock kept our fancy fan secured to the leg of my desk . . . which had been bolted to the concrete beneath the worn blue carpet.

Even after my shower, I had failed to clean all the filth from beneath my fingernails. My teeth still crunched dirt and grit, and after blowing black gunk from my nose, the stink of cat piss and dead things lingered in my nostrils. My skin felt itchy even in an LAPD T-shirt and yoga pants. Two ice-cream sandwiches and a large bottled water had helped me move past the scene at the Washington property, and with pain eased by Advil, my pulse slowed, the sound around me muted, and I could think, I could plan, I could *be present*.

You need more time.

In August, I'd returned to work after my car accident up in Bonner Park back in March, an accident that I'd caused by ramming a Toyota SUV into a parked truck as Zach Fletcher held a gun to my head, an accident that had ultimately saved my life and ended Zach Fletcher's. Yes, I'd returned to light duty and spent a month working the warrants desk until I'd climbed, sprinted, jumped my way toward full medical clearance. Ignoring the pain that still existed just to return to my version of normal. And I'd succeeded until the heat wave from hell—in one-hundred-degree heat, the simple act of blinking took incredible effort, even for the able-bodied. And my body still needed . . .

More time.

But I didn't have "more time." "More time" meant going out on long-term disability. "More time" meant raising the eyebrows of my colleagues and superiors. It was already difficult to receive recognition for a job well done each time I closed a case. I'd be stupid to admit defeat, to admit weakness. Yeah: my body hurt, and certain smells made me freeze, and the sound of some men's voices made me jump. Yeah: since March, I had avoided Bonner Park and the strip mall where Zach Fletcher had run a community medical clinic—and lured girls to their deaths. And yeah: I always switched lanes whenever a RAV4 drove too close to me.

Even while battling all these things, I did not have "more time."

People needed me. Eugene Washington needed me. And I needed to track and uncover the person who had killed him just hours after he'd celebrated his birthday.

With his hands behind his damp head, Colin sat at his desk and squinted at me. He had changed out of his suit and taco-sauce-stained shirt for blue jeans and an LAPD polo. "You look better. You take something?"

I grinned. "Yep. A shower. You should try it sometimes. Warning: the soap may burn."

He said, "Ha," grabbed his steno pad, then rolled in his chair over to my desk.

My eyes watered, and I sneezed twice. "Geez, you use the whole bottle again?"

He blushed. "That house killed my sense of smell."

I opened my binder—grit in the creases of the book—and swiped at the dusty pages. "It's gonna be like a trip to the beach. I'm still gonna find dirt in my notebook six months from now."

"I've been to some jacked-up places since I've lived in LA—"

"Like your desk and your apartment—"

"But *that* house?" Colin ran his fingers through his hair. Since arriving in Los Angeles a year ago, he had discovered hair-styling product—for the second consecutive day, he wore his hair weirdly mussed. "It takes a special kind of nut to live with fifty cats and a herd of cockroaches. How could he breathe?"

"Don't know, but please stop disparaging our victim and his pets."

He twirled his pen between his thumb and index finger. "No lie. You got PTSD from Zach Fletcher, and I got PTSD—"

I snatched the pen from between his fingers. "I don't have PTSD."

"PTSD" equaled "permanently disabled," which equaled a future walking the beat between Macy's and Wetzel's Pretzels.

"Lou—" Colin said.

"I don't. Shut up now."

Colin shrugged. "Whatever you say, bro."

"Shall we get on with detective-ing now?"

"Yep. Detective away."

I handed him his pen, then sent my numb fingers to peck the keyboard.

The first picture of Eugene Washington blinked onto my monitor, courtesy of the DMV. Smiling for his driver's license, his eyes crinkled in the corners. His salt-and-pepper beard had been trimmed, and his black-and-white dress shirt pressed.

The next three pictures showed a less joyful man, younger, more pepper than salt. Dead eyes. A scowl. He wore the orange jumpsuit sported by all those booked into police custody throughout Southern California.

"He got a jacket?" Colin asked.

"Yep. Let's see . . ."

"*Muchachos y muchachas!*" Luke banged into the squad room. He wore the same sweaty brown suit he'd worn at Eugene Washington's house.

"Where's Pepe?" Colin asked.

Luke thumbed behind him. "Down in Evidence." He grabbed a can of Raid bug spray from his desk drawer. "Critters in the car. *Que asco.*"

My eyes returned to the computer screen. "So: Eugene Washington's offenses. A few DUIs between 1981 and 1985. An assault in '87. Another assault in '92 . . . Two citations from the city about the house."

"When?" Colin asked.

"Back in 2010 and then this past January."

"So he was an angry drunk who wouldn't throw shit away?" Colin asked.

"And a veteran. Don't forget that." I continued to click around the World Wide Web to learn more about my victim. "A self-employed carpenter . . . He's owned that house on Victoria since '82."

Results also included a brief mention in the May 2012 issue of *Black Vets* magazine; and a "New Member" announcement in the August 2011 electronic bulletin of Blessed Mission Ministries.

"He got the Holy Ghost," Colin said.

"And gave up the spirits," I added.

"You think Miss Bernice is gonna show up tomorrow?"

"Nope." A few taps on the keyboard and Bernice Parrish's DMV picture popped up on the screen. Full-drag makeup and finger waves like RuPaul. Smoky eyes and pouty lips like Tyra Banks.

"A few parking tickets," I said. "Possession of drug paraphernalia fifteen years ago, and . . . interesting." Detective Google told me that Bernice Parrish owed the State of California so much money that they'd tried to publicly shame her as punishment—she was now listed as a deadbeat on their tax cheats Web site. And since 2012, Who Do Yo Hair had been sued six times in civil court.

"Did you ask her why she was dating a man like Eugene?" Colin asked.

I shook my head. "A woman in deep debt will overlook a house of trash if she needs to. Women overlook a whole lot of things. Hell: I did." Then, I typed in "Joseph Rice."

The screen filled with a list of offenses longer than *Infinite Jest*.

Colin tsk-tsked. "Joe problems, Joe problems, Joe problems."

From fraud and armed robbery to trespassing and indecent exposure, Joseph Rice broke the law as though breaking every one of them resulted in a new set of tires and 30 percent cash back.

"Born in '55?" Colin marveled. "Wow. He's a lot older than he looks."

"Black don't crack," I said. "I'm actually 106 years old."

"What up, C.T.?" Vince O'Shea, red-faced, pockmarked, and shaped like a tuba, grinned at me as he steered a handcuffed *cholo* toward the interview rooms.

"You all right, Taggert?" O'Shea's partner asked. Dennis Whitaker resembled cotton candy wearing a bow tie. To me, he asked, "Run into something good today, Norton?"

"If she did," O'Shea said, "bet they'll make her mayor."

Both men laughed.

I flipped them double birds, then said, "Why don't you both go catch a bus in the face?"

Whitaker grabbed his crotch and squeezed.

"Call me when you find it," I said, "cuz sources say you're no bigger than a jumbo Tampax."

Both men reddened. The *cholo* and Colin snickered.

"I've seen the pictures," I said, twisting the knife in. "Should I share them?"

Whitaker muttered something—a curse or a plea.

The *cholo* said, "You got a little pecker, *ese?*"

O'Shea said, "I call bullshit."

I plucked my phone from the desk.

He held up his hands. "Don't run me over, Sarge." He cackled, then ambled back to his messy desk.

Colin gnawed his bottom lip, then said, "They're assholes."

"And they were assholes last September, too," I said. "The accident is just giving them more material to work with. They've never liked me, Taggert. It's cuz of my boobs and the way I always talk back to the movie screen." I grinned, then shouted, "Gurl, don't go in that room!"

He didn't speak or smile.

"Does it look like I'm stressing over them?" I asked. "What? You embarrassed to be my partner now?"

His blue eyes darkened as he glared at me. "Hell, no."

"Then, relax before you pop a blood vessel." In truth, my skin smoldered with anger. "C.T." didn't mean "Colin Taggert." It meant "Crash Test." Whatever. Crashing the RAV4 into that Park Services truck netted me a dead villain, a $300 Trader Joe's gift card from the NAACP, a promotion, and a Medal of Valor.

Colin yawned and stretched. "So, what now?"

"We send Eugene's will over to the lawyer who prepared it," I said. "Then, we wait for the autopsy and forensic results to see if he was shot or intentionally poisoned. And we'll bring in Bernice and Joe for a lengthier chat. Call the Oswald guy since he's getting the house."

Colin said, "Great," then rolled in his chair back to his desk.

I sat back and surveyed the squad room.

Luke was still out killing roaches.

O'Shea and Whitaker were huddled over O'Shea's desk, a shrine to Big Macs and Monster Energy drinks.

Quiet for a moment.

Until Colin hit the voice-mail button on his phone. A man's voice boomed from the speaker. "This is Detective Andreoff in the Internal Affairs—" Colin grabbed the receiver. He listened to the message with his eyes closed, then dropped the handset back into the cradle.

"Why is Andy calling you?" I asked. "He want you to snitch on somebody?"

"Who knows?" He blushed, then his hard eyes settled on the computer screen.

I watched him in silence, then asked, "I know it's ancient history now, but we never really talked about . . . Do *you* believe my decision at the park . . . ?"

He canted his head. "You had no choice. Either you would've had to let Zach Fletcher take you to that spot on the trail where he left Chanita and Allayna, hoping he didn't take your gun away, hoping he didn't kill you; or end that shit in the RAV4 and not take a chance, hoping that God would save you in the end. Killing Zach Fletcher via windshield saved Taylor, Trina, and who knows how many girls. I would've done the same thing, Lou." His face softened. "You're right—O'Shea and Whitaker are bastards who just want to poke at nonexistent shit. Yesterday, today, until the end of time. Jealous jerks who think . . ." He forced a smile to his lips. "Screw what they think, right?" His smile wavered.

But then again . . . maybe I was seeing things.

8

Seeing things.

Like dead people.

Zach Fletcher. Napoleon Crase. My sister Victoria.

On the street. In the corner of a room. In the backseat of my car.

Something, something brain structure, neurobiology blah blah blah according to my neurologist.

Quite common, my psychotherapist had explained. *Not psychosis. Just your mind's way of coping with loss.*

At Southwest Division, loss happened every day—outside this old building, certainly, but also in every squad and break room. Loss smelled like lilies, cigarettes, and assorted fresh fruit, like the basket now in my arms. The Edible Arrangements gift came courtesy of Angie Darson, who had suffered greatly at the hands of her husband Cyrus and Max Crase. Lips trembling, she said now, "Like it or not, you and me? We're linked forever by men who took away people we loved."

Like me, Angie nightmared every night.

Unlike me, Angie had borne two daughters, Macie and Monique, with a monster. She'd loved Cyrus, had shared his bed and taken his name without ever knowing that he'd joined Max Crase in the rape and murder of my sister. It wasn't long ago that Crase had strangled Monique and left her hanging in a closet of his father's condominium before he finally shot and killed both Macie and Napoleon, Max Crase's father—and owner of the liquor store that had also been the grave for my sister's bones. That afternoon, he had also turned his gun on me, but my fist in his face stopped him from being great. Still, as Max Crase's murder trial came closer to its start, shame, fear, guilt, and anxiety kept Angie from moving forward in her life.

I feared she would succumb to the pain. That she'd smoke herself to death if she didn't use a gun or pills first. Twenty pounds lighter, and hair almost completely gray, she allowed her grief to moor her, to make her heavy.

"I'm just worried about you, Ang."

"I'm worried about you, too." She looked past me to the woebegone families, the handcuffed thugs, and the weary-faced rookies all sprinkled around the lobby. "This place—it ain't healthy."

I chuckled, even though my gut twisted. "Can't disagree."

"What's the point?" she asked.

Nothing I did prevented a damned thing. For ten years now, I had picked up the pieces after that Very Bad Thing. Cleaned crazy up. Prayed that the monster I caught would pay the price before I turned to *another* monster who'd done a Very Bad Thing. Clean. Pray. Clean. Pray. So many monsters.

I carried Angie's fruit bouquet down the corridor of the fallen en route to my desk. On the walls were pictures of Southwest Division officers slain while on duty. Aiden Colletti, an asshole who had come up the ranks of the ex-chief Daryl Gates's LAPD—Crips had smoked him during a raid at a crack house. Patrick Nicholson, another dinosaur who'd rather eat glass soaked in lye than work beside blacks and women in the force. Tom Larson, who had championed community policing and *talking* to people instead of shooting them.

For weeks, I'd avoided this route—its dark energy made my knees quiver.

How long will I last? Avenging the dead, finding the monster, and receiving cupcakes, fruit, discounts on oil changes, and free dry-cleaning from the ones left behind.

Back in March, I could've been on this wall, easy. And there would've been cops standing where I now stood, thinking about what an asshole I'd been before my demise, griping about the commendations I'd received but didn't deserve. How I obviously *wanted* to die because of my divorce or because I just couldn't cut it anymore with the boys.

While cops were six times more likely to commit suicide than Joe Public, black women had the lowest suicide rates of all races and gender. So, hell no: I wasn't ready to leave this earth yet. I still needed to see the first black woman president run the world from the Oval Office. After that, though? Y'all could do what you want. Check, please.

She gave you fruit again?" Colin complained.

"You ain't gotta eat it," I said. "In fact . . ." I sat the basket on my desk, searched the cellophane wrapper, then gasped. "Your name's not even on it."

Colin winked at me as his cell phone chirped. He viewed the number, smiled, then answered. "Hey you."

Luke entered the bullpen, devouring a wet plate of something that smelled like onions and musty socks. "That dessert?" he asked, nodding at my fruit.

I grimaced. "What the heck are you eating?"

"You insultin' my heritage?" He shoved the last bits of his heritage into his mouth.

Colin, eyes closed, was still on the phone—but he now held it away from his ear. His plum-colored face meant that the chick on the phone was giving him the blues. "Libby," he said, rubbing his eyes, "I'm hanging up now. I'm . . ." He stuffed the phone into his shirt pocket. "Is it me or does every woman in LA have a serious mental problem?"

"You meet a loon on one date," I said, "you've met a loon. You meet loons on every date . . . Maybe you're the asshole. Luke, where's Mr. Kim? We need to get started."

Pepe's chair was empty—the fan twisting on his credenza cooled no one. Packs of Starburst chews and Camels sat on his desk. He never went anywhere without either.

"Another phone call with them people," Luke said between bites.

Many rank and file considered cops in the Internal Affairs Bureau to be out-of-touch, pearl-clutching snitches. They dinged you for breaking rules, dinged you for taking shortcuts, and suspended you for wielding your baton and badge too wildly. I'd been called before the IAB to answer for Max Crase's nose ("Yes, sir, I broke it"), Eli Moss's nose ("Yes, sir, I broke it"), and Zach Fletcher's . . . body ("Yes, ma'am, I . . . broke it"). With a pamphlet addressing proper use of force in hand, I was then sent back to my desk to do better.

Pepe didn't care—he had worked homicide for three years now. The son of a Korean grocer and a Mexican seamstress, he had been the only one of us who'd made his parents proud. But once he came out to them, his parents joined the support group founded by my mother, Colin's father, and Brooks's parents—parents who were profoundly disappointed in their kids' choices. I couldn't pass the state bar and chose to be a cop instead. Colin had cheated on the daughter of Colorado Springs's chief of police while on duty. Brooks had chosen to carve up the dead instead of carving out a successful career as a surgeon. But the Kims' membership to this club of Profound Disappointment would be short-lived if Pepe landed a spot in the IAB. Better suits. Nicer offices. More visibility.

"We'll wait five more minutes," I said, "but then, we need to meet. We got work to do."

While waiting, I nibbled pineapple wedges and checked e-mail: Police Foundation (give), Police Chief Beck's Fund (give). Pressure had lodged over the ridge of my forehead, and I had taken enough Advil for at least two more hours. Still . . .

I tossed casual glances around the squad room—no one was looking at me. I opened my bottom drawer and pawed around my bag, finding the Altoids tin that held mints and ibuprofen caplets. *You need it.* My hands shook as I touched a pill, hesitated—*I can wait*—then slipped a mint into my mouth instead.

"You okay?"

I startled and closed the Altoids tin with a *pop.*

Pepe, over at his desk, was staring at me. In his tailored suit and conservative haircut, he looked like he already belonged to the IAB.

"Yep. I'm good." The mint slowly dissolved in my mouth. I grabbed my bottled water near the computer monitor and took a gulp. "We're meeting now."

"I'll only be a minute." Pepe said. "You sure you're okay?"

I flicked my hand. "All good. Go get your nicotine fix." I picked up Angie Darson's basket. "I'll bring refreshments."

He said, "Okay," grabbed the candy and Camels, then hurried back to the exit.

After Pepe's smoke and fruit chews break, he joined Colin, Luke, and me in conference room Freedom.

Despite its new moniker, fresh coats of cerulean blue paint, and updated audiovisual capabilities, the room still reeked of mildewed carpet and grilled onions—and with the boxes of evidence from Washington's house sitting around, it now also stank of cat pee and roach dust. A few roaches from those boxes ran across the walls and table—but Luke smashed and sprayed them before they could mate with our native population. Pictures of the house and victim that we had taken before that afternoon had been tacked into the cork wall. At least the air conditioner worked, although it made the smells sharper. One day, I'd work in a place that smelled of vanilla, lavender, and Weight Watchers entrees.

I pulled skewers of strawberries and pineapple from the fruit basket (the best-smelling thing for miles), then connected my laptop to the cables of the sixty-inch television monitor. "The Washington house is secure, right?"

Pepe nodded. "Two uniforms will be rotating on, rotating off until you give me the word."

Luke's eyes widened with panic. "We don't have to go back, right?"

I opened my laptop. "If we gotta, we gotta. Especially since those gold coins are in there somewhere."

"We did see a car right as we were leaving," Pepe said. "A silver Chrysler 300 moving real slow. I ran the plates."

Colin pulled off a cantaloupe skewer. "Lemme guess: Joseph Rice."

Pepe popped a lemon Starburst into his mouth. "Yep. That's Bernice's special friend, right?"

"Yeah," I said. "Did he stop?"

"Nope."

"Was she in the car?"

"Couldn't tell," Luke said. "Tinted windows." He opened his notebook. "I've been a cop for fifteen years, and I ain't never seen no house like that. I'm *still* killin' roaches in my car."

Colin popped open a can of Diet Coke. "When I get home tonight, I'm gonna clean the hell out of my apartment."

I walked over to the whiteboard and wrote TO DO. Item number one: WARRANTS FOR MED RECORDS. "Pepe, could you handle that?" Then, I made another heading on the whiteboard: WHODUNIT? "So who could've killed our vic? And remember: the locks weren't forced, and the windows weren't broken. Eugene Washington probably opened the door and invited his murderer in for a forty ounce and a game of checkers."

"Ain't poisoning a girl thing?" Colin asked.

"Typically." I wrote BERNICE as my first suspect.

"Put down her real boyfriend," Luke added. "He coulda used that gun."

JOE RICE went second.

Pepe tossed me two strawberry Starburst. "Mr. Washington got any family?"

I tapped Bernice's name, then opened the fruit chew. "Not according to her. Let's look at the will again."

As Colin read aloud, I wrote more names beneath Bernice's. OSWALD LITTLE . . . ISAAC UNDERWOOD . . . ASSOCIATION OF BLACK VETERANS . . .

I underlined the second name on the list. "Oswald Little is getting almost everything valuable—the house and the car. The vets get the medals. This guy Isaac gets the vinyl records. And Bernice, the gold."

"Who are Oswald Little and Isaac Underwood?" Pepe asked.

"We need to find out." I made a note to contact both men. "Oh. Insurance policy—we're supposed to check."

We searched the boxes but found no forms.

"Bernice says he had an old policy and was getting another," I said. "Let's keep it in the front of our minds from here on out."

"All those people on the board," Luke said, "who'd want him dead quickest?"

My marker tapped BERNICE, then slid to OSWALD LITTLE. "Sell the house, make half a million."

"I think Bernice is our best bet," Colin said. "Especially with shifty-ass Joe. And didn't you say she's been sued, like, fifty times since yesterday?"

"Six times since 2012," I said. "You're right—she needs money."

"Who gets the guns?" Pepe asked.

I scanned the will. "I don't see anybody listed. Where *are* the guns, including the one found near Washington's armchair?"

"In the evidence locker," Pepe said. "What's his face in Ballistics will check to see if any of them have been fired recently."

"I guess it's kinda normal for a vet to have that many weapons sitting around," Colin said.

"He hoarded everything else, so why not guns?" I pointed out.

"And that cash we found in his wallet," Pepe said. "Seventeen hundred dollars, right? Why so much?"

I tapped the marker against the whiteboard. "Good question. We know he was a carpenter—folks may have paid him in cash. Luke, sniff around and find out where he got his income, and if he has a bank account."

We rummaged through the boxes again and through all the items that had seemed important this morning, like the picture of Eugene and his friend on the red boat and the church services program. A battered camera case contained a wide-zoom lens and a folded piece of yellowing paper with letters written in fading ink. M.S., A.A. O.L., R.T. MM. Some letters had checks by them while other letters had been crossed out.

"What does it mean?" Colin asked.

"It means . . ." I held the paper to my forehead and closed my eyes. "Who the hell knows what it means on this, the first day of our investigation?"

"So now?" Luke asked.

"*Now*, Colin and I will talk to Bernice again," I said. "And we'll talk to Oswald Little and Isaac Underwood and then, just for background's sake, folks over at Blessed Mission. Luke's handling the old man's finances. Pepe, you're on phone records and medical history. We cool?"

Pepe and Luke eyed each other, then Colin and me. "That's it?" Pepe asked. "Our suspects are a gold digger and a church?"

"Is that a problem?" I asked.

"Usually, there's more," Pepe said.

"That's our job," I said. "To find more. Someone's probably hoping that we'll wander away from this case cuz he was an old man who died in a filthy old house on a filthy hot day. But our superpower, gentlemen, is figuring out why someone died."

Pepe sighed and scribbled in his notepad. His necktie had remained knotted—only the button on his blazer had come undone.

I cocked my head. "Tired, Peter? Bored, maybe?"

"Nope," he said, eyes on his pad. "Just don't wanna waste time on something so . . . vague."

I raised a finger. "To paraphrase Ghostface Killah—"

"Oh, hell," Luke said, rolling his eyes, "you got her quoting Wu-Tang now."

I smiled. "To paraphrase: stars, sky, look up, was I meant to be here? Dolla-dolla-bill, y'all."

Colin waved a hand in the air. "Amen, sista."

A roach—the small German kind—skedaddled from his home in an evidence box toward the fruit basket in the center of the table. One of Colin's size 12s sent it home to the roach lord in the sky.

Lieutenant Rodriguez knocked once on the door before he shoved his massive bulk into an inch of open space. The fleshy bags beneath his gray eyes declared that he hadn't slept much. And he'd been chain-smoking—his tobacco scent mingled with Pepe's. Without uttering a hello, he barked, "Taggert, my office. Now."

Colin flinched, then gathered his things.

Lieutenant Rodriguez nodded to me. "You feel all right today?"

My heart sent up a flare as my partner shuffled to the door. *Today?* "Just digging into the Washington case. Everything okay?"

"Yep," Lieutenant Rodriguez said. "Everything's good."

And just like he came, my boss left without saying good-bye.

Pepe, Luke, and I sat there in the quiet. Then, Luke grabbed the last skewer of strawberries from the arrangement. "What was *that* about?"

"You two screw up again?" Pepe wondered. "Other than probably making this case bigger than what it should be?"

You feel all right today?

Maybe Lieutenant Rodriguez had discovered that I wasn't 100 percent yet.

That I still popped an occasional Vicodin.

That I nightmared every night that I *did* sleep.

Sometimes, I look up at the stars . . .

9

In the county of Los Angeles, there were six entries in the public directory for Oswald Little. The first three numbers I called did not know Eugene Washington; the fourth and fifth possibilities did not answer their phones; and number six had been disconnected.

"You need to hang up the damn phone and stop working. You'll never get laid with that thing glued to your face." Lena poured more red wine into her glass, then settled deeper into the deck chair. "If your eyes are rolled back in your head from sheer ecstasy, time will pass and the case will solve itself. It's like, not watching for the water to boil, or whatever the hell the saying is."

I tossed her an eye roll while standing in the open patio door of my condominium. I'd taken Lena's advice a month ago and spent half of my divorce settlement to purchase a beach-community, one-bedroom condo in Playa del Rey, just a mile from my marital Shangri-La. Being near the ocean calmed me. The white noise of crashing waves eased me into sleep (theoretically), and the lagoon on the condo's backside provided me with ducks to feed.

And now sunlight glinted off the ribbon of liquid sapphire across the street. A flock of seagulls circled in the sky above the Pacific Ocean, adding to a cool breeze—the first I'd enjoyed that had not come from a fan.

"Who needs a man when I have all these seagulls," I said. "I could sit out here and watch these birds all day. Just—"

My phone vibrated with a text from Greg. *Thanks for calling Mom and for sending Det. Zamora. I know there's not much you can do. Still, TYVM.*

"Who's that?" Lena asked.

"Mr. Norton thanking me." I clenched, and waited for Lena's French barb regarding this interaction with my ex-husband. When she didn't speak, I gaped at her.

Brown eyes wide, she clasped her hands together, then said, "So . . ." She tugged at her pink booty shorts.

"So . . . what?"

"Before we have drinks with Ethan and Dominic, we're going upstairs for dinner—"

"I told you that I didn't want to eat with—"

"It's not with *them*." Hope and worry colored her face and twisted her mouth. "Chauncey called. He's in town. *He's* buying us dinner." She smiled, frowned, then smiled again.

Despite his affair, his coming-out, their divorce, his marriage to his personal trainer the former Brando Gooch, despite Lena's various Eastern European and Israeli lovers, she loved Chauncey Meadows. And she hated Chauncey Meadows. She was an ex-wife.

"What does he want?" I asked.

She shrugged. "Maybe he went to one of those 'pray gay away' churches."

I grinned. "The ones where you get healed and don't like men no more? Just women, women, women?"

"I know—*c'est impossible*." She plucked my romance novel from between the chair's cushion and then read the back cover. "What's up with you and Sam?"

"He's still extricating himself from the case. So nothing's up." With that, I shuffled into the living room and kneeled before the last moving box. It was the "precious memories" box, the one that stowed my framed commendation from the city of Los Angeles, the blue velvet box that had held my Medal of Valor, and my wedding album.

Lena grabbed her glass of wine from the deck table and slinked back into the condo. "That's it? No other comment or observation about Sam? Or about Chauncey?"

"Nope, nothing about Sam. But Chauncey? Don't trust a big butt and a smile."

"You're quoting Bell Biv Devoe at me? What the hell does that mean?"

"That *means*, last time Chauncey was in LA I had to hold a cold pack to his face after you beaned him with your BlackBerry."

She laughed, then adjusted a strap on her tank top. "Ah. Memories. BlackBerry—they still make those?"

"Do I have to go on this date then?" I asked. "Don't you want some quiet time with your ex?"

She pointed toward my bedroom. "Go ye into the closet and put on something breathtaking and marvelous, *oui?*"

"*Oui.*" I trudged to my room and opened the window. Jonathan Livingston Seagull and his friends were still circling above the waves.

"Get dressed," Lena shouted from the living room. "And stop looking at them damn birds."

I groaned. Cement in my belly, I moped to the closet and stood there, idling the way women did before dreaded blind dates. Stacks of jeans (flared, boyfriend, skinny, boot-cut), rows of shirts (V-neck, scoop neck, Oxford, short-sleeved), and rows of shoes (heels, flats, sneakers, boots) surrounded me, but I didn't want to wear any of it.

I pulled off my LAPD T-shirt and yoga pants. Glared again at the clothes on the shelves and hangers, then reached for—

"And don't you dare pull on jeans," Lena shouted.

"Leave me alone," I yelled back, swiping at the hangers.

I hate Greg. And I hated him for making me go through this "dating in the twenty-first century" crap.

I hated the chitchat.

You ever kill somebody?

Did you see that post on Facebook about the cops who [insert horrendous thing done in the name of justice]?

What do you think of those cops in [insert city with a jack-ass police force]?

And I hated the strong cologne, the teeth kissers, the skinny jeans, the lack of curiosity in things outside his side hustle, the app he planned to build, his explanations about chem trails being real and the reasons he stopped eating red meat.

I want Sam. There were no stupid police questions with Sam. He wore light cologne. He used his tongue. He wore old-school Levi's. Laughed easily. Enjoyed Porterhouse steaks. Wasn't trying to get me to buy vitamin supplements or phone cards or his latest demo.

But I couldn't have Sam. I needed Max Crase in jail more than I needed a lover.

And as I stood before the mirror, I saw that I also needed my hair done, just like Bernice Parrish had suggested. I texted my hair stylist and scheduled an appointment for Monday. Then, I turned back to the closet. *What to wear? What to . . . ?*

Screw it.

Gold Stuart Weitzman stilettos only worn once, and a clingy scoop-neck dress with no pockets to hold a phone card or vitamin samples.

Chauncey Meadows had pitched for the Los Angeles Dodgers for three seasons until he needed Tommy John surgery to reconstruct his ulnar collateral ligament. He recovered from the procedure, but by then the team had replaced him. Chauncey quickly pivoted and became a sports agent, using his natural talent for business and the connections he'd made as a starter. One client became three clients, and now he operated one of the most successful boutique agencies in the country.

But he still possessed the knobby knuckles and broad shoulders of a jock. He'd grown a thin mustache and goatee to hide the scars from cleats in his face and fights on the mound. His suit, with its high thread count, enamel buttons, and hand stitching, cost more than my last paycheck.

And now I wondered why the hell he'd come to Los Angeles, and I watched as he greeted his ex-wife as though he hadn't cheated on her with his personal trainer.

"*Bienvenue à la maison,*" Lena cooed.

"*De rien, ma cherie.*" Chauncey kissed both of her cheeks. "You look beautiful." Then, he grinned at me. "You, too, Lou. Especially after that accident." He wrapped his arms around me and squeezed. "The city of Los Angeles doesn't deserve you." Then he held out Lena's chair as she sat at our table.

Redheaded server Amy wore a white apron that was cleaner than a surgeon's scrubs. She draped stiff napkins on our laps as we grabbed cocktail menus. After she welcomed us to Mastro's, she said, "If you're thinking soufflés for dessert, you should order now."

And so we did.

Lena ordered a dirty martini, and Chauncey ordered wine for the table.

Then, it was my turn. "A coconut ginger mojito. That's nonalcoholic, correct?"

Chauncey and Lena were gaping at me. *Virgin?*

Amy smiled. "Sure is."

"You still on the clock?" Chauncey asked.

"Nope," I said.

"Are you pregnant?" Lena asked.

"Stop asking silly questions."

"You've just never . . ." Lena squinted at me.

"And I ordered our favorite Cab," Chauncey said.

"Just trying something different," I explained. Honestly? After today's trek through Hoarded Hell, I needed a drink crammed with rum, vodka, and moonshine. But my blood pressure was high, and I'd promised Dr. Popov to adopt better living initiatives.

To avoid my friends' scrunched eyebrows, I found interest in the polished cutlery, in the mounds of Caesar salad on the plates of diners at the next table, and, finally, in the leather-bound menu that listed six million ways to eat three thousand kinds of surf and turf. "So Chauncey," I said, "what brings you back to Los Angeles? Business?"

"No, actually." He sipped from his water glass. "Personal stuff."

The server returned with my mojito. It was bubbly and gold—fool's gold. Amy then presented Chauncey with the 2010 bottle of Silver Oak Alexander Valley Cabernet Sauvignon.

My mouth watered, and a whimper escaped from my lips as Amy poured that eggplant-colored liquid into two glasses instead of three.

"You sure?" Chauncey asked me.

I nodded, sipped my virgin mojito, and winced. Tasted like sugar and fake coconut, neither of which complemented a sixty-dollar rib eye. "Brando fly out, too?" I asked.

"Bran stayed home," Chauncey said, "even though he hates to miss staying at the Four Seasons. I had hoped"—he smiled at Lena—"to stay out at the house. I love Connecticut, but I miss the Pacific Ocean."

Lena sipped from her wineglass. "I'll think about it. May not be enough room."

"Last time I checked," he said, "there were five bedrooms."

Lena rolled her eyes, then gulped more wine.

"Lou, I hear congratulations are in order," Chauncey said. "Finally, detective sergeant and a Medal of Valor. That deserves a toast."

Lena squinted at him. "What the hell do you want, Chauncey?"

"There *is* something." He squared his shoulders, then pushed out a breath. "Brando and I have been married now for three years."

"And?" Lena said.

"*And* we want to start a family."

"What the hell am I supposed to say to that?" Lena demanded. "Why am I here, Chauncey?"

The ex-pitcher futzed with his napkin. "Well, it's obvious that neither Brando nor I can naturally carry a child—"

"You don't say." With her tiny hand trembling, Lena reached into the dirty martini for the skewer of olives. She tore off the green globes with her teeth, broke the long toothpick in half, then dumped it on the table.

I held my breath as my shoulders automatically tensed—a cop all these years, I knew that danger lay ahead.

Chauncey forced himself to smile. "We—Brando and I—would like *you*, Lena, to carry him. Or her. A baby. For us."

Lena glared at her ex-husband, then screeched, "*What?*"

Over at the next table, the family celebrating Nana's birthday stole peeks at us. No one cared about Uncle Siggy's appendectomy, not with family drama featuring an ex-wife, two husbands, and a baby happening just a yard away.

"I just . . ." Chauncey shrugged. "You know I still love you. You are the most beautiful woman in the world. So exciting and vivacious and . . . The baby, our child, should have a strong woman in his life, her life, and . . ." His eyes shimmered with tears. "We'll adopt if you say 'no' because we trust no one else with this responsibility. We'll pay all of your health bills, your clothes—I know you love you some Versace and Tom Ford."

Then, Chauncey explained that he'd done research about surrogacy and in vitro fertilization, that Brando was totally for it, and that Baby Meadows would be very much loved. "If you want," he continued, "you can stay in the cottage on our property."

Oh, boy. That landed a punch in *my* chest and I coughed.

Lena's hand flexed around her steak knife. "Stay in the cottage . . . Like a wet nurse or a mammy."

"Don't get that way," Chauncey said, oblivious to the danger zone he'd just entered. "You'd just be closer. We'd really be a family. *Our* family."

I placed my hand over Lena's and squeezed. A silent plea for her to release the knife.

Her grip only tightened. She had dreamed of having two kids with Chauncey—Josephine and Noah Meadows. They'd vacation three times a year, play Monopoly on Friday nights, and watch *Annie* and *The Wiz* on Saturday nights. Graduation, weddings, grandchildren—she'd planned to celebrate each milestone with this man. And now . . .

BlackBerry in the face all over again. This time, with knives.

But Lena released the knife. She folded her arms and glared at the broken toothpick. Then, she closed her eyes and a tear slipped down her cheek.

"I think . . ." I swallowed, then started again even though my heart beat so hard I couldn't hear myself talk. "I think she needs time to think about it, Chauncey."

He nodded. "Of course." He tried to smile at his ex-wife. "Take as much time as you need."

A server sat my sizzling plate of steak before me, then did the same for Lena and Chauncey. Even with bowls of lobster mashed potatoes and sautéed brussels sprouts before us, no one moved.

Lena wouldn't look at Chauncey. She wouldn't look at *me*. She sat silent, barely breathing, arms wrapped around her torso like a straitjacket to keep herself together.

But Chauncey had already broken her.

Again.

Wednesday, September 2

10

The devil lies beside me in bed, ready to slaughter me as I sleep.

Blood and brain mats his black hair. Pale skin hangs from his face and arms like molted snake skin. His eyes are as black as an abandoned coal mine.

My reflection shines there, in those coal-black eyes. My mouth opens, ready to scream.

The devil shrieks. His dank claws grab my left arm.

Pain rips through me like wildfire. I thrash against his bloody, shredded body, losing the battle as that fire consumes me. Give up. Let it happen. It's okay.

Zach Fletcher crawls on top of me. His breath smells of a thousand corpses. Bloody foam drops from his lolling tongue and splatters on my face.

I squeeze my eyes shut. My heart hammers in the red. My end will soon come.

He shakes me, urges me to fight. "Open your eyes. Open your eyes and see."

But I won't fight. I refuse to see. Trapped like an animal in tar, I lie there, trembling, hands jammed into my armpits.

He licks my quivering cheek, then slips off the bed and creeps from the room. Beyond the door, waiting for him is my sister Victoria.

I'm alone. Again.

But in sixteen hours, we will see each other once more. The graveyard shift.

I opened my eyes, ready to fight daytime monsters, sweating, already tense, and trusting absolutely nothing.

Muted light glowed behind the closed window sheers. The red digital numbers on my bedside clock claimed it was seven thirty.

Didn't trust that, either. Not with the heat waves and rolling blackouts. Not with the clock's six-dollar price tag and its almost-Sony-Samsung-sounding name.

After my mind stowed my nightmare in its steam trunk for the day, I grabbed my iPhone from the nightstand. Barely trusted *that*, especially with the new, glitchy OS.

7:53, six text messages.

I stink-eyed the lying digital clock, then sat up in bed. Just as they had during my nightmare, my muscles burned and any area surrounding a pulse point ached—but not the good ache that came from physical therapy squats or Krav Maga hammer fists.

"You okay?" Lena stood in the doorway. Her eyes looked silvery—was she crying? "You were screaming and I didn't know if I should've shaken you awake or . . ."

I scrutinized the twisted comforter and sheets on the hardwood floor. Back on the nightstand, the bottled water and Glock hadn't moved since I'd sat both there last night. "I didn't knock anything over this time, so *that's* progress."

"Yeah. . . ." Her gaze cartwheeled around the room—dark television screen, Ed Ruscha print, that gun. She refused to meet the eyes of the mess wearing the "On Wednesdays, we wear pink" tank top.

My new state had unnerved the baddest bitch in the world.

Indeed, the last days *were* upon us.

Lena rubbed her arms to ease the chill. "Do you really need the gun so . . . close? Cuz what if . . . ?"

My Glock sat on the nightstand like some women's reading glasses and hand creams.

"Didn't mean to scare you," I whispered. "I told you I wasn't ready for male company yet." I chuckled because I'd just *had* male company. Not the *living* kind.

She closed a slightly open dresser drawer, then said, "You're *not* ready. Glad I listened."

"Lena, I—"

At the window, a flash of darkness moved beyond the curtains.

Him. Again.

My eyes widened and my breath caught in my chest.

Lena tiptoed over to me and touched my shoulder. "No one's here, Lou." She nodded at the window. "No one's out there, either."

Ice-cold panic still crackled across my skin. "I know. I just can't . . . I know."

But he *was* here. Lena just couldn't see him.

I couldn't tell her or anyone else that I saw Zach Fletcher every night. The three-month, short-term disability leave I'd taken had already made Captain Wyatt cock an eyebrow at Lieutenant Rodriguez. Which then made Lieutenant Rodriguez cock an eyebrow at me. Didn't need either man reading in my file that post-traumatic stress disorder kept me seeing dead men anytime I closed my eyes for more than five minutes. Didn't want Wyatt or Rodriguez to learn that, despite my protestations (no, I'm fine; no, I don't need time off; no, that doesn't hurt), I still felt more broken than a 1970 AMC Gremlin.

The secrets women keep.

Colin: he knew *something* was wrong. He had mentioned PTSD yesterday, but only because I'd slipped enough so that he could peep past my mask. Couldn't do that again.

"I'm fine, Lena." I forced myself to smile as I scrolled through the texts on my phone. "Hey! What's his face already sent me a message."

Lena settled beside me in bed. "You gonna text him back?"

I smirked. "Uh, no."

Dominic Campbell had been a beautiful man with teeth as white and straight as piano keys. His muscles had muscles. Over drinks (Pellegrino and lime for me), he chatted about his battalion chief, his trip to 9/11, and his Rottweiler, Ace. He asked how long I'd been divorced and how many children I had. He loved kids. He had six kids, and they each lived with their mothers.

"What about you?" I asked Lena while reading Colin's text: *See you at LACCO!* "Ethan's no Israeli arms dealer or Russian oligarch, but he seems nice enough. Like a cocker spaniel."

She wiggled her nose. "I'd never get my private island on a civil servant's salary."

Lena, already sour from dinner with Chauncey, had ended the date once firefighter Ethan said, "If you wanna go halves, we can—"

"But I could tell that you didn't like him before that," I said now. "Reluctant hugs and great-aunt kisses from the woman who brought us fellatio in a Ferrari on the 405."

She shrugged. "I was a little distracted. Chauncey and his . . . *proposal.* And he really expected me to let him sleep in the house after asking me *that?* What was your excuse? Dominic too hot for you?"

I smirked. "I checked out the moment he said that we'd make pretty babies."

"Too soon?"

"That man's penis has more miles on it than Halley's Comet." I stood and winced as I shuffled to the bathroom.

"Want breakfast?" Lena asked.

"Yes, please." Like a tonic, the cold from the marble floor oozed from the soles of my feet up my legs and to my neck. I glimpsed my reflection in the mirror: scar over my left eyebrow, scar above my hairline, shoulders tense and slightly misaligned. My satin scarf had fallen off my head, and now my hair shot this way and that. I needed more sun—my skin was not as bronze as it should've been.

I pulled open the vanity's drawer. Squirreled-away vials of Percocet and Vicodin rolled forward. Only ten Vicodin and three Percocet remained with no refills on either prescription. I hadn't taken Percocet since May—but winter was coming.

Or was it already here? Could my current 7 on the pain scale, with its jagged aches and scratchy colors, be negotiated down to a 4 with prayer and caffeine?

I sighed, then closed the drawer—it had to. I whispered a quick prayer-mantra mash-up. *Dear Lord, make the pain into nothing, into the wind, just the wind.* I needed to think today since the easiest tasks— pointing at crap to take, pointing at the dead body I couldn't take—had already been done yesterday.

Eugene Washington deserved all of me.

I roller-balled Icy Hot in key spots, then checked my blood pressure: 135/80. Crappy but better than yesterday—guess that came after twenty-four hours without wine. I flat-ironed my hair and successfully avoided my scalp wound. After eyeliner and bronzer, I pulled on dress jeans and a pink Oxford shirt, throw-away-ables if I needed to return to the Hoard on Victoria.

Twenty minutes later, I strolled into the kitchen like the chill California girl I was born to be.

"Penny's friend has stomach mumps," Lena reported. She was staring at *Good Times* now, playing on the small television bolted to the cabinet.

I cocked my head and placed my hands on my hips. "Girl, look around. This isn't a finishing school—"

Lena spread her arms. "It's the *ghetto*!"

I settled at the breakfast bar and stared at the strawberry Pop-Tart sitting on a saucer. "*This* is breakfast?"

She poured fresh-brewed coffee into our mugs. "You ran out of the brown sugar ones. But I toasted it to make it even more special. *Bon appétit.*"

I reached for the dimmer to the kitchen lights and lowered the switch. I loved the white and pearl mosaic tiles and platinum-colored cabinets, but on mornings like this? Too much. "Any plans for the day?" I asked my friend.

She pointed in the direction of my bedroom. "First, I'm climbing into your bed to sleep for a few hours. Then, Chauncey wants to talk again before he flies back home."

"You decide what you're gonna do?"

She tucked her head between her wrists, then groaned. "Am I evil if I tell him no?"

"Evil for not wanting to become his womb for rent?"

She said, "Ha," and then broke apart my Pop-Tart and nibbled on the half. "There *are* pros."

"And plenty of cons," I said.

"Pro: I get a cute baby."

"Con: it ain't just your baby. And it just ain't Chauncey's baby, either. It's the third guy's, too."

"Pro," Lena said, "Chauncey will never be a deadbeat dad."

"Con," I said, "what *sane* man will wanna deal with two men, you, and a baby?"

Lena groaned. "This is some Bay Area nonsense. I'm from effin' New

York. What the hell am I doing?" She sighed. "If you were me, what would you do?"

"I wouldn't do it. I can't commoditize my uterus like that. It's not like a kidney or a piece of my liver. And to be a babymomma to a man who hurt me like Chauncey hurt you?"

"I may not get another chance," Lena said.

"Bullshit," I said. "There's sperm all over this city. I wouldn't be surprised if you're standing in a puddle of it right now. We'll go to Target or log on to Amazon—it's the everything store. You can buy uranium *and* sperm."

Lena smiled. "And since I'm a Prime member, I'll get it today before three."

"Exactly. Again: what do you gain by doing this?"

"I'd get a baby."

I folded my arms. "No—you're the surrogate, *not* the parent. Unless you two draw up custody papers, the baby will belong to Chauncey and Brando. Again: what do you gain? You don't need the money."

She shrugged, then bit the inside of her cheek. "That was the only benefit, I guess."

I sipped coffee, then said, "Dominic the fireman is cute, and he's also anxious to make more pretty babies. You should call him." I moved to the living room to grab my bag.

"If this were Greg—?"

"Hell no."

"If this were Sam?"

I raised my eyebrows as words tumbled out of my mouth. "I'd have Sam's baby."

She ambled toward the hallway. "That requires sex, you know."

"I'm gettin' there. Don't rush me. These things take time."

"For a lame snail, *ma chérie*. Not for a healthy, sexy Homo sapiens."

"Good night, Lena."

"Good night, Elouise. Have a lovely day avenging the dead."

11

A *venging the dead.*

So many tasks to complete to accomplish that—the first would be attending Eugene Washington's autopsy. I thought about those blue splotches on Eugene Washington's face as I grabbed my car keys from the coffee table. Brooks had mentioned arsenic poisoning as a possible cause, but would arsenic cause all that swelling?

The morning air smelled of car exhaust, jasmine, and burning hillsides—the official scent of late-summer Los Angeles. And it was hot. But "hot" was nothing new in this town. What that white disk in the sky was now sending our way? More than heat, and whatever it was swirled throughout our bodies and cooked us like frogs that would never jump out of the pot.

The county coroner's office was now in possession of hundreds of cooked frogs, most of them senior citizens. The rest of the dead represented the usual demographic: people who hadn't moved quickly enough—out of a bullet's path, away from a knife's swing or a drunk driver's front bumper. No meat wagons occupied their parking spaces—each van now trundled around the city, ferrying the deceased to the coolest spot in town.

Colin paced in the shade of the science building. He had already sweat through his tan dress shirt. Once he spotted me, he tapped at his wristwatch. "You know autopsies make me nervous." On cue, the nerve over his right eyebrow jumped and twisted.

"I know. Apologies."

He loosened his tie and unbuttoned the neck of his shirt. "You know that you being late only makes me crazier. Cuz I hate autopsies."

"Wasn't on purpose, Taggert. Calm down. I'm here now."

"Company?" He winked, then bit his lower lip.

"Yes. Salma Hayek's in my bed right now."

He beamed at me. "Hot damn. You shoulda called me."

I rolled my eyes. "Cuz real life *is* a Cinemax channel. I couldn't pry myself out of her arms long enough to give you a ring."

My phone vibrated as we headed to the entrance. Another text from Dominic Campbell. *Really want 2 cU. 4your eyes only.* He posed naked on a balcony that overlooked a pool flanked with swaying palm trees. He held the phone in one hand and his . . . *hose* in the other.

Well, damn.

Something trembled inside of me—the same trembling that resulted in too many wine coolers in the backseat, panties left in the ashtray, and nine months later a stroller in the back of your SUV. And if anyone could make baby furniture appear in my Porsche, it was the fireman with the six babymommas.

My thumb moved toward the trashcan to delete Dominic's picture, but it stopped. It really was an artful shot. Inspirational, even.

"A naked selfie from the hero?" Colin held open the door, and the aromas of formaldehyde and Pine-Sol swirled around us.

I squinted at him. "How did you know?"

He said, "Your face changed. Doesn't he have chili to cook? Recliners to do nothing in?"

I showed him the picture. "But he has all *this* going for him."

Colin shrugged. "Balconies are overrated."

"I've seen your balcony. It's small."

"You saw it in March, during that freaky weather. It was cold, then. Everything's smaller in the cold."

"That's what they all say." I pointed to his face. "Your eyes look better."

"I used the drops again. Really: your fireman needs to be putting out all the fucking fires around here instead of tryin' to get you on your back."

"True. The pictures?"

"I sent them to Brooks last night."

"Not just of the scene but—"

"The casserole dish and gun, too. Yep. Sent 'em all over."

At the locker rooms, we separated to change into scrubs. Minutes later, we reunited in the hallway. Colin rubbed his arms, welted now from his nervous scratching.

I poked a red slash. "You're gonna bleed to death, you keep it up."

He winked. "You'll rub some Neosporin on it later?"

I winked back. "Yep, then I'll hold a lit match to it." We reached the autopsy suite. I peeked through the door's window.

Brooks's assistant, Big Reuben, with his earbuds in place, pulled out drawers. His large brown hands grabbed all things sharp and stainless steel. Dead bodies lay beneath sheets on the three exam tables. In the corner of the room, Brooks filled out paperwork. He examined one of our crime scene photos taped to the cabinet door, then wrote onto his pad.

During his residency as a surgeon, Brooks had been the pride and joy of Susan and Spencer Brooks II, M.D., Ph.D. To their profound disappointment, Brooks decided that the living had enough help but the dead needed brains. He had smiled at his zombie pun that afternoon at Duke's restaurant in Malibu. Syeeda and I had also giggled, but the elder Dr. Brooks had snarled, ". . . throw away your life," while Mrs. Brooks nursed her aching heart with a third glass of Chardonnay. After dinner, Syeeda and I had taken our depressed friend to the hood for the Cork's too-strong Long Island Iced Teas and delicious Buffalo wings. Once Brooks and Syeeda began making out on the dance floor, I slipped out of the club and fell asleep in the backseat of Brooks's Yukon.

And now, years later, the deputy medical examiner regarded me as though I'd placed fifteen items on the 12 Items or Less conveyor belt of life. His eyes brimmed with concern—it was the doctor in him. He asked, "How are you?" as he handed me a face shield.

"Been better," I said, pulling on the mask.

Brooks grunted, then said to Colin, "Hello."

And now, the three of us huddled over Eugene Washington.

Colin stood with his legs apart, arms crossed, and chin dipped to his chest. His lips were tight, his jaw clenched. Nothing in that blond head of his except, *Don't throw up, don't throw up.*

But there were so many noxious things before us. Splashes and splatters, gooey cherry-red objects that glistened beneath the overhead lights. Smells, stinks, and sounds that existed only because you no longer did.

Laying on the table, Eugene Washington didn't look like he hoarded cats and trash. On Brooks's table, he was a naked, grizzled seventy-three-year-old, freckled, scarred red, and splotched blue. Purplish lividity had spread across his buttocks, the backs of his thighs, and his feet. Since our time together, he had bloated, grown stiffer and colder. He heard nothing as Brooks described him into a microphone.

One hundred sixty pounds. One hundred eighty-five centimeters. Angioedema—the swelling around Washington's eyes and lips.

"Petechial hemorrhaging in both pupils." The tiny red spots were caused by ruptured capillaries brought on by asphyxia. Brook opened the man's mouth and used a tiny flashlight to scour the darkness. "The patient's tongue is swollen and . . . his throat is constricted. Pharyngeal and laryngeal edema. Mucous plugging present in the airway." The old man hadn't been able to breathe.

Brooks scraped Washington's tongue and dropped the swab into a glass vial.

Behind the face shield, Colin's eyes were squeezed shut.

And his eyes stayed shut as Brooks examined Eugene Washington's internal organs. "The lungs appear hyper-inflated," Brooks said. Both organs resembled balloons and took up most of the room in his chest.

And still no evidence of a gunshot.

I held up a shaking hand.

Brooks switched off the microphone.

"You'd mentioned poisoning yesterday because of the blue splotches," I said.

"Possibly." Brooks then pointed to the blue splotches. "Caused by a lack of oxygen in the blood. Has anyone told you of a food allergy?"

I shook my head. "We're still looking around the house."

Spots of red colored Colin's cheeks, and he lurched out of the double doors.

Brooks viewed the digital clock over the sink. "Twenty-six minutes."

I smiled. "A record."

"But this is strange," Brooks said, nodding at the body. "Some things

I see say cyanide, like the blue splotches. Other indicators say anaphylactic shock."

"From eating something he's allergic to."

"Yeah." Then he turned to the photographs taped to the cabinet. "Look at the second picture on the right."

I found the close-up shot of the casserole dish filled with that goop.

"You said a witness thinks this is peach cobbler?" Brooks asked.

"Right."

"The flecks, then," Brooks said. "Those could be peach leaves. And the grit that looks like cracked pepper? Crushed peach pits, perhaps. Both of which contain cyanide."

"Hopefully, Zucca's results will be in soon."

"I'll test Mr. Washington's hair and stomach contents. Take some bone as well. If it's arsenic, it'll show itself, and I'll be able to determine if he'd been poisoned over a span of time or just one big event."

Colin slipped back into the chamber. "Sorry 'bout that." He blushed, then dabbed his clammy face against his shoulder.

"We'll get a warrant for Washington's medical records," I said. "See if his recent blood tests showed anything."

"Do you know when he saw the doctor last?" Brooks asked.

"His girlfriend said he had a physical last week," Colin offered.

"But he didn't take the blood tests," I said.

"Did she bake the cobbler?" Brooks asked.

"She denies it," Colin said, "but she'd never admit it if she did."

"Hopefully," I said, "there are prints on the dish."

"So the gun?" Colin asked.

"Wasn't used to kill him." Brooks then pointed to the tattoo on Eugene Washington's left bicep. "Vet, huh?"

"Found a few medals in a box at his house," I said. "Including a Purple Heart."

Brooks sighed. "How did he come to die in a place like that?"

In my own understanding of PTSD, I'd learned that black vets especially were more likely to develop the disorder. Too many of them didn't seek help for their problem—and so, too, many of them committed suicide. Eugene Washington had served in this country's most unpopular war. Anyone could tell from the hoarded mess he called home that he hadn't benefited from any mental health programs. A Purple Heart and Medal of Freedom stowed in a box hidden beneath a hill of cat skeletons?

As F. Scott Fitzgerald wrote, "Show me a hero and I'll write you a tragedy."

12

So is it official, Lou?" Pepe asked as he settled in a conference room chair. "That Washington was murdered?"

I shrugged as I pawed through the evidence boxes. No insurance policy papers but I did find a yellowed sandwich bag filled with tangled and tarnished chains. "According to Brooks, after ingesting cyanide, your respiratory system stops working after ten, fifteen minutes. Your heart stops a little after that. He sent hair, nails, and bone to be tested to see if he'd been poisoned over a long period of time."

"That's a fucked-up way to die," Pepe said.

"Did they find prints on the beer bottle or the cobbler dish?" Colin asked.

"The prints on the beer bottle were the vic's." I returned to my seat and glanced over Zucca's preliminary autopsy report on the laptop. "No matches yet found on the casserole dish. And Bernice Parrish is supposed to come in today to leave her prints."

Colin nodded. "I'll call her again as a friendly reminder."

"I didn't look," I said, "but did that dish come from a set in Washington's house?"

No one spoke.

I sighed. "So when we go back in—"

"No," Colin shouted.

"Let's look and see," I continued.

"Peach pits can kill you?" Luke asked.

"Cherry, plum, nectarine . . ." I said.

"Who knew that?" he asked.

Pepe, Colin, and I raised our hands.

Luke blushed. "But we eat them *saladitos*."

"But you don't consume the *pit*," I said. "You just suck off the salt."

Zucca's report now filled the screen of the sixty-inch monitor. I double-clicked to open the enlarged picture of the casserole dish, then placed the cursor on the dark flecks suspended in sugary goo. "The cobbler tested negative for cyanide *and* arsenic as well as other . . ."

No one spoke.

My heart dropped. He wasn't poisoned—and I'd just wasted a day and thousands of dollars on a feckless crusade.

Colin tapped my shoulder. "It's okay, Lou. You wanted to be sure. That's our job."

"Yeah." I studied the plastic sandwich bag sitting on my binder, then dumped the chains onto the table. "Whoa." From the tangle, I pulled out a medic alert bracelet. The red snake emblem was still bright against the dust. The front of the bracelet listed Eugene Washington's name and phone number, and the back listed two lines.

Allergic:

Coconut.

13

Zucca didn't say anything, but I heard him breathing on the other side of the phone line.

"Is that a problem?" I asked.

"Testing the beer and cobbler for coconut? Not really. But I'm not understanding . . ."

"If Mr. Washington died as a result of ingesting coconut—"

"But people die from anaphylactic shock without nefarious—"

"True but . . ." *But what?* My mind whirled. "Can you do it, please? For me?"

Brooks was harder to convince.

"Where was his medic alert bracelet?" I asked the pathologist over the phone. "A man this old with a food allergy should have been wearing his bracelet." I pulled from the expandable file that picture of Eugene Washington on the boat with Ike Washington. "The photograph I'm looking at right now? He's wearing the bracelet, but back at the house, it wasn't on him when we found him."

Brooks grunted.

"And at the picnic," I continued, "wouldn't he ask, 'Hey, what's in this cobbler,' if he thought it could possibly be unsafe to eat?"

"Sure."

"Please do the test, Brooks. Pretty please?"

"Do you think someone *took* the medic alert bracelet?" Brooks asked. "Because an easier explanation is that the bracelet fell off."

"And another explanation is that someone removed the bracelet after poisoning the man with coconut." I squeezed my eyes shut and prayed, *please, please, please.*

Brooks sighed, then said, "Guess I could do tryptase and IgE analyses which would help me determine if he could've died from anaphy-laxis—"

Yes! "That means allergic reaction, right? Sounds good. And I'll get the medical records to confirm the coconut allergy. Thanks so much Brooks."

"And if you're wrong?" he asked.

"Then, my critics will dance on my career's grave and I'll soon be walking the beat between Claire's and See's Candies."

And as I ended my call, I prayed again. *Please let me be right.* A tragic prayer to pray, that someone murdered an old man. A selfish prayer. But I'm only human.

Colin and I exited the building for the parking lot. The fiery urgency of 2,500 burning acres of Douglas firs, lodgepole pines, and chaparral shrub forests in a zero-percent-contained blaze slammed us in the nose. Two layers of California snow made my blue Crown Vic look silver.

"Car's filthy." Colin ran a finger through the ashy buildup. "Didn't you wash it last week?"

"Yeah," I said. "So, yesterday, when L.T. called you out—"

"Are we still investigating Washington's death?" he interrupted.

"We are."

"As?"

"As a poisoning."

"Because of the medic alert bracelet?"

"Yep."

He shrugged. "You're the boss. Wanna drive?"

I shook my head. "I'm a little beat."

"I hear ya. Let's grab some drive-through before we head over to Blessed Mission."

A little beat. If he kept a primer, Colin would know that "a little beat" meant "low-grade headache with slight pain in my left arm."

Two tacos and a Diet Coke helped dissipate my headache, but the ache in my arm only grew stronger.

Colin chomped the last of his second burrito, and taco sauce dripped onto the cuff of his shirt.

"Maybe you should eat something clear for lunch," I said. "Like water."

He dabbed at the stain with a tired napkin. "Where am I driving?"

I scanned the map on my phone. "Blessed Mission's over on La Brea in Inglewood."

The church's digital billboard advertised this week's sermon: THE JŌB/ JŌB EXPERIENCE.

"Wait a minute," I said. "I've been here before. Well, not this exact . . . It was much smaller back then." During my childhood, Blessed Mission had been one of two churches on this stretch of La Brea. On the block before reaching Blessed Mission sat Mount Shiloh Baptist Church, along with a barbershop, auto collision garage, stationery store, a U-Buy-We-Fry fish market, and a locksmith. But Mount Shiloh had been torn down and that land had been developed to become Blessed Mission's parking lot. The digital billboard now stood in place of the locksmith and stationery store. The auto collision shop had survived, and its three bays were filled with smashed-up clunkers.

Colin passed through the tall wrought iron gates of Blessed Mission Ministries. Gold letters bolted into dual brick retaining walls read BLESSED MISSION on one side, and BISHOP SOLOMON TATE—PASTOR on the other. The boulder positioned between the walls carried the church's logo: a tall leafy tree with its trunk protected by a golden shield.

This was not your grandma's church with its brick façade, potholed parking lot, and weather-beaten cross stationed above the double doors. Nope. Palm trees lined the long, private driveway. The tropical plants filling the porte cochere reminded me of time-shares in Hawaii.

Colin drove past the patio and parked near the fire hydrant. "And I thought my folks' church was swanky. This place makes Divine Light look like Chernobyl."

The parking lot was now a quarter filled with cars and SUVs. People scurried all around the campus, some carrying weed whackers and leaf blowers while others rushed about with buckets and vacuum cleaners. A squad of six cleaned the long rectangular fountain that started in the lush courtyard and ended near the church's glass double doors.

We entered the main building and stood before golden-brown way-finding signs. Stainless steel columns, high windows, a grand staircase, and recessed lighting—like an airport or a LEED-certified convention center. We wandered to the round welcome desk. I plucked a pamphlet from the acrylic brochure stand. WELCOME HOME, it said. Beneath the greeting was a black, white, and spot-red photograph of Bishop Solomon Tate group-hugging a light-skinned black woman with shoulder-length twists, a preteen boy with a flattop, and a curly-haired grade-school girl missing her front teeth.

After we'd wandered the lobby without anyone stopping to help us, Colin and I were rescued by a woman wearing a purple sweater set and a lapel pin of the church's tree logo. Though she had perfect silver hair, her wrinkle-free face looked closer to fifty than sixty. "To get to the bishop's wing," the woman said, "go up the stairs, turn right, and walk all the way around the rotunda."

Colin said, "Thank you, Sister . . . ?"

"Elliott," she said and smiled. "Sonia Elliott. Have a blessed day."

On the way to the stairs, I spotted a giant giving tree on the wall. Leaf-shaped pictures of member-donors filled the branches. An ATM sat just a few feet away.

Subtle.

"Where are the pictures of Jesus and heaven and Charlton Heston holding the Ten Commandments?" I asked. "And why is there an ATM in the lobby?"

Colin said, "To get money, duh."

"And I thought it dispensed vaccinations. Why?"

He cocked his head. "I get to know something you don't know?"

I started up the stairs. "Sure. Enlighten me."

"Big churches don't exist on their own goodness, Lou," he explained. "You need lots of cash to keep 'em going. My church at home has at least four offerings each Sunday. Building fund, regular tithe, special offering, and children's ministries." He held up a finger. "*And* church members gotta submit their tax returns. It's required."

I gaped at him. "You're kidding me."

"To make sure everybody's paying their ten percent."

A pang of anger flicked within me. "My taxes ain't nobody's business."

He shrugged. "Malachi 3:10 says bring the whole tithe blah blah blah."

"But . . . But Jesus died."

He studied the high ceilings and tall windows. "This place isn't *that*

big. Now, down in Orange County and Atlanta, those churches are massive." He grinned as his eyes shimmered with memories. "Gotta admit
that I miss it sometimes. The community, the music. The day I got—"
He made quotation fingers. "—saved? One of the best days of my life.
Never seen my folks look so happy. Dad bought me a Jeep for baptism,
and—"

"May I help you?" A woman's husky voice drifted from the top of
the staircase.

My back was turned to her but Colin's wasn't. He blushed and his
blue eyes widened. A smile broke over his lips like waves over rocks.

I turned around and saw the woman from the "WELCOME HOME" brochure, the one with the long twists, high cheekbones, and Sophia Loren
eyes. I startled—gosh, she was pretty. "We're looking for someone on
the pastoral staff," I said.

The woman's whiskey-colored eyes left mine to linger on Colin. "I'm
Charity Tate, the bishop's wife. Is that 'pastoral staff' enough for you?"
She had a tired jazz singer's voice, a voice treated with menthol ciga-
rettes and cherry cough drops.

Colin grinned. "Guess that's enough."

I badged her, then introduced Colin and myself.

Charity Tate's perfect eyebrows furrowed. "Uh oh. What did my husband do this time?"

I opened my mouth, but no words came.

She giggled. "It's a joke, detectives." She smiled and said, "Sol's in
his office."

As we passed the audiovisual room and the entrance to the balcony's
seating, we chatted about the weather, the fires, and then the weather
again.

"And here we are." Charity led us into a suite with khaki-colored
walls, chocolate leather furniture, and French doors overlooking a
patio.

Bishop Solomon Tate leaned against a cold fireplace with a Starbucks
Frappuccino in his hand. His outfit—a Gap for Seniors gray polo shirt
and light gray chinos—seemed more Neighborhood Watch captain than
church pastor. He had been the pastor during my single visit back when
I was a kid. He seemed old even then. And he was married to *Charity*?

She couldn't have been in her fifties. Hell, she couldn't have been in her forties.

"We have visitors, honey." Charity made the introductions.

She reminded me of my high school friend T'keyla with those cat eyes and Nigerian nose. Born round-the-way but now living the dream with Louis Vuitton bags, Whole Foods produce, and a monthly wine club.

We settled on the couch, then smiled politely as Charity chided her husband about the Frap and his waistline.

Bishop Tate tossed her an icy glare, then unbuttoned the top of his shirt. To Colin and me, he said, "How can we help?"

"As you've probably heard," I said, "Eugene Washington died in his home yesterday."

Blank faces from the couple. *Huh?*

Charity cocked her head. "Who?"

"Older," I said. "Thin. His house . . ."

"Yes, his house," Bishop Tate said. He then described our victim to his wife.

"That's Ike's friend, right?" Charity asked.

Bishop Tate nodded.

I pulled out a copy of the picture we'd found in Eugene Washington's den. I pointed to the man standing next to him in the red fishing boat.

"That's Ike Underwood," the minister confirmed. "Sorry to say, but we haven't heard a thing about this. How did Gene die?"

"We're still trying to determine that," I said.

"We do know that he attended the church picnic on Sunday," Colin said. "We heard that he ate a lot. Maybe got a little sick. You know if anyone else came down with a stomach bug?"

The couple shook their heads. The bishop considered his beverage. "Brother Washington . . . He was an incredible man. Fought in Vietnam. Gave back to the community tenfold."

"How long was he a member of the church?" I asked.

"About three, four years," he said. "Came in through Ike Underwood."

"I like Ike," Charity peeped. "He's good with his hands."

Bishop Tate glowered at her.

She rolled her eyes. "*You're* the one with the dirty mind. Stop being an old man."

"I *am* an old man," he mumbled.

She swiveled her neck to look at me, all *anyway*. "Ike's in construction, so, yes, he's good with his hands." She tossed a last smirk at her husband.

Charity also reminded me of my sister—that is, if Tori had grown up and married a preacher. A wild child with a sweet heart.

"Could you give us Ike's number?" Colin asked.

Bishop Tate pulled his phone from his pocket and read off Isaac Underwood's contact information.

"Have you been out to Mr. Washington's house recently?" I asked, writing in my pad.

The minister grimaced, then shook his head.

"What's wrong with the house?" Charity asked.

Bishop Tate's throat reddened. "It's . . . in shambles some."

"*Some?*" I asked, eyebrow cocked.

"It's in shambles *a lot*." He swirled the melting Frap around the cup. "Ike and the men's group tried to address that situation. Went to clean it up a few times. Found Gene a therapist and . . ." He crossed, then uncrossed, his legs. "And we prayed for him. Nonstop. Covered all the bases. There wasn't anything else we could do."

"What happens to the house now?" Charity asked.

The minister took a sip from his beverage, then said, "He probably left it to Ike or Oz."

"I believe we have a call out to Oz," Colin said, looking at me to confirm.

I nodded. "Do you know if Mr. Washington had an insurance policy?"

The couple shrugged, but Charity's eyes darted to the table.

My gaze lingered on her as I said, "We heard that the seniors of the church were forced to draw up their wills."

Charity and Bishop Tate laughed. She poked her tongue against her cheek. "Not forced," she said. "Strongly recommended."

"Because?"

"*Because* people are messy," she said. "And when death is involved, they're *really* messy. Then, the probate courts get involved and the . . . mess hits the fan."

"Sweetheart," Bishop Tate chided. The vein in the middle of his forehead hardened.

"I said 'mess,' Solomon," Charity said.

He can't control his wife. One of the so-called witches had mentioned that yesterday.

She plucked the Frap from his hands. "Anyway, we brought in planned giving people and encouraged *everyone* to get their houses in order. 'To Heal and to Help.'"

"That's our vision statement," Bishop Tate said.

"Mr. Washington have any family?" Colin asked.

The pastor shook his head. "Not that I know."

"So then the funeral." Charity pumped the drink's straw up and down, then sipped.

"We'll handle it," her husband said, taking back his drink. "And I'll contact the VA since he was a vet."

Charity peeped at her wristwatch—the ring she wore on her left hand caught the light and temporarily blinded me. "Honey, it's almost time."

"Right, I know." He stood, then offered me his cold hand. "I have an important teleconference with our councilwoman." After apologies and more apologies, he walked us to the door.

"We'll probably have more questions," I said.

Charity was already bustling around the desk and the telephone.

"You know where we are," he said, warm smile in place. "We're here to help."

As we trotted down the stairs, I grinned at my partner, and whisper-sang, "Colin and Charity sittin' in a tree—"

He blushed. "Leave me alone."

"P-r-a-y-i-n-g."

"You're going to hell."

"And you're gonna need a better job. You see her ring? It was as big as the moon."

He didn't respond.

"And talk about May-December romances. More like—" I elbowed him. "Why so serious?"

"They didn't seem too broken up about Washington dying. And you notice how they didn't know who the hell he was, and then, all of a sudden, he's the greatest soldier since General Patton?"

"I noticed that. And she looked weird when I asked about an insurance policy."

We stepped out into the hot air. My eyes burned, no longer soothed by the HEPA-filtered environment of the church. My radio chirped from my hip.

"Lou, you copy?" Pepe asked.

"Yep," I said, radio to my mouth. "I'm here."

"One of Washington's neighbors wants to talk to you," he said. "Something about a church van coming to the house on the night before Washington died."

14

Even after death, Eugene Washington kept the city of Los Angeles busy. Zucca's enormous Yukon hogged any driveway space left over from the dead man's rust bucket and mounds of junk. Cats, stationed on the porch, in boxes, and in the magnolia tree, watched us with the detached disdain that only cats possessed. On the sidewalk, an old woman wearing a fuchsia tracksuit yelled at Pepe and Fitzgerald. A jackass misogynist to me, Fitzgerald displayed patience and understanding with cranky old people. His dark face showed concern as he listened to the old lady rant. She spat one last thing at him, then stomped back to the white-and-blue Spanish-style home on the right side of Washington's house. The two men snickered, then shrugged.

An animal control truck was parked at the curb, and two workers were unloading carriers from the bed of the truck.

"Can't go in yet," I called out to the cat catchers. "We're still processing the scene."

Zucca, with his Tyvek suit pushed down to his waist, walked out from the house to stand on the porch as visual confirmation.

The chubby cat catcher pointed to the old lady's white-and-blue Spanish-style. "Tell *her*, then. She's called, like, thirty times since yesterday."

"I'll go talk to Hot Pink," Colin said to me with a grin. "This should be good."

"Bring any pastries?" Zucca asked as I approached the steps to Washington's house.

"You find my soup pennies?" I asked in turn.

"Lou, we need to talk," he said. "You've been neglecting me recently."

CITY OF SAVIORS | 105

"Blame technology. I don't have to visit the labs in person as much now, with all the Skyping and FaceTiming and whatnot."

"Delivery works."

"Tell me something good, then. Like, 'Yes, Lou, I found gold bullion in the bathtub,' or 'Hey, Lou, I know whose fingerprint that is on the cobbler dish.' You do that, and you'll immediately receive a dozen Sprinkles cupcakes."

A gray minivan rattled down the block and parked across the street. The three prophetesses climbed out of the van and drifted to the perimeter tape surrounding the yellow Craftsman. Once they took their positions, they stretched their arms, closed their eyes, and began to pray.

I tore my eyes away from the trio and said to Zucca, "Where were we?"

"At chocolate marshmallow cupcakes."

"You mean, at gold bullion."

He zipped up the Tyvek suit, then said, "I'm looking, I'm looking, all right?" Then, he retreated into the house.

Time to join Colin and Hot Pink.

The old lady liked wrought iron—and there wasn't a bar or a fleur-de-lis spear she hadn't chosen from the catalog. The crowned bars surrounded her house like Pinkerton guards. As she actively ignored Colin, she held a garden hose to water her white roses. Gelled chignon. Pink Chanel slip-ons. Giant diamond studs in her ears. She belonged in this neighborhood as much as a tarantula belonged on the 405. Definitely not holding that water hose. And definitely not living beside a man who sheltered more vermin than all of Santa Monica. She told me that her name was Judith Ainsley, and that she now had roaches because of the filthy hoarder next door.

"I know that sounds awful," she said, hazel eyes hard, "and I typically don't speak ill of the dead, but he was filthy and he let that beautiful house go to *hell*—excuse my French. You smell it. I know you do. In the cold. In the heat. In the morning, evening, all day, every day. It stinks to high hell—excuse my French—and I don't pay eight thousand a year in property taxes to serve as a hostel to cats, rats, and roaches. Lord, forgive me, but I'm sick and tired of smelling that stink."

"I understand, Ms. Ainsley," I said, my own stomach queasy from the smell. "We're trying our—"

"*Really? Are* you?" She squinted at me. "People coming and going, everybody got a badge but it still stinks to high hell, and you all got me cursing and my pressure's up."

Mine, too, lady, and you ain't helping.

"We're here today," I said, "to try and finish. Then, we'll allow a cleaning crew to come in and . . ." I waved to the Washington property. "Do what needs to be done."

She harrumphed and now aimed the water hose at the gray rosebushes.

"Anything you see or happen in the last few days that you haven't seen before?" I asked.

"We had a blackout Monday night," she offered. "Around seven. Lasted about an hour."

According to his liver's temperature, Eugene Washington had still been alive during the blackout.

Colin motioned toward the house. "Has it always been this way?"

"It's always been messy," she said, "but not always uncontrollable." She pointed at the tower of milk crates and recyclables. "Most of that wasn't there when we moved in. It started getting ridiculous around the time Katrina hit. Like all that trash from New Orleans washed up in his yard."

"So August-September 2005," Colin said, "that's when—"

"That's when he started building the Great Wall of China's Trash over there." She sucked her teeth, then shook her head. "Reminds me of that TV show. You know, with the hoarding people? Wouldn't be surprised if he was crushed under some trash. Is that what finally did it? A tower of trash?"

"No, it wasn't," I said. "He have any visitors over the last couple of days?"

"His girlfriend or whoever she is came over last weekend. And she came by yesterday morning like she do every Tuesday. Glad she found him before he added to the stink." She squinted at me again. "Especially since the city wasn't coming out here with us just complaining. Somebody had to die first; then they sent you two."

"Well, that's the only time we get sent places," I said. "When folks die."

She harrumphed again, then switched her watering hand. "Some folks from his church came to visit him on Monday night, around—No!" She aimed the hose at a rangy gray cat that had wandered over from Washington's property to drink fresh hose water. "Y'all gon' get this?" Judith Ainsley shouted at the animal control workers.

The two men shrugged and eyed me. *We gon' get that?*

I nodded, and the animal control workers scooped up the gray cat with a butterfly net.

"One down, thirty million to go," Judith shouted.

I turned back to Judith. "How'd you know that the people visiting Monday night were from his church?"

"Because they drove up in a blue van that said Blessed Mission," she recalled.

"Were the visitors—?" Colin pointed to the trio still praying at the tape.

"No, but I'm glad *somebody* over there praying. The couple I saw . . . He was tall. And there was a woman, but I couldn't really see their faces because it was dark. The van, though. The van definitely said Blessed Mission. And I know he attends Blessed Mission because he'd always hand me flyers about their events. Like to the church picnic on Sunday."

"Did you go?" Colin asked.

She grimaced. "If they can't help *him*, then they can't do a damned thing for me. Excuse my French."

"Anybody else visit over the last few days?" Colin asked.

Judith scratched her arm as she thought. "Sometimes, the girlfriend would bring a big guy—bald, dark-skinned, scary-looking fella—with her. Sometimes, he'd go in the house with her. Other times, he'd sit in his silver thug-mobile."

Joe Rice and his silver Chrysler 300.

A black Volvo pulled into the driveway of the dusty pink bungalow on the other side of Washington's property. A tall white woman climbed from behind the steering wheel. Back in the day, my grandmother would've called her "handsome" because of the Katharine Hepburn jaw and top-heavy, dark blond bun. Unlike Hepburn, this woman carried a giant container of roach spray. She wore tight jeans and a gold T-shirt that read THICK CHICKS.

"Hey, Nina," Judith shouted at the woman. "Come on over here." To us, she said, "That's Nina. We call her 'Tiny.'"

"Did you know Mr. Washington?" I asked Nina.

The woman laughed and rolled her eyes. "Gene hated me more than he hated anybody else on the block. Probably because I called the city on him two times—"

"Four times," Judith corrected. "You called four times. That giant possum was three, and the bees, that was four."

Nina scowled. "And I love bees but having a hive as big as a piñata was not safe. After my second call, the city came out. That's when they threatened to tear the house down. And that's when he cleaned up some. It's been this way since."

"This is *cleaned up*?" Colin asked.

"Uh huh. So the rest of us just have to deal with the smell, the cats, and the bugs. And giant possums. And raccoons. A lot of raccoons." She held up the container of pesticide. "This is my second container in two weeks. I'm thinking we need to hire professionals to do the job right, but they're not *my* bugs so why should I pay? Judy, we should sue his estate and recoup some of our costs."

"Emotional and physical distress," Judith said, nodding. "I'm sure my asthma is worse now."

"I'm just guessing here," Colin said, his skin flushed, "but neither of you are sad he's dead."

Nina sat the pesticide on the sidewalk. "I mean, yes, it's awful when people die. But one, Gene was old, and two, Gene was disgusting. The way he lived . . . I mean, how can you *not* die after living in all that?" She shivered and goose bumps rose on her pink skin.

Judith tossed the garden hose into the lavender. "My asthma is just ridiculous now. I run through two, three, four inhalers a month."

"They'll have to knock that house down," Nina said. "Salt it, turn the ground, then drop an A-bomb to kill all of those roaches."

Colin clenched, and the nerves all over his face twitched.

"Is that how he died?" Judith asked us. "Poisoned from all that . . . everything? His lungs must've been petrified. Is that why you all were wearing those alien suits yesterday?"

"The conditions are . . ." Colin swallowed. "They're a little . . ."

"Dangerous?" Nina completed. "Toxic? Radioactive?"

"It was just best to wear the protective gear," Colin explained.

"They're gonna find Tupac and Jimmy Hoffa playing spades up in the attic," Nina said. "With Amelia Earhart making waffles in the kitchen."

Judith cackled, then slapped her knees. "Tiny, girl, you are *crazy.*"

"Judy tell you about the woman who was always coming and going?" Nina asked.

I nodded. "His girlfriend Bernice?"

Nina frowned. "*Girlfriend?* Are we talking about the one with the three different hairstyles all on one head?"

"Yeah, that's Bernice," I said.

"If Mr. Washington was her boyfriend," Nina asked, "then who's the man always feeling up on her?"

"I told them about him," Judith said. "I was about to get to that part."

"When did you see him feeling up Bernice?" I asked.

"Back on Saturday night," Nina said. "They were parked in the Chrysler in front of my house, making out like teenagers. I was just about to call the police—really, hand on the phone—when they stopped."

"Because Gene came out," Judith added.

"He started yelling at her," Nina continued, "saying that she was nothing but a whore and how she only wanted his money, that she didn't love him, that nobody loved him. And then he started crying and . . ." The woman blushed, then shook her large head. "And now I feel like crap. That poor old, nasty-ass, roach-loving man."

Judith grunted. "Well, now he's out of his misery. And maybe the city will now do something about all that mess." She smiled, and her hazel eyes brightened. "Ooh. Maybe some of the new techie people will buy the land and build a new house."

"You mean *more* white people?" Nina asked, winking.

"You know it," Judith said, "and you know what *that* means?"

Better breakfast spots. Starbucks returning. A place where salads

meant more than iceberg lettuce and cherry tomatoes. Increased property values. And much, much more. Judith talked about potential white
neighbors like the Munchkins talked about the Wizard of Oz.

Anger simmered in my blood—I hated these women. "Is it possible
that either of you helped Mr. Washington meet his end? I mean, he *was*
bringing down your property values."

Both Nina's and Judith's eyes bugged. Their mouths moved, sputtered words like "what," "ridiculous," and "excuse my French."

Colin hid a smile behind his hand.

I squinted at the two women. "The motive is there. Get rid of the
nasty old man and—"

Over at the prayer line, the tambourine started jangling as Idell
shouted, "Yes, yes, now, Lord." Ebony swayed as her lips moved. Dorothea
waved her lace hankie in the sky and chanted, "Thank you, thank
you, thank you."

"What the hell's gotten into *them*?" Nina asked.

"Lou!" Zucca called from the front porch.

"What's up?" I shouted back.

He smiled. "I think you can go get me those cupcakes now."

15

So . . . we're going in?"

I zipped the front of the Tyvek suit without answering Colin's question.

"I didn't plan to . . ." Pepe held out his arms. "This is my nice suit. It cost over—"

"It look like I give a fuck?" I asked. "Or that I have time to give said fuck?"

Colin and Pepe grumbled as they snatched biohazard suits out of the supply box.

"So lemme get this right," I said, my face hot. "Two grown-ass male detectives who get paid to solve crimes are giving me grief over getting their girdles soiled? Is that an accurate assessment?"

"Lou—" Pepe began.

"Nope. Not today." I stomped out of the staging tent with the fury of a thousand dragons. Because *I* didn't wanna go back into that house. I didn't wanna don industrial plastic and face gear just to bump against towers of papers and islands of cat crap. Really: don't complain about your job to another cop dressed in a damned bunny suit. Don't do it.

"I was pulling prints off the fridge's door handle," Zucca told me in the hallway, "and I just decided to open the freezer out of morbid curiosity."

"Okay," I said, "but I wanna go back to the den really quick."

"For?"

Eugene Washington's soiled armchair sat in the room, waiting for a butt that would never sit on that cushion again. With my flashlight, I searched beneath the seat—dust and vermin, both dead and alive. I stuck my gloved hand between the cushions.

"We searched yesterday," Zucca said.

"I know but . . ." My hand slipped into the torn fabric—coins, pens, crunchy things that weren't pistachio shells. As I dug, I told Zucca that Washington was wearing the bracelet in the fishing trip picture. "Where is his current medic alert bracelet?"

Zucca shrugged, then added, "We haven't found any EpiPens anywhere, either."

"You guys should look again," I said. "Really: if he was allergic enough to wear a bracelet, then he must have a bracelet and those shots around. Okay. So. Tell me about the fridge."

Colin, finally suited up, met us in the hallway. "Pepe's skipping this part," he told me.

"Oh, yeah?" The intense need to careen out the house and scream, "Gimme your badge, Kim," clawed at my skin.

"Yeah." Colin sighed. "I guess that's that."

"That is so not that. First things first, though." I forced a smile to my face, then turned back to Zucca.

As we followed Zucca into the kitchen, he said, "I'm gonna start wrapping up soon. Everything else is too dusty, and I can't pull anything cuz I can't *see* anything. But we took pretty good pictures and video."

Yesterday, the firemen had cleared a pathway from the front door to the den. That had allowed Brooks and his team to safely remove Eugene Washington from the house. But now those ordered columns had collapsed because of the cats, reuniting vinyl records with ancient *Life* magazines, and cat food tins with empty shoe boxes.

The kitchen resembled everything and nothing—like those puzzles that make you find hidden objects. This puzzle, though, was stinkier and more toxic.

We did a quick search through the cabinets for anything "coconut." We found shattered jars of clouded this and dented cans of rancid that. The refrigerator door was covered in souvenir magnets and caked-on grease and dirt.

I made the mistake to look down—a troop of earwigs wiggled near my feet. A shiver zigzagged up my spine, and I tasted the Pop-Tart from breakfast.

"Well, I guess you should open it," Colin said to me.

"I guess so." I pulled the freezer's door handle.

Stacks of freezer-burned meat. Tupperware of every size. Loaves of bread and who knows crammed into the shelves. One plastic tub had been labeled SOUP with black marker.

"Go ahead," Zucca said. "I already took pictures."

I eased the tub from its spot and pulled off the lid. "Oh, boy."

Gold coins filled the container. Some had buffalo imprints; others had imprints of eagles and Native American chiefs.

Zucca whispered, "Wow."

"How many you think are in there?" Colin asked.

I shook the tub and the coins jangled. "More than fifty."

"There's more," Colin whispered, pointing inside the freezer.

Behind the crushed container of ice cream sat two more tubs marked SOUP.

Footsteps clomped somewhere behind us. "Anybody in here?" a big-voiced man shouted.

"Who's that?" Zucca asked.

"Where the hell is Pepe?" I snapped.

Colin happily darted out of the kitchen. "You can't come in here," he told the intruder.

The tall black man now standing in the hallway clutched trash bags and wore black Wellingtons and Dickies. An elegant figure. Silver Fox, Mod Squad Uncle Linc with a sensible haircut. He was also the man in Eugene Washington's fishing boat picture.

"Sir," Colin said, "who are you and why are you here?"

"Ike Underwood," the man boomed. "Gene was my . . ." He gawked at our bunny suits. "Y'all from . . . NASA?"

I told him that earth was our realm and that we were at the house to investigate Eugene Washington's death.

Colin stayed with Zucca to catalog the bullion, and I escorted Ike Underwood to the big magnolia tree in the front yard.

"Gene and me," Ike said, "we been buddies for over twenty years. Thick as thieves. We were in Vietnam together. Came back here and worked construction together and . . . Can't believe my brother's gone." He pulled a baseball cap from his back pocket but didn't slip it on his head. He glanced back at the house. "I came to start cleaning up, and to find his dress uniform."

"When was the last time you saw Mr. Washington?" I asked.

"At the church picnic back on Sunday." He rubbed his stomach and grimaced. "I didn't stay long. Ate something that didn't agree with me."

"Any idea what that was?" I asked.

Ike squinted in the distance as he recalled Sunday's dinner. "Potato salad, baby-back ribs, fried chicken . . ."

Listeria, e-coli, and salmonella—all mixing together on one of the hottest days of the year. It was a wonder Ike Underwood now stood before me.

"Did Mr. Washington eat any of those things?" I asked.

He chortled. "He ate *all* of those things and more. By the time I left, he had piled another helping onto his plate. Gene liked him some potato salad."

"He have a food allergy?" I asked.

Ike shook his head. "He ain't ever mentioned one to me."

"So eggs, wheat, mango, coconut," I said, "he could eat all of that?"

Ike nodded. "I've seen him eat all of that."

"He got any family?" I asked.

"Nobody I know of. He ain't ever married. All of his brothers are dead. No nieces or nephews. Just the church. And me. I'm paying for some of his service, but since he's a veteran, the government will cover his plot."

I canted my head. "What about his girlfriend?"

Ike snorted. "I told Gene to stay away from Bernice. She's a gold digger whose field is the church. But he still liked having her around—she's younger than us, understand. Can't blame a man for wanting to feel young and vibrant."

I tried hard not to roll my eyes. "How long were they together?"

"Oh . . . A few months."

"They get into it recently?"

Sadness draped over Ike, and his shoulders slumped. "He called me—I guess it was late Saturday night. He caught her with some man she'd been passing off as her cousin. Argued with her and did all that carrying on that young men do." He scratched his gray head, then toed the heap of tangled wires near the tree trunk. "Guess they made up cuz they was holding hands at the picnic the next day. She made his plate, carried him drinks, and . . ." He bit his lower lip, then clapped the cap against his thigh. "Got him on tape. Wanna see?" Ike pulled out his cell phone, then swiped at the screen.

In the video, Eugene Washington appeared fuller than the swollen shell I'd met back on Tuesday. Maybe it was the sweat on his face or his buck-toothed grin. He sat at a picnic table with a plate loaded with chicken, monkey bread, and potato salad. Seated behind him, a woman shoved a chicken bone into her mouth. Over to his left, a neon-orange Frisbee glided and a grade-school girl danced to a Chris Brown song.

And he wore his medic alert bracelet on his left wrist.

"You got enough to eat there?" Ike's off-screen voice had asked.

Eugene Washington had smiled at the camera. "Almost."

Charity Tate had entered the shot with a red cup in one hand and a small bowl in the other. She wore that huge diamond ring as well as diamond earrings the size of lima beans. With those rocks, she weighed an extra ten pounds.

"What's all that, Sister Charity?" Ike had asked.

She placed the cup and bowl before Eugene Washington. "Sweet tea and more potato salad for the birthday boy."

"Ain't got nothing I can't touch, do it?" Eugene Washington asked.

"You can eat 'delicious,' can't you?" Charity asked. "Cuz that's all I have."

The old man laughed. "If I keep eatin' all this food, y'all gon' have to put me in the grave. I won't be around to see seventy-four."

Charity smiled, then squeezed his shoulder. "You're not going *any-where*, Brother Gene. Solomon said, 'For through me your days will be many, and years will be added to your life.'"

"Bishop said that?" Ike had asked.

"Not *my* Solomon," Charity said. "*King* Solomon." She kissed the top of Eugene Washington's head, then said, "Save room for dessert."

"Good stuff?" the birthday boy had asked.

"Your favorites," she said, nodding. "Sock-it-to-me cake, cupcakes, and peach cobbler."

Eugene Washington had then tucked into his bowl of potato salad as Ike said, "Here's to another happy birthday to my buddy." From the right edge of the shot, Bernice Parrish, arms crossed, had glowered at the camera.

"That's it," Ike said to me now, turning off the phone.

Just an hour ago, Charity Tate had acted as though she'd never met Eugene Washington, but here they were solid, like Ashford and Simpson.

"Did you ever talk to Mr. Washington about his living conditions?" I asked.

"Oh yeah," Ike said. "Before I retired, I owned a construction company, and Gene worked for me. Carpentry, electrical, a few other things clients needed done. But he told me to keep my hands and tools off his property." Ike scratched his head. "It was worse than this, believe it or not. He had a few old clunkers sittin' around and some dangerous broken appliances. I'd sneak and clean up a little here, a little there, but he knew where everything was and he'd get mad and wouldn't talk to me for days." He chuckled. "But on Sundays? He'd show up to service in a nice suit, clean, and shaved. If you didn't know Gene, you'd never think he lived like . . ." Tears welled in his eyes, and a single drop slipped down his grizzled cheek. "Where'd you find him?" he asked as he swiped at his face.

"In his armchair," I said. "Watching television, drinking a beer, eating peach cobbler. Maybe from the picnic?"

Ike shrugged. "If you look in that fridge, you're gonna see food in there that's been expired for months. He'd eat it, too. Hell, knowing Gene, that cobbler coulda been from last Christmas. Bet you won't ever see *me* eating anything from that kitchen." He held up the trash bags. "So can I get to work?"

"Soon."

"Soon, like an hour? Two hours? I know the neighbors gonna be happy."

"Possibly," I said. "But no promises."

Ike nodded, then frowned. His temples twitched, and he swiped at his face again.

I squinted at him. "Is there some kind of time crunch?"

His face brightened some. "No, not at all. I'll just hang around a little while longer. I got a cleaning crew coming. And then, I guess, a funeral to plan."

I offered my condolences, then left Ike to himself.

Dying alone . . .

Eugene Washington had not been surrounded by a daughter or a wife. No. His last companions had been parasites, rodents the size of roosters, sick cats, and old things. He had been a sick man—not physically, perhaps, but certainly mentally ill. What kind of church family allowed someone to *live* like this? What kind of girlfriend? What kind of fishing buddy?

And who cared enough to want this man dead?

16

Oswald Little had not called me back, and now I wondered if I'd left messages for the right man. Bernice Parrish had also broken her promise to stop by the station and leave her fingerprints. Luke called her again—no answer. I called her, but she wouldn't pick up. I left a message using my inside voice, really nice-like and ended my message with, "Don't make me send a squad car over there." But real nice-like.

Colin watched as Ike Underwood found his friend's army dress uniform in a bedroom closet. Protected by a suit cover, the gold buttons gleamed, the ribbons looked crisp, and the soft cap looked clean.

I took a trip over to the barrier tape and the prophetesses. Two days ago, where were they with their outstretched arms and prayers and Bible verses? They knew so much, why didn't *they* warn Eugene Washington about the killer cobbler?

"Who says we didn't warn him, Sergeant Norton?" Dorothea said to me with soft, shimmery eyes. The lace hankie she clutched today was pink with green bows on the edges.

"Tate will receive his due," Idell said, lightly tapping the tambourine.

"For treating us like this," Dorothea said.

"Portraying us as demonic," Ebony added.

Then, together they said, "And say to them, 'O dry bones, hear the word of the Lord.'"

"You've only just begun," Ebony said to me.

"They banished us," Idell said. "Will they do the same to you?"

Dorothea touched my arm. "You don't need them for this mission. You only need Him—" She pointed a pink polished finger to the sky. "To be great."

"Pray with us," Idell requested.

"You'll see," Ebony added.

I said, "No, thank you."

The three women considered each other, then turned away from me. Arms out, tambourine and hankie ready, eyes closed, they sang. "*Standing here wondering which way to go . . .*"

My radio chirped. "Lou," Lieutenant Rodriguez barked, "you copy?"

I tore my attention away from the trio to say, "I'm here."

"Release the house."

I closed one eye, stuck a finger in my ear to block the jangling cymbals. "I didn't catch that. Come again?"

"You're done there. Let them clean it, burn it down, whatever. Just wrap it up and—"

"But we're still—"

"This is coming from the captain," he said. "One of the neighbor's husbands called, and the guy is some blah-blah-blah in some blah-blah-blah. You already got the gun, the dish, and the goop and gold. So just call it. Release the house."

A battered pickup truck carrying six men of Hispanic origin pulled up to Washington's driveway. Ike waved at the group, then met them in the front yard.

Also arriving: the dull ache in back of my left shoulder and the anxiety that bubbled like a geyser in my gut at each onset of pain. The heat was making the impossible insurmountable today, tomorrow, and three hundred years from now.

"You copy?" Lieutenant Rodriguez was asking me.

"Yep. I'm gone, sir."

Whatever. Didn't care anymore.

Just the wind. Just the wind.

Colin did the honors of completing the last bits of paperwork. I directed the patrol cops to tear away the yellow barrier tape; then I shared the good news with Ike and his crew. "But if you find anything weird," I told them, "anything that will help with the case, call me ASAP." Then, I handed Ike and four of his workers my business card.

Ten minutes later, Colin sauntered off the property. And, like me, he paused to look at the three women still praying at the fence. "The witches are still here?"

"Don't call them that, Taggert." I tossed him the car keys. "You drive."

I sank into the passenger seat as the ache oozed toward my neck. My breathing slowed as though pain constricted my throat. The heat. The stink, cats, bugs . . . I was done. My hands shook so much that I couldn't shove the seat belt's tongue into its buckle. I succeeded on my third attempt, and the click pounded like a sledgehammer and sent concussive vibrations up my arm and to my head.

Colin glanced over at me. "You okay?"

"Uh huh."

"We'll count the coins, log 'em in with Evidence, call it a day?"

"Sounds good."

He clicked on his seat belt, then pulled away from the curb. After a minute of silence, he asked, "What are you gonna do about Pepe?"

I covered my eyes with a hand. "In regards to what?"

"Insubordination. He didn't follow your direct order."

"You're certainly concerned."

"Friend or not, you can't let him get away with that. You're a sergeant now."

"Wow, am I?"

"You're not acting—"

"Stop." I looked at him, so tired. "I'm not doing my job now?"

His knuckles whitened around the steering wheel.

"Don't worry about Pepe," I said. "He'll be handled accordingly." I gave him the side eye. "What? Are folks gossiping about me again?"

He didn't respond.

"I'm not hard. I'm too hard. I work too much. I don't work enough. I kill the guy. I arrest the guy. It's never enough for you white boys and your moving goal posts."

"What's that supposed to mean?" His face had turned cherry red.

"None of you think I deserve—"

"None of *you*? I'm one of *them* now?"

"Why are you inferring that I'm not—?"

"I just asked—"

"And I answered."

"I'm concerned."

"Don't be."

"I don't want anyone taking advantage of you not being . . ."

"Being what?"

He swallowed, then shook his head. "Nothing. Forget it."

I slipped sunglasses over my eyes, then took deep, deep breaths. *For being what?* But I knew.

Neither of us spoke as we carried the tubs of gold coins back to our desks.

I logged on to my computer and searched the Web for the bullion's value. "A one-ounce American Gold Eagle is worth eleven hundred dollars," I told Colin. "And the buffalo is worth a little more."

He had organized the coins into stacks of twenty. "We have 375 total."

My skin flushed. "That's almost a million dollars."

Colin whistled. "Bernice is about to become a very rich lady."

"Not if she killed him."

We took pictures of the coins. Completed more forms about the coins. Told Luke and Lieutenant Rodriguez and anyone who cared to listen about finding the coins in the freezer. Then, we carried the tubs down to Evidence. On the way back to the squad room, Colin said, "I'm not one of *them*, all right?"

I nodded.

Done for the day, he grabbed his bag and trudged to the exit.

I also rounded up my things but stopped at Pepe's desk. I scribbled on a sticky note, then slapped it on his dark monitor. *We need to talk in the morning. Lou*

Back in March, the rain had never ended. The constant moisture meant Los Angeles soon wore a coat of moss and mildew—and we cursed it all. Now, months later, dust and ash covered the city, and we all prayed for water, for heavy fog, for anything wet to wash off the scum, to wash away the dead carcasses, to make us sparkle again. Everyone on my drive from the station to my condo all looked shriveled, like Shrinky Dinks left in the oven too long.

In my driveway, Syeeda McKay slouched on the trunk of her Benz. Even though my friend topped out at five foot six in the wedges she now wore, her smooth brown legs were Naomi Campbell long. With that car and those legs? Postcard ready. Just chillin' beneath the white disk, hangin' out in ninety-degree heat, moments away from spin class or hot-tub book-club to discuss Ta-Nehisi Coates's latest book on the State of Us in America.

She offered me a reluctant smile as I pulled the Porsche into my second parking spot. After our big fight back in March, we hadn't spoken much—Syeeda, too, had wanted to bring awareness to the murders of teenage girls in our childhood neighborhood. Rumor had it that convicted sex offender Raul Moriaga—and neighbor to one of the dead girls—was responsible. Without doing enough background checking, Syeeda and her assistant editor, Mike Summit, published a misleading article about Moriaga being a suspect—even though I (the lead detective on the case) had not named him as a suspect. As a result, folks in the neighborhood took up torches and pitchforks, and Raul Moriaga, the wrong monster, was killed. Syeeda had been there, though, after my accident. She'd brought me food and changed my bandages, acting like the friend she'd been to me since elementary school. But we hadn't officially made up, nor had we been alone together since that fight.

Guess that was about to change.

Syeeda held up a four-pack of ginger beer and a frosty bottle of Grey Goose vodka. The tangy scent of barbecue wafted from the greasy bag sitting on the Benz's trunk. "The Moscow Mule fairy left this under a tree in my backyard," she said. "Hope you have some mugs and lime juice."

I smiled. "I do. I even have mint."

She slid off the trunk and held out a greeting card. "And the Hallmark fairy left this. Congratulations on your promotion. You deserve it, of course."

I took the card and hugged her. "Thanks. Yes. I *do* deserve it."

Her eyes darted around my face, taking in the scars, bags, and general weariness dusted about me like talcum powder. "You look . . . You look . . . So you said you had mugs and lime juice?"

Inside, I opened the patio door for fresh air. Syeeda started on dinner and cocktail prep.

I padded to the bathroom and stripped. As I showered, the tight bundles in my neck and shoulders unwrapped and slipped off of me like soap lather. I pulled the blood pressure machine from the cabinet, but then decided against checking my status. False readings with the shower and all that. Instead, I checked the wound in my hair. It was dry and starting to scab over.

Relaxed now in shorts and a tank top, I retreated to the patio. The sun sat in its six o'clock position, and the bruised nectarine sky had darkened with the pinks and purples smearing the golds. Surfers threw their boards into white water, catching one last wave before they all washed out. Filled copper mugs sat on the coffee table alongside a slab of beef ribs and a tub of macaroni and cheese.

In between sips of Moscow Mules and mouthfuls of hickory-smoked rib meat, I recapped my date with Fireman Dominic. "He sent me a dick pic this morning."

Syeeda shrieked. "Lemme see." Together, we admired Dominic's gift that kept giving and giving until there had been six kids with his eyes. "God is good—"

"All the time," Syeeda said. "Are you gonna text him back?"

"No."

"You have to say *something*."

"I ain't gotta do nothing except stay black and die. Did Lena tell you about Chauncey?"

"Every time I try to root for that man." Syeeda frowned and shook her head. "What the hell does that mean, would you mind having my baby for me and my husband?"

"He needs to have a seat."

"He needs to have *all* the seats," Syeeda said. "I told her she cannot say yes to that."

I stabbed a clump of macaroni noodles with my plastic fork. "What's scary is, she's actually thinking about it."

"That's Lena, though. Drama mama, bless her heart. And what's up with you?"

Syeeda licked the barbecue sauce off her fingers. "Writing a feature about the Eriksens."

"The family we thought had fled to Mexico but turned up dead in the desert?"

"Yup."

We sat in silence and watched the water.

Out there, the ocean did what it always did. Crash, foam, undulate. Smooth as a mirror in some places. Chaotic and spiky at the rocks. Like life on solid ground.

Syeeda shook the ice in her mug—she wanted to ask, "What are *you* working on," but she knew better. Instead, she cleared her throat and asked, "And you're feeling . . . ?"

I one-shoulder shrugged. "It hurts when I do that."

"And it's not going to get better at this rate. Maybe you shouldn't have rushed back to work."

"I didn't rush. And I feel bad cuz of the heat. Everything is worse when you're sweaty."

"So sweat is your excuse?"

"Yup."

"I'm glad you're going to therapy," Syeeda said, "but you need more time off. And if they're being assholes, then you need to call your union rep. See what your rights are."

"Yeah." I sipped my Mule, then said, "Some say I didn't deserve my promotion."

Syeeda grunted, then slumped in her chair.

"Okay, fine. I couldn't ride the desk anymore. It was driving me ef-fin' crazy, riding the pine like that." I swallowed the lump forming in my throat. "I had to go back, Sy."

Her head rolled in my direction. "I know."

"I feel like . . . like they're all watching me, waiting for me to fail just so they can say, 'Well, we tried.'"

She sighed. "I know."

"Then, throw in all the race baloney," I said. "Ferguson, Baltimore, New York. A lot of them are pissed because they think they can't do their jobs anymore."

"Without being accountable to the people?"

"Without beating *up* the people."

She cocked an eyebrow. "You keep saying 'they.'"

I smirked. "A black woman with two degrees? I was never a 'they.' The gap's just becoming more of a canyon. And sometimes it feels like Colin's on that other side, too, judging me." I lifted my mug to drink. "Something's going on with him. Pepe, too."

She squinted at me. "And something's going on with you."

"Yep." I drained my mug. "Not enough of these in my life."

Down on the bike path, a teen boy tried to climb a palm tree. The girl, wearing that cute floral sundress we all wore at sixteen, captured the boy's show with her phone.

Syeeda sat a rib on her plate. "I'm . . . You . . . I . . ."

"Yeah?"

"When Lena called and told me that you were in the car accident . . ." She took a deep breath, then slowly exhaled. "You and me—we hadn't made it right before that and I was so . . ." Her voice quivered—she wanted to cry. "Nothing is worth us being angry at each other, Lou, and I'm sorry, okay? I just wanted to do the right thing, and I shouldn't have trusted Mike Summit and I only wanted those girls to be honored and avenged and . . ." She unwrapped a napkin from a slice of white bread, then used it to dry her eyes. "I'm sorry. For everything."

I entwined my arm through hers. "I love you, Sy, and I'm sorry this went on as long as it did. Thank you for helping me recover."

"But you're still recovering, from injuries inside and out, and . . ." She tapped my knee. "Just don't sent send him away. Don't you dare."

I unwrapped my arm from hers, then grabbed my mug. Sadness blistered in the back of my throat and I choked out, "Sam's . . . We can't right now. Soon, though. Really."

"I said that all the time with Adam, remember? Kept finding things to keep from moving forward. And now look at me."

"Gorgeous and successful as ever," I said, crunching ice. "Sam's keeping himself busy. Isn't he going out with one of the mayor's advisors?"

"He told me he's just biding his time until he's freed from the Crase case."

My heart shimmied. "*You* talked to Sam?"

She shoved a piece of bread into her mouth. "I saw him at that Community Coalition fund-raiser last week. He had a little too much to drink. I did, too."

"The Beverly Hilton does give a generous pour."

"Yeah, and so it all just . . . Blah. You were a part of Sam's word vomit."

"Alcohol may be a man's worst enemy—"

"But the Bible says love your enemy." Syeeda lifted her mug.

I raised my own to complete our toast to Frank Sinatra.

We lingered on the patio until the sun dipped below the horizon, until the sky turned Yankees blue and the waves resembled soggy tissue paper. When we retreated inside, Syeeda read my commendations, then kicked off her wedges.

I marched to the bathroom and pulled the blood pressure cuff around my bicep. After squeezing and squeezing, the machine beeped its verdict. *130/90.*

Progress.

I tossed Syeeda a T-shirt and boxer shorts, then watched as she pulled the bed out from the sofa. She popped popcorn. I melted butter. We slipped beneath the comforter in the sofa bed and watched bearded Kirk Russell rescue a suspicious Husky lost in the Arctic. My nerves were soothed by all of it, all of tonight.

Friends again.

And when I screamed from being chased in the dark forest by a man in a gold mask, Syeeda woke me from my nightmare, and whispered, "You're okay. I'm here."

Thursday, September 3

17

In the living room, Syeeda converted the bed back into a sofa. She nattered on about something, but from my place at the patio door, I couldn't hear her over the crash of waves and squawks of sea birds. The pain between my eyes moved like those waves and hung low like those clouds in the sky.

Back in my bedroom, the early-morning news anchor announced, "Another scorcher in the Basin today."

Didn't need specifics—"scorcher" at ninety-six degrees was no different than "scorcher" at one hundred. But I let the meteorologist ramble on about humidity and low pressure as I stood in my closet, hands on my hips. Wondering. Waiting. Yellow linen pants? Lime green silk shell? Black slacks? Black T-shirt? Get dressed? Climb back into bed?

I missed clouds. Not the angry, humid ones filled with hurricanes and thunderstorms. Not the ones that gave you headaches and made 70 degrees feel like 148 degrees in the shade. No, I missed the friendly spring clouds. Puffy, tall, and white like bunny tails. Cool breezes and crisp blue skies came with those clouds.

The clouds in today's early-morning sky hated humanity and had conspired with that famous rock star in the sky to cook us like frogs in a slow-to-boil pot of water. The ocean looked flatter than usual, a murky blue-gray. A few surfers stood in clumps on the shore with their hands on their hips. Wondering. Waiting. The doorbell rang.

"I'll get it," Syeeda shouted.

I grabbed those yellow slacks and green shell, then considered the inaccurate nightstand clock: six thirty. Which meant it could've been midnight. I dressed, then padded into the living room. The aromas of cinnamon, warm sugar, and fresh-brewed coffee greeted me. "It smells like Christmas in here." The scent wafted from the basket and cardboard carafe now sitting on the breakfast counter.

Syeeda tugged on my gray Gap hoodie, then readjusted her ponytail. "So Lena *was* telling the truth. Food fairies *do* exist."

"You know," I said, "in some cultures, Satan is depicted as a type of fairy." I aimed the remote control at the television and found *Good Times*. Penny's mother was back, this time, wearing a fur coat.

Syeeda smirked. "Well, Santa spelled backward is . . ."

"Atnas."

She read aloud the greeting card that always accompanied the food delivery. "Lulu, I know we haven't settled things between us, but a good breakfast will make you feel better. You loved cinnonomin (that's what you used to call it) as a kid. Love, Dad and June."

While Victor Starr had paid for the deliveries, I'm sure Good Eats had been his second wife's idea. June had probably heard about it on a morning show or at her book club meeting, and had truly believed that freshly prepared French breakfast delivered to my house three times a week would feed my heart, not fuel my hate. Ha! Victor Starr had abandoned my mom, sister, and me decades ago. He hadn't contacted us once, even after Tori had been kidnapped. Not a card, not a check. Silence from him up until a year ago, when he elbowed his way into my life and tried to make me accept him. Food was now his ploy. On Thursdays, I received cinnamon buns; on Sundays, chef's-choice quiche; and on Mondays, fresh brioche, applewood bacon, and a variety of cheeses. Each basket was delivered by a slight blond man named Rory who drove a butter-colored Fiat and always threw in an extra jar of raspberry preserves.

Syeeda didn't care who had arranged the hot buns or the coffee. She moaned as gooey frosting and melted brown sugar covered her fingers. She shoved dough into her mouth, moaned again, then tore another strand from the roll. "So . . . question: do you do that every night?"

I squinted at her. "Do I do *what* every night?"

"Have nightmares." She licked away a glob of frosting lodged beneath her fingernail. "Lena said that—"

"You and Lena really like talking about me, huh?"

Syeeda blanched.

I sighed, then said, "My shrink says it's normal. That they're caused by some really big words and sophisticated concepts too early in the morning to try and describe. He said I'm just like any other person who suffers the trauma of almost being killed twice in one day."

"Have you tried sleeping meds?" she asked. "They don't let you dream."

I grabbed two coffee mugs from the cabinet and set them on the counter. "Not dreaming leaves me slow. And then not dreaming means I wouldn't be able to sleep with Idris Elba. That's all kinds of jacked-up."

Syeeda poured coffee into both cups. "You're not gonna indulge?"

"I drink the coffee, but this?" I waved to the rolls, then grabbed the last two Pop-Tarts from the box. "Anyway, I'm about to be very full after eating this strawberry-flavored breakfast square." I tore away the foil packet, nibbled the pastry from its corner, then rubbed my belly. "Yum. So good."

Syeeda licked her fingertips. "I'm not saying that you need to integrate Victor Starr into your life. All I'm saying is this: don't deprive yourself of delicious fresh pastries to prove a point to someone who doesn't know you're depriving yourself of said pastries." She pulled off a piece of sweet dough, then offered it to me. "Seriously: it's the most wondrous thing you'll put in your mouth today, unless it's Sam's—"

"Yeah. Okay. You do know that sugar goes straight to your gut." I tossed a quarter of my Pop-Tart at her, then retrieved my bag and badge from the living room coffee table.

"That's what lipo's for." She coaxed another roll onto her plate. "Since you don't want the food, have you told your father to stop sending the food?"

I clipped my badge to my belt loop, then scooped my leather shoulder holster from the area rug. "I told Mom to tell him since she insists on answering the phone every time he calls. And I never *waste* the food—I take it to Colin, Luke, and Pepe."

Syeeda considered me with soft eyes and whispered, "Elouise, maybe if you ate some of these weekly offerings, you'd recover quicker. Emotionally. Physically. Think about it."

Lightness trickled over me, and I laughed. "Next time on *Dr. Phil . . .*"

A nerve twitched at the corner of her mouth. "See, that's why black people can't succeed."

"That, and O. J. Simpson." I wandered back to my nightstand as she continued to rant about Our People's Problems. I said, "uh huh," when she asked if I was listening, then grabbed the Glock from its new home on the nightstand.

"We can't expect Jesus and Obama and the ghost of Malcolm X to fix our problems," Syeeda was saying as I returned to the kitchen.

"Why don't you write an editorial in that paper you run," I suggested. "I pay attention better if it's in print. And everything sounds doable on paper."

She grabbed her purse from the couch cushions. "Keep mocking me. I know things."

I pushed her toward the front door. "The world needs an enema, Sy. Sorry to say, but I'm part of the shitty problem."

Syeeda followed me in her car as I sped east. The glass and aluminum headquarters of M80 Games glinted in the sunshine. The parking lot was almost empty—it wasn't crunch time, so folks wouldn't start rolling in until ten. No lights shone in Greg's corner office on the second floor. The urge for me to turn into the parking lot had diminished some since last week. One day, I'd drive by M80 and feel the same as I did while driving past a storage warehouse or a business that sold rope.

At Crenshaw Boulevard, Syeeda pulled her car to my left. She rolled down the passenger's-side window, then lowered the volume on NPR. "Lena just called," she shouted through the window. "She wants to talk to us."

"I'll call her later," I shouted back. "You got the pen; I got the sword. Go be productive."

She blew me a kiss and turned left—she'd reach *OurTimes* in under a minute.

I continued my eastward trek.

The sky was already tinged pink and gray as the fires surrounding Los Angeles continued to blaze across drought-stricken forests. Down here on the ground, crackheads, heroin addicts, and garden-variety drunks were taking the deliberate, gimpy steps of people trying to appear sober. Working folks stood with the working girls at corners and bus stops. Near the carwash, a homeless man performed jumping jacks. Another morning in Los Angeles.

My phone chimed—a text from Colin. *Brooks sent the autopsy report for EW.*

As I texted, *Almost there,* my phone caw-cawed. "Yeah?" I asked my partner.

"Just read the report," Colin said.

"Was I right?"

"There was coconut in his system. Yep, you were right."

18

The detective's bureau on Thursday mornings resembled the detective's bureau on Sunday mornings. A hard Wednesday had led some exhausted Angelenos to drink away their despair, to wallop that jerk in the Cork's parking lot, to smack his babymomma for demanding money for diapers and formula. On Thursday mornings, our clientele transformed back into respectable men that sat with bowed heads and gaped at their swollen, bloody knuckles, lamenting their tempers for drinking too much tequila, for the oppressive heat and that petty bitch who'd finally pushed him so far that he'd landed in jail.

Nothing more exciting on a Thursday morning than reading an autopsy report. Brooks had run tests looking for certain antigens in Eugene Washington's blood—and had found a high concentration of proteins that were released during allergic reactions. That—combined with the throat swelling, the expanded lungs, the mucous plugging the airways—screamed anaphylactic shock.

"But it could still be accidental," Colin said as he rolled over to me in his chair. He wore a clean tan shirt with a smart blue-and-cream tie. No taco sauce stain on the cuff, but it was only eight in the morning.

"True." I continued clicking through the report. "Where's stomach contents?"

"Didn't see it. Does it matter? We know he ate something with coconut."

"But I want to be sure." I clicked "reply" to Brooks's e-mail, then typed, *Missing stomach contents report.*

"By the way," Colin said, "Luke and Pepe went to pick up Washington's medical records. They're very happy that we don't have to go back in the house anymore."

The sticky note I'd left on Pepe's monitor last night was still stuck there.

"Luke uploaded the pictures, and I sent them to you." Colin rolled back to his desk to update the murder book with the new report. "I had to remind him to do that—just didn't want them disappearing like the pictures from the Jackson case. You were out for that one. Total clusterfuck."

"You're taking care of business, aren't you? Combed hair, Tic Tacs stowed—who are you? Captain America?"

He smiled, shrugged. "Just doin' my job."

I opened the pictures taken at my victim's home, not really paying much attention until I clicked on pictures of the envelope found in the camera case and the wallet filled with seventeen hundred dollars in cash. The postmark in the upper right corner of the envelope had been stamped on December 1, 2005. The sender had mixed cursive writing with print—for "Eugene," a printed lower case *g* and a scripted upper case *N*. The return address: 43239 Chariton Drive, Los Angeles, Calif. 90056.

"A lot of money to carry around," I said, "especially for an old guy."

"Maybe he didn't want the IRS to know it exists," Colin said. "He was in construction, right?"

I nodded. "Maybe Ike didn't put him on the books for payday?" I then searched for Blessed Mission's Web site. "I think Miss Bernice will have to wait a little while longer for her coins. She's gonna be pissed."

The incredible busyness of the church's Web site should've come with a warning similar to those for video games and Japanese cartoons. Everything blinked, moved, and glimmered—from the Blessed Mission header to the tree-shield logo and copyright language in the footer. Links to videos and sermons and testimony, "Ways to Give," and "Watch Services Live" sparkled, and some words even twirled. Every bit of the site had been casinoed.

> Founded in May 1977, Blessed Mission seeks to change the
> lives of people so that they may grow in Christ and thrive—
> here on Earth and in the kingdom of Heaven.

Bishop Solomon Tate, dressed in a tailored gray suit, and First Lady Charity Tate, resplendent in a stormy sea-blue dress, greeted cyber visitors to their online home.

I clicked "Message from Bishop Tate." My computer's speakers boomed with gospel music—Mary Mary encouraging me not to give up now.

"What's up with all the soul singing?" Colin asked.

I laughed, then hit the side of my monitor. "I think I won, but where does the money come out?" I muted the sound, then clicked here, there, and over there. "Can't tell what they believe. A little holiness, a little Methodist, and a little Oprah."

There were three services on Sundays. Tote bags and rugs with the church name and logo were on sale.

I clicked "Building Fund."

The tree logo filled the screen—its bottom third was shaded green. The tree's leafy top half—marked "$1 Million by December"—was gray. A PUSH PAY button sat in the soil beneath the tree's trunk.

"They need to raise seven hundred thousand dollars by the end of the year," I said.

"Or?"

"Or they turn into a pumpkin."

"What else could they possibly build on that property?" Colin asked. "A Jiffy Lube?"

I kept clicking around. "Four thousand parishioners at Blessed Mission. Maybe Sister Charity really *didn't* remember Eugene Washington yesterday. They got a kajillion people in the pews—how many of them are old gray black men? Forty percent?"

"My family's church has close to fifteen thousand people," Colin said. "The site used to be a Walmart. And give Charity a break—being first lady of a megachurch is hard work. Oh—she called me."

My breath caught in my chest. "Pardon me?"

Smiling, he leaned back in his chair, hands behind his head. "Last night, Charity Tate called to say thanks for everything and to talk about Mr. Washington. She feels bad about the way he died."

Cold prickled along my arms. "She say anything . . . interesting?"

"Like, 'I poisoned that old coot and let's you and me run off to Aruba with his money'?"

"Yeah, like that."

"No, nothing like that."

I left the Web site and searched for "Blessed Mission" in Google.

The *Times* had included Solomon Tate in its investigation of popular ministers around the country. "Seven-hundred-fifty-thousand-dollar salary," I read from the article, "and a six-bedroom home in Ladera Heights."

"Not as bad as what's his face with the private Lear jet," Colin said. "Or the fleet of Bentleys."

"Ha. But that's like saying chlamydia ain't as bad as syphilis."

"Bernice Parrish killed Washington." He held up his index finger. "First, she's shifty." Another finger. "Second, that Joe Rice guy she's sleeping with? He's shifty, too. Or it's that Oswald Little guy."

I cocked an eyebrow. "Oswald Little: he hasn't shown up yet to collect his prize."

"You gonna call him again?" Colin asked.

"Sure." I tapped on the public records icon on the desktop, but an e-mail response from Brooks made me click away. *I didn't send over the tox report for stomach contents yet. Re-testing them again. Strange results. Shouldn't take more than a few hours.*

"Wonder what he found?" I asked.

Colin snorted. "Fresh vegetables."

My desk phone chirped. Lieutenant Rodriguez was calling. "What's up?" I asked.

"In my office," he said. "*Now.*"

19

My boss twisted back and forth in his leather chair. Chin in his hand, he used his other hand to direct me to sit.

"Good morning," I said, opening my binder. "So, we're slowly making progress—"

"I didn't call you in here to discuss the Washington case." He squinted at me, then covered his mouth with his hand.

"Oh. Okay." I closed the binder, then relaxed in my seat. "What's going on?"

"How you feelin'?"

I shrugged. "Great."

He grunted, then shifted in his seat. His gray eyes narrowed. "You havin' any pain or having a hard time sleepin' or anything?"

I tilted my head and stared at him. "Umm . . . Nothing remarkable."

He considered me without speaking for several long moments. Then: "If you had to take a pee test right now, would they find anything?"

A flare shot in my gut. "*Huh . . .* ?"

"Answer the question: would HR find anything stronger than Tylenol or ibuprofen in your urine test? Like Vicodin, Percocet, Demerol, oxy?"

"Of course not. I haven't taken anything."

"Which is a problem since you're in pain, right?" He cocked his head. "The vultures are circling, Lou. And you know they are, which is why you aren't medicating."

I bit my lip, then said, "I'm fine."

He sighed. "Starting Sunday, thirty days. You're taking vacation."

"Excuse me?" Fear enveloped me like cold slime. "Why? I haven't done—"

"You need the time, Lou."

"Bullshit," I shouted. "Someone's trying to get me fired—" *Banish me.*

"You're right," he shouted back, "and I'm keeping that from happening right now. This ain't a negotiation, Sergeant. Thirty days. You have plenty of time on the books, almost four months of vacation. That's too much time." He slid over a sheet of paper that he'd already prepared. "There are some who want you to take administrative leave or be put back on restricted duty. You know what that means. But this way, you get the rest you need using time that belongs to you. You get to keep your badge, your gun, your mobility. You can pop as many pain relievers as the doctor prescribes without guilt or worry. Now: sign on the X."

I considered the document, but tears in my eyes kept me from reading a damned word. "I was injured within the course and scope of my job. I worked that shitty warrants desk job pushing paper for a month. I passed my physical and psych exams to return to normal duty, and now, you're telling me . . . ? Maybe I *should* have my union rep put in a call."

He sighed, squinted at me. "Will you trust me on this? Please?"

I glared at him—he wouldn't glare back. Those gray vampire eyes had turned the color of doves.

Someone knocked on the door, and Lieutenant Rodriguez left his desk to open it.

Behind me, I heard Colin say, "We have a guest."

"She'll be there in a minute." Lieutenant Rodriguez closed the door. "I'm gonna get a cup of coffee," he told me. "Stay here and get yourself together."

"So what do I tell my team?"

"That you and your girlfriends are going to Tahiti. The rich, crazy one can make that happen. Aloha."

"But why *now*? Why am I taking time off all of a sudden?"

"Cuz the Groupon's expiring." He rolled his eyes. "Let me worry about that. Sign." Then, he left me in his office.

I sat there as hot tears seared my cheeks. The three sisters had warned me.

What do men do to women they can't control?

They banished us. Will they do the same to you?

Someone had sold me out.

Who?

For five minutes, I tried to come up with a list of rats, but my brain had shorted and I could only glare at the signed form.

Thirty days of vacation?

"Fine," I muttered. *Screw all y'all.*

With Joe Rice behind her, Bernice Parrish strutted into the detective's bureau like she held a key to the city. Wearing a zebra-cheetah print dress with a ride-or-die girdle beneath it and heeled ankle boots with peekaboo toes, Eugene Washington's girlfriend dressed as though Queen Elizabeth would be taking her fingerprints in Buckingham Palace instead of a fat Latino detective with a mustache full of *pan dulce* crumbs in interview room 2.

Colin and I sat across the table from her. He then reintroduced us since my mind still remained on that signed form left on Lieutenant Rodriguez's desk.

She stared at my head. "And you still ain't gone to get your hair did."

That brought me into the moment. I swiped at my bangs. "I haven't—been busy trying to find who killed your boyfriend."

"Where y'all got my cousin Joe waitin'?" she asked.

"He's talking to other officers," Colin said. "And Sergeant Norton and I will chat with him once we finish our time with you."

Then, we went over the timeline again—the moment she reached the house, discovered Eugene dead in his chair, and the time she dialed 911.

"How come Ike Underwood can go off in the house now?" she asked. "He's stealing what's supposed to come to me."

"What's your relationship with Ike?" I asked.

"Ain't got one."

I waited for more.

She shrugged. "Ike don't mean nothing to me."

"You have no opinions about him?" I asked.

She poked out her bottom lip, then said, "He need to get himself a woman. That way, he can mind his own business. Now, about my soup pennies—"

"Yes," Colin said, snapping his fingers. "We *did* find the bullion. So Ike won't be able to steal that, if that's your concern."

Her eyes had widened. "Why ain't y'all call me sooner then?"

"I *did* call." I held up three fingers. "This many times. You didn't call me back."

"Cuz you ain't mention that you had my coins. I just want what's coming to me."

"Bernice, you'll get all that's coming to you," I assured. "What do you know about Oswald Little?"

Her mouth twisted. "Who?"

"He's a friend of Gene's," I said.

"Don't know him." She swiveled her head on her shoulders. "Y'all gon' let *him* in before me, too? And them witches. They're over there every time I drive by. And they're over there right now. Why ain't you told them they was trespassing?"

"Because they're on the sidewalk," I said. "How many times a day do you drive by?"

She futzed with the hem of her dress. "Just four, five, six times. Joe thinks we need to make sure . . . you know."

I didn't know but I said, "Yeah. So Joe: you know he's a convicted felon, right?"

She waved her hand. "He ain't done half the things they say he done did."

"No?" Colin said. "If he's so upright, why didn't you want him to know about the coins that Eugene left you?"

She squinted at him but then turned to me. "I didn't want him to know cuz niggas are like fish—they like shiny shit, and gold is shiny. You know what I'm saying?" Then, she cracked up laughing, and then ripped a hanging string off the hem of her dress. "That's why Gene had all them guns. He thought someone was gonna figure out he had money hidden off in his house."

"But why so many guns?" Colin asked.

Bernice gaped at him, then laughed. "Why so many records? Why so many cats? Why so many—child, he a *hoarder*. He ain't got one of *nothing*." She laughed again, then shook her head. "Bless your heart."

"But he never *fired* the guns," Colin said, "and other than that one gun we found in the den—" Colin blushed—we weren't supposed to mention that gun. He gulped, then continued. "Other than that, they weren't in places he could've easily retrieved them."

She smirked. "Somebody crazy if they wanna go off in there on their own."

I cocked an eyebrow—she was right about that. "Neighbors said that you and Mr. Washington had an argument on Saturday night out there on the front lawn."

She waved her hand again. "He said that I was cheatin' on him. It was just a misunderstanding."

"A neighbor also said you were kissing Joe Rice that night in the front seat of his car."

She stuck out her neck. "I can't kiss nobody now? No kissin'—that ain't biblical. And one kiss don't mean I'm sleeping with the man. That's just ridiculous. Do *you* sleep with every man you kiss?" She hugged herself, then rocked in the chair. "Gene got all upset for nothing. See, Joe's like a baby cousin to me, that's all. Them people need to mind they own business and get a life."

"I'm thinking Gene discovered that you didn't care about him," I said.

"I cared," she said.

"Then why were you and Joe Rice making out for the world to see? Neighbors told us—"

"All that is my private business." She folded her arms. "Ain't nobody know how me and Gene felt about each other."

"Speaking of your private business," Colin said, "we learned a little something about yours."

"Yeah?" She used a pinky finger to dig in her ear. "What you learn?"

"That you've been sued a few times. Bankrupt—"

"Is that illegal?" she snapped. "What does that have to do with me getting what my man left behind?"

"You need money," I said.

"Who *don't* need money?" she asked. "You don't need money?"

I smiled. "I do, but you're the one with liens and judgments against you."

She stared at me and sat back in her chair. And she kept staring at me even as Luke interrupted our interview to take her fingerprints.

Afterward, as she wiped her fingers on a wet nap, she said, "I didn't kill Gene, so you don't need to go there about my shop."

"Oh, but I must. It's my job to go there." I flipped back to my notes regarding Bernice's finances. "Yes, so . . . two hundred and fifty thousand dollars to LaQuisha Follett—you'd left the perm in too long. Another two hundred and fifty thousand to Amber Treviste—another burned and bald client. Failing to pay taxes last year, and . . ." I looked up from my notes. "Shall I continue?"

Her eyes blazed. "You. Ain't. Got. To go there. I pay my bills."

"But you need a little help, right?" Colin asked. "And you asked Eugene and he told you no, even though we now know that he could afford it."

Tears filled Bernice's hot eyes. "He was gonna help but—"

"No, he wasn't, Bernice," I said, shaking my head. "He knew about you and Joe, and he had a meeting scheduled *today* to take you out of his will."

A lie, sure. Why not?

Her lips trembled. "I ain't heard no such thing."

"Yes, you have," I said, "and you couldn't have that, right? So you made him a cobbler and you soaked it in poison, killing him before he could make that change to his will. A change that would've left you broke."

"Nuh uh," she said. "No, no, no."

"You didn't care about him," I said. "You didn't even know he was allergic—"

"To coconut," she said, and snapped her fingers. "*That's* what he can't have. You asked me the other day, and I couldn't remember. My mind was all messed up cuz of all that was going on, but I remember now. And he wore the medical bracelet that tells doctors that he got an allergy. And he used to keep one of them pens you stick yourself with just in case you eat something."

Bernice nodded so hard, her head was moments away from snapping off. "He kept a pen on his TV tray, next to the remote control. Always."

"Did you ever touch that pen?" I asked.

"Never. I ain't never-ever-*ever* touched that pen. One time, it rolled off the tray and I went to go pick it up and Gene nearly bit my head off. He didn't want me messin' with his pen."

"Cuz I have that pen," I lied. "And we're running the fingerprints on it through our system."

Colin pointed to the door. "*And* we have Joe Rice in the other room right now, telling us everything."

Her wild eyes darted to me, to the door, then back to me again. She took shallow breaths, then held her breath before shouting, "I didn't kill Gene. I may not have been . . . *right* with him all the time but . . ." She shook her head. "You got one of them lie detector tests laying around?"

"We do," I said, "and he just happens to be here today."

Officer Ruben Lipsky was not here—he was wrapping up tests at Seventy-seventh Division, but he promised to be here by ten. As he drove, I told him about the case and about Bernice Parrish. Then, I e-mailed him questions my number 1 suspect needed to answer.

After getting her a can of Sprite, I led Bernice to the polygraph exam room and introduced her to Officer Lipsky. A moment later, I joined Colin in the AV room and plopped into the empty chair.

"Sorry about mentioning the gun," he said, flushed.

"Heat of the battle," I said. "No worries."

Lipsky was now strapping Bernice's right arm onto the padded armrest of the chair. Officer Elaina Sills joined them and helped apply monitoring equipment around Bernice's chest and stomach. Then, Lipsky shared with Bernice questions he'd be asking and gave her the chance to bring up any concerns she had about the polygraph exam.

Bernice Parrish smiled at him and shook her head. "No questions—I seen this on TV. I'm ready."

He started with control questions—name, date of birth, residence, today's date—to help him and the machine gauge truth from deception. Then: "Have you ever prepared food for Eugene Washington?"

"Yes, several times," Bernice said. "He always liked—"

"Please keep your answers to yes and no," Lipsky requested. "Have you ever prepared food for Eugene Washington?"

Bernice said, "Yes."

"Did you prepare peach cobbler for Eugene Washington in the last week?"

"No."

In August, July, June?

No.

In the last year?

Yes.

"Did you put coconut into the cobbler you baked?" Lipsky asked.

Bernice shook her head. "No."

"Did you put coconut into other foods you prepared for Eugene Washington?"

"No."

"Did you handle Eugene Washington's EpiPen?"

"No."

Luke knocked on the door to the AV room. "Hey. They just ran Bernice's prints against the prints we took in the house, including the set found on that cobbler dish."

My pulse jumped, and I sat up in my chair. "Please tell me it hit." With that good news, a monthlong vacation wouldn't be so bad.

"She's touched every damned thing in that house." Luke shook his head. "Except for the cobbler dish. Sorry, Lou."

"Damn it." I slumped in the chair.

Colin pat my arm. "Doesn't mean she didn't do it. Just means she didn't leave the print. Somebody else could've carried it for her."

I thought about that and an ounce of hope surged through my veins. "True. You're good for something, Taggert."

"Well, that girl I—"

"You just can't help yourself, can you?"

He winked at me. "That's what *she* said."

Thirty minutes later, Lipsky, unlit cigar clamped between his teeth, found Colin and me in the AV room. "She's crazy as hell and the Joe Rice question about him sprinkling the cobbler with coconut made the machine wiggle a little. She claimed she needed to pee, which, you know, anxiety and whatnot."

"Ultimately?" I said.

"She passed."

I groaned and rubbed my face. No hit on the print. No lies on the polygraph. Bernice Parrish didn't kill Eugene Washington.

But Joe Rice was still in play.

"Let's hook him up now," I said.

"Sure," Lipsky said. "Oh—one more thing. Miss Parrish wants her soup pennies or she's gonna sue."

20

Joe Rice, a man as slick as spit and seaweed, passed the polygraph exam. He was a great deceiver in his professional life but anything related to poisoning Eugene Washington? Just call him Booker Effin' T. Washington.

"You need a new suspect," Colin said as we entered the parking garage.

"I know. Where do you think we're going?" I spotted the Crown Vic in its space—sparkling chrome, shiny blue paint and wheels. "You washed the car." He had even cleaned the car's interior—the scent of pine almost masked the pervasive stink of mildew and pickles.

"Don't ever say that I don't do nice things for you," he said, turning the key in the ignition.

At a little past noon, the sun had shot us with the worst it had for the day. Angelenos continued to sweat, yes, but they walked a little quicker and swung their hips with more zest and ease. The heroes in the San Gabriel Mountains were successfully containing the fires, and now the sky was almost light beige again.

And despite Bernice Parrish and Joseph Rice washing out as suspects, despite being forced to take a thirty-day vacation starting Sunday, the day did not hurt as much as I'd expected.

Colin hummed a Maroon 5 song as he navigated through midday traffic.

In the passenger seat, I reread a text message Sam had just sent. *Sometimes it snows in April.* Code for "I miss you and it makes me so sad being away from you." The Crase case had kept us apart when I needed him most—but we'd both rather wait so that a murderer remained in jail forever.

Blessed Mission Ministry's digital billboard had changed since yesterday. DO YOU NEED SPECIAL PRAYER?

Yes, I do. I closed my eyes. *No more snow. No more separation. Let me win. Amen.*

Colin didn't notice my praying. He kept looking in the rearview mirror to check his teeth, to check his hair, and to pry grit from the corners of his eyes. He fished a roll of Pep O Mint Life Savers from his jacket pocket, then popped a lozenge.

"You're so breaking the tenth commandment," I said.

He offered me the roll. "Which commandment is that?"

"The adultery one." I slid a mint beneath my tongue.

He smirked, then tossed one last look into the rearview mirror. "I ain't broke nothing . . . *yet*."

The houses surrounding Blessed Mission were mostly remodels or all-new construction, with a McMansion shoved between dilapidated bungalows and weathered ranches. The Googlers, Twitterers, and NFL were coming to the hood and brought with them higher rents and property taxes. Colored folks had a little money to get that new roof, and white folks had discovered cheap land.

"Old house, new house, new house, old house," Colin said. "What a strange little neighborhood."

"Ah," I said. "Noticing something other than your teeth?"

The Craftsman next door to Blessed Mission was a little rundown but still boasted great bones. A sweaty construction worker gleefully shoved a Bobcat into its living room. Metal and wood crunched and groaned.

I winced and tightened just hearing those sounds again, and from smelling gunpowder and talcum powder—the few memories I had from the car accident in Bonner Park were of gunpowder from Zach Fletcher's gun and the talcum powder from the airbag that had exploded in my face.

Colin didn't see me go rigid—his attention had returned to his teeth and hair. All this grooming for Mrs. Solomon Tate.

And as we sat with her in Bishop Tate's office, I had to admit . . .

That lopsided smile. Those Sophia Loren eyes. She was one of God's showroom pieces, His "look what I can do" *haute couture*. A face pretty enough to trick Eugene Washington into eating killer cobbler so that she could put in a sauna behind the baptismal pool.

Charity smiled as she handed Colin a glass of sweet tea. "Sol flew to Arizona last night for meetings, but you can call him at his room at the Hilton in about an hour." She pushed up the sleeves of her salmon-colored sweater.

"When's he coming back?" Colin asked.

I cocked an eyebrow at my partner. *For his sake or yours?*

She smiled at him. "Tomorrow night. *Late* tomorrow night." She sat the pitcher on the coffee table, then swiped her hands on her salmon slacks.

The room smelled sweet and smoky, like vanilla candles that had been snuffed out. With Charity looking at Colin like that, with Colin looking at her like that, and with the room smelling like the honeymoon suite at the Bellagio, it was obvious: I was the third wheel.

"Why do you have an ATM down in the lobby?" I asked.

Charity tore her eyes away from Colin's. "You know this area—it's not the safest. The members, especially our seniors, can get money out without the fear of being robbed or harassed."

Colin sipped his tea, then said, "We have an ATM in our station lobby for the same reason. Safer place to get money. Makes sense." He nodded at me. *Right?*

I rolled my eyes. "Guess it also helps with the offering plate."

Charity chuckled. "It does. We need our members to give. Nothing's free—our Homeless Ministry *especially* ain't free. There are more than twenty-five thousand homeless people in this city." She paused, then added, "Even Jesus had a group of women supporting him."

"That article you're quoting about the homeless," I said. "The reporter also mentioned high rent and gentrification as causes."

Charity nodded, then made a sad face. "People can't even afford the 'poor' nowadays."

The sound of clicking shoes against the tiled floor outside the office grew close, then stopped—someone was listening. After a moment, the clicking started again, this time, moving away from the pastor's office.

"Back when I was a kid," I said, "Blessed Mission had a small lot. No fountains or porte cocheres. No massive parking lots."

"I remember those days, too. Back then, folks were giving me the side eye because I was thirty years younger than Sol when we got married. But I proved them all wrong. This little ghetto butterfly got them all of *this*." Charity held out her arms and a smile crept across her face. "We *did* purchase surrounding property, Sergeant Norton, but we paid the owners a fair price. No one went homeless because of Blessed Mission."

"So what's the building fund for?" Colin asked, a cop again. "One million dollars, right?"

She fluffed out her twists, then said, "Yep. We need to retire some debt. Do a few renovations here and there. And we're building a senior residential facility next door."

"The craftsman coming down as we speak?" I asked.

Charity nodded. "We purchased that lot and two more. And the building fund is long-term so that members won't have to come up with a lot of money at one time if something around here breaks." She held up both of her hands and that planet on her ring finger threw prisms against the walls. "Again, none of what we do here is free. The literacy program, the substance abuse program, Spanish ministries . . . We feed and clothe thousands of people a year. We give back, and then some. Not to brag, but I'm not like some other first ladies around the country." She smirked. "I drive a Honda, and my husband drives a Toyota with cloth seats."

"Well, that counts for something," I said. "I listened to one of the services posted on your Web site. During offering, your husband said something like, 'If you give, God will rain down upon you health and wealth.'"

"That promise is biblical," Charity pointed out. "Psalms, Jeremiah, Proverbs . . . You can find it in each of those books. Exodus 23:25 says, 'Worship the Lord your God and His blessing will be on your food and water. I will take away sickness from among you.'"

Beads of condensation trickled down the sides of the iced tea pitcher, and a wet ring was now forming on the coffee table.

Charity moved the issue of *Black Enterprise* and a framed family portrait away from the puddle, dabbing it with a napkin. "We don't hold a gun to people's heads, Sergeant Norton. This ain't a stickup."

"No," I said, "but if they don't donate, then they won't get on that giving tree."

"That's because you have to *give* to get on the *giving tree*," she said.

"I'll be honest, Mrs. Tate. I loathe that tree. Sure: I only went to church six times in my life, but I do remember hearing that Jesus said to give in secret."

She nodded. "To not perform your acts of righteousness before men. But that was then. A long time ago."

I blinked at her as blood filled my ears. *That* was her answer?

Love your neighbor. *Oh, that was then, a long time ago.* Thou shalt not kill. *Oh, that was then, a long time ago.*

Charity folded her arms and tilted her head. "Why do you think we're crooks? Is it because you did some digging and found out how many bedrooms I have?"

"I'm charged with finding out who killed Eugene Washington," I said, "and now that we've discovered that he was a very wealthy man—"

"You think *we* had something to do with it?" She gaped at Colin. "Seriously?"

"When we first asked about him yesterday," I said, "you didn't seem to know who I was talking about."

She shrugged. "Right. So?"

"But we saw video of you and him together at the church picnic. You actually kissed the top of his head."

"We have a lot of people here," she said. "I kiss a lot of heads. My job as first lady is to make every member feel like family."

"Over at Washington's house," I said, "we've met some very interesting people who are members of your church. There were three women—"

"The soothsayers?" She laughed, then shook her head.

"You kicked them out," I said.

"They were being disruptive."

"How?"

"Trying to take over services. Interrupting Sol as he spoke. They'd stand over people and start praying, waving that hankie, banging that tambourine, finishing each other's sentences." She shivered and rubbed her arms. "Honestly? They were freaking people out. They were freaking *me* out. So we asked them to stop. They refused, and so Solomon had to ask them to leave. He was very nice and extremely patient. Because, you know, they all have *history*. And then they tried to take people with them to start another congregation, which was just ridiculous. Anyway, ignore them—they bring nothing but conflict and chaos to anything they touch."

"Neighbors say that they saw a van from this church at Mr. Washington's," Colin said. "They said a man and woman visited him back on Monday night. Were you with the van recently?"

Charity closed her eyes, thought for a moment, then shook her head. "No, that wasn't me."

"Where were you?" I asked.

"On Monday night? Football practice with Brandon, my twelve-year-old. And Solomon was in Pasadena, at All Saints Episcopal for a meeting."

"Did you make a special dessert for Mr. Washington on the day of the picnic?" I asked.

"Me?" she asked, pointing at herself. "I don't cook nor do I bake, to my husband's chagrin."

"Your fingerprints, then, wouldn't be on a casserole dish we found near Mr. Washington on Tuesday morning?"

She squinted at me. "Why would it be?"

"Stranger things have happened," I said. "Could you come down later to leave us your prints? And when Bishop Tate returns, we'll ask the same of him."

Eyebrows crumpled, she regarded Colin, then me. "Sure, but I don't see why you need my fingerprints."

"No one's exempt in a homicide case," I said.

"But . . ." She tried to smile. "We're innocent."

I shrugged. "Says everyone I've ever questioned in my hundreds of years as a police officer."

Colin's skin flushed and he cleared his throat. "So what happens if you don't raise the seven hundred thousand by the end of the year?"

Charity smiled her Cheshire Cat smile and her whiskey eyes sparkled. "No idea. The board came up with that deadline. Somebody read a book about fund-raising, and said we needed a deadline." She turned back to me. "I thought y'all said his girlfriend killed him."

I regarded Colin. "*We* never said that to you."

"Oh," she said, her eyes flicking at my partner. "Yes. Anyway . . . You're gonna have to talk to my husband about budgets and deadlines. I do know that every cent we raise goes back into Blessed Mission and our programs. Every cent helps people in this community." She sniffled, then dabbed her fingers at the corners of her eyes. "Forgive me—this is a little stressful. I'm not used to dealing with the police in this capacity."

"We have to ask questions," Colin assured her. "And don't worry: we know you do good work here." He smiled and lifted his glass. "And you make great sweet tea. Thanks again."

As we stomped back to the car, Colin wouldn't speak to me.

"What the hell?" I said. "Why are you talking to her about the case?"

He didn't answer.

"Why are you telling her about suspects?"

"Are you gonna write me up like you wrote up Pepe?" he spat. "Oh, wait. You haven't written up Pepe."

"Don't change the subject," I snapped. "I'm not there to be nice."

"And I'm not there to beat up—"

"Beat up?" The cords in my neck stood against my skin.

"Yeah. With your words and your attitude."

"If she looked like Phyllis Diller, would you be this pissed at me?"

"Who the hell is Phyllis Diller?"

"Blessed Mission has just as much motive as Bernice Parrish," I said. "Stop and think with the head on your shoulders, not the one dangling between your legs." I blinked at him. "Why are we having this conversation?"

Ben Davis. During the Chatman murder investigation, I had cozied up to Christopher Chatman's best friend to get answers. Was Colin doing the same with Charity Tate? Was this his strategy for gaining a confession?

But my partner was done talking to me. He threw himself behind the Ford's steering wheel and turned the ignition.

The Bobcat driver over at the yellow Craftsman had ditched the heavy machinery. He and two others now sat on the tailgate of a battered pickup truck and guzzled bottles of Gatorade.

This was now the third day of my investigation, and all I knew for sure was that I had lost my partner to a pastor's wife with Sophia Loren's eyes.

My phone rang.

"Sergeant Norton?" The man speaking had a Spanish accent. "You don't know me, but I a'work at Mr. Gene's house right now. You should come cuz my friend . . . ? My friend . . ." He stopped, then whispered, "My friend found something."

I opened the car's passenger's-side door. "Well, that's expected, sir. That house is filled with all kinds of things."

"Yes," he whispered, "but my friend . . . ? What he found . . . ? He found hands."

21

Protected by bunny suits and respirators, we crowded the tiny bathroom off the den at Eugene Washington's. The medicine cabinet mirrors reflected nothing—just a platter for decades-old layers of dust, cat hair, and cobwebs. Fossilized porno magazines, including the issue that had forced Vanessa Williams to surrender her Miss America crown, had been ripped from their petrified stacks. Roaches of every variety roamed around a large cherrywood humidor sitting in the center of the tower of boobs. And inside the wooden box: a pair of mummified hands.

"Are they . . . real?" Colin asked.

"Just eyeballing," Zucca said, "I'd say 'heck yeah.' Geez . . . This house is like Ripley's Believe It or Not!"

The skin of the hands smelled musty and resembled turkey jerky wrapped around bone. No smell of decay wafted off of them.

Standing there, in that bathroom, with those hands made my stomach churn, and Charity Tate's sweet tea burned my esophagus.

"This box has been here a few years," Zucca said. "I'm not a forensic anthropologist, though, so I'll rope in Dr. Goldberg."

Just a year ago, Douglas Goldberg, M.D., Ph.D., had helped search the basement of Crase Liquor Emporium near my childhood home. He had examined the bones we'd found there and identified them as my sister's.

The thick gnarled fingers in the humidor looked like they'd belonged to a man. On the left ring finger, there was a tarnished gold ring with an onyx center engraved with the square-and-compasses symbol.

"Z.," I said, "get good pictures of that ring. Looks like he was a mason."

A moment later, I clomped out of the house with my team behind me. I unzipped the front of my Tyvek suit and exhaled as cool air hit my sweaty shell.

The three sisters stood a few yards away, arms outstretched, eyes squeezed shut. They had greeted Colin and me as they'd done before: *The detective and the chief join us today.*

Ike and his men were huddled on the sidewalk—once again, police tape surrounded the property. They had made great progress during their short time cleaning. They had attacked the living room, and now countless black trash bags were piled in the room's center. Ike had rented a giant Dumpster trailer, and a lot of the junk from the front yard sat in its bowels. Cats camped about the mountains of plastic. Some had ventured forth and perched on the top bag.

"We need to look for bodies with missing hands," I told the team. "John Does. Dead homeless. We'll search the house, and if we don't find him here, then we'll search citywide."

"We can't do this alone," Pepe groused. "It took us three days just to find the hands. Which *we* didn't find."

Colin's face reddened. "Dude, stop whining so fuckin' much. What the hell's wrong with you lately?"

Pepe took a step toward Colin. "You know what, Taggert? You can kiss my—"

"Hey," I snapped. "Chill the hell out, both of you. I'll get cadets from the police academy to help out, all right?"

Hands on his hips, Colin watched Pepe and Luke zigzag to their car. "We in trouble?" he asked me.

"For?"

"Not finding the hands."

Vises were locking down my joints, and dull aches pounded in my left arm. "L.T. called me off yesterday, remember? Told me to release the house? I have a signed, dated form saying that. And I dare *anybody* to soar while working two days in a junkyard. What matters now is what we do next. I'll need to get a search warrant for an extended amount of time."

"Like, for how long?" Colin asked. "Another week?"

I gazed back at the house—at all the broken and junky and . . . "Make it two weeks."

"Miss?" The heavily accented voice belonged to a sweaty man with rust-colored skin covered in scars. His strong hands twisted a dusty Margaritaville baseball cap.

"I'll call for the cadets," Colin said, "and start on the extension request—the pair of mummy hands should make it a 'gimme.'"

I smiled at the worker and beckoned for him to meet me at the end of the tape. "Thanks so much for contacting me." After reassuring him that I didn't care about his or anyone's immigration status, he told me that his name was Guillermo Velasquez and that he'd come from Guatemala to work and provide for his family. And then he looked past me and froze.

Behind me, Ike Underwood paced closer to the driveway. He tried not to look in our direction but couldn't help stealing peeks.

My stomach kept churning iced tea and acid as I led Guillermo Velasquez to a side yard and out of Ike's line of sight.

"Don't speak so good English," Guillermo Velasquez said.

"*Donde esta cerando* . . . box? Umm . . ." I made a square. "*Caja?*"

"*El baño.* I was a'working. Shovel. All this trash." He pantomimed digging with the shovel. "Boom. I hit a'somethin hard, and I a'dig and it was there. Mr. Ike, he told us not to open but I open and it was there. *Los manos.*" Tears filled his eyes as he swiped his mouth.

"What did you do then?" I asked.

"I call Mr. Ike. He get mad. He say . . ." He pointed his finger at me. "You not supposed to go through Mr. Washington's a'stuff. I say 'sorry' and . . ." He shook his head, kneaded the cap. "You give me card a'yesterday to call. So I sneak to call. Mr. Ike, he don't look like he call. He tol' me, *trabajo, trabajo.'* And I go back to work and he close the door and walk away. You come in time."

"*Trabajo mucho con Ike?*" I asked.

The man nodded. "He give me a'many job. I need work."

I thanked the man for his courage and honesty. Then, I asked him to come to the station for a formal interview.

Ike, hands on his hips, was now glaring at Zucca and the forensics team.

"Mr. Underwood," I shouted.

He peeped in my direction.

I beckoned for him to come over to me.

We retreated farther down the block, away from the noise. "You seem very interested in all that Mr. Velasquez was telling me," I said.

"His English ain't so good. I just didn't want him to, you know, say one thing when he meant something else."

I cocked my head. "So, why don't *you* tell me what happened."

Ike took a deep breath, then launched into his account. He paralleled Velasquez's story until: "And I closed the bathroom door because I didn't want him taking the box and selling it. The guys were breathing and talking over it, and I seen *CSI* and I know about the DNA in people's spit and the open air messing up evidence. I was just trying to protect it."

"Why didn't *you* call?"

He gaped at me. "Did he say that I didn't?"

"Well, you didn't. I talked to *him*."

"Billy, he didn't wanna call cuz he thought you all would run his name and call Immigration." He plucked a soiled hankie from his back pocket and mopped his face.

"Do you know why Mr. Washington would have a man's hands in a wooden box?" I asked.

"No. Who'd think a thing like *that*?"

"Do you know of a man who's missing his hands?"

"No."

"Did you know that you could possibly find hands in this house?"

Ike glanced back at the house—at Judith and Nina, the prophetesses, and the patrol officers manning the perimeter. He scratched his nose, then swiped it with the hankie. "Gene collected all kinds of things. No telling *what* he got off in there. And after finding those hands, I now know that *anything's* possible."

Hundreds of thousands of dollars in gold bullion. Collectible *Penthouse* magazines. A man's hands. *Anything's possible*. No truer words.

It couldn't get worse than this.

But then Brooks called.

22

I tapped SPEAKER on the phone, then sat it on the Crown Vic's center console. "Okay, Brooks. Let me have it."

Colin pushed the seat back from the steering wheel, then found a clean page in his notebook.

"So we've already established that his last meal was the cobbler and the malt liquor," Brooks said. "I'm pretty sure now that had been his dessert because tests found something else."

"What was the main course?" I asked. "More poison?"

"Umm . . ." Brooks paused, then said, "Human flesh."

My pulse damn-near stopped. Nausea washed over me, and I covered my mouth with a hand.

Colin had also paled. Eyes closed, he said, "Whuh-*huh*?"

"There was flesh in Mr. Washington's stomach that tested positive for human DNA that did not belong to Mr. Washington."

No one spoke.

Outside the Crown Vic, an LAPD van of fresh-faced police academy cadets wiggled out of their seats. *Real police work, yeah!* But then, they *saw*. Enthusiasm dwindled, they stumbled in their steps with their faces crumpled. The horror, oh, the horror.

I swallowed. "Umm . . . Brooks?" Goose bumps formed on my arms, then spread across every inch of my skin. "Can you tell us . . . like . . . from where or from whom?"

"I cannot identify the specific location from which the flesh derived," Brooks said. "Nor can I tell you whose flesh it is. Stomach acids destroyed those specifics."

I closed my eyes and groaned. "But I guess 'who' and 'what' ultimately doesn't matter right now."

"Our vic's a fucking . . . *cannibal?*" Colin asked. "No wonder some-body killed his ass."

Even Brooks had to say, "Yeah."

With numb fingers and a weak will, I scribbled notes even though Brooks's words had seared into my memory. "So, we're . . . uh . . . We're back at Mr. Washington's house right now," I said, "cuz some workers found a pair of hands. Hands that have been separated from the owner."

Silence, then Brooks said, "What the hell?"

Colin grinned—it wasn't every day to hear the deputy ME use non-clinical terms.

"The flesh you found," I said, "could be the hands' owner. But we wouldn't be able to determine that, correct?"

Brooks said, "Correct."

I sighed. "I'll keep this information about Mr. Washington's . . . *diet* a secret for now. We're already in Bat Boy territory with all the people here knowing about the hands."

"Anything else?" Colin said, chuckling.

"Nope." Brooks then offered one last "what the hell" before hang-ing up.

Colin and I sat in the car, gawking at each other, until he said, "I need a drink."

"There's not enough wine in Napa Valley. So. Well . . . We need to take the food that's in the fridge." I shuddered with revulsion. "This is crazy."

Colin cocked an eyebrow. "And we're keeping the cannibal part . . . ?"

"On a need-to-know basis." I closed my notebook, then exhaled again. "We'll tell Zucca, L.T., Pepe, and Luke. Eventually, we'll need to wran-gle in a few more dicks cuz . . . The *original* case combined with the case of those hands and meat, and now . . ."

We sat in silence for a few moments more. The police cadets were now listening intently to Zucca about the proper ways to search a crazy scene like this. He was so calm and so level-headed . . . until we told him about Eugene Washington's main course.

Zucca's eyes bugged, and he lost his ability to speak. In silence, we tromped back to the kitchen.

I opened the refrigerator door.

Even without the tubs of hidden gold coins, there were other count-less plastic containers and foil-wrapped who-knows-what shoved into the freezer.

"Well?" Zucca said. "Do we take everything or . . . ?"

My heart pounded in my ears. "I'm sick of coming to this house."

Colin grunted. "We lucked out, you know? Ike's men hadn't reached the fridge yet. This could've all been gone."

I pointed to a tub of frozen dark gravy. "You think he kept the hands in the bathroom and the guy's spleen in one of these?"

"Dahmer had four heads and a heart in his freezer," Zucca said. "And a box of baking soda. Nothing like your milk tasting like dead male prostitute."

I sighed, then closed the freezer door. "Let's just seal it and take the whole damn thing." I tapped Zucca on the shoulder. "Merry Christmas."

After stepping out of that house, the ordered disorderliness found in the streets of Los Angeles was a welcome sight. The weeds, the traffic cones, and the illegal lamppost posters advertising Reggae Fest seemed quaint, old-fashioned, and honest, especially compared with a closed home filled with poisoned cobbler, severed hands, and tubs of human meat.

So.

Eugene Washington was a cannibal.

When I said that aloud, the person on the other end of the phone line didn't speak.

"L.T.," I said, "you there?"

Colin chuckled, then dumped Tic Tacs into his mouth.

"Yeah," our boss said. "I'm . . . What the hell else are you gonna find in that house?"

A body, maybe?

23

No Thursday night Krav Maga.

"You were doing so well coming in," my trainer, Avarim, told me.

But as Marie Curie said, progress is neither swift nor easy.

Zucca's crew rigged up bright lights in the front and backyards. And like moths to flames, one reporter and cameraman and then another reporter and news van found us digging through junk just in time for the six o'clock news. The blonde reporter from KTLA5 was interviewing Nina and Judith. I'd already thrown a bunch of "no comment" to whomever asked. I'd let the public information officer do her job and talk to the media. I had other crap to do.

Neighbors stood on their front porches and driveways. All the noise from the newcomers had scared the cats, and they escaped deep into their Igloos and Magnavox boxes.

"You ain't heard one word I've said," Lena complained. Then, she pushed a bunch of numbers on the phone's keypad.

"That's because I'm working, and I'm only taking a break now—"

She pushed the keypad again to show her displeasure.

I snapped a selfie of me dressed in a bunny suit and sent it to her. "Does this look like I'm cavorting about? Do I look like I'm having the time of my life?"

"You look like a Hefty bag," she said.

"Thanks, pal. I have two minutes. Answer the question: are you gonna have Chauncey's baby or what?"

"*Qui sait.* You texting Dominic back or what?"

"After the day I'm having, I may just call him. See if he Photoshopped all his goods, then make him slather Icy Hot all over my naked, broken-up body."

"It's that bad?"

"Worse. Way worse. Right now, I'm standing near a window of a room piled high with cat skeletons, old *Sunset* magazines, and broken souvenir plates from Delaware, Nebraska, and Texas."

I didn't tell Lena that, in the kitchen, CSI techs were taping up the refrigerator with intentions of testing whether the foil-wrapped loin in the fridge came from a pig or a man. I didn't tell her that another tech would have to study the fingerprints of a pair of dismembered hands to find their owner. That I still needed to catch the person who had murdered my cannibal-victim.

Lena told me that my job depressed her, then said, "Fortunately, the two minutes you had are up. *Adieu.*"

Pepe found me sitting on the veranda's banister, still taking my much-needed breather. His hair lay mussed and limp against his scalp after being trapped in the Tyvek hoodie. He sat next to me, then asked, "Why is Z. wrapping the fridge with red tape?"

"This is between us. I'll tell Luke later." And then, I told him about Eugene Washington's last supper.

Pepe's craggy face crumpled as he listened to my story. Shoulders stooped and glassy-eyed, he whispered, "I can't do this anymore."

I squinted at him. "Are you aware that you've been a tremendous asshole lately?"

He grunted, then folded his arms.

"And until you're up and out of Homicide, you can't ignore your duties, nor can you disregard my orders. Understand?"

He snorted, and stared at the floorboards.

"That's a ridiculous request to you?" Anger seeped through my pores like beads of sweat. "I can tell Luke that he was a homophobic jerk when you came out to him back in March and he rejected you, but I can't tell you to stop being an old-fashioned jerk toward me? I threw my power behind you, and yet—"

He held out his hands. "Okay, okay. I get it."

I squinted at him. "I don't think you do."

He shrugged. "Doesn't matter."

"You do know . . ." I stood from the banister and squared my shoulders. "No one's talked to me yet about your IAB application."

His eyes glazed, and the vein over his left temple jumped.

"Nope. What's his face had to cancel last week. But we rescheduled for Tuesday."

Pepe's eyebrows raised, then scrunched.

I folded my arms. "Oh, so *now* you care."

"It's not that," he said. "It's just . . . I can't do *this* . . ." He waved at the house and the yard. "I'm tired of dead bodies and cannibals and fucked-up families and secrets and roaches in my car. I will never be you—Lockjaw Norton who always gets her man. I don't care enough, all right? Not anymore. I give zero fucks about this weird fucker in this weird hoarded house who's now eating people. Screw him, all right?"

I studied him, his slumped shoulders, his pursed lips. "I'm not going to give this conversation too much weight—we've been at it all day in the worst conditions. Exhaustion is making you say these things—"

"No," he said, shaking his head. "I'm burned out on being murder police. Give me crooked cops and a cubicle and I'm good."

I squinted at him again. "What if you don't get this position with IAB?"

He took in a deep breath and slowly released it. He pulled on his hood, then said, "Then, I'm telling this job . . . *Banghaehaji mala*. I'm ghost."

24

Banghaehaji mala. Translation from Korean to American English: *Fuck off.* That's what Pepe planned to tell us if he didn't get the position with the Internal Affairs Bureau.

And there was nothing I could say to him at that moment except, "Good luck."

Alone again on the veranda, I tried to take deep cleansing breaths— but the air was crunchy with cancer-causing dust, amping my anxiety into the red. I pulled my phone from my pocket and found Fireman Dominic's last text and picture. I flushed—biology.

"I am only a woman," I muttered as I sent him a one-word reply. *Impressive.*

Over on the sidewalk, the PIO had stepped into the spotlight to offer the official LAPD statement. A bunch of words that meant nothing to the team of forensic anthropologists who'd also arrived to strategize the search for a body.

Back in the parking lot at Southwest Division, my Porsche was where I'd left it nearly fourteen hours before. Since then, my desk phone had been stuffed with voice-mail messages.

This is Solomon Tate. Charity said you needed to talk to me . . .

Hi, Sergeant Norton. My name is Mira Roberson, and I'm with Farmers Insurance. I have questions about a claim . . .

This is Bernice. When can I get my coins?

It was almost eight o'clock. End of watch. I wasn't answering jack. Done for the day.

Really: there was nothing else hard and sure I could do about those hands until the print team came back with results from AFIS. The Automated Fingerprint Identification System stored and analyzed millions of fingerprints taken from millions of people across the country. Hopefully, this database contained just one more hit for the hands.

Bishop Solomon Tate did not pick up when I called back. And my linen pants—so lemony-crisp that morning—couldn't wrinkle any more than they had. So I did as most Americans after working my ass off all day: ordered a dozen marshmallow and chocolate cupcakes to be delivered to my favorite criminalist. Then, I stopped at Trader Joe's for bottles of Orangina and two bags of cinnamon-sugar pita chips.

My next-door neighbor Misty sat on her porch and watched as I trudged from the driveway to my front door. She pulled her long auburn hair into a ponytail and then continued to lace her Rollerblades. "You're late," she said.

"If you watched the news tonight," I said, "you'd know why."

"Guess you can't come out again and skate?"

I shook my head. "Catch me next week. I'm taking some time off." Ha. *Some* time.

"It's a date, then." She slipped a pair of headphones over her ears, then tapped the volume on her iPod. "Dancing Queen" drifted past the ear pads as she rolled toward the bike path.

Perfect weather for skating—marine layer was now drizzling the parched earth. The moon offered no heat but plenty of light, and the slight chill motivated muscles to burn. Across the street at the lagoon, lovers walked arm in arm, enjoying air that no longer hurt.

Inside, hundreds of untouched vials of pain meds crowded the coffee table, and the basket of cinnamon rolls still sat on the breakfast counter. I placed the Trader Joe's bag next to the pastries just as my phone chattered with Ewoks.

A text from my ex-husband, Greg. *You home?*

I texted back—*Yeah. Just got here*—then, scratched my head. Sticky dampness made me yank away my hand. But it was too late. Bright red blood glistened beneath my fingernails. *Damn it, Lou.*

After undressing and stowing the baby Glock in its case and its big sister on the nightstand, I dragged myself to the bathroom. Avoided my reflection as steam from the shower clouded the mirror. Each thought I had lasted no longer than ten seconds—brain in hummingbird mode. Clean and dry, I rolled Icy Hot over my arm and shoulders, then pulled on shorts and a tank top. I considered the blood pressure machine on its shelf—*nope, not today*—then dabbed Neosporin on my head wound.

My phone chimed—a text from Dominic. *I'm on tonite but if u ask nicely, I'll make a special house call just 4u.* My heart thudded so hard that I coughed. Before I could text back something hopelessly unoriginal like *Put out my fire* or *It's so hot, you wanna touch it*—the doorbell rang.

Greg Norton, my forever-love and ass of an ex-husband, held a bag of Korean fried chicken in one hand and a six-pack of Limonata in the other. "You. Have. Mail." He smiled, but his lovely teeth and beautiful brown eyes no longer made me tingly.

I stuck my head into the Kyochon bag. "Doesn't smell like mail. Smells like kimchi wings."

"Mail's back here." He twisted so that I could see envelopes shoved into the back pocket of his cargo shorts. "May I come in?"

He'd gotten a tattoo on his left bicep—it was peeking from beneath the cuff of his T-shirt. It was tribal-looking, and sexy enough that I would've licked it if I still liked poison. He was still muscular, but now clean-shaven—no more five o'clock shadow. He also wore a new woodsy cologne, and that new scent enveloped me as he wandered from the foyer over to the patio door. "Really nice place," he said.

"Yep."

"Eli Moss's attorney called. He wants to know more about our bitter divorce and your substance abuse problem."

Eli Moss had burned homes all around Baldwin Hills. We thought that he had also set fire to the home of Christopher and Juliet Chatman —a fire that took the lives of Juliet and her two children, Chloe and Cody. He hadn't set that fire, but Eli Moss had set fire to my condo, and that night I ran after him. Just as I had with Max Crase, I sent my fist flying into his face. He didn't appreciate that and was suing me for excessive force.

I rolled my eyes. "Did you tell him just how *bitterly* we're divorced? Substance abuse problem—you're kidding, right?"

Greg shook his head. "He asked if you being an angry, bitter drunk contributed to our demise. Then he asked if you being an angry, bitter drunk led you to breaking that fire-starter prick's nose, and if I'm gonna let you—"

"An angry, bitter drunk—"

"If I'm gonna let you take me down."

"And you said?"

Greg smiled. "I told him to get the hell off my phone. And then I sicced the Terminator on him."

The Terminator aka our attorney, Wesley Ibarra.

Greg stepped out onto the deck. "Great view. This a condo or an apartment? How much you paying?"

"You with the IRS and Zillow now?"

His phone rang from his front pocket. "Just looking for somewhere else to live."

"You don't like Santa Monica?"

"Too crowded. Too many people who don't believe in vaccinations or meat or plastic bags. I can take two of those things, but all three?" He stepped back into the living room. "I still like this area. The beach but not a lot of tourists." His phone continued to ring.

I held up the Kyochon bag. "Thanks for dinner. Off to a late-night meeting now?"

He cocked his head. "Nope. You gotta go step in somebody's brains now?"

I tugged the belt loops on my shorts. "Not dressed for that—Glocks are already asleep."

"I didn't have a chance to congratulate you," he said. "A medal and a promotion. Just had to crash into shit and nearly die for them to give you props. Bastards." His phone rang . . . rang . . . vibrated . . .

"Yeah, but they're *my* bastards." I pointed to his pocket. "Are you gonna talk to her or are you just gonna keep being annoying?"

He pulled out the phone, then pressed the power button.

"Uh oh. She's gonna be pissed. Whose credit card will she use now to rent *The Maze Runner*?"

"Ha ha. So you're doing okay?"

"I'm great. I'd ask you to stay—"

"I was hoping you would—"

"But I don't want your company."

He offered a crooked smile. "We're still friends, aren't we?"

A nerve twitched above my left eye. "No, we're not. By the way: how's

Michiko doing? And the one with the cheek fillers. Willow. That's her name, right?"

He closed his eyes. "C'mon, Lou."

"We're not friends, Greg. Let us not define that, you and me. Or maybe we should, but not tonight since that would require you staying, and, again, I don't want you to stay."

My phone now acted out, playing the *Star Wars* theme from the breakfast bar. The selfie Sam had taken on our first rainy-day lunch at Johnny's Pastrami back in March brightened the phone's screen.

Greg stared at my ringing device. "Listen Lou, I . . ." He dropped his head, then crossed his arms. "I really don't know how to say this . . ."

My stomach growled—those peppery wings were waiting. I plucked from his back pocket the mail he'd brought: Cheryl's baked goods catalog, a credit card offer from Discover, and the Dream House raffle circular. "*This* is my mail you carried all the way from Santa Monica?"

"Elouise, listen." He came to stand close to me. Heat rolled off his body and crashed against mine. But he didn't touch me—he knew better than to touch me.

I cocked my head. "Did someone ask you to come over here tonight?"

He squinted at me. "And who would that be? Sy and Lena hate me."

"My mother, then. Did she ask you to come?"

"Nope."

"Yeah, she did," I said, "and she asked that you bring me something to drink that didn't contain alcohol, right?"

"I love you, Lou."

Quiet filled the condo. Not even the faint roar of the ocean penetrated the silence.

Spots of red brightened Greg's cheeks. "I'm not asking you for anything, but you should know that. How I feel about you. Still."

After my accident, Greg had visited me in the hospital twice a day. He'd brought Mom, Lena, and Syeeda food and sat with them, even hugged them as they cried. He read to me and paid for care that my insurance wouldn't. I thought he'd done all of that out of guilt—for cheating on me during the last two years of our marriage. I thought he'd done all of that out of fear—I'd been so close to death, by my own actions and by Zach Fletcher's design. I thought he'd done all of that out of loneliness—his twenty-two-year-old girlfriends were too young to appreciate old-school hip hop, Los Angeles in the eighties, and Frogger. That's what I thought.

"Remember when you called my mom the other day?" he asked.

I nodded. "Yeah. No big deal."

"She didn't tell you," he whispered. "She's sick. Like, *really* sick." He scratched his chin. "This is all so very fucked up."

Angry tears burned in my eyes. Now, the condo was *too* loud. My heart beat. Greg's shallow breathing. Whale songs. Abba. The moon. The wound scabbing over in my head.

I sighed, then grabbed the six-pack of Limonata from the breakfast bar. "You get glasses and some ice, and I'll get two plates."

Friday, September 4

25

My phone vibrated from the nightstand and pulled me from sleep.

It was a little after seven o'clock on Friday morning, and the dim bedroom glowed with soft light. Beyond the sheer cream curtains was a blue sky and the blur of seagulls soaring and diving for breakfast in the Pacific Ocean.

I lifted my head, then froze—brown spots of blood speckled my pillowcase. Beneath my fingernails, more crusted blood. My tear ducts burned, but I refused to cry so early in the morning and in my bed. I *did* whisper "not a good start" as I grabbed my phone and then retreated back beneath the warm comforter.

The early e-mail sender was Alexander Levitt, Eli Moss's civil attorney. Moss had already pleaded no contest to setting at least six fires around Baldwin Hills, including his attempts to burn down my condo in Playa Vista.

Levitt had included an attachment with his message.

I advise that your lawyers contact me to discuss possibilities that will not take us into court—and embarrass you any further.

There was one picture of me standing out on the deck with a pill vial in my hand. Another picture, out on the deck again, showed a bottle of wine on the table. The last picture captured me with my right hand to my mouth and my left hand holding the wine bottle.

My anger made me push off the comforter and sit up in bed.

The first and second pictures: Lena had visited that morning only two months after my accident—she had successfully cooked omelets, then failed at making mimosas since I only had white wine in the fridge. I'd gone out to the deck to call in a refill when I spotted the bottle of wine on the table. I had lifted that bottle to show her—*it's wine, not champagne*—and not to guzzle.

For a moment, I stopped breathing as a more insidious realization dawned on me: Levitt had a private investigator watching me. He was attempting to further his portrayal of me as a pill-popping, excessive-force-using, angry drunk.

I forwarded Levitt's e-mail to the Terminator with a simple message: *Happy Friday. Help me.*

At least my morning's blood pressure hovered at 132/90. Not great, but better.

After applying Neosporin to my head wound and pulling on jeans and an LAPD T-shirt, I stepped into the living room. It was still dark, and the curtains were still closed.

In the sofa bed, Greg stirred beneath the blankets, then slowly sat up with a yawn. After dinner, he had hooked up my Xbox One, and we had played soccer until I fell asleep with the controller in my hands. I didn't invite him back to my bedroom, but he did show up in my nightmares—he stood in front of my sister Victoria on a hill, looking down at me. I tried to scramble toward him as that man in the golden mask grabbed at my feet. Greg did nothing except watch me struggle.

And now my ex-husband's eyebrows crumpled and worry darkened his pecan eyes.

I considered my blue jeans, T-shirt and Doc Martens boots. "No fur and sequins today. We're digging for a body."

"It's not your outfit." His Adam's apple bobbed. "I came in a few times last night and had to shake you awake. Are you okay?"

My empty stomach dropped. "Sorry about . . . the . . . and the . . . Lately, my sleeping gets a little . . . *imaginative.* I apologize for scaring you."

Greg bit his upper lip, then said, "It's okay. Glad I was here. It's just . . . Is it a new thing?"

"It is a new thing." I had never nightmared like this during our marriage. Even after investigating brutal murders with body parts, buckets of blood and evil everywhere, I'd never suffered "wake up sweating, almost shooting people, scratch myself to death" nightmares. In some

ways, Greg kept me sane and slumbering even as he banged purse de-
signers and marketing managers from sea to shining sea.

Hunh.

I retreated to the kitchen, where the breakfast counter now served
as a buffet for Victor Starr's cinnamon rolls and Greg's kimchi wings.

Men—always trying to shove something in your mouth.

"Coffee?" I asked Greg.

"Sure." He pulled his cargo shorts over his boxers, then joined me
in the kitchen. He poked at the basket of cinnamon rolls. "Can I heat
these up?"

I pulled coffee beans from the cupboard. "Enjoy. I was done the
moment they arrived."

"You need to gain a couple of pounds." He slipped the last three rolls
onto a paper towel.

"Not a weight thing—Victor Starr sent them."

Greg placed his breakfast in the microwave oven, then licked his
sticky fingers. "Nothing says 'forgive me' like fancy sweet rolls."

"Or a Porsche." I dumped coffee beans into the grinder.

He said, "Ha," then stared at me with glassy wide eyes.

"Stop worrying," I said.

"I'm not worrying."

I squinted at him. "I know that look, Gregory, and you're looking that
look at me right now."

He pulled the now-heated rolls from the microwave, and the warm
scent of cinnamon and sugar filled the kitchen. "If it's the drugs, Lou—"

"Greg, I hardly take any drugs."

My phone played the *Star Wars* theme. Sam had texted. *Good morning. You didn't call back. You around?*

I grabbed my phone from the counter and messaged him back.
*Sorry. Was in the middle of an intervention last night—and it's still happen-
ing right now.*

"I can tell," Greg was saying, "but are you getting a restful—?"

I hit the coffee grinder's ON button, and the loud whir drowned out
his voice. Once the beans couldn't be grounded any finer, I released the
button.

He said, "But are you getting—?"

I hit the ON button again.

He smiled.

Off.

He said, "Restful—?"

On.

I smiled at him.

He held up his hands.

My nerves jabbed my skin like millions of tiny needles. "Just because I let you stay," I said, "doesn't mean we're 'us' again. Your mother was always nice to me, and I know her situation is worrying you, but—"

"Let me say this and I'll shut up."

"Sure." I dumped the ground coffee into a paper liner.

"Get another shrink," Greg said. "Maybe you *do* need to take something to keep you from nightmaring. I mean, how can you do your job if you don't get enough rest? You work hard, Lou. And I'll say this while I still have the floor: you're not failing if you take some more time off."

With a shaky hand, I filled the coffee pot with cold water, then poured it into the coffee maker. "Where was all this *caring* before?"

"I've always cared for you," he said, "and you always pushed me away."

I smirked. "There were so many chicks' asses in my face, I couldn't help but push you away. Oh, right. The multiple side pieces—they're *my* fault. I'm the cart *and* the horse. The chicken *and* the egg."

"I didn't mean that," he said with a quaver in his voice.

"Oh. I misunderstood. My fault. Again."

Greg leaned against the counter and scratched his thumb against his lips as the coffee machine burped and gurgled. "You can confide in me, Lou," he whispered. "You can tell me how you *really* feel. You can tell me what's scaring you, why you're having nightmares. I've never told anyone your secrets, and that still goes, even now. You can trust me."

I squeezed his shoulder. "Greg, that's very sweet of you but . . . no." Twitching with repressed rage, I held out my arms and said, "You helped to create who I am today." I gave him a thumbs-up, then grabbed two coffee mugs from the cabinet.

"I love you." He crossed his arms and nodded. *There, I said it.* He flushed, and the vein in the middle of his forehead pulsed.

I wanted to say, "I love you, too." And then kiss and kiss and live happily ever after.

But I didn't want to do any of this with Greg.

26

I wanted to say "I love you" to Sam. Even though we'd spent no romantic time together since March, Sam—or the thought and promise of Sam—made me swoon and daydream of cabins and books, quiet and rib roast, a little girl with pretty eyes and the Cirque du Soleil Big Tent every fall. It made no sense to me—I didn't know if Sam could give me that or even if he *wanted* to give me that. Still, I loved the possibility of us both sharing this fantasy of Normal together.

And now, as I drove to work with a sea of cars all going ten miles per hour, I didn't care about traffic or getting to my destination. I'd watched the clock roll from eight thirteen to eight twenty without getting any closer to the traffic light. Didn't care—and my lack of caring was so profound that a Honda, a city bus, and a dump truck all merged in front of me as I talked to Sam on the phone. And as I glimpsed my reflection in the rearview mirror, I saw bright eyes, an easy smile, and no cords standing in my neck.

I told him about Syeeda's and Greg's attempts to save my life.

"Greg . . . stayed the night?" Concern etched Sam's voice.

My phone vibrated with a text from Colin. *Headed over to the house.*

"Don't worry," I told Sam. "It was not sexy. It was an intervention mingled with the news of his mother going in for a biopsy."

"Hunh."

"Jealous?"

"Very."

"I should be, too. You and the Italian hottie."

He chortled. "It is not a thing. She knows that I'm distracted."

"By?"

He sighed. "My fantasies of you are better than real-life her. I must admit, though, waiting for you is becoming a challenge in some ways."

"Hair where there was no hair before?"

"Something like that. Yeah. That. But enough about my struggle with onanism—"

"Big word for?"

"Self-pleasure."

"Oh, dear."

"Indeed. And how are you?"

I punched the button for the air conditioner—the outside thermometer had ticked up to ninety-three. "Well, Eli Moss's attorney sent me a lovely e-mail this morning. It included out-of-context pictures of me holding a wine bottle."

"You send it to Ibarra?"

"Yep."

"Then, don't worry about it anymore. How are you *physically?*"

"Been better," I said. "I keep scratching the wound in my head. Keep dealing with some other things that kinda suck."

"Tell me."

"I'd rather do it in person and then you can see with your own eyes."

"Sounds bad."

My throat clutched some, and I choked out, "It is."

"Next week this time, you can show and tell me as much as you want without fear of Crase running free. I miss you, Elouise."

"I miss you, too, Samuel." My stomach jitterbugged just saying that. "That means you're on schedule to being released?"

"First thing Monday morning. Lucille's taking the case."

"Wonderful."

"Until then," he said, "stay away from Greg."

My face ached from smiling so hard. "And you stay away from Isabella."

"Deal. Next week, then?"

"Yes. I want the works. Roses, dinners, movies, Broadway shows, that gondola thing in Long Beach and . . . naked. Lots of naked."

"You got it. Whatever you want, it's yours."

That's what I wanted to hear. And now, the idea of vacation *really* didn't seem offensive. Sam naked combined with a night at the Pantages Theatre? Why the hell would I deny myself that kind of gift?

I'd only reached the third mile of my eight-mile trip when my phone rang again. After making the slowest left turn in the history of left turns, I answered.

Lena's face brightened the phone's screen. *"Bonjour, ma chérie!"*

"Good morning in American," Syeeda shouted, forcing her way into the shot.

Heading into the sun, I slipped on my aviators, then flipped down the visor. "So I just realized that neither of you checked up on me last night or this morning. It's like you knew Greg would be there."

Neither friend responded. In the background, an espresso machine hissed.

"Hello?" I said.

"Did anything . . . *happen?*" Syeeda asked.

"We played FIFA soccer, ate Kyochon chicken, then gave each other head."

Together, Lena and Syeeda shouted, *"What?"*

"That was a joke," I snapped. "He slept on the couch. I slept in my room, which he didn't enter until he had to wake me up from my nightly nightmares." And now, I let no car ease its way into my lane. Happy Lou had skipped away to her secret garden.

"We just . . . you could . . ." Syeeda sighed. "It's just that . . ."

"That I may OD or shoot myself?" I asked.

Silence from my friends.

"Hello?" I said again.

"We'd rather make sure you're safe," Syeeda said, "than wonder if you're safe."

"I'm not taking drugs," I said. "My pee is clean."

Silence again.

"Hello?"

"We know that," Lena said. "Still . . ."

"We did all this because we care," Syeeda explained. "Don't be mad at us. We love you. We don't want you to be alone if you don't have to be."

Lena sang, "*That's what friends are for.*"

Then, Syeeda joined in with, "*I'll be on your side forever more.*"

And they sang that 1980s friendship anthem until an irritated smile found my lips. And as I finally reached Leimert Park and turned onto Victoria Avenue, smiles today would be rarer than tanzanite.

Pulling up to Eugene Washington's house was now almost routine. The three women stood in their regular positions along the sidewalk with their hands out, eyes closed, lips moving in silent prayer. The Dumpster was now half full with trash bags. The cats still perched everywhere. This morning, though, Ike Underwood and his crew watched police cadets search through the junk piles. A cadaver dog with his nose to the ground and wearing protective argyle socks pulled his lady trainer around the front yard. In the driveway, a man in a FORENSICS Windbreaker leaned against a Bobcat and waited to push junk out of the way.

Colin, eating a granola bar, stood beneath the magnolia tree. He pushed his sunglasses to the top of his head as I approached. "Traffic again?" he asked.

"Yep. The tech boys conspired against me getting here on time. The dog alert yet?"

He nodded, then slipped the aviators back over his eyes. "I'll show you where."

I followed him to the backyard.

Dirty workers wearing khaki flap hats were now clearing the last bits of junk from a six-by-twelve piece of land at the rear fence.

I sighed. "This is gonna take forever."

My partner popped the last third of his granola bar into his mouth. "They're gonna find a bunch of cat and raccoon skeletons all over this property."

"You don't think we should be doing this?"

"Didn't say that."

"What *did* you say?"

He shrugged. "They're gonna find a bunch of—"

"Well, that's expected. We have disembodied hands and a dead man with a gut full of human meat—"

"I know that. I'm not stupid." His face had reddened.

"Why are you second-guessing every decision I make?" I snapped.

"Whoa," he said, hands out. "That escalated quickly." He pushed up his sunglasses again. "I meant nothing by my comment, Lou. Damn. Chill out."

The dog's bark pulled us out of our asses. He had alerted in Washington's garage and now lay beside a stack of Del Monte boxes in various stages of rot. Paige, the dog's handler, praised her pup as a forensic tech placed a yellow tent at the spot.

Forensic anthropologist Douglas Goldberg found Colin and me back beneath the magnolia tree. His hat hadn't protected his face from burning, but sunburn didn't hamper his eagerness. "Three spots so far," he reported. "Once we clear the way, we'll bring out the GPR buggy."

While ground penetrative radar would not provide traditional pictures of those things buried, it would still alert us to differences below the surface.

"When do you think you'll start with GPR?" I asked the scientist.

"Oh . . ." He pushed back the hat and scratched his damp head. "Probably by tomorrow. I'll alert the medical examiner when we're ready to dig, just so they'll have somebody ready to come in the event we find human remains."

I thanked the doctor, then watched him hustle into the garage.

Colin glanced at his wristwatch. "Please tell me we're not staying here all day."

"We're not staying here all day." I opened my leather binder. "We have a lot on our to-do list, so let's get started."

"Where to now?" Colin asked as we walked to our cars.

My phone rang again—this time, Zucca was calling.

"Where you at?" he asked.

"The Washington house," I said, "watching them grid out the junkyard for GPR. You get the cupcakes?"

"Yes, thank you. Already inhaled two. Can I meet you back at the station?"

"Will it take long?" I asked. "We got a lot to do before the sun sets today."

"Well . . . Those hands the workers found?" he said. "We got a hit in AFIS on the fingerprints. And the guy the prints belong to? He's still alive."

27

Millions of fans stationed around the squad room twisted back and forth. But the man-made breezes failed to cool anyone wearing a tired suit or filthy Dickies—and the place still stank of burned coffee and dying deodorant. Summer at Southwest Division.

"Are you ready for your miracle?" Seated in my guest chair, Zucca sounded as though his equipment budget had increased a hundredfold over the next decade.

I smirked. "I'm ready for it, but my partner ain't."

Over at his desk, Colin held the phone to his ear. He smiled like a goof, then glanced in my direction.

I motioned for him to end his call.

He nodded, said, "Talk to you later, Charity," then rolled over in his chair.

"Did you just say what I think you said?" I asked.

Colin nodded. "She was just callin' to let me know that the bishop was coming back tonight."

I cocked an eyebrow. "She stopping by today and leaving her prints as requested?"

"Didn't ask," Colin said, "but I can go over later with a print kit."

I squinted at him, then turned to Zucca. "So, what's the miracle?"

Zucca pulled from his accordion file pictures of the hands as well as pictures of fingerprints tagged with dots. "Fortunately, the left hand still had fingerprint ridges on the index and pinky fingers."

"Is that normal?" Colin asked. "Them sticking around a long time after you're dead?"

"Depends," Zucca said. "That cigar humidor preserved them really well. So, I was able to cast the fingers in latex to get better ridge detail. That was miracle number one."

I made notes in my pad, then said, "That means there's a miracle number two."

Zucca beamed. "Uh huh. We ran the prints in AFIS."

My stomach tightened. "And?"

"*And* we got a hit." Zucca pulled another sheet of paper from that accordion file and placed it on my desk. "Lady and gentleman, meet Oswald Little."

Colin and I gaped at each other. "He's the guy who's supposed to get Eugene Washington's house and car," I said.

"We've been trying to reach him," Colin said.

The black man's receded salt-and-pepper hairline matched his beard and mustache. Born January 7, 1940, in Belmopan, Belize, he now resided at 7170 Corning Avenue in Ladera Heights. He had the easy smile of a self-made, self-satisfied man.

"According to public records," Zucca said, "Mr. Little is still alive. So, he'll be happy to hear he's a beneficiary."

I shivered and ice formed between my eyes—an ice-cream headache without the ice cream. "Let's pay him a visit today. Maybe I had the wrong number—or maybe it's under someone else's name." Back in my married days, Greg paid the phone bill, but it had been under my name.

"How the hell is that even possible?" Colin asked. "Him being alive? He has no hands."

"You can live without hands," I said. "You'd wear prosthetics. Like that double-amputee guy a few years ago on *Dancing with the Stars*."

"Or like Jaime Lannister on *Game of Thrones*," Zucca added.

"The dancing guy had those blade things for legs," Colin said to me. To Zucca, he said, "And Jaime Lannister isn't real."

I held up the picture of Oswald Little. "Maybe he lost 'em in a hand of poker. Came up short-handed."

"Got his ass and hands handed to him," Zucca said, smiling.

Colin groaned. "You two gonna appear in the Starlight Lounge after dinner?"

"Anything else, Z.?" I asked.

He nodded. "The cobbler contained coconut—the flour was a mixture of regular wheat flour with coconut flour folded in. There was also something—possibly coconut extract—in the filling."

"Any flaked or shredded coconut?" I asked. "Big enough to catch in your teeth?"

"Nope. Just looking and feeling, you wouldn't know that you were texturally eating coconut. By the time he realized it, he'd already eaten more than half the dish. I'm sure Brooks will tell you that he was probably dead within the hour."

"Because his throat was swollen and his lungs . . ." I grimaced. "That's a jacked-up way to go."

"We also tested the contents on a few of those tubs we found in the freezer." Zucca slipped another report on my desk. "No coconut, but it was more roast beef than human, but still . . . The other stuff was . . . you know. People."

"People," Colin said.

"People who eat people," I said.

"Are the luckiest people, in the world," Zucca sang.

"Any DNA hits?" Colin asked.

Zucca shook his head as he packed up his things. "The meat in the tubs doesn't match the DNA from Little's hands."

I offered a weak grin. "I don't know if that's good or bad."

In this case, "good" meant "tomatoes" and "bad" meant "tomatoes." And because of that, I needed a helluva primer and decision tree to tell me if it was good that the DNA in the two human samples (the tubs and Washington's stomach) were not a match because that meant Eugene Washington didn't have parts of the owner of those hands stuck between his back molars but that he'd eaten someone else.

I grabbed the phone to return Farmers Insurance agent Mira Roberson's call. But her line went straight to voice mail. I left my cell phone number and told her to call me at any time. No such thing as after hours during a murder case.

Luke and Pepe had gathered Eugene Washington's medical records and had left a folder on my desk.

Colin flipped through pages that provided a glimpse of our victim's health. "Oh, wow," he said.

"What?"

"About five years ago, Eugene Washington ate something that had coconut in it. And he didn't have his EpiPen with him. Fortunately, he was close to a fire station, and the heroes saved him." Colin looked up. "He has a prescription for epinephrine—it was renewed and filled during his appointment last week."

"Again," I said, "I didn't see EpiPens anywhere *in* that house."

"Me, neither," Colin said, "even after digging down in that filthy armchair."

"Do they test for human remains in your blood work?" I wondered. "Or do they simply suggest that you lower your cholesterol? Eat less red meat?"

Then, I opened the folder that contained Washington's financials. Two sheets of paper. "Looks like he had a checking account at Excelsior Bank of California." The balance: $17,053.66. "Seems like a lot of money but . . ." My eyes jumped around the page. "How did he get income?" The next page in the folder came from the Veterans Administration. "According to this statement, he received checks from the VA each month."

"Maybe he cashed the checks at the bank, then pocketed the money." Colin pushed away the medical records. "Do we tell the church that Brother Washington ate people?"

I said, "Hunh. What *is* the protocol for that?"

"Hell, yeah," was Luke's response.

We found him and Pepe at the taco stand across the street having late breakfast or early lunch. Luke was attacking a breakfast burrito as thick as my thigh while Pepe smoked and nibbled a greasy torta. Colin ordered a smaller breakfast burrito for me and a tamale plate for him, and as we ate I caught Pepe and Luke up on the Washington case.

"And how's the house search going?" I asked.

"They gridded out that narrow swatch of land on the north side of the house," Pepe said. "No more alerts from the dog."

"So that's three possible sites," Colin said. "North side, back fence, and garage."

Pepe lit his third cigarette. "How long you think those hands were in the box?"

Luke swiped egg from his mustache. "Can you live without hands?"

"They're *hands*," I said, "not lungs."

We finished our meal, then lumbered across the street to the parking garage.

"Where to?" Colin asked as he climbed into the passenger seat.

I twirled the car keys around my index finger. "Let's see if the man with no hands is at home."

Ladera Heights was one of three neighborhoods comprising Black Beverly Hills. From cardiologists to sports stars, residents enjoyed backyard tennis courts, swimming pools, and breathtaking views of Los Angeles—and at a cheaper price than 90210. Despite the benefits of segregation, the residents here suffered with the same ninety-degree heat as their northerly neighbors. Survival came via Frappuccinos, tank tops, and paisley-printed umbrellas. The entire city perspired enough to fill our drought-stricken reservoirs.

I made a right turn onto Corning Avenue and eased past an atrocious three-story Tudor, a pleasant ranch, another ranch, and a Mediterranean. FOR SALE signs. Glistening Bentleys. Hispanic gardeners. Quartets of power-walking seniors wearing shorts and polo shirts.

At 7170 Corning, a bronze Mercedes-Benz sat in the circular driveway of a yellow house that combined the rambling sprawl of a California bungalow with the front-door-flanking windows of a Cape Cod. A butter-hued woman wearing a brown wig and a violet housecoat opened the massive front door. She clutched a shih tzu to her bosom and scowled at Colin above her readers as though he'd already tromped crap-covered shoes across her shag carpet. Wagner's "Ride of the Valkyries" blasted from a stereo system somewhere in the house.

I flashed my badge. "Good morning, ma'am. Is Mr. Little in?"

She blinked her enormous eyelashes, sending my way a draft of gardenia, jasmine, and musk. "You'll have to speak a little louder, honey, if you want me to hear anything you're saying. My hearing's bad today. See, I've been down all week with this horrible cold goin' round."

As Wagner's soprano soared over the horns, reeds, and bass drum, the old woman scratched the dog's ear and told us about her bronchitis misdiagnosis. Then, she shared her son's opinion that she was suffering from earwax buildup and her opinion that big pharma controlled the weather and therefore controlled everyone's health.

The dog in her arms didn't flinch. Such an obedient, quiet dog. Such a stiff . . . stuffed dog.

"So I've been going on," the woman said as she scratched the taxidermied pooch's head. "How much money do you need?"

Colin chuckled. "We're not fund-raising. We'd just like to speak with Mr. Little."

She squinted at him. "*Who*?"

Colin shouted, "Oswald Little, ma'am."

She shook her head. "Ain't no Orenthal Miller living here."

I wrote Oswald Little on my notepad, then showed it to her.

"No. Nobody by that name lives *here*." Then she told us that her name was Hermie Bellman, short for Hermione, and that her husband, Donald Bellman, bought their house a few years ago. "But wait a minute," she said. "Oswald . . . His name sounds a little familiar. He may have been the previous owner. See, my husband handled all of that, but he died two years ago, on Thanksgiving. Heart attack."

Back in the car, I booted up the Crown Vic's ancient laptop. According to the county assessor's records, Hermione and Donald Bellman had purchased the property at 7170 Corning in 2012. It had four bedrooms, three bathrooms, and a swimming pool.

"Oswald Little pulled permits for construction in 2011." I scrolled down the page. "The house was put on the market in 2012. Sold for 1.5 million."

Colin whistled. "He probably took that money and flew to Fiji."

I googled "Oswald Little." A formal portrait of the man popped up on the "About Us" page for Excelsior Bank of California—senior vice president. Two more links to a PDF from July 1995 from the Most Worshipful Prince Hall Free and Accepted Masons located on Figueroa Boulevard announced that Little had been elected Grand Junior Warden. The second Prince Hall PDF, this one from 2000, announced Little had received a service award.

Oswald Little also drove a 2000 Jaguar, was not an organ donor, and had donated $6,000 to Al Gore's presidential campaign.

"Another connection," I said. "Eugene Washington's only bank account was at Excelsior."

And then, the laptop died. It would resurrect in three hours as it typically did.

I pushed the dead computer away from me, then said, "I'd just come back from T.J.Maxx and there was my baby Puccini, dead on his favorite chaise. Now: how much money do you need?"

Colin exploded into laughter. "How long did it take *you* to realize the dog was dead?"

And then, we laughed and laughed.

Poor lady.

Gina Cisneros at Social Security owed me a favor since I'd arranged for her heavy-handed husband to be picked up on a bench warrant. She paid me back now by telling me that Oswald Little, Social Security number ending in 6539, had been receiving Social Security checks ever since his retirement in 2010.

"Do you have an address for him?" I asked.

"Yep," Gina said. "He's at 11317 Garth Avenue, Los Angeles, 90056."

"As recent as . . . ?"

"As last week," she said.

"Garth Avenue: that's still Ladera Heights, right?" Colin asked after I'd ended my call.

"Yep. Two streets over." I turned the key in the ignition. "Let's go see a man about his hands."

28

Driving two blocks felt like driving three miles. Behind me, the sun had drifted to its late-morning spot in the sky, and I feared that my traditional workweek—and the last Friday before vacation—would end without resolution. Part of me saddened—every victim deserved their case to be solved, no matter their prior villainy or their diet. If I had to pick a case that had loose threads, though, it would have been this one. Eugene Washington did not have a widow blowing up my phone with a voice wet with tears and sorrow. But he had Bernice and Ike, and they loved him for their own reasons. And, ultimately, solving any case was for those left behind.

On Garth, I parked in front of a ranch-style house a few yards away from the Mediterranean two-story with the blue-and-gray flagstone driveway and an address plaque that read 11317.

Colin whistled. "Nice."

"But one of these things is not like the other," I said.

"Which thing?" he asked. "The Jaguar parked in front of the three-car garage? Or the banged-up truck with planks of rotten lumber in the back?"

"That truck looks mighty familiar."

Colin swiveled the laptop computer in his direction, then mashed the power button. "Still dead." He smacked it, then squinted out the window. "That truck looks like Ike's—" The computer monitor blinked on, and Colin started typing across the keyboard before it died again. "It *is* Ike Underwood's truck, and the DMV has him living here at this address."

My nerves exploded like tiny firecrackers all over my body. "You mean, construction guy and Eugene's fishing buddy Ike Underwood? He lives *here?*"

"Yep." He tapped the keyboard. "But the 2000 Jag belongs to Oswald Little."

I sighed, then sank in my seat. "Remember back on Tuesday when I thought this case was gonna be easy? All so simple then."

"We going in?" Colin asked.

Dread churned like pancake batter in my belly. I kept my eyes on that truck as though it would disappear at any moment. "No," I said. "Let's just watch."

"Why?"

I turned Colin's question over and over again in my mind—and the answer kept slipping between my fingers like mud. "Something's not right, and my gut's telling me to just . . . watch. It's Friday—my gut's never wrong on Fridays."

And so we sat. At the gray colonial, a teenage girl talked on her cell phone as a toddler boy rode his tricycle around the driveway. On the sidewalk, dog walkers carried leashes in one hand and golf clubs in the other. The water-delivery truck stopped in front of the ranch-style. A postal carrier passed over the vacant-looking contemporary without leaving mail.

Colin took a few selfies—Colorado smile, Colorado steel, Colorado bored.

I gave him the side eye. "Who are those for?"

He blushed and his ears turned bright pink. "For future use."

Thirty minutes and ten liters of sweat later, we were still watching Oswald Little's home from the car. As we sat, my mind fluttered like a butterfly from one subject to the next.

Is Lena gonna have Chauncey's baby?

Is Sam gonna come through and take me away?

What's my blood pressure right now?

Who did Eugene Washington have for dinner?

Who is he texting?

Even as his eyes remained primarily on the house, Colin's fingers never stopped tapping his phone.

At the house, both the water truck and the postal carrier had delivered mail and two bottles of water, but no one opened the door to retrieve either. Water bottles meant someone lived there. There were no newspapers or circulars languishing on the lawn to suggest vacancy.

At one thirty, Colin said, "Think somebody's gonna come out and get the water?"

"Don't know."

"We going in?"

"Give me a minute."

His stomach growled. "You hear that?"

"Nope. My son says I got earwax buildup."

"You realize we haven't eaten since—oh, hell." He pointed to his right.

A resident of the ranch-style wandered from the house and down to our car. The plump woman had the same nose as the pug in her arms.

Colin and I pasted on smiles as she bent at the window. She smelled like sweet melon and vanilla, and thanks to being around Eugene Washington for four days, I had the strange urge to bite her chubby cheek.

Colin said, "Good afternoon."

She placed the panting pug on the grass. "Y'all are cops. Is there something going on? Should I be worried?"

Smiling, I said, "Absolutely no reason to worry. We're just observing."

"Nothing to see really," she said. "It's pretty quiet up here. A few parties every month but nothing dramatic. Ain't no drive-bys in this part of town."

"Do you know all your neighbors?" I asked.

"Pretty much." She pointed to the colonial. "She's a lawyer. He's an executive something at Sony. Two kids." She pointed to the Tudor. "He's a surgeon. She's stay-at-home. Big Democratic-party donors." Up and down the block she went. Consultant, judge, professor, Black Republican—can you believe it? At Oswald Little's Mediterranean, she said, "He owns a construction business. Widowed. Really sweet."

Confusion flicked inside my head. *Construction?* According to my search, Oswald Little was a senior VP at Excelsior Bank.

"How long has he lived there?" I asked.

"Since 2012, at least," the woman said. "So, about two, three years."

"What about his roommate?" I asked.

The woman narrowed her eyes. "I don't know anything about a roommate."

"You know his name?" Colin asked.

"Oz," she said. "Can't recall his last name."

"Is he bald? Beard, mustache, short?" I asked.

"Nuh uh. Tall, broad, head full of hair. Reminds me of, oh . . . what's his face." She closed her eyes as she tried to remember. "You know who I'm talking 'bout. The black guy."

"Oh yeah," I said. "He was in that show with what's her face."

She snapped her fingers, and pointed at me. "Yeah. Him. That's who Oz resembles."

But Oz didn't have a head full of hair.

We thanked her, then watched as she led the pug back into the house.

"Who's what's his face?" Colin asked.

"No idea. Nor can I figure out if Ike lives here or not."

Colin brought out his Tic Tacs from his pocket. "What do we know for sure?"

"That Oz Little's name is on that house and on that Jag."

The door to the pug owner's house opened again. "Excuse me," she shouted. "The black guy in *The Matrix*. That's who Oz looks like. Just older."

I gave her a thumbs-up, then turned to Colin. "She's talking about Laurence Fishburne."

"And that's not Oz. That's more like Ike."

I flipped through my binder and found the phone number for Ike Underwood.

After three rings, he answered. In the background of his world, heavy equipment beeped and scraped. Men shouted above the noise.

"Hey, Mr. Underwood," I said, putting light into my voice. "How are you?"

He chuckled. "Just confused, you know? Tryin' to help out around here but you all won't let me."

"I'm calling to change all of that—we do need your help. In a big, big way. My partner and I, we're out and about right now, but can you meet us back at the station around six o'clock?"

Ike paused, then said, "You want me to leave the house?"

"Only for twenty minutes or so."

With great hesitation, he finally agreed.

"He sounded thrilled," Colin said.

"I know. Can't wait to hear how all of this is connected."

"Maybe he'll bring Oz."

"Who, according to Social Security—"

"Is still alive and lives at this address."

I tugged at my ear as snippets and space junk whirled through my mind—I needed time to think and to connect the dots by discarding that junk. But my cell phone rang and interrupted my brain's slow-mo analysis.

"Glad I caught you." It was Mira Roberson from Farmers Insurance. "It's Friday before the holiday, and I know some people leave work early on Fridays before holidays."

"I am not one of them," I said, smiling. "How can I help you, Mira?"

"I have a claim," she said, "but I wanted to talk with you first before we pay it out."

"Sure. Who are we talking about?"

"Eugene Washington. He died early this week."

"That's correct." I grabbed my binder from the backseat, then put the phone on speaker so that Colin could hear. Then, we explained to the claims agent the condition in which we'd found Eugene Washington's records.

Mira Roberson was silent for a moment before saying, "Wow."

Colin said, "Yeah."

"So the policy is for two hundred and fifty thousand," she said. "Taken out last September. I know you're investigating his death right now, but is there any reason to deny the claim?"

"It depends," I said. "Who's the beneficiary?"

"Let me check. The beneficiary is . . ." Her fingers pecked at a computer keyboard. "The beneficiary is Oswald Little."

29

With Friday-evening holiday traffic and after a quick roll through McDonald's drive-through, we reached the Prince Hall Grand Lodge on Figueroa Street an hour later. Although the long stone-gray building took up most of the block, it did not exude the ostentatious magnificence of the marble-clad Scottish Rite Temple on Wilshire Boulevard. This lodge needed more white columns and fourteen-foot statuary of historic men made of travertine. And then . . . everything else.

"So this is a Blacks-only kinda thing?" Colin asked, then slurped the last of his Diet Coke.

"Yep, cuz, you know, slaves and descendants of slaves weren't allowed to join George Washington's masons." I tapped his shoulder. "I know that's hard to believe since racism is over."

"Exactly. So why is this still around?" Colin asked, nodding toward the building.

I blinked at him. "That was sarcasm. Racism isn't over."

He chuckled. "Right. I know."

Developers had yet to gentrify this part of Figueroa. Just a few miles from Watts and almost twenty miles from the airport, forced improvements seemed far off—Chicano lesbian president of the United States far off. Instead of Trader Joe's, megachurches, and a BevMo, residents would have to get by with the Numero Uno Mercado, modest houses of worship, and liquor stores.

At the entrance, Colin whispered, "Can we go in?"

I knocked on the door, then rang the doorbell. "We're the police. We can go wherever the hell we wanna go."

"We're a little underdressed," Colin said, looking down at his jeans and T-shirt.

"Do you wanna go wait in the car?" I asked.

Too late.

A Lurch of a man opened the door. He had stooped shoulders and a caved-in torso and stood at least forty-nine feet tall. His name was Dr. Rodney Riley, and, as the lodge's grand secretary, he didn't give a damn *who* we were—we weren't moving beyond the lobby without a warrant. "Members only," he boomed. Behind the closed double doors of that members-only section, chairs scraped against the floor. "I can answer your questions out here."

Out here was a black-and-white tiled lobby with bright white walls and oak and glass cabinetry filled with fancy plaques and mystical-looking scrolls. Framed pictures of men wearing black suits, white aprons, and top hats hung on the walls alongside banners of the lodge name and the square-and-compasses symbol.

"We're looking for Oswald Little," Colin said. "We know that he's a part of this lodge."

"Well, when you find him," Rodney Riley said, "tell him that we miss him."

"When was the last time you saw Mr. Little?" I asked.

"It's been about five years," Rodney Riley said. "We gave him a retirement party, and a few months after that, he stopped coming to meetings. I can check our attendance records and give you a better date."

He led us to an office that smelled of cigars and fresh-brewed coffee. He sat at the computer and moved the mouse with his massive right hand. He wore a ring similar to Oswald Little's.

"Does every member of the lodge get a ring like yours?" I asked.

"They may order one if they so desire," he said.

"Would you give something like that away?" I asked. "Like, as a gift or . . . ?"

Riley gave a curt shake of his head. "Never. I will be buried with mine." He double-clicked on a record, and Little's picture—balding, mustache, beard—blinked onto the monitor.

"Was he an active member?" I asked.

"Oh, yes. One of our most committed. He'd made plans to run for grand secretary. Sometimes, brothers are so gung ho when they join, and then they just lose interest. Find other things to do, especially after retiring." He scrolled down Oswald Little's member page. "Looks like he stopped coming to meetings back in . . . October 2010."

"And he didn't tell anyone why?" I asked.

"I only know that he didn't tell any of the officers. Unusual only because of the type of man he is."

"And what type of man *is* Mr. Little?" I asked.

Riley leaned back in the chair, then templed his fingers. "He was a banker before he retired. Smart with money. Generous, almost to a fault. Always buying luxury items—not just for him, though. He doesn't have a wife or kids, so he spoiled the brothers all the time. For Christmas one year, he dropped almost two thou on a prime-rib dinner for all of us at Lawry's. He likes eating and drinking with friends. He travels all the time—flies home to Belize a lot, but he also goes to France and Spain, parts of the Orient every year. Nice guy—never brags about his wealth. He'll talk your ear off, though. That man can talk the dead back to life."

"I have a weird question," Colin said. "Do you know if he's ever been in any accidents?"

The giant mason stared at the ceiling as he thought. "He got banged up pretty bad in a four-car pileup on the Grapevine right before he retired. That didn't stop him from his duties here or at work, though. And he still kept spending money on us. But he was definitely slower after that accident."

"Did he like . . . ?" Colin paused, then said, "Did that accident cause him to lose limbs or anything?"

Rodney Riley eyed him. "I don't know about all that, but he *did* hit his head pretty hard. It's a miracle he survived."

"Did you send any notices to him at the house on Corning?" I asked.

"We did." Riley gripped the mouse again, then clicked into "Address." "Everything we sent came back marked 'return to sender.' A few of us stopped by the house, but no one answered. And he didn't return our phone calls, so, you know, we stopped trying."

"What about the house on Garth just a few blocks over?" I asked. "You send mail there or stop by?"

Rodney Riley clicked around the address history. "We don't have an address on Garth. I do know that a few of our brothers attend the same church as Oz."

"Eugene Washington?" I asked. "Or Isaac Underwood?"

"I don't know those names," Riley said, shaking his head. "But Oz's pastor—Bishop Tate—belongs to our lodge."

"So Oz is a member of Blessed Mission?" I asked.

"Oh, yes. He gives a lot of money to that church."

Blood filled my ears. "You asked Bishop Tate about Oz?"

Riley nodded. "Of course."

"And what did he say?"

"He'd heard that Oz went back to Belize to take care of his mother." The man cocked his head. "What's this all about again?"

Colin told him that a friend who'd just passed had listed Oz as beneficiary of the policy as well as property. "It's a nice amount: two hundred and fifty thousand dollars, and I'm sure the house will be worth a good amount. The car, not so much."

The tall man checked his watch, then pulled his large body from the chair. "Well, again: when you find Oz, tell him that I said it's bad form to drop off the face of the earth and not tell anybody."

Bad form, indeed.

30

The current senior vice president of Excelsior Bank of California, a woman named Lisa Greene, hadn't seen Oswald Little since his retirement in 2010. The car accident on the Grapevine had hastened his departure. "That head injury destroyed his gift of running numbers," Greene told me over the phone. But neither she nor anyone else at the bank remembered Oz Little losing his hands. "I'm sure I'd recall that," Greene said.

Next, Colin called Bishop Solomon Tate.

"I'm about to board the plane," the minister said over the speakerphone.

In the background, I heard the roar of jet engines, people talking, traffic-cop whistles, and blaring car horns.

"Well, we really need to talk to you, sir," Colin said.

Bishop Tate said, "Could you stop by the church in the morning? My wife mentioned that you wanted our fingerprints for some reason?"

"Correct," Colin said. "Just as part of the investigation."

"Oh, well that's fine, but it will have to be tomorrow," he said. "I have to hang up now—FAA regulations." He chuckled, then said, "Have a blessed evening."

Colin tossed his phone on the dashboard.

I grinned. "Was that awkward? Talking to the minister whose wife you wanna bone?"

Colin squeezed the bridge of his nose. "It was easier than you'd think, boss."

Back at Southwest Division, men—free and in custody—shuffled between interview rooms and restrooms. Despite the efforts of those ten overworked fans, the mingled stink of sweat and a backed-up toilet

clobbered my senses. All afternoon, I had lucked out—whatever nerves
the ibuprofen had been engineered to target had been successfully hit.
No pain today, not really, and despite searching for a man with no
hands and not finding him, today had been a decent day. At almost five
o'clock, though, my boss was trying to change that.

We had all congregated in conference room Freedom for a final Friday check-in. I opened the murder book to the first page, and to the
eight-by-ten photograph of Eugene Washington, alive, smiling wide,
freckles dancing across his skin like fireflies.

"This Little guy," Lieutenant Rodriguez said. "He been reported
missing?"

Colin cut a look at me. "He hasn't, sir."

Lieutenant Rodriguez grunted, then sipped from his RC Cola can.

"The city of Los Angeles says he's alive," Colin continued. "He's still
getting Social Security checks each month and lives over on Garth in
Ladera Heights."

"No one's actually *seen* Oswald Little, though," I pointed out. "His
neighbor described him as looking like someone else. Someone completely different from the pictures we've seen. His lodge brother and
former coworkers haven't seen him since September 2010."

Lieutenant Rodriguez rolled his eyes. "You do know that adults can
disappear if they so desire. As long as we don't want 'em, nobody says
they gotta stick around."

My cheeks burned, but I squared my shoulders. "I understand that,
sir. And believe me: I know that firsthand, sir. But *this* is not *that*."

"So the summons you want," Lieutenant Rodriguez said, "it's for . . . ?"

"For Oswald Little to show up," Colin said. "To show up and claim
his hands and his bequeathed property."

Lieutenant Rodriguez sat back in his chair. "What if he's seen that
house and doesn't want that piece of shit? And what if he's over his
hands? Doesn't care about those hands? Has new hands? Better hands?"

I sighed. "I have to do *something*, sir."

"Does he have Alzheimer's?" Pepe asked. "Is he mentally . . . you
know, slow? Impaired in any way?"

Colin flipped through his notes, then said, "He was in a bad car
accident. Had some type of head trauma."

Lieutenant Rodriguez pointed at me. "So was she—bad accident, head trauma—and she's not impaired."

I cracked a smile, and wanted to say, *Are you kidding me? Why are you forcing me to take some time off, then?* Instead, I said, "Argumentative."

My boss chuckled.

"We're not missing persons, guys," Pepe complained. "We got enough crap on our plate with dead people."

"Eugene 'Lechter' Washington," Luke added, "we *know* that fucker's dead."

Lieutenant Rodriguez pointed to the warrants we'd prepared. "The end game for these is what, exactly?"

"To confirm that Oswald Little is either dead or alive," I said.

"And to do all that," I continued, "we need to access Ike Underwood's finances as well as Oswald Little's finances and phone records." I darted to the whiteboard and wrote a schematic that started with Eugene Washington, then added arrows pointing to Ike Underwood and Oswald Little. "It's all connected to our victim. Little's hands were discovered in Washington's house. Ike's DMV records say that he lives at Little's house. Eugene Washington has an account at Little's bank. Little is the beneficiary on Washington's insurance policy and will. And each man attends Blessed Mission Ministries."

"*So,*" Colin said, "we wanna grab any documents that have signatures that we can compare—"

My phone rang. I said, "Gotta get this," then put the phone on speaker. "Dr. Goldberg, how goes the dig? We're all here, listening and hoping you have news for us."

"We've identified four sites now," the forensic archaeologist said. "The back fence, both side yards, and the garage. Just because it may be easier—and more discreet a location—I plan to start concrete removal in the garage sometime tomorrow morning."

"Yes." I pumped my fist. "Do you need me to call the medical examiner or . . . ?"

"I've already done that, and someone will attend. Maybe Dr. Brooks, depending on his schedule."

After I ended the call, Lieutenant Rodriguez said, "That's good news."

"Hope he finds something after all this," Pepe said.

I dropped back into my chair. "Back to Ike and Oz."

Lieutenant Rodriguez stretched his arms and the conference room shuddered. "Maybe they lived together. Ike and the hands guy."

"Yeah," Luke said. "Maybe they're boyfriends."

Pepe blushed, probably waiting for the rib, or the entendre.

"Maybe they are," I said. "We're talking to Ike any minute now so I'll ask. Still: why would Eugene Washington have Little's hands in his house?"

"A weird Ripley's Believe It or Not! souvenir," Lieutenant Rodriguez suggested. "Little didn't want 'em, but he didn't wanna throw 'em away, either. Looks like Washington collected all kinds of shit in that house."

"He's one *tipo loco*," Luke said.

"When do you plan to walk into that house on Garth?" Lieutenant Rodriguez asked.

"After we get a better lay of the financial land," I said. "We'll ask Ike to invite us over for coffee or something. If he refuses, then I'll escalate it with the second warrant."

Lieutenant Rodriguez's cold gray eyes stayed on me as he tapped his pen against the battered table. He read the warrants again, then cocked an eyebrow. "I'll okay *this* warrant for Judge Keener to sign—to go into the house as well as the warrants for Ike's finances and Oz Little's phone. But the summons for Little to claim his hands? Nope." He scribbled his signature on the requests. "Time for you to take the bar again and do the lawyer thing, Norton."

I took the signed papers and slipped them into my binder. "And leave all of this?"

Lieutenant Rodriguez laughed. "Talk to Zapata about *maybe* putting out a bulletin for Little." Then, as we gathered our things to leave the room, he pointed at Colin. "Stay back."

Colin sank back in his chair.

A flare shot in my chest. "Is everything okay? Do I need to stay?"

"Not necessary," Lieutenant Rodriguez said, his heavy gaze on my partner. "You should fax over those warrant requests before she leaves for the weekend."

My heart pounded in my ears. "May I ask what's going on?"

Both men turned to me with hot eyes, but only Lieutenant Rodriguez spoke. "You should send over the warrant requests now."

What was going on?

Were they going to talk about me?

My gut, once again, told me that they were and that I *should* be concerned. My gut could be wrong, but again, on Fridays . . .

Back at my desk, I reached for the trio of envelopes that had been placed in my mail tray. The first had come from Frank Webber at Mandalay Bay Hotel and Casino. I tore open the flap to find a gift certificate for a week's stay that included breakfast and transportation courtesy of . . . V-Starr Cars.

French breakfast three times a week, and now an all-paid vacation? Victor Starr really thought he could buy my love. What would he send next? A seat on the Virgin Galactic space flight? A bathtub encrusted with hand-applied Swarovski crystals?

After ten minutes alone with our boss, Colin returned to his desk. He thumped into his chair and logged on to his computer.

"I ordered Thai for dinner," I said.

"Thanks." His eyes stayed on the computer screen.

"Wanna talk about it?" I asked.

A flash of a smile hit his lips. "Nope. I'm good."

We worked in silence until Jimmy the Thai guy dropped off our meal. Before the late-night drunken brawls and drive-by shootings, we all enjoyed regular conversation.

Who you got for the Stanley?

. . . and she was wearing this thong, I kid you not . . .

And that son-of-a-bitch pulled beside me and just . . . Boom!

As I dug into my carton of pad Thai noodles, sharp pain shot from my shoulder to the back of my head. The sudden spark made me gasp and drop my chopsticks. I blinked and spots swirled before me. The pain paralyzed me for a second.

"You okay?" Colin asked.

I nodded, then took a long pull of Diet Coke. "Don't know what that was."

Luke banged into the squad room. "Hey, Lou. You got a special guest."

I thanked Luke, then smiled at Colin. "Let's go see who's downstairs."

Colin wouldn't look away from me. He now knew for sure that I wasn't 100 percent.

And now, *I* knew that it was possible that my thirty days could stretch into forever. And I could almost smell those Wetzel's pretzels baking.

31

For the sixth time in two minutes, Ike Underwood shifted in the metal chair—its cold hardness was getting to him. He had worn suit pants and a sports coat, dressed for throwing back Old Fashioneds at Musso and Frank's with a buxom brunette named Roz instead of fidgeting in a cold room with shedding foam walls, jaundiced fluorescent lights, and hooks in the table to attach handcuffs.

From the AV room, Colin and I watched our guest fidget.

"We can't keep him," Colin said.

I crossed my arms. "Have I said anything about arresting him?"

"I know—I'm just saying that we really don't have—"

Anger hurtled up my spine and fired from my mouth. "Colin, dude. We have more than you think."

He nodded. "I just want us to be careful, is all."

Seated across from our guest, we all talked about traffic and the heat, weekend plans, and the heat again. And then it was time to start.

I flipped to the beginning of my notepad, then said, "Ike, I just realized something. You never asked us how Gene died."

Ike's pulse jumped in his neck. "Huh? I didn't? I thought you said . . . I *know* I did."

"No, you didn't." I turned to Colin. "You tell him?"

Colin shook his head.

I shrugged.

The man's lips sputtered like a carp on dry land. "Guess I assumed how he died since we were talking about food at the picnic. I figured that he, you know, ate something bad." He chuckled, and that chuckle sounded fake, like "other natural flavors" found in fruit juice. But then, again, on Friday nights around seven fifteen, I'm usually an asshole and so everything sounded fake.

I pointed my pen at him. "Speaking of Washington eating . . ."

"He got any unconventional appetites?" Colin asked. "Strange things he likes to eat?"

"Besides him eating old food?" Ike shrugged, then said, "May I ask . . . ? Why am I here? I haven't done anything wrong."

"All these questions come standard with death investigations," I said with a smile. "Just like my next request."

Colin pushed forward the fingerprinting kit.

Ike's eyes narrowed. "But I was over at Gene's all the time. My prints are gonna be everywhere."

Colin gave him gun fingers. "Exactly. So when we find prints that *aren't* yours, we're one step closer to solving the puzzle."

Ike nodded. "So how did Gene die then?"

"He died from anaphylactic shock," I said. "He ate something he shouldn't have eaten."

Ike's shaky hand covered his mouth and his eyes filled with tears. "What did he eat?"

"Can't tell you that," I said. "So: You've noticed that we're digging all around Mr. Washington's property."

"Uh huh." Ike dabbed at his wet cheeks with the heels of his hands. "Hopefully, y'all find what you're looking for."

"About that," Colin said.

"Oswald Little," I said.

Ike nodded. "Oz is one of my oldest, dearest friends."

"We hear that he had a bad car accident several years ago," Colin said.

"Uh huh." Ike then told us about the trip up Highway 5, the icy road on the Grapevine, and the four-car pileup. "You know, Oz came out of that with a renewed spirit. But his body . . . He had to retire earlier than he'd planned. Couldn't do the day to day anymore, not with his injuries."

Colin shifted in his chair. "So say we dig tomorrow at Gene's house. Will we, like, find Oz buried in the garage?"

Ike's eyes bugged, and he laughed. "You're a funny guy." He shook his head and laughed some more. "You're gonna find dead cats, maybe a raccoon. But you ain't gonna find Oz anywhere *near* Gene's house."

"But we found his hands there," I pointed out.

That didn't knock the smile off Ike's face. "Trust me. Oz ain't there."

"You live where?" I asked.

"I've been living over at Oz's. It's just easier that way because of . . . you know." He made crab-claw hands. "Lemme tell you: we had no clue that Gene stole them hands. Why the heck would he do something like *that*? Who'd want somebody else's hands? That makes absolutely not one lick of sense. But then you've seen Gene's house."

"How did Oz lose his hands?" I asked.

"You ain't gonna believe this." Ike's finger traced the etched letters of ROLLING 60S on the wood table. "You asked me if Gene had a strange appetite. Two years ago, Oz ate some weird type of fish. Now, Oz—there's your man, you wanna talk strange. Anyway, he ate the strange fish, got sick, and finally went to the hospital. Doctors found all kinds of bacteria floating around his body, brought there by that fish. It's some Japanese fish—I don't know. Anyway, Oz is sitting there in the exam room, and his hands and feet start turning purple. *Right there in the room*, gangrene was setting in, and the doctors just couldn't believe it. So they told him, 'If you wanna live, we gotta cut off your hands and feet.' Flesh-eating bacteria—that's what took his limbs."

"You're right," I said, eyes wide, "I *don't* believe it." On my pad, I scribbled, *Check hands for bacteria??*

"You're shitting me, Ike," Colin said.

Ike held up a hand as though he was taking an oath. "I'm telling you the God's honest truth. He woulda died right there in that exam room. Wasn't no other way but to cut 'em off." Ike chuckled, then sighed. "Oz was always doin' that, eating exotic stuff. That's cuz he travel all the time. Sure as hell didn't think Gene woulda taken . . ." He shrugged. "Oz don't get out much now, even with his prosthetics. Real nice ones, too—he can afford 'em. Don't travel abroad unless he has to. He's embarrassed."

Colin nodded. "Understandable."

"First, the car accident," I said, "and then hands and feet chopped off cuz of bad sashimi."

"Yeah," Ike said. "It gets him down sometimes."

"Oz is a mason, correct?" I asked.

Ike nodded. "But he hasn't been active since the operation."

"And he'd just toss his ring like that?" Colin asked.

Ike blinked. "His ring?"

"His mason's ring," I said. "It's still on the left hand."

Ike shrugged. "Maybe, since he stopped going, he doesn't care about it anymore." He tapped his fingers against the table. "Will Oz be able to get that back? The ring? If he wanted it?"

"After we no longer need it," I said, "I'm sure he can. I'll be happy to deliver it to him myself."

"Is Oz alive, Mr. Underwood?" Colin asked.

"Most definitely," Ike said. "He's in Belize right now—that's where he's originally from. His mother, Raquel, passed away last week, but he's been down there for months now cuz she'd been sick. We can call him if you'd like."

I slid my cell phone over to him. "Sure. Let's call."

"Does he know that Gene died?" Colin asked.

Ike nodded as he dialed.

I studied him, looking for shaky hands, or a sweaty brow. Nothing.

The line rang . . . and rang.

My stomach tightened, and something in me reached like hands wanting to touch Oz and confirm that he was real.

The room grew cold, and now my metal chair worked my tail bone. I dusted flecks of soundproof foam off the table, then swiped my hand on the leg of my jeans.

Ike whispered to us, "He's not answering. Should I leave a message for him to call you?"

I nodded.

"Oz, hey," Ike said into the phone. "Listen, I'm still working on Gene's house, and guess what? He had your hands in all that mess. Yeah, I don't know how he got 'em since the doctors were supposed to have thrown 'em away. Maybe he paid somebody or something . . . But you know Gene—if there's a will, there's a way. Anyway, a coupla detectives wanna speak to you. An Elouise Norton and a Colin Taggert. Could you give them a call as soon as possible at . . . ?" Ike read my number off the business card I'd given him, then ended the call. "It's a little late now," he said to us. "Belize is two hours ahead."

"That's not much of a time difference," I said.

"For an old man with health issues, it is." Ike grinned at me. "You're just a kid, so you don't understand."

"We'll probably have more questions for you after we talk with Mr. Little," I said.

Ike's face brightened. "Anything to help." Then, he waggled his fingers. "So you still want my prints?"

32

AFIS was down again.

The fingerprinting system's crash brought tears to my eyes—this case was killing me.

Yes, my work always affected my worldview. This one, though, with the trash, the hands, the hoard? Its evil was like tentacles that puckered at and stung my skin. This evil was real and tangible, with smells and jagged dark things. And as I drove home, I grew convinced that behind every closed door, at every home address, were secret piles of junk worse than the ones we already acknowledged. That husband wasn't just *mean* to his wife—he beat and kicked her 'til she lost consciousness. That mom wasn't only a drunk, she undressed in front of her teenage son and climbed next to him in bed.

As I veered off Jefferson Boulevard and onto my crooked street, my own junk—tangible, emotional, psychological—crowded my mind. Not necessarily Eugene Washington's level of collecting, but there were countless broken things in my life that I continued to keep but no longer needed. Spaces that would never see light, not over my dead body. Shit I didn't even know about—or that I told myself didn't exist.

No one knew that I was home. A moment away from forty years old and trained in martial arts and weaponry, I didn't need a babysitter. I could take care of myself.

Can you? Really? Did Eugene Washington say the same thing after accumulating that first pile of crap?

There it was again. Self-doubt dressed as reflection.

That now-familiar lump crowded my throat—*See? You're weak. A baby.* I swallowed and sent that knot to my stomach.

Why was I feeling this way? What was *wrong* with me?

Eyes closed, I let the hot spray from the showerhead beat my over-worked muscles. The day's filth sluiced off of me and swirled at my feet. I wanted to cry. I wanted to sit somewhere and just . . . *weep*.

My head pounded as my skull squeezed my aching brain. I opened the drawer and the vial of Percocet rolled to the front. With clumsy fingers, I plucked out two pills, then placed both on my tongue.

Winter had come.

I strapped the blood pressure cuff around my bicep.

The machine beeped three times: 138/90.

Back to where I'd started.

Something needed to change.

"I'll call Dr. Popov on Monday," I told my bedraggled reflection.

He would be disappointed. More disappointed, though, if I had a stroke on his watch.

I pulled on a fleecy sweatshirt, then took my phone out to the deck. The temperature had dropped as the sun abandoned us for Asia. Now, the steel-blue sky twinkled with stars and the blinking white light of airplanes. The shadows of couples walking hand in hand along the shore filled me with acid and envy.

I hated them. I hated the people on the planes. I wanted . . . *something.*

The 2010 Cabernet Sauvignon from the central coast of California—that's what I wanted. I wanted to laugh again. To sleep soundly through the night. To know that I was okay. Because everything was supposed to be okay. I'd followed the rules. I'd caught my share of bad guys. I'd remained faithful and loyal and hardworking. Yet . . .

The dull stupor that came with Percocet shrouded me as I left the patio. My mind still pitched from Eugene Washington's case to leaving Los Angeles with Sam to that bottle of Joel Gott sitting on the counter beside the big bag of Doritos. I ignored the wine but grabbed the bag of tortilla chips and a Limonata from the pack Greg had brought. I dragged to the living room and turned on the television to avoid the silence, to keep from admitting that the quiet scared me.

Bewitched . . . Girl Meets World . . . The Walking Dead . . .

On HGTV, a couple hunted for a home in beautiful Costa Rica.

Fine.

Dominic had texted. *Hey, baby.*

I sighed, then blocked his number. "No more, don't wanna," I whispered, then aimed the remote control at the television. If I was going to hate-watch TV, I preferred something less topical. Like *Sanford and Son.* Lamont was dating a woman who hadn't told him about her divorce and her young son.

My phone vibrated again, but now my limbs had gained weight and couldn't move. My body sank deeper into the couch cushions.

Fred was now working at a restaurant . . . Bubba came by . . . Tide detergent . . . Yoplait . . . snoring . . . so tired . . . so . . .

Thwump!

I bolted upright from the couch. My pulse raced like a bird trying to escape a cage. My eyes darted around the living room. The television was still on—*227* had replaced *Sanford and Son.* The floor lamp in the corner still burned, and a cobweb floated in the golden light. The empty Doritos bag had fallen from the couch to the hardwood floor.

The *thwump* had come from . . . I couldn't tell where it had come from, but it sounded as though someone had hit a door with a wet mop.

Am I dreaming?

That was the other possibility.

Frozen on the couch, I tried to hear past the rush of blood in my ears. My eyes moved around the room as my mind tried to wake up, to make sense of a very real thing.

Maybe someone kicked the door.

The room was shaking.

I was shaking.

Maybe, it's . . . I stood, then crept to the front door. Peeped out the peephole.

Lit porch. No one there.

I turned back to the living room.

My bag sitting on the armchair . . . Marla Gibbs dispensing advice to Sandra . . . the almost-empty Limonata can sitting dangerously close to the edge of the coffee table . . .

"I'm losing my mind," I whispered. "I'm finally—"

Over at the patio door, a crimson splatter stained the glass and was dripping down the pane.

Is that . . . blood?

I slid open the glass door. The salty scent of ocean enveloped me, and a thick breeze tickled my ears. Down at my bare feet, on the bleached wood, lay a sea gull. Its neck was twisted into a U. Blood stained its gray and snowy-white feathers.

"Oh no," I muttered. "No no no no no."

Mariners were cursed if they killed an albatross. Were there folktales about dead gulls? Would I be punished even though this accident was not my fault? Did I now need the additional psychic burden of a dead animal placed on my back?

Sure.

The gull wavered before me—I was crying. Even though Percocet had taken away the hurt, something inside of me remained broken. My warm, fat tears beaded atop the bird's feathers as I wept out there on the patio, as I wept until I had nothing left.

Spent, I scooped the bird into an empty shoebox, then carried it down to the beach. The ocean licked my feet, and I shivered and waited for the last couples to kiss and to piggyback ride away from me. Alone at last, I swung the box.

The bird glided through the air, then splashed somewhere out there in the foamy deep.

I lingered beneath the moonlight a few minutes more. Inhaled that soft scent of sea wood and sea life, of cigarettes and bonfires. Icy water rushed around my ankles and sand shifted beneath my toes. As the ocean pulled me closer to its darkness, a voice whispered that I should just do it, that I do the unthinkable. *It won't hurt if you just give up.*

I moved back one step, then another step, and then another until my feet touched dry sand again. "No. I won't go."

There was nothing out there beyond the waves for me.

Saturday, September 5

33

It was Saturday morning, and my third hour laying awake in bed, the third hour I had watched shadows twist and play on my ceilings and walls. I should've popped Unisom, but that thought came in the middle of the second hour. At six o'clock, the sun glowed like a dying flashlight through my bedroom curtains. My eyes burned as though I'd pulled an all-nighter at a crime scene. I felt like I'd been run over by elephants and a thousand Shriners in little cars. I should've reached for the phone and called in sick.

I didn't.

Stumbled to the bathroom, bedroom, and closet. Pulled on gray slacks and a black T-shirt. The material scratched my skin like hay and cornflakes. Stood in front of the fridge but didn't wanna eat anything there or anywhere. Since this was my last day before *vacation*, I threw my hands up and said, "Fuck it." Chased a Vicodin with two gulps of tap water. Grabbed my guns, holsters, and bag, no more awake or aware than I'd been brushing my teeth.

The doorbell rang. I glanced at my watch: it was ten minutes before seven. It *was* the right day of the week but too early in the morning for a visit from neighborhood Jehovah's Witnesses or Mormons.

As I opened the door, waves of muggy heat rolled in and puffed my shirt.

My mother, Georgia, and her boyfriend, Martin Paysinger, stood on the porch as crisp and sweet smelling as an April morning. Mom held a potted yellow orchid in her hands. Together, they sang, "Good morning!"

Wide-eyed, I said, "Hi."

Mom's smile faltered as she considered her white pants. That grin brightened again as she shrugged, and said, "I'm in California, Elouise, and I want to wear white pants. And it's not Labor Day yet, so hush." She handed me the orchid. "Happy housewarming!"

Martin, wearing khaki cargo shorts and leather flip-flops, held up a bag from Noah's Bagels. "We brought breakfast, too."

Across the street, joggers canted around the sun-flecked lagoon. Over in the grassy area, a group of seniors slowly moved their arms and legs for morning tai chi. The white disk in the sky beat down on all of us, promising a high today of a hundred degrees in the basin.

Mom's smile faltered again. "Are . . . are you alone?"

My cheeks warmed at her round-the-way query about my sex life. "Yeah. Yes. Come in."

Mom's scent of coconut and vanilla combined with Martin's oniony bagels to permeate the foyer.

"Even a mole would say it's too dark in here, ladybug," Mom complained.

I sat the orchid on the coffee table, then yanked open the drapes.

Martin unpacked the Noah's bag—bagels, cream cheese, lox, onions, tomatoes, and capers.

Mom regarded the hallway that led to the bedroom. "Are you sure you don't have company?"

I shook my head. "Just me."

Relieved, her shoulders slumped. She pulled a greeting card from her handbag. "This is for you."

I took the envelope. "I'll have to open it later cuz—"

"It ain't *War and Peace*," Mom cracked.

Glitter and "love" and bluebirds filled the front of the card. Mom's assured cursive filled the inside.

The world is a better place because of you. Even with everything that's happened, I am the luckiest mother in the world. I have finally found peace, love, and acceptance—and it's all because of you. I am so proud of you, ladybug. You're so brave, so selfless, so uniquely you. Stay strong. Love you more, Mom.

My eyes stung with tears and something heavy lifted from my heart.

She pulled me into a tight hug, then kissed my forehead. "I mean every single word."

"I know," I said, "and thank you, but I really need to go."

She cocked her head. "But . . . we're having breakfast. Why are you acting surprised?"

I attempted to smile. "Because I am."

"You shouldn't be. I told you we were coming over today."

I shook my head. "No."

Mom and Martin considered each other with exasperation. Mom's lips thinned before she said to me, "Elouise, you and I agreed last week, and then, on my last text message, I said, 'see you Saturday,' and today is Saturday, sweetheart."

I pulled my phone from my pocket and found her last text. My cheeks numbed—there it was. "Oh. Yeah."

Martin wandered over to the wall where I'd hung my Medal of Valor and framed commendation. "Really proud of you, Elouise. Georgie, you gonna . . . ?"

Mom cleared her throat and forced a smile to her lips.

A flare shot through my heart and pierced my soaring lightness. "What's wrong? What happened? Did Victor Starr—?"

"No," Mom said, shaking her head. "Nothing like that."

Martin picked up the bottle of Cabernet from the coffee table that Lena had enjoyed before dinner back on Tuesday. He walked it to the kitchen, and placed it into the recycle bin with the other empties.

"Sounds like a lot of bottles in there," Mom said with a nervous laugh.

I shrugged. "Not really."

"But you're the only one living here," she said. "How many bottles—?"

"Lena stays over a lot," I said. "Like she stayed over Tuesday night. And sometimes, Colin . . ." Couldn't complete the lie—Colin didn't even drink wine.

"I know you and the girls enjoy your reds," Mom said, "but you guys really need to slow down. You're not the same as before the accident."

"It's just four empties, sweetheart," Martin said even though he gave me the Dad Eye.

Mom pointed to the roller-ball bottle of Icy Hot and the tubs of

Advil and Tylenol on the coffee table. "You have an entire pharmacy in your living room. Are you still in a lot of pain?"

"Not really. They're just sitting there. I haven't had—"

"Elouise, do you really take me for a fool?"

"I haven't cleaned up in a while," I explained. "But when I do pop pills, I don't chase them with wine. The 2010s ain't cheap, so I drink Everclear and liquid crystal meth."

Mom pointed at me. "Don't talk to me like that."

"And don't talk to me like I'm some kind of *addict*," I shouted. "Yes, I take meds every now and then, but I—" *I been clean now a whole week.* In that movie, I was now Bernice Parrish's crackhead buddy.

Mom rolled her eyes. "I guess I *am* a fool. You couldn't even remember that we were coming over today."

"That's because I'm busy," I explained. "Not because I'm *high* or drunk. You know what I do for a living—regular interactions can be distracting and all-consuming."

Mom held her hands to her lips, prayer-style. "Every time I visit you, I notice more bottles of wine and more medications. Every time I visit you, you look worse."

I snorted, then folded my arms. "Thanks, Mom. *That* helps."

"Roll your eyes if you want," she said, "but you look like hell. And it's because of your accident, yes—"

"Mom, listen—"

"No," she snapped, then pointed at me. "*You* listen. I did not raise you to be . . . *this*. Despite our horrible situation, I raised you better than—"

I raised my arms. "Can I get a break, for once? I'm just getting back to normal—"

"You're *far* from normal," Martin said.

I glared at him, then turned back to my mother. "I just got divorced. I just moved here—"

Mom was shaking her head. "I refuse to let you do this."

My shoulders slumped, and I squeezed the bridge of my nose. "Do what?"

She didn't respond.

"Do what?" I asked, louder this time. "Tell me how I'm disappointing you. Tell me how I'm ruining my life."

She clamped a shaky hand over her mouth. Her eyes shimmered with tears, but she was too pissed off to cry.

Martin rubbed the small of my mother's back. "We just don't want you—"

"Is this any of your business, Martin?" I wanted to laugh—because now, I sounded like a fourteen-year-old. My life had become an ABC Afterschool Special.

"I know I'm not your father," Martin said, "but I don't want you—"

"ODing on Tylenol?" I asked, blinking. "I don't have time to stand here and discuss my imaginary substance-abuse problems. If you want the truth, I'm not taking *enough* drugs because I don't wanna be a fucking stereotype. If you wanna know the truth, I wish I could take as much Vicodin and Percocet as I want and without judgment from anybody because hurting every day is bullshit. But I can't, okay? And yet, I *still* lose because here we are."

Tears rolled down my mother's cheeks, and that made me shut up.

Martin pulled Mom into his arms, and whispered, "It's okay, it's okay."

My feet had grown roots into the carpet. Helpless and horrified, I stood there, pulse pounding, watching my mother cry as though I already lay beneath dirt and sod.

Not wanting to look at her, I looked everywhere else. At the last unpacked box. At the Pop-Tarts' silver wrapper on the breakfast counter. At the empty wine bottles in the recycle bin. There were no crack pipes or heroin-tinged aluminum foil scraps on blood-spotted, vomit-stinky carpet. The guns in my leather holsters were legal. The drugs in my system? Prescribed, and I'd denied myself their curative goodness for weeks and weeks. And I hadn't had sex in ohmylord, don't know how long. So why did I now feel like a pissed-off crack ho in my $700,000 beachside condo? Why was my mother crying?

Mom pushed away from Martin. "I think that *we*, as a family, must address this. You, me, Tori, your father—it's all related. I haven't said anything to you about my worries because you're an adult."

I snorted again, then closed my eyes.

"But I'm saying something now," Mom said, "before it's too late."

"Too late for . . . ?" I asked.

Her eyes found mine. "I wasn't the best mother sometimes. I know that. Between your father leaving and your sister . . . That's no excuse. I should've been more present. When Greg was acting up, I shouldn't have insisted that you work it out." She squared her shoulders, then said, "I'm so sorry, Elouise. For everything."

She needed to say these things. I had *waited* for her to say these things. But not at seven in the morning. Not after having a night with no sleep.

A woman in white pants. A man in leather thongs. A drunk, meth-head cop carrying a Glock . . . Eugene Washington was doing better than all of us.

She dabbed her wet face with a napkin she'd plucked from the break-fast counter. "We will go to family counseling. We'll go together. You are an adult—you can say no, but I think this is important."

With weak legs, I wobbled before her. "Whatever you wanna do, Mom."

She nodded as she stroked my hair. "I'll find us help, okay? We'll get you—*us*—healthy and happy again." Her stroking my head had scraped the new scab on my scalp. I clasped Mom's hand in mine, and the pain caused by her touch eased . . . but not completely. "Whatever you want, Mom. Whatever you want."

I'd say anything to stop the pain.

34

As I buckled the seat belt in the Porsche, then started to cry again for no reason, I should've climbed back out of the car. When the world turned fuzzy and flames crunched at so many parts of me, I should've taken my black ass back into the house and called *somebody*—Mom, Lena, the *mayor*—to help me.

I didn't.

I just . . . sat. And cried. And burned.

Outside, the sun had gone from glow to psychedelic blister. Everything glinted—chrome car bumpers, windowpanes, the surface of the lagoon—and no one seemed to notice. Joggers trotted around the water. Old people moved slowly with dog leashes or canes. Toddlers waddled in front of their mothers.

Didn't they *see*? Couldn't they *feel* that?

"Make it stop," I whispered, not even sure what 'it' was but knowing that whatever 'it' was left me weak, achy, and so tired.

So . . . tired . . . so . . .

My iPhone caw-cawed from the ashtray.

I jerked in my seat, then wiped drool from my cheek.

The phone played Colin's ringtone again. That noise pierced my skin, now as thin as rice paper.

I'd fallen asleep.

"You coming in or what?" Colin asked.

"Yeah." That one word sounded strained, too try-hard. "Had a hard time sleeping. Well, I *didn't* sleep. Oh. So, I'm also late because my mom and her boyfriend stopped by thinking it was the best time for an intervention."

I told him about the greeting card, the worrying clink of empty wine bottles, and the cocked eyebrows at the pill vials. "She started crying," I said, "then asked if I'd go to family therapy and church with her."

"And you said . . . ?"

"I told her okay just to get out of there." I sighed. "So, what's happening?"

"They're starting the actual dig this morning."

"I know."

"It's cooled down some," Colin said, "so we'll be able to get some work done."

"I'm in the car, Taggert. Relax—the fuckery will still be going on in twenty minutes."

The Porsche's dashboard clock claimed it was now a little past nine o'clock and ninety-one degrees.

I'd spent two hours sleeping in my car, still buckled up in the driver's seat, head flung back, mouth open, spit flowing back to my ear, dentist-visit style.

Thanks to the nap, I didn't feel as fragile as a chipped teacup—but I still felt . . . *fractured*. Like that broken-necked seagull I had flung into the Pacific Ocean just hours ago.

"You got this, Lou," I whispered. "You got this. You're good. It's cool."

Sure.

I landed at my desk close to ten thirty, the latest I'd clocked in since voting on Election Day 2008 and standing at my polling place in a line that snaked all the way to Zanzibar. And I just . . . *sat there*, staring at my computer monitor, thinking about nothing, caring about less.

The shifty-looking crackhead bleeding all over the carpet? The weeping babymomma collapsed near the water cooler? Didn't care. So what?

Colin was staring at me. Then, Pepe's and Luke's eyes joined his from their desks.

I *still* didn't care. I was okay with just sitting, letting them look.

My partner tossed his LAPD Koosh ball at me. "You okay over there?"

I forced myself to smile. "Umhmm."

Luke and Pepe came over to Colin's desk. "She okay?" Pepe whispered.

"Couldn't sleep," Colin whispered.

"You should tell her—"

"I can hear you," I said, staring at the computer monitor. "And I can still talk. See how I'm talking?"

"Lou, are you okay?" Luke asked, his brow furrowed.

"Yes. I am okay."

No, I wasn't. Half of me lay on the beach and the other half sat in the car, and dribbles of me dotted the asphalt like spilled gravy between the two locations. And my stomach growled—I'd fed it nothing even though Mom and Martin had brought me bagels and fixings.

"Is AFIS back up?" I asked.

Luke said, "Not yet."

The red voice-mail light on my phone was blinking. *When did I get a call?* I winced as I jabbed the button to listen to the message.

"Detective Norton." A deep voice boomed from the phone's speaker. "Good morning. This is Oswald Little. Isaac Underwood told me to give you a ring." He had a lilt and rhythm in his voice, more "gud maanin" than "good morning."

Colin had grabbed his notepad and rolled over to my desk.

"My mother passed last week," the man was saying, "and I been down here in Belmopan since June, just to be wit' family. I'm still shocked that my old friend Gene has passed. I've known him for a long time. I wish I could make it for the services, but no. It takes great effort for me to travel anywhere—I'm sure Ike's told you of my condition. As far as my hands are concerned, blame it on adventurous eating in Seoul. A dish didn't agree wit' me. I got so very, very ill, and then I had a decision to make. So: off wit' my hands and feet. But the Lord, He continues to bless."

In his world, the ocean crashed against the shore, and children shrieked as they splashed around in water.

"I'll be down here for another month or so," the man said. "Takin' care of family business. Hope that's not a problem. You can call me if you must, but Ike—he can tell you everything you need to know." He rambled off his phone number with the country code 501 for Belize, then bade farewell.

Colin leaned back in his chair. "Whatcha think?"

I shrugged. "How do we know that's actually Oz Little?"

"Guess we don't." He placed his hands behind his head, then studied the cork ceiling. "But how do we find out for sure? Ask him to Face-Time or Skype? I'm down for a trip to Central America, if you wanna go."

"That's an option. Here's another." I grabbed the receiver, then flipped in my notebook to yesterday's entries. "Let's ask someone who's had his ear talked off by Mr. Little and would know his voice."

Twenty minutes later, Dr. Rodney Riley sat in my guest chair. The mason—an emergency room physician in his other life—looked crisp in his blue scrubs and spotless white Adidas. His eyes were closed as he tried to listen to the voice mail for the third time over a weeping woman shouting, "He ain't done nothin', I swear, he ain't. I put that on my babies!"

Colin and I held our breath and watched Riley tilt his head and bite his lips.

The voice-mail recording ended with Oswald Little reciting the same phone number Ike had offered me last night.

Riley opened his eyes, then shook his head. "Nope. That's not him."

Colin and I exchanged glances. "How can you tell?" he asked.

Riley chuckled. "Oz's favorite saying is, 'Sleep wit' yo' own eye.'"

"Which means?" I asked.

"Rely only on what you know for sure, not what other people tell you." Riley pointed to the phone. "And this guy, he's telling you to do the opposite. That you should trust in what this fellow Ike says. And Oz's voice isn't that deep. And then, there's the accent—Oz is Belizean, you know."

I cocked my head, then said, "This caller had an accent. Plus, Oz has lived in America for decades now. He may have—"

"No. I'm telling you: Oz's accent is *thick*," Riley said. "Even living here and picking up our speech pattern, he *still* sounds like he got off a plane from Central America—maybe not two days ago but a week ago. This guy . . ." He pointed to my phone. "This guy sounds like an American who vacationed in Belize for a week. Trust me: whoever called you? He ain't Oz."

35

Colin navigated a bleached-out but still bustling King Boulevard. We didn't talk much during the drive—every time I uttered a word, my teeth rattled in my head, and the whites outside the car got whiter. I needed to bank all my wits and strength to simply exist today. I needed silence.

But the radio crackled and calls filled the cabin.

. . . shots fired.

. . . suspect is a black male . . .

. . . stabbing . . .

. . . suspect is a Hispanic woman . . .

Colin turned down the volume.

I looked at him, then laughed.

"What?" he asked.

"We're dressed the same today."

He gazed down at his gray slacks and black polo shirt, then at my gray slacks and black shirt.

"We're twinsies," he said.

"It's just like high school," I said.

"Except with more guns."

I smirked. "What high school did *you* go to?"

A block away from Eugene Washington's house, we heard the jack-hammer breaking through concrete. Colin smiled. "What's her face and the big white girl must be thrilled with us." His grin widened.

"You're a little overjoyed that our efforts are disturbing the peace, huh?" I asked.

"Hell, yeah," he said. "But once we find Jimmy Hoffa in Washington's basement, their property values are gonna skyrocket."

"We're not gonna find Jimmy Hoffa," I said, "cuz Gene Washington ate him."

"That's just . . ." Colin shuddered. "What . . . ? How . . . ?"

"The Donner party. Those guys in the plane crash in the Andes . . ."

"But that's desperation," Colin said. "That's eat or die. Washington—"

"Ate people when there's soul food less than a mile away?" My phone rang—Bernice Parrish. I didn't answer because I knew what she wanted. And her voice-mail message confirmed that she wanted her gold.

Patrol officers had set up sawhorses at the intersection before the house. Lookie-loos had camped out with cameras and curiosity. Two news crews had parked, and both reporters scribbled notes into their little pads.

After being waved through, Colin rolled past a criminalist van, a coroner's wagon, patrol cars, and LAPD trucks loaded down with heavy equipment.

My nerves were Christmas-morning giddy, seeing all this activity surrounding my case. "Man, I hope there's a body in there somewhere."

Colin threw the car into park. "If we don't find anything, I'm blaming the dog."

A plastic blue tarp now covered the entrance to the open garage. Men in khakis, work boots, and face masks waited in the corner as workers shoveled rubble from a spot that had been taped off. White light from portable stands illuminated the dusty air.

I gave a "Hey, I'm here," then ducked back out to speak with Brooks and Goldberg.

The two doctors stood a few feet away from the garage. A group of medical students were picking through bigger rocks while more experienced researchers ran smaller particles through sieves.

Spencer searched my face, then whispered, "You okay?"

I gave a one-shouldered shrug. "Same as it ever was."

He shook his head.

"Worse as it ever was?" I put my finger to my lips. "Ssh. Our little secret." Louder, I said, "Any luck so far?"

Goldberg swiped at his sweaty forehead. "Nothing yet, but we just cracked through. I don't expect to hit anything for a moment."

"Seems that the concrete in the garage was poured in the last seven, eight years," Brooks said. "The concrete in and around the house is older, made of different sand."

"And the dog alerted again in the garage, in that spot," Goldberg added.

"Should we stay then?" Colin asked.

"If you can't," Goldberg said, "how close will you be?"

"Inglewood," I said, "so no more than five miles away."

Both Goldberg and Brooks shrugged. "We find the first bone," Goldberg said, "we'll stop and call you immediately."

Colin and I trudged back across the lawn. He pointed down the block. "Your homies are here."

The three sisters stood at the sawhorses with their arms out, their eyes closed, and their lips moving.

"Why the hell are they here?" Colin asked. "Gene's been dead for five days now. Don't they need to do laundry, go to Target, find a brunch near the marina or wherever?"

"They know something," I said, "but refuse to speak anything other than King James."

"So it's like you when you know something," he said, "and you hold it to your vest."

I slipped my glasses over my eyes. "You're keeping things to yourself, too, Cowboy."

He smirked, then moseyed toward the Crown Vic.

"Fine." I moseyed to the car, too, but couldn't feel my feet—all the blood had rushed to my head. "I guess it's like that now."

"What are you talking about?" he asked.

"Your big secret."

"I don't have any secrets."

"Bullshit. You're different now."

He laughed, gawked at me, then laughed harder. "*I'm* different? *You're* the one who's different. Since you've come back, you're one big tense muscle, constantly trying to prove shit."

"I'm *always* trying to prove shit," I said. "I've had to prove shit since my first hours on earth."

"Here we go," he said, flushing.

"Race and tits, right?" I cocked my head. "Those things don't matter to you since—"

"I'm a white dude, correct?" He stopped in his step. "We're partners, Lou. I'm not O'Shea. I'm not Whitaker. I don't want your job. I think you're better at this than all of us."

I blinked at him.

A nerve stood out in the middle of his forehead. Spit had gathered at the corners of his thin lips. His eyes had turned stormy blue. "You have one big ol' target on your back right now."

"I know that," I snapped.

"But I didn't put it there, all right? I'm not aiming at it, either."

"Uh huh."

He studied me with narrowed eyes. "What's that supposed to mean? You think I'm—"

"What have you told L.T.?"

"About?"

I rolled my eyes. "Really?"

"Nothing," he said. "I've said nothing to anybody about how you've been feeling. How I think that—"

"What? What do you think?"

"You should've taken more time." He sighed, then slumped. "I didn't like partnering up with that jackass Moreno, but I would've preferred you taking the time you needed. That you *still* need."

My eyes burned, but I pushed tears away with a sigh. "We need to get going."

"Lou—"

I held out my hand. "Gimme the keys."

He stared at me, then tossed the keys on the roof of the car. His glare softened, and he started to speak.

I had already opened the car door and slammed myself into the driver's seat.

He was looking at me with hands on his hips and the sun on his back.

"You comin' or what?" I shouted.

He climbed into the passenger seat. "I'm sorry—"

"Don't apologize because you're right." I tried to toss him a smile. "Your wish for me is coming true."

He squinted at me. "What does that mean?"

And I told him that Lieutenant Rodriguez was forcing me to take vacation. "But that's between us, all right?"

He gulped, then nodded. "Right." He frowned, then glared out the passenger's-side window. Pissed.

But then, weren't we all?

36

The edge had abandoned Colin's face by the time we parked beneath the church's shaded portico.

Before I could take the key out of the ignition, my phone rang. The number showing belonged to Neil aka Bang-Bang, our division's quartermaster and on-site geek. "So that call from Belize," he said from the phone's speaker.

I slipped the pen from my binder, ready to write. "What about it?"

"It didn't hit any towers in Belize," he said. "Or any towers in Central America."

"Huh? Where did it hit?"

"Malibu."

Even after Bang-Bang had ended our call, I continued to stare at Malibu in my notepad.

Colin's mouth hung open.

"Talk about being as far from Central America in every effin' way," I said.

"So, who left you that message then?" he asked.

I shrugged, then turned to stare at the church. "But when we talk to *them*, we don't know any of this, right?"

"Call?" Colin asked, mock confused. "Yes—that call from Belize with Oz Little. Yes, he did sound very sad and very Belizean. Too bad he's not around right now."

We stepped into the air-conditioned lobby of Blessed Mission Ministries. Members of a uniformed cleaning crew stooped to shine brass and chrome fixtures while others swept, mopped, and emptied garbage cans. At the welcome station, a woman arranged a grand bouquet composed of orange, red, and yellow roses.

Colin wandered over to the giving tree, then pointed at a foil leaf. "There's our man with no hands."

The picture of Oswald Little on the cherubim branch was the same picture I'd found on Excelsior Bank's Web page just a day ago.

"You're back." The woman's familiar voice was soft and warm.

I tore my attention from the donor recognition to connect the voice with the face.

Perfect silver hair. Young-looking face. Instead of a sweater set, she wore a pink designer sweat suit and blue Nikes. She clutched a walkie-talkie in one hand and a tumbler filled with lemonade in the other.

"Sonia Elliot," the woman reminded us.

"Church secretary," I said, nodding.

She beamed. "That's me."

"Bishop and Mrs. Tate are expecting us today," I said.

Sonia cocked her head. "News to me. I don't think Charity's here, but Bishop Tate's in a meeting right now."

I winked at her. "We'll wait."

"You can wait upstairs," she said. "I'll walk you up."

"He have a good trip?" I asked as we followed.

"Oh, yes," Sonia said. "He was only gone for a few nights, but we always miss him when he's away from the fold."

"So I hear Brandon plays football," Colin said. "I did, too. High school and college."

Sonia looked back at us. "Brandon's gonna be a star. He has his daddy's quickness."

"And practice was Monday night, right?" I asked.

Sonia narrowed her eyes. "Must be a new schedule. He usually practices on Tuesdays and Thursdays, right after school."

I regarded Colin with a cocked eyebrow. Charity Tate had claimed she'd been at football practice on Monday night and not dropping by Eugene Washington's house with a killer cobbler.

As Sonia led us up the stairs, the walkie-talkie chirped and crackled with voices.

"Sister Elliot, the florist said we need another arrangement beneath the lectern for balance . . ."

"Sister Elliott, I just picked up the robes from the dry cleaner's . . ."

"Sister Elliott, we need two signatures on this check . . ."

"You're a busy lady," I said.

"Blessed Mission can't do one thing around here without me." She keyed the radio, then said, "I didn't authorize anybody taking a check to him. He hasn't serviced the organ in over two months. If he has a problem, he can call me." She shook her head, then shoved the radio into her jacket pocket. "These people are gonna kill me by the end of the day. Thank goodness you're here so you can arrest 'em."

Colin and I offered the polite chuckles we kept in our pockets like mints and matchbooks.

"Any progress on poor Brother Washington's case?" Sonia asked. "I saw the digging machines this morning."

"You must live nearby then?" I asked.

She nodded. "Up the hill. And because I'm the church secretary, people—even the bishop—rely on me for information. I make it my business—"

"To know everybody's business?" I asked.

She wiggled her nose and her brown eyes twinkled. "Exactly."

Sonia had been pretty back in the day—a nonthreatening, pasteurized pretty. Like a stewardess on a second-rate airline carrier. She was clutching to it—and to her relevance—with the track suit and the gray, coiffed hair.

I told her that we still had not resolved the case, that the machines and the digging involved a search for Eugene Washington's will, and that his murder had turned into a real head scratcher. "Maybe it *was* just bad potato salad," I said with a shrug.

On the second floor, she led us in the opposite direction of Bishop Tate's office. "You can wait in here," she said.

The conference room had modern oak chairs and a stylized oval table. Framed photographs of Bishop Tate—smiling with a councilwoman, shaking hands with the mayor, shaking hands with the governor, shaking hands with Stevie Wonder—covered the walls.

"Would you like something to drink?" Sonia lifted her tumbler. "Lemonade? I just made a new pitcher."

"That would be wonderful." My stomach growled—a request for that, along with a burger and fries.

Colin wandered over to the window and peeked out. The growl of earthmovers and the *beep-beep-beep* of trucks in reverse was faint but still audible.

Sonia frowned, then said, "All that noise. You'd think they'd give it a rest on the weekend."

I sat at the table. "No one said progress was quiet."

"I suppose it's a positive thing, all the building." She twisted her lips. "This neighborhood *is* safe again, so that's good. And the politicians— they pay us some attention now that we're not some rinky-dink church in the ghetto, like we used to be." She laughed, so I laughed.

"You've been a member for long?" Colin asked.

She cocked her chin and smiled. "I've been with Blessed Mission since the very beginning, when we worshipped in that tiny, tiny space where the digital billboard stands. About fifteen years ago, we really started digging deep into the Lord's work. Being faithful. I helped get the bishop and board of directors focused. Bake sales, rummage sales, magazine drives. We got busy, you know? And we bought some land, and then we bought some more land, and the Lord kept blessing us again and again. Tenfold. Let me show you."

We followed her into a smaller space off the conference room. More like a walk-in closet, the space smelled of dust and old glue, stale breath and ancient memories. The pictures on these walls were of the smaller Blessed Mission building, when it had been as big as a donut shop. The bookcases were filled with photo albums of differing colors and sizes. The spines wore labels of years 1977–78, 80–82, and on and on.

Over twenty years ago, Mom and I had sat in the pews of Blessed Mission's original home. We had clutched "Have You Seen Her?" flyers to our chests and had hoped that someone in the congregation would help us find my missing sister Victoria.

"And then we bought the business next door." Sonia was pointing to the framed shot of Solomon Tate wearing a business suit. A young, fresh-faced Charity Jackson, her hair styled in an asymmetrical bob, stood with him in front of an old car lot. The large sign on the fence to their right said, "Future Site of Blessed Mission Ministries—coming 2011!"

"That's where we're standing right now," Sonia said.

"The church has come a long way," I said. "Bishop and Mrs. Tate's work paid off, it seems."

"They didn't do it alone," Sonia pointed out. "Trust me: they had a lot of help, if I do say so—"

The radio in her pocket chirped. "Sister Elliott," a woman whined, "you gonna get back to me?"

"In a minute, Margie." Sonia rolled her eyes. "Charity never has to deal with any of this." There was an edge to her voice—it was thin as a razor blade, but that blade had been slicked with venom. "She throws up her hands, then tosses it to me. I have to handle it. Even something as simple as the mission statement."

"To help and to heal," Colin said. "Catchy."

"Thank you." She pointed to her chest. "That was me, not that I'm looking for credit." She shrugged, then offered a good-natured smile. "To God be the glory. It's all for Him in the end, isn't that right?"

My smile and lifted eyebrows had frozen—someone was a little *bitter*. "That's right. So you handle all the church records?" I asked. "Birth, death, baptisms, all that?"

"Me and my assistant secretary," she said, nodding. "We're a little behind our archiving with all the recent growth—people having lots of babies, old folks dying. My nephew tells me to make our records digital but . . ." She winced, then touched her neck. "I don't trust computers."

"Did you know Eugene Washington?" Colin asked.

She pinched her fingers together. "Just a little. He mostly kept to himself."

"What about Oswald Little?"

She furrowed her eyebrows. "I thought he left Blessed Mission?"

"You tell me—you're the secretary." I winked at her.

"If you need, I can find out." She sat her tumbler on the table. "Not that I'm complaining, but with so much growth, with so many people, I don't get to know folks too good, you know? Especially the younger members and the members who don't come as frequently. I hate that, but it is what it is."

I gestured to the photo albums in the bookcase. "This is everything? Or should I say, 'everyone'?"

"Can't say yes to that. Only because I may not have every single announcement." She tapped a large photo album with the spine labeled 1971. She then slid her fingers to the newer violet album three shelves over. "Like I said, so many people, it's hard to keep up. And sometimes, folks drop off the radar."

Like mom and me. No one had called us after that Sunday's visit.

"May we look at a few albums?" I asked.

"Certainly." The radio in Sonia's hand chirped again. "What year do you wanna see?" she asked, her face showing strain.

"This year, 2015." A shot in the dark.

She pulled the last violet album from the shelf and placed it in Colin's hands. She touched it like a mother touching her baby. "Just don't take anything—we don't have extras."

Colin said, "Yes, ma'am."

"Now," the woman said, smiling, "I'll get you those glasses of lemonade and I'll go check on Bishop Tate." Away too long from knowing all, Sonia keyed the mic on the radio as she quickstepped out of the small room.

Colin sat the album on top of a credenza. "You wanna see if Oswald Little's in here?"

I flipped to the album's last page. "He wouldn't be. He's still alive, remember? And Eugene Washington's program won't be in yet since his funeral isn't until next Wednesday."

Out in the conference room, a thin woman silently sat a tray holding glasses and a pitcher of lemonade on the conference room table. She padded out of the room as quietly as she came.

Colin left me in the archives nook, then returned a moment later with two glasses of lemonade. "I'll hold your drink as you look," he said. "I don't think Sister Elliott would appreciate wet spots on her precious memories."

I guzzled half my glass, handed it back to Colin, then dried my hands on my slacks. "Let's see . . ."

Back in January, Sister Helen Montgomery had died. She had been ninety-two years old, but for the funeral program, her family had chosen a picture circa 1958 when she'd resembled Lena Horne's darker cousin. She was survived by her twin daughters Bess and Tress and countless grandkids and great grandkids.

Handsome Marcus Sandford, fifty, former marine, thick lips, goatee, gingersnap skin, passed on Valentine's Day. He was survived by members of Blessed Mission.

Sixty-seven-year-old Thomasina Jacobs succumbed to cancer in May. She resembled Ella Fitzgerald in her heyday, with chubby cheeks, raisin eyes, and a lovely smile. She was also survived by members of Blessed Mission.

Three more seniors had passed this year and had been survived by countless grands and greats.

"Could you take pictures of these programs?" I asked.

Colin plucked his phone from his pocket. "May I ask why?"

"Because I'm nosy. And because I have a niggling."

Sonia Elliott popped back into the room. She no longer wore her jacket, and her phone was now strapped to her bicep. Her eyes darted over to the album and then to the programs I held. "Bishop Tate's available now. Did you find everything you need?"

"I think so," I said with a grin. "And don't worry. I'm not taking programs. Just reading." That niggling, like tingling and spiraling combined, poked from my gut again. I'm sure I *had* found everything I needed—I just needed to put it all together.

37

I handed Bishop Tate a wet wipe to clean his hands of the fingerprinting ink, then said, "Oswald Little is a cherubim."

"A *what?*" The minister wore pressed chinos and, despite the heat, a sweater of many patterns. A simple gold wedding band and a Timex with a worn leather band were his only adornments. A purple-and-white robe with velvet cuffs hung on a coat rack near his desk. Probably cost him a fine nickel, that robe, but the man seated in the armchair across from us, in that Cliff Huxtable sweater, did not present as a Lear-jet-flying, Armani-suit-wearing, Bentley-driving man of God.

"Mr. Little is a cherubim," I repeated. "A donor level on your giving tree. That's several thousand dollars a year, right?"

He waved a dismissive hand. "No idea. That's Charity's thing. I'm not much of a fund-raiser." He tossed the soiled wipe on the table, then regarded Colin and me as though we were dusty ficuses in the corner of his office. "You're not much of a churchgoer, are you, Sergeant? I can tell—you seem to have no idea why we need money." He chuckled. "To be honest, someone could be just as suspicious of you."

Sonia Elliott and her tray of lemonade entered the office. She moved differently now—more hips swaying than before. Glossier lips, too. She sat the tray on the coffee table in front of the minister and poured lemonade into each glass, then handed them out.

Bishop Tate, a smart man, knew to keep his eyes off of the secretary's ass, and instead he watched me, or he watched Colin, or he stared at the sleeve of his busy sweater.

"Anything else?" Sonia Elliott asked with a smile. "I made some of my famous coffee cake this morning."

"Sister Elliott's one of our best cooks," the minister told Colin and me.

"*One* of the best?" she asked, hands on her hips.

Bishop Tate smiled. "*The* best."

"That's right," the woman said with a triumphant smile. "Would you like some?"

Bishop Tate shook his head. "We're fine. Thank you, Sonia."

After she slinked out of the room, I said, "You were saying someone could be suspicious of me?"

"I'm a taxpayer." He pointed to me. "I pay your salary. Not just yours, of course. All of LAPD's. I could ask, 'Well, why do the cops need all those fancy Mustang patrol cars and body armor and all that?' Back in the day, police only needed batons, a service revolver, and a good pair of shoes. Crime rates were much lower back then than they are today— so what good is the slick car and the high-powered rifles?"

"Well, back then," I said, "in those good old days, there was no drug war, nor was there a proliferation of assault and automatic weapons in the hands of ordinary citizens. Back then, in those good ol' days of William Parker, our first police chief, Negroes couldn't vote or enjoy a grilled cheese and Coke at Woolworth. Man, those *were* the good ol' days, weren't they?"

Bishop Tate's eyebrows rose and a small smile played on his lips. "Anyway. I mean no harm or disrespect. And if you ever need someone to talk about what's going on with you *personally*, Sergeant Norton, I'm here. And I'm not talking about Eugene Washington or Oswald Little. I'm referring to your pain. The Spirit has whispered in my ear about you, and this may not make sense or it may sound weird but . . ." He squinted at me, then pointed to my left and right shoulders. "At this very moment, demons are camped all about you."

"Not sure how to respond to that," I said.

The minister grinned and pointed at Colin. "*You're* saved. I see it in the set of your jaw, and in the way you glow."

I rolled my eyes—guess the spirit didn't tell him that Colin had a thing for his wife.

"Thank you, sir," Colin said, "but we're here to investigate a murder and a missing congregant who has lost possession of his hands."

"And demons are usually present around those who do our type of work," I added. "And I'm not referring to the supernatural kind. To be honest, the supernatural kind can take a number and wait in line." My words came out dangerously slow as lava.

Bishop Tate cocked an eyebrow. "Them's some bold words."

"God's on my side," I said. "Whom shall I fear?"

He winked at Colin. "Keep praying for her."

"Like you prayed for Mr. Washington?" I asked.

His smile dimmed some, and he grew so rigid that he vibrated from the strain. "I can't help those who don't want to be helped. You see, while I may provide this congregation with the Word, members must also take an active role in their daily living, in their own salvation. Jesus said, 'Open the door.' That means verb-ing. That means action. He cannot open the door for you. Nor can He clean your house."

I nodded, then said, "Idell Messere, Dorothea Tennyson—"

"The so-called prophetesses," he said with a wry grin. "More like witches. Predicting the future is not the same as hearing and sharing the word of the Lord."

I shrugged. "Predicting? In my few conversations with them, no one has told me what I'd find, where I'd find it, whodunit. A few gospel songs and a lot of daily praying—that's all I've gotten from them."

"Why do you think they're coming to Washington's house every day?" Colin asked.

He sighed, shrugged, rolled his eyes. "No idea, Detective Taggert. I just couldn't allow them to remain members of this congregation. Any other questions?"

"On the first day," I said, "they mentioned Mr. Washington trusting when he shouldn't have. And that others trusted him when they shouldn't have. Do you know what they—?"

"I don't fill my mind with their sorcery," Bishop Tate said with a wave of his hand. "Anything else?"

"Yes," I said. "Oswald Little."

"Oz was a member of Blessed Mission. A church deacon. Helped us win several development loans. Great guy."

"Was a member of Blessed Mission?" Colin asked. "So he is dead?"

Bishop Tate froze, then blinked at us. "As far as I know, he's alive. Unless you've heard something?"

"We're told he's alive," I said. "He's also your brother, correct? Masonic brother, to be specific."

The minister leaned back in his armchair. "Yes. Oz and I attend meetings at Prince Hall."

"The grand secretary," I said, "says Mr. Little stopped coming to meetings in October 2010. Why is that? Why did he stop being active?"

The minister shrugged. "After his accident—"

"Which accident?" I asked.

Bishop Tate pointed to his head. "Oz changed after that. He's a banker, so he was very methodical. After his head injury . . ." Tate whistled. "No one knew what he'd do from one moment to the next. *He* didn't know sometimes."

"Any other injuries?" I asked.

The minister squinted as he thought. "Can't think of anything else."

"And he's still a donor to the church, correct? Despite that head injury?"

Bishop Tate nodded. "Good habits never die."

"When was the last time you saw Mr. Little?" Colin asked.

Bishop Tate crossed his legs, then rubbed his chin. "Let's see . . ." He stared at the ceiling as though the correct answer had been scribbled there.

"Blessed Mission has, what?" Colin asked. "About four thousand members?"

"Six thousand."

"That's a lot of people," I said. "You can't personally keep track of everyone."

His eyes bit into me. "I do my best, Sergeant Norton."

I nodded. "I'm sorry—I interrupted. You were figuring out the last time you saw Oswald Little."

A bead of sweat slipped down the bishop's forehead and soaked into his right eyebrow. As though it was connected to his biorhythms, the air conditioner clicked on. "Do you mean at Sunday service?" he asked.

"On Sunday, Tuesday, Wednesday, picnics, weddings, Christmas, Easter, whenever."

He shrugged, and his face relaxed. "I'm embarrassed to say that I can't recall. Despite our political power and community influence, not knowing everyone and where they are at any given month is a problem with a church this size. I must do better. I *will* do better. Thank you for bringing this to my attention. Like I always say: you only improve by recognizing your problems. Anything else?"

"Yes, sir," Colin said. "Where were you on this past Monday?"

He patted his stomach, then pointed to the empty space on the couch. "Asleep right over there, recovering from Sister Raymond's potato salad she made for the picnic."

"Was anyone here with you?" Colin asked.

He nodded. "My staff, including Sister Elliott, the head deacon, several elders—they were also with me that night at the board meeting in Pasadena, at All Saints."

"And then later this week," I said, "where were you?"

"I've had meetings in Arizona."

"With?"

"Our national board of directors."

"Which city in Arizona?" I asked.

"Tempe."

"Not Phoenix? Your wife said—"

"I flew *into* Phoenix," Bishop Tate said, "but the meetings took place in Tempe."

"And you stayed where?" Colin asked.

"With a colleague and his family."

"How'd you get to Tempe?" I asked.

"I drove."

"A rental?"

The minister stared at me, his hatred pulsating like radiation from the sun. "Of course, since I *flew* in."

I smiled through this attack, asking, "On Monday night, do you know where Mrs. Tate was?"

"She . . ." He cocked his head and squinted. "She had dinner with an old friend."

"Not football practice with Brandon?" Colin asked, paling.

The minister shook his head. "No. Football's on Tuesdays and Thursdays. She told me . . ." He shifted in his chair and his Adam's apple bobbed.

I gave Colin a side eye—his Adam's apple was also bobbing in his throat.

"Who has access to the church vans?" I asked.

"All the officers, Ike Underwood, and my wife have access."

"Is there a checkout system or tracking of who took which van at what time?" Colin asked.

Bishop Tate shrugged. "You'll have to ask Sister Elliott that question."

"Where do you think Mr. Little is right now?" I asked.

He swiped his sweaty eyebrow. "In Belize—at least that's what I've been told."

"Who told you that?"

"Ike Underwood. He's in constant contact with Oz—Ike is his caretaker and stays with him at the house."

I leaned forward. "So when you told me that Mr. Little was in Belize, you didn't know that firsthand?"

Bishop Tate shook his head.

"Why is Mr. Underwood taking care of Mr. Little?" Colin asked.

The minister reached for his glass of lemonade. "The head injury diminished Oz's ability to take care of himself."

I cocked my head. "And yet he traveled to Belize all by himself." I flipped pages in my notebook. "So you have seven hundred thousand to raise before the end of the year."

Bishop Tate traced shapes in the condensation on the glass's side. "Sounds impossible, but we can do all things through Christ. What does any of this have to do with Eugene's death?"

Colin plucked a picture of the mummified hands from the expandable file, then placed it near the pitcher of lemonade.

Bishop Tate slipped on his reading glasses, then studied the picture without touching it. "Brother Underwood told me that workers uncovered these at Eugene's house. That they belong to Brother Little. Is that true?"

"You don't seem shocked," Colin said.

The minister snorted, then took off his glasses. "To be honest, I don't believe that the hands are real."

"Oh?" I asked.

"In my line of work," the minister said, "I've witnessed unexplainable, sometimes strange things. Demon possession, a child aging backward, inexperienced billionaires running for president. And I've witnessed staged things—demon possession, a child aging backward, and inexperienced billionaires running for president. These hands look like props in a magic show."

"The hands are real, sir," Colin said, "and we've confirmed that they belong to Mr. Little."

Bishop Tate blinked . . . blinked . . . "So the hands I've seen on Oz . . ."

"Are prosthetics," I said.

"When did that . . . ?" He pointed to the picture.

"Mr. Underwood told us the operation occurred in 2013," Colin said.

"I guess no one told you?" I asked.

The minister stared at the picture, then shook his head.

"You have any idea how Mr. Washington came into possession of Mr. Little's hands?" Colin asked.

Bishop Tate took a deep breath, slowly exhaled, then shrugged. "Other than stealing them? No idea."

"Do you trust Mr. Underwood?" Colin asked.

Bishop Tate opened, then closed his mouth without answering. His knee jiggled a bit, then stopped. "I *did* trust Ike, but with everything going on and your questions . . . I don't know what to think. Of *anybody*."

"Could we get check copies of Brother Little's most recent donations?" I asked.

Bishop Tate shouted, "Sonia?"

A moment later, Sonia Elliott entered the office. "Yes, Bishop?"

"Could you get the detectives check copies of Mr. Little's recent donations?"

The church secretary shuffled over to a file cabinet and pulled out a drawer.

Bishop Tate pointed at me. "Believe me when I say He's gonna do something wondrous for you."

I cocked an eyebrow. "I need wondrous nowadays." To Sonia Elliott, I said, "In addition to current checks, I'd like to see old ones, too, from Mr. Little, say . . . 1999, 2000, even 2004. I know you have them for auditing purposes. Thank you." I snapped my fingers, Colombo-style. "Oh. The church vans—is there a log of who had keys on any given day?"

Sonia Elliott blinked at me, then swallowed as though a pill had been stuck in her dry throat. "Of course, but to be honest, I'm not a stickler for people to fill out the log. So many other things for me to be obsessed about."

I nodded. "Totally understand. Still: could you provide me a copy of this week's log? Thanks so much for your help."

Sonia flipped and flipped in notebooks, selecting a page here and there, then flipped some more.

"Last thing," I said to Bishop Tate. "Where can we find your wife?"

His face darkened. "Why?"

I picked up the print kit and waggled it. "We need her fingerprints, too."

38

Bishop Tate didn't know where we'd find his wife. "Obviously, her schedule is more fiction than I thought," he said, as he flipped through Charity's blank desk calendar.

"Do *you* know where she is?" I squinted at Colin as I tossed my bag into the driver's seat.

His face flushed all the way to the roots of his hair. "Why would I?"

I folded my arms and leaned against the car's hood. "Really, dude?"

He cleaned the lenses of his sunglasses with the tail of his polo shirt. "I have no freakin' clue where she is."

"Call her," I said. "Tell her we need her prints and that I'm gonna stop asking nicely."

He slipped on his Ray-Bans, then dialed Charity's number.

Cars pulled in and out of the parking lot. The janitorial service carried mops and spray bottles to a van rumbling beneath the porte cochere. Back across the street, Sonia Elliott had wandered to the courtyard with a phone to her ear.

"Hey, Charity, it's Detective Taggert." Colin paused, then cleared his throat. "Thought I would see you today—we're here at the church. I know this sucks, but we still need your fingerprints. Also, umm . . ." He scratched the inside of his free ear. "There's some discrepancy about where you were back on Monday night, and we need to clear that up. So just give me a call as soon as possible. Thanks." He left his number as though she needed it, then ended the call. To me, he said, "Now what?"

I placed the copies of Oswald Little's checks as well as the church van log into my binder, then looked back at the church. "Was I imagining things or does Sister Elliott—?"

"Have a thing for the bishop?" Colin asked. "Yeah, I thought she was gonna sit on his lap."

"Anyway," I said, "let's do some footwork on their dead church members, shall we?"

On the car's laptop, I searched public records for all things Helen "Nell" Montgomery.

The DMV's picture of the old woman was stingier than the photo used on her funeral program. The glam was gone, and beneath the harsh, institutional fluorescent lighting, she was an angry-looking woman with mottled skin and a dull-brown wig.

"She lived over near Leimert Park on Edgewood," I said.

Colin pulled out of the parking lot and headed west.

Once upon a time, the house had probably been a small California bungalow, but now it lived out its days as another two-story behemoth. In the driveway, a gorgeous family of four unloaded groceries from the back of a minivan. The middle-school boy and girl carried toilet paper and paper towels into the house.

"It's like they're in a Honda commercial," Colin said.

He stayed in the car as I approached the couple now wrangling an economy-sized tub of laundry detergent and dog food from the van's trunk. Their eyes widened before I could open my mouth. May have been the badge on my left hip. May have been the holstered Glock on my right. Or maybe they smelled death on me—I wore it like some women wore Chanel No. 5.

I introduced myself, then smiled to ease their fears. "How long have you folks lived here?"

He pushed back his maroon Morehouse College baseball cap. "Just moved in about three weeks ago."

"Did you know the previous owner?" I asked.

He shook his head.

She tugged at her Spelman College tank top. "Oh, no. Did someone die here? Cuz there wasn't anything in the papers. Cuz they have to disclose that, right? They have to."

"They have to disclose if it's a murder," I said, "but I'm not here . . ." I blushed—I *was* here about someone's murder. "Do you remember the realty company that sold you the house?"

She snorted, then rolled her eyes. "No, but they charged too much commission."

"Was it a remodel or a complete tear-down?" I asked.

"They kept two walls," he recalled. "Added the second level, enlarged the kitchen, new paint, new roof. It's a great house."

I thanked the HBCU homecoming king and queen, then returned to the car.

"Well?" Colin asked.

I sighed. "Nothing strange."

He pulled out a roll of fruit Mentos. "You know who we haven't heard from yet?"

"Dr. Goldberg?"

He popped a candy, then offered me the roll. "True, but we haven't heard from Ike, either."

"You're absolutely correct." I took a pink Mentos, then said, "Let's check in on our good buddy." I dialed Ike Underwood's number.

He didn't answer.

That didn't stop me—I left a message for him to call me back immediately.

Then, I called Oswald Little's phone number.

It rang and rang until an automated message told me that the voice-mail box was full.

Back on the laptop, I typed "Thomasina Jacobs," and then "Phoebe Oleander," "Ulysses Benjamin," and "Florence Tatum"—all dead members of Blessed Mission. No property records listed for Phoebe, Ulysses, and Florence. Finally, I typed "Marcus Sandford."

The deceased veteran had lived on Olmstead Avenue down in Leimert Park. He'd purchased the house there back in 2000.

As a result of construction on the Crenshaw Boulevard subway route, major streets had been closed. The businesses on these arteries had either been shuttered entirely or clutched at survival by posting desperate STILL OPEN!!! signs that no one saw.

After a detour from Crenshaw Boulevard to Coliseum Avenue to Buckingham Road to King Boulevard and then back again, Colin pulled up to 9919 Olmstead Avenue. The new, two-story California-Spanish featured a dead lawn filled with sanders, tile cutters, and leftover pieces

of drywall. Squeezed between two tiny bungalows, the house also featured a FOR SALE sign jammed into the ground. The metal whir of machines and the unrelenting joy of Norteño music drifted out from the
house to the sidewalk.

Colin and I stepped into the foyer and into the cacophony of whir-
ring and tuba-oomphs. Men shouted at each other in the great room—
and the guy hammering nails into drywall was the same guy who'd found
Oswald Little's hands in Eugene's Washington's bathroom.

Guillermo Velasquez spotted Colin and me and his ruddy complexion darkened.

We waved at him.

Guillermo Velasquez set down the hammer, then trudged over as
though he owed us a million dollars. And he did owe us—he never came
in to give his formal statement.

"I didn't have no car," he explained. "So sorry."

"Ike working here today?" I asked.

Guillermo Velasquez shook his head.

"He come by at all?" Colin asked.

"He come early today. He a'stop at Mr. Gene's house, see them digging, then come here. I work on this for now." Velasquez offered a weak
smile. "*Es* okay. *Es* clean here."

Both Colin and I laughed. And so Guillermo Velasquez laughed.

"When did construction on this house start?" I asked.

He shrugged. "*No se.*"

"Who's selling it?" I asked.

He shrugged again.

"What's the name of Ike's construction company?"

"*No se.*"

Frustration roiled inside of my stomach like gas. "Well, who's paying
you, then?"

"Mr. Ike, he a'pay me."

"What *name* is on your check?" Colin asked, face flushed.

"Cash. He give me cash." Velasquez lifted his hands. "*Los manos?*
Who?"

"They belonged to Oswald Little," I said. "Do you know that person?"

Guillermo Velasquez shook his head. "No. I don't know Oswald a'Little."

"You know how much they're selling this house for?" Colin asked.

Guillermo Velasquez didn't know.

So we asked Mr. Gatlin, the stoop-shouldered owner of the bungalow across the street.

"Probably high eights. Values here have gone up since I bought back in eighty-eight." The older man scratched his snow-white head and considered the newest McMansion on the block. "Too big. Doesn't fit the neighborhood. And I'm sure it ain't energy efficient. Damn shame."

"Did you know Marcus?"

"A little," Mr. Gatlin said. "He was quiet. Pretty religious. Involved a lot with his church, but after his tours of duty—Iraq, Afghanistan—I wouldn't blame him, you know? I'd be on my knees all the time."

"Mr. Sandford have any family?" Colin asked. "Anybody who stopped by a lot?"

"He lived here alone," the old guy said. "No women staying overnight. Like I said, pretty religious. He always asked my wife and me to attend service. We went once. Nice enough, but not a place for us. Anyway, he worked out all the time. He was a pretty healthy guy. Well, I thought he was."

"How did he die?" Colin asked.

"He was about to go to the gym but had a heart attack in the front seat of his car." Mr. Gatlin pointed to the driveway now crowded with bags of cement. "He died right over there in his Lexus. Ain't *that* something? The church gave him a real nice service, made sure he was buried in the veterans' cemetery over in Westwood. His pastor offered a lovely eulogy, too. Really nice." He snapped off a lavender bloom and twisted it between his fingers.

"How long after Mr. Sandford's burial did all of this"—I waved to the construction—"did all of this start?"

Mr. Gatlin laughed, then said, "*Burial?* Day after Marcus passed, folks was cleaning out the house."

My heart lurched up and into my throat. "Who is 'they'?" I asked. "The folks who cleared the house?"

"All I know is that they were from his church," he said, "and I know *that* because I saw the church van a few times."

"Heart attack," Colin said. "They do an autopsy? He was a young guy, right?"

"Don't know about any autopsy," Mr. Gatlin said. "He was barely fifty."

Colin and I chewed on this over oxtails and smothered pork chops at Dulan's, a stone's throw from Gene Washington's house and a better alternative than eating someone's thigh. We sat at a corner table next to an open window with a view of Crenshaw Boulevard. Aretha Franklin sang about freeways and pink Cadillacs from speakers nailed next to autographed pictures of Muhammad Ali and Roger Troutman. No other diners stood at the counter as one cook poured a pot of red beans into a stainless steel tray.

"No family, so they leave their big-ticket items to a friend," I hypothesized. "Then, the friend tears down the old house, rebuilds it, and sells it for a small fortune. Gives ten percent or more to the church." Eating had given me heft again, and the hard pounding all around my body eased.

Colin shoved a wedge of pork chop into his mouth. "That's not illegal. Come again."

My cell phone rang before I could offer another theory.

Ike Underwood sounded exhausted. "My clients got me going all over God's creation nowadays." He tried to chuckle. "Y'all finish digging over at Gene's?"

"Hardly," I said, "but we need to talk with you again. What time today can we stop by the house?"

"Uh . . . I can come to the station," he offered. "That's no problem."

"We're not sure when we'll be back at the station," I said. "So we'll just stop by later today or tomorrow."

Ike Underwood said, "Sure," but his tone was anything but certain.

"I don't think he wants visitors," I said to Colin. "We've been very nice to him, haven't we?"

"You haven't even cursed at him." He shoved more pork chop into his mouth. "When are we gonna look at the copies Sister Elliott gave us?"

I took a long gulp of my Arnold Palmer, then said, "When we get back to the station. And you'll also send Solomon Tate's prints over to the lab."

"Sounds good, but I just wanna say again that when you die, you can leave your shit to whoever you want, and said shit receiver does nothing wrong when they take it and sell it."

I twisted my lips—Colin was right.

And so I was stuck again.

Until God sent me Peachy Yates.

39

I twisted in my chair to study the room around me—paused at the gnarled cords of the million desk fans meeting near the overstuffed power strip behind the watercooler. Stopped at the tangled dreads of Keyshawn Eastman—the shot caller for the Jungle Bloods was dripping sweat all over the worn blue carpet and kicking O'Shea's desk with his shoe and being a general, all-around asshole. He guffawed once a kick knocked O'Shea's Big Gulp to the floor.

Peachy Yates threw a glare at Keyshawn. "What's wrong with you, boy?" she asked. "You retarded?" The seventy-five-year-old woman wore blue jeans, a jean jacket, and nurse shoes and didn't wince when the handcuffed Blood mean-mugged her as his response. Earlier, she hadn't blinked when a half-naked hooker threw her heroin-addled body against the coat rack and screamed, "Excessive force." Peachy just patted her thin silver hair done up in wispy curls and clutched her purse handles tighter—not out of fear but to use it for knocking someone the hell out.

Had Peachy Yates been sent back from the future? Was I now seated across from Lou Norton, senior citizen, who had returned to warn Lou Norton of today about Skynet and the Great Cabernet Sauvignon shortage of 2044?

A stream of amusement trickled up my spine, and I smiled.

The old woman shot me a glare. "I say something funny to you?" She had a voice that had been seasoned by unfiltered Kools and bottles of Jim Beam.

My face flushed. "No, ma'am."

Her baggy eyes squinted at me. "Why you smiling then?"

A woman named Shirley Hawthorne served as a head deaconess at Blessed Mission and had told Peachy about two police officers (Colin and me) visiting Bishop Solomon Tate twice now. Peachy had been Thomasina Jacobs's best friend since their childhood back in Mississippi. And she had grown suspicious about her friend's death.

"Two years ago," Peachy Yates was now saying, "I told Tommie to leave that church. I left, and that's why I'm still here, *alive*, talking to *you*. Don't know what happened to Bishop—once he married that *child*, he ain't been right. Folks don't wanna show their W-2 forms, and they're tired of special offerings for this and special offerings for that. And Bishop ain't preached a true message since 9/11. Now it's all about death and money, money and death. 'Getting your house in order,' he calls it.

"It was starting to feel Jim Jones off in there. Giving all your money and property to this *man*. And the Tates got enough—vaults and secret rooms, men with guns and people tied up."

I must have sighed as I shifted in my chair.

"You ain't gotta believe me." She moved my stapler from near the tape dispenser over to the pen holder. "Not one Bible gotta open during service now. No more, 'thus saith the Lord.' So I went over to Faithful Central. That's where I worship now."

Colin returned to my desk holding a can of Dr Pepper. "Ma'am, I checked, and we don't have any bottles."

"You don't need to tell me all that." Peachy Yates took the soda can, then popped the top. She motioned at my desk. "Where the cup at?"

Colin's face reddened as he marched back to the break room for the third time.

Keyshawn Eastman shouted, "Get me a Mountain Dew since you goin' back."

The old woman's eyes settled on me. "I ain't lying when I say they got gold coins and vacation houses down in Central America."

A shot whizzed from my belly to my brain. "Gold coins and . . . Who has all of that?"

"Who we talkin' 'bout? And I could care less about material things. I'm here about Tommie. She was only seventy-five years old when she died from colon cancer. And when she got it, it was only stage two, and it wasn't in no other organs yet."

According to Yates, her friend had taught middle-school math at Orville Wright. Tommie Jacobs had never married, didn't have kids, took three cruises a year, and loved the Lord with all her heart and with all her soul.

"She had a wonderful doctor over at Cedar's," Peachy Yates said, although she didn't smile as she said "wonderful." "He was a Jew, so he *knew* what he was doing. And after he cut the tumor out the first time, she was doing well, but there was still some disease left and it came back. Worse this time."

Colin, pink-faced and tight-lipped, approached my desk again. Flustered yet still polite, he sat a plastic cup in front of the old woman as though it had been made of nitroglycerin. "Need anything else, Mrs. Yates?"

She glared at him. "How about quieting down and not interrupting when a lady is speaking? And it's '*Miss* Yates.'"

Colin dropped into his chair without a word.

And I no longer wanted this woman to be Lou Norton, Senior Citizen. This gnome in my guest chair never laughed. And she had obviously ignored her mother's warning: *you keep frowning, your face is gonna freeze that way.* Let Skynet, terminators, and wine shortages come cuz *fuck this.*

"So Miss Jacobs was doing well on her treatments at Cedar's?" I asked.

She nodded, then pushed the OFF switch on my fan. "Somehow, though, folks at the church convinced her to take some natural healing medicine. God's cancer treatments, they said. There was a woman in the congregation claiming to be healed by beets and carrot juice. All this talk about coffee enemas, apricot seeds, cabbage juice. So Tommie was all excited, took all of that, and waited for her miracle. I ain't agree with none of it, but I bought her a juicer and whatever vitamins she needed."

"But there *is* proof," I said, "that some foods—garlic, for example—taken with cancer treatments will help reduce the effects of—"

"Who do you think you are? Dr. Oz? You ain't heard one word I said. Tommie didn't *go* to the doctor *at all* once Blessed Mission got to her." Peachy's lemony skin darkened. "She told me that medicine was sorcery and that God spoke out against sorcery in the book of Psalms, and that He gave us herbs to heal. And so she'd sip her beet and carrot juice and . . ." Her thick lips clamped together. "The cancer kept attacking her and you could just *smell* it. And I begged her, 'Let me take you back to Dr. Eisner,' and she told me that I was being unfaithful, that I needed to trust in the Lord with all my heart and with all my soul.

"And I called on Bishop Tate, and he quoted John at me, the verse about my Father's house having many rooms? So we're duelin' back and forth with our 'thus saith the Lord' and Tommie back there in the bedroom, dying, thinking she around the corner from her miracle and—"

The room dropped into silence.

Peachy Yates closed her eyes as her mouth moved in silent prayer. A tear, then another, slipped down her cheeks. "We used to go square dancing twice a month. We wore them big can-can skirts and . . ." She opened her eyes, then poured more soda into her cup. "When Tommie died, she weighed eighty-seven pounds." She took the tissue I offered her, then shook her head, wiped her face, and sipped Dr Pepper. Her lips and cheeks quivered, and the cup shook in her hand.

I asked, "What did her family—?"

"She ain't *had* no family," the old woman said. "I was *it*. And I was expectin' a call from the lawyer who handles both our papers."

"But the lawyer didn't call you?" Colin asked.

"Oh, he called me, and I got her diamond rings, the watch, all her clothes and purses. When I asked him who got the baby grand, the Buick, and her house over near Village Green, he wouldn't tell me."

"Do you know who was supposed to get those things?" Colin asked.

"Her sorority was supposed to," Peachy Yates said. "Tommie was a Delta."

"But the Deltas didn't?" I asked.

"No, they didn't. And the Road Runners? Her CB club? They were supposed to get her radio equipment."

"But they didn't?" Colin asked.

She shook her head. "Whoever got the house ain't wasted no time. Ain't even been a year yet, but they tore most of it down and put it on the market for a fortune."

I asked, "Do you know Oswald Little, Marcus Sandford, Ike Underwood, or Eugene Washington? They all attended Blessed Mission."

She poked out her bottom lip. "That church is too big now to get to know people. Folks are all strangers there. Just one more reason why I left." She paused, then said, "But I bet you this: Blessed Mission got

Tommie's house. And I bet you this, too: they had an insurance policy on her, one she didn't know about. And I bet you they have policies on every single member of that church." She pushed away the cup of soda, then glared at Colin. "How old is this can of coke? The mixture's off."

40

She said, 'Can I get a coke?'" Colin said as we huddled in conference room Democracy.

"But then," I said, "she followed up with a request for a Dr Pepper."

"But she said 'coke.'"

"She wanted a Dr Pepper."

"Then why didn't she say get me a pop, a Dr Pepper if you have it'?" Colin asked.

"Because she says 'coke', and you say, 'pop,' and you're both wrong cuz it's—"

"Soda," Pepe and Luke shouted together.

My phone vibrated—Greg had texted. *Want company tonight? Tix to Hollywood Bowl.*

My heart tripped in my chest—was my ex-husband asking me out on a *date*? I typed back a single word. *Nope.*

Pictures had been tacked on every wall—from Eugene Washington's blue-splotched body to the heaps of junk in every room to the gold coins in the freezer and the pair of hands in the cigar humidor. Pepe had created a "family tree" with Washington as the trunk and connecting branches holding leaves—people in his life like Ike Underwood and Bernice Parrish. Some leaves—Marcus Sandford, Thomasina Jacobs, and Peachy Yates—were waiting for me to make the connection.

Two pizza boxes sat at the center of the long table alongside foam containers filled with Dulan's peach cobbler. I hated this room—pipes above us whooshed each time a toilet flushed somewhere in the building.

"Do you think she's right about the church?" Colin asked as he took a second slice of pizza from the box. "Or do you think she's a crazy old lady with no manners?"

I nibbled a slice of pepperoni as I thought. "Peachy Yates may have been sour and rude, and suspicious of everything and everyone, but then so am I." I grabbed a blue marker and approached the dry-erase board. Under TO DO FOR MONDAY, I wrote CHECK LIFE INSURANCE POLICIES FOR TOMMIE & MARCUS.

"Really?" Colin asked.

"Totally," I said.

"So I," Luke said, "a random-ass person, can take out an insurance policy on anybody I want? Without them knowing?"

"Basically," I said. "You have to prove that their death could impact your finances. And one less person paying tithe to a church that needs to raise seven hundred thousand—"

Pepe held up his hand. "You really think the *church* killed a seventy-five-year-old woman with stage two colon cancer?" He gaped at Colin, who gaped back at him. "What pills you been popping, Lou, cuz . . . wow."

I dropped back in my chair and rubbed my temples. "Just do it, okay? Next?"

"But the church isn't a beneficiary of Washington's policy," Pepe continued, "Oz Little is."

"Oz whose hands were found in Eugene Washington's bathroom?" I asked. "The one man we can't find cuz he's in Belize but calling from Malibu—that Oz Little? Shall we move along, then, like to the copies that Sonia Elliott made us this afternoon?"

"Who's Sonia Elliott?" Luke asked.

"Blessed Mission's church secretary." I opened the PDF. "This is Sunday's log."

A ledger with different signatures filled the slots beneath IN/OUT/TIME headings.

"Lot of vans out," Pepe said. "I count five."

"The picnic was on Sunday," I said. "Probably used them to cart people, including Eugene Washington, to Bonner Park." I clicked to the next page. "And here's Monday."

Two vans in, with van number 6057 checked out by Q. Lessing at 9:15 a.m., and then returned at 1:50 p.m. The second van, number 6381, had been checked out at 12:10 p.m. There was no signature until it was checked back in on Tuesday at 10:00 a.m.

"That says 'Ike Underwood,'" Pepe said.

I cocked my head. "So Ike had the van. And it looks like there were no other vans out on Monday night."

Colin nodded. "So the van Gene's neighbors saw in his driveway on Monday night—"

"Had to be number 6381," Pepe said. "The van Ike was driving."

"I thought he claimed he didn't see Washington after the picnic," Luke said. "Cuz he had a tummy ache."

"We'll ask him again tonight," I said. "Maybe he *misremembered*."

"And wasn't there a woman with him?" Luke asked.

Colin and I exchanged glances—had Charity Tate gone along for the ride?

My partner's jaw tightened, and his blue eyes darkened, and this time he said, "Next?"

"Charity Tate," I said.

Colin blushed. "What about her?"

"We have Bishop Tate's fingerprints now," I said.

"And I sent them in for analysis," Pepe added.

"But we still don't have Charity's." I arched an eyebrow. "She call you back?"

Colin tore his pizza crust in half. "Not yet."

"When you gonna get 'em, *amigo*?" Luke asked. "When she climbs on top? If that's your plan, just put the inkpad next to the pillow."

Colin turned flamingo pink, and the nerve beneath his left eye twitched.

I patted his wrist, then cooed, "It's okay, buttercup. Anyway, we'll drive by Thomasina's house en route to talking with Ike Underwood."

Colin gave a thumbs-up.

"And on Monday, should we call her oncologist?" Pepe asked. "Or on Tuesday, after the holiday?"

"Either day is fine." A small part of me clenched—I wouldn't be at my desk on Monday or Tuesday.

Luke passed out photocopies of Oswald Little's phone bills. "So I went back."

"How far back?" Colin asked.

"To 2011, a year after his retirement. This is the landline from the house on Garth." On the laptop, Luke double-clicked on a PDF. The digital version of the phone bill blinked to the screen. "You can see . . ." He clicked forward to last month's bill. "Five calls in a row to one number. There's a lot of that—lots of calls, then nothing. Lots of calls, then nothing again. That's Eugene Washington's telephone number. But the most interesting stuff happened a few weeks ago."

"Did Oz call Eugene before August third?" Colin asked.

Luke said, "Nope." Then, he pointed to the pink highlighted rows. "August fourth, there were more calls to that number, and then incoming phone calls, one right after the other."

"Whose phone number is that?" I asked.

"Don't know," he admitted. "Came from a public phone off Western and Vernon, near that Louisiana Fried Chicken. And then the landline number wasn't used for any outgoing calls. Incoming from telemarketing, election robo calls, that kind of stuff."

Pepe pushed back a lock of dark hair that hung over his eyebrow. "Maybe Mr. Little switched to using his cell phone. If he has disability issues, calls are easier with voice activation and whatnot."

Luke flipped pages in his notepad. "Oswald Little *does* have a cell phone. It's the one that called Lou from Malibu."

"And who is he calling from *that* phone?" I asked.

"Other than you? No one." Luke double-clicked to open another PDF. "Ike Underwood also has a cell phone in his name, and this is his last bill." Three green highlighted rows of outgoing calls made on August thirty-first, the Monday before we found Washington dead in his armchair. "Calls to and from another pay phone," Luke said, "but this time, the pay phones are downtown, near Sixth and Central."

"Who's he talking to on Skid Row?" Colin wondered.

"Other calls Ike has made and received," Luke continued, "are to you, Lou, and to Blessed Mission's main number, and to Solomon Tate."

I stared up at the dark corpses of dead insects collecting inside the fluorescent lighting tubes. "Were there any calls from Oz Little's phone to the church or to Bishop Tate?"

"Nope."

"That's strange, right?" Colin asked. "Little's a big donor to the church. He's a mason in the same lodge. But he has absolutely no contact with Solomon Tate?"

I grabbed the container of peach cobbler we'd just purchased from Dulan's—the one without coconut and roaches. The sparkly sugar crust, brown syrup speckled with cinnamon, firm and sweet peaches . . . I took a bite and my head exploded, my pulse raced and the stars collided. "While you were out fetching a coke, Miss Peachy said something very interesting."

Colin dunked his spoon in the cobbler and cut away a wedge. "Yeah? Besides calling 'pop' by the wrong word?" He shoved the spoonful of cobbler into his mouth.

I laughed. "The word's 'soda,' dude. Anyway, she said that Blessed Mission was becoming like Jonestown. Men with guns—"

The guys snorted, and rolled their eyes.

I cocked an eyebrow. "She mentioned gold coins and vacation homes in Central America."

The trio froze and their smirks died.

"Uh huh." I waggled my cell phone. "And speaking of Central America, Oz hasn't returned my call yet. Not from Belize. Not from Malibu. Where he at?" Then, I shouted at my phone: "Where you at, Mr. Little?"

Next, we turned to financials, with Pepe passing around stapled hard copies before turning to the computer. "And the bank sent me copies of checks from Underwood's checking account." Three years ago, Ike Underwood purchased a Ranger Bass fishing boat for eight thousand dollars. It was a fancy thing with a sonar unit, stereo, and trawling motor. "The boat we saw in that photograph of him and Washington," Pepe said. He flipped through his notes. "And the trailer's license plates are linked to the Corning Avenue address, where the old lady with the stuffed dog lives. Ike doesn't pay a mortgage or a car note. He buys a lot of junk at Home Depot.

"And then, there's Oz Little. He's footing the bills in the relationship. He pays the mortgage, the Jag's note, food. He made a big buy at Tiffany.com back in February, around Valentine's. That's it. His bank statement lists no major stores. Well, Target's on there, but no bill over one hundred fifty dollars. And income taxes—they both filed.

"Ike made about thirty-five thousand dollars, and Oz Little almost sixty, mostly from investment income, Social Security, and his pension plan. He gave charitably—a couple grand to Blessed Mission."

"Let's not forget," I said, "he's also getting Washington's house and he's the sole beneficiary on Washington's life insurance policy."

"That's quarter of a mil, right?" Colin asked.

Whoosh. Somewhere, a toilet flushed and water rushed through the pipes. *Whoosh.* Another flush. *Whoosh* again.

"Uh oh," Luke said. "Sullivan broke the crapper again."

I picked up copies of Little's checks that Sonia Elliott had provided. "Let's look at these."

Colin double-clicked the PDF.

The first check was payable to Blessed Mission for three thousand dollars and dated November 17, 2010. Spidery cursive especially on the signature line with those *L*s and *T*s that comprised "Oswald Little."

"And now a check from this year," Colin said.

Another check payable to Blessed Mission for three thousand dollars.

"Is that the same writing?" I asked.

No one spoke.

Colin cleared his throat. "May I ask the obvious question again?"

Pepe crushed his Diet Coke can. "How can a man with no hands write a check?"

"Prosthetics," I said. "And robots—they're taking over, don't you know. Let's look at the checks dated in 2000, when Little was still working at the bank."

Pepe squinted at the screen and those checks. "So . . . what am I supposed to see?"

"No idea." I grabbed my phone. "But I know someone who knows someone who will."

An hour later, a balding Asian man wearing squeaky shoes bustled into the room. William Wu, Ph.D., had a cool superpower: he could look at a document or a person's handwriting to determine its authenticity, authorship, or alteration. "You wanted to look at checks and signatures?" he asked.

He placed the check from Oswald Little's checking account in 2000 next to a check he wrote to Blessed Mission just last month. "No one writes their name the same way ten times," Wu said. "And then, when they're injured, it all changes—letter form, lines and pressure, formatting. So the thick start, and shakiness *here* . . ." On the latest check, Wu pointed to the O in "Oswald" and the darkness of the *e* in "Little." "This may not be of any concern. However . . ." He pointed to the 2000 check. "Here, though, we don't see the weird O or the dark *e*." He minimized the recent check on the screen and opened a check from Ike's account, payable to Bass Pro Sporting Goods. He pointed to the *d* in "Underwood" and the *d* in "Oswald." "Same decisive finish," he said. "Same slope and upward lift at the stem."

"And the *e*, too," I said.

Wu nodded. "Correct."

"Is it possible the same person wrote *both* checks?" Colin asked. "Bass Pro Ike and last month Oz?"

Wu nodded again. "It is possible."

After Wu left, I said, "What about the envelope I found in Washington's house? The one with the initials on the back."

"What about it?" Colin asked.

I clicked to the copy of the envelope, and my pulse jumped as I noticed two initials. "O.L.," I said. "Could that be 'Oswald Little'? And N.M. Could that stand for 'Nell Montgomery'?"

No one spoke.

The other initials: A.A., R.T., M.M. were not Marcus Sandford or Thomasina Jacobs.

"Think there are fingerprints still on this?" I asked.

Pepe said, "Maybe."

"If this *is* a list on the back," I said, "who are these people, and why are their initials crossed out? Because they're dead now?"

"O.L. and N.M. could be anything," Colin said.

"Including Oz Little and Nell Montgomery," I countered. "So I wanna check for that *and* . . ." I studied the envelope and the still-closed flap that sealed it. "See if Zucca can grab any DNA from the adhesive—the sender probably licked it."

Luke held up his hand. "I'm confused."

"It's Saturday," Pepe said, "of course you are."

My phone rang: Brooks was calling. "Gotta take this, guys."

I rolled my chair away from the table and into the corner of the room. "What's up, Doc?"

"I think we hit something," Brooks said.

"Like?"

"Teeth."

"Cats, maybe?" I asked.

"We found a few skeletal bones, too. And unless cats have now evolved to have thumbs, what we've found are human remains."

41

A week of fires and smoke, murderous heat and no breezes would now pay off. In the west, the five o'clock sun dipped closer to the horizon. Soon, the sky would turn the color of orange juice and red popsicles, bruises and dragon scales. The windows of cars were rolled down, and Notorious B.I.G. and Drake drifted from stereos. Grandmas bopped their heads to Roberta Flack or Andrae Crouch as they drove. Iced coffees and wide smiles and little girls wearing Krispy Kreme hats . . . it no longer hurt to live in Los Angeles.

Death happened. Poison, cancer, heart attacks. Murder for profit. Insurance policies on dead church members. "But the show must go on." Colin navigated the car west on King Boulevard to reach the neighborhood of Helen "Nell" Montgomery.

Butterflies swirled in my stomach. "I know this will sound hyperbolic, but I'm with Peachy on this—I keep thinking about Jim Jones and Peoples Temple and the almost thousand people who were bilked out of everything they had. And for what?" They thought they'd done the right thing, only to be betrayed by their leader. Only to be *murdered* by their leader.

"So you're still convinced the church is involved?" Colin asked.

I gaped at him. "You're not? What are you waiting for?"

He gripped the steering wheel tight, and his knuckles whitened. "My gut's telling me that . . . I don't know. It just feels wrong, blaming people of God."

Throughout Baldwin Vista, OPEN HOUSE signs sat on street corners and pointed us to Helen Montgomery's remodeled contemporary. It had a high-pitched roof and big windows, trimmed white rosebushes, a new garage door, and a CPT PROPERTIES sign jammed into the too-green-for-a-drought lawn. A gay white couple, each man holding the hand of a black toddler with Afro puffs, stood on the porch. At the curb, a middle-aged woman and teen girl climbed into an Audi. Another young family walked up the brick pathway, ready to see what $818,000 bought you in 90008.

"I'll stay here," Colin said, sinking in the driver's seat.

The house's open floor plan boasted dark wood floors, a stone fireplace and modern light fixtures. It smelled of new paint and fresh-baked chocolate chip cookies.

In the foyer, a real estate agent with flawless brown skin and a short Afro frowned at me—I had refused to sign the visitor's book. "It's beautiful," I told her, "but I'm just looking, so no need for a name. When did it go on the market?"

"Last week," she said.

In the kitchen, the gay couple marveled at the quartz countertops. Their daughter jumped up and down, making her tennis shoes sparkle with pink lights.

"And why are the owners selling?" I asked the agent.

She gave the couple in the kitchen a "one minute" finger, then said to me, "The owner died, and now the investors want to sell."

"You can go help them," I said, nodding to the potential buyers. "I'll just wander around."

The glassed-in dining room had a great view of a redwood deck and the backyard. Out in that yard, a pretty grade-school girl with hair twists and pink shorts frolicked on the jungle gym. A preteen boy sat in a swing, his eyes glued to a cell phone.

A husband, kid, jungle gym, dining room, badge, and gun. Once upon a time, that's what I'd dreamed about. And still wanted. Some women *did* have it all—and such creatures existed throughout the LAPD.

So what's my problem?

Breathless, I scratched my scalp, grazing the never-healing wound never healing there.

"Surprise, surprise." The woman's voice pulled me from my family planning. "Didn't know you're looking to buy." Charity Tate had snuck up on me. Worse, she flaunted near-perfect foundation even in this heat.

"I'm not looking," I said. "But you are?"

She shook her head. "I'm the selling agent. That sign out front? CPT Properties? That's me. Charity Patricia Tate." She curtsied and smiled.

That churning in my stomach returned—but not because of my fears of dying alone. "You help run the church *and* you sell houses?"

She raised a finger. "*And* I'm raising two kids. Yes—I *am* an over-achiever. No—I will never slow down, not until God forces me to." She touched her temples. "And all that church business drives me insane. I need to get out sometimes."

"Speaking of getting out," I said, "you told me that back on Monday night, you took Brandon to football practice."

"That's right."

"I talked to a couple of people who told me that practices are on Tuesdays and Thursdays."

She hesitated, then said, "Usually, but not this week." Her eyes darted to the shield on my hip. "The coach changed it. Something about park permits."

I said, "Ah," with the tiniest smile on my lips.

"Who told you that?" Her brows furrowed, but then she shrugged. "Doesn't matter. Whoever it was *obviously* doesn't take Brandon to practice."

"Helen Montgomery owned the original house, right?" I asked.

"Helen?" She narrowed her eyes. "Oh. You mean Nell. I don't know her by Helen."

Then, you must not know her. But I didn't say that.

"So if you're not buying then, you're here . . . ?" Charity asked.

"To learn more," I said.

"About?"

"Helen Montgomery."

"Because?"

"Police business."

She turned to light a cookie-scented candle. "Well, let's see. Sister Montgomery passed back in January—"

"From?"

She struck a match. "She died peacefully in her sleep."

"Was there an autopsy?"

Charity didn't blink. "She helped George Washington Carver plant that first peanut, Sergeant."

I laughed. "Yes, she was old. Had she been ill?"

"Diabetes. And she was kind enough to bequeath us her house. We remodeled, and here we are, overlooking the—" She blew out the match. "Entertainer's backyard." She pointed to the kids. "Brandon and Mica don't come with the house—they're mine."

I snapped my fingers. "Gee whiz. And I was gonna pay cash right now. Oh, well." I leaned against the banister. "Were you also the selling agent on Thomasina Jacobs's house and now Marcus Sandford's house?"

"I am." She leaned beside me and gazed out to the yard. "Marcus was such an honorable man. Served in the US Marine Corps for almost fifteen years. Saw all that Mideast action, and then to survive all that only to die at home."

"Strange way to die."

She turned to wave at her kids. "Since when are heart attacks strange?"

"When they happen to fifty-year-old men."

She shrugged. "So Brother Washington's house: Ike told me that you're at a standstill."

"Yep."

"Any ETA on when he can start back to cleaning again?"

I faked a smile. "Lemme guess: you're selling that house, too?"

She grinned and nodded. "This girl is on fire."

"How long has Ike worked for you?"

"He's worked for *Sol* since the eighties or something. Way before me." She blew a kiss at her daughter, now a pilot in the play set's wheelhouse. "Guess you could say Blessed Mission is Ike's rehabilitation program."

I arched an eyebrow, surprised that Charity knew Ike Underwood's background.

"He was in jail for, oh . . . two years or so for burglary and assault," she said. "But Ike has a kind heart. Solomon realized that Ike was good with his hands and put him to work, kept him busy. And the rest is history." Her perfect eyebrows scrunched. "So I want to continue keeping Ike busy, know what I mean?"

I stepped back into the dining room. "So Marcus Sandford's family—?"

"Marcus had no family." Charity followed me, tossing a last wave to her daughter.

"Oh, so he left the house to . . . ?"

"A friend of his in the congregation, Richard Trudeau. I don't know all the details, but I do know that Marcus had a will."

"And Tommie Jacobs?"

"She drew up her will once she was diagnosed with colon cancer."

"Know what else is strange?" I asked. "Having to show something as private as your tax forms to your church."

Charity's mouth tightened, and those Sophia Loren eyes narrowed. "If we are to do the Lord's work, everyone must give their fair share. And the only way we can ensure that is—"

"To invade the financial privacy of your congregants."

"*Invade?*" She sucked her teeth. "Not at all."

"The church told Thomasina Jacobs to stop chemotherapy."

"It's poison," Charity announced, standing straight. "It's poison and she was old."

"So you killed her. Basically."

Charity laughed. "Are you *kidding* me? You are, right? You're not. Look: People live. People die. There are different approaches to cancer treatment, and patients succumb all the time on chemo."

"When did she change her will?" I asked.

"Who?"

"Tommie Jacobs," I nearly shouted, "or are there other old women you've convinced to surrender their only shot at survival?"

She glared at me and crossed her arms. "Maybe you should go now."

I smiled and my teeth dug into my lip like knives. "You got me confused with them little church ladies you direct. Don't get it twisted."

She shrunk some. "What else do you want from me, Sergeant Norton?"

"Your fingerprints. You were supposed to give them to me three days ago."

She shrugged. "I've been busy."

"Yes, I know. Taking Brandon to football practice."

She smirked. "Yes, and if you had a family, you'd know that your life is not your own. But you obviously don't have kids—and if you do, you obviously don't have custody."

My face must've contorted and darkened because Charity flinched and took a step away from me. "Anything else?" she whispered.

"Oswald Little."

"Oswald Little is a church member in good standing." She canted her head. "Even without hands."

"When was the last time you've seen him in the flesh?"

Charity thought for a moment, then shrugged. "But I've talked to him plenty on the phone. He's one of our most committed . . ." She sighed. "Sergeant Norton, I still don't understand why you have such a problem with us. I know I'm about to sound snotty and not first-lady-like but . . . Did God do something to you? Not give you a puppy after you prayed for one or something? And so now you're cynical and critical of those of us who still believe He answers prayers?" She pointed at my head. "You're . . ."

I touched my hairline, then inspected my fingers. Blood. Fresh. Bright. I plucked a crumpled tissue from my pocket and dabbed at the wound. "And the insurance policies you have on your members?" I asked.

A stab in the dark.

"We don't take policies out on members," Charity claimed. "Sister Walker died two weeks ago. She had a nice home on Denker. We didn't inherit that. Sister Benetiz died, and she had *two* houses and some land down in Louisiana. We didn't inherit any of that. I could name you twelve members who've died in the last year where we didn't receive one cent, including Marcus Sandford. Other than the commission I'm getting for selling it, Richard Trudeau is getting the rest." She pushed out a breath, then shook her head. "I'm sorry. We aren't who you think we are."

The Tate children charged into the dining room. Mica, the girl, hugged her mom around the waist.

"You said we could go to Dave and Buster's now," Brandon whined. He held up his phone. "It's five thirty."

"Umhmm. A promise is a promise." Charity kissed the top of Mica's head, then gazed at me with tear-filled eyes. She shook her head, a silent plea to not discuss death and murder around her kids. "Is there anything else I can do for you, Sergeant Norton? I really do want to help."

The blood in my hair turned cold. "No. It's time for chili cheese fries and video games. But I still need something from you before you go."

The cool air kissed my skin as I retreated to the car. Residents were watering their lawns with hoses and movable sprinklers. Teens sat on the curbs, laughing, chatting, texting. Purple-gray smoke that smelled of meat and onions wafted behind the California ranch. Charity's agent slid an OPEN HOUSE sign into the back of her Nissan Pathfinder.

Colin was snoring.

I plopped back into the passenger seat of the car and elbowed him. "Get up."

He startled awake, then rubbed his face. "Yep."

I pointed out the window. "Get her prints, will you?"

Charity Tate locked the front door while her kids somersaulted and cartwheeled across the front lawn.

Colin wiped the drool from his chin and scratched crust from his eyes. He reached to the backseat for the print kit, then climbed out of the car.

I slapped down the visor to scrutinize my head wound—blood made that patch of hair glisten. I dabbed tissue at that spot, wincing from the sting as well as Colin's strained conversation with the preacher's wife.

My phone rang and Luke's number popped on the screen. "What's up?" I asked, still dabbing at the freshly opened wound.

"AFIS is back up."

"Finally."

"The prints on that cobbler dish we took from Washington's house?"

"Yeah. What about them?"

"One set of prints are still out, but we got a hit on the second set."

My hand froze. "Whose prints are they?"

"Isaac Underwood."

42

Ike Underwood had touched the casserole dish of killer cobbler.

"But we don't know if he actually *baked* the cobbler," Colin argued.

I blinked at him. "True, but he lied about going to the house."

"Maybe the killer borrowed the dish from Ike," Colin said. "There's still that second set of prints we haven't IDed."

I rubbed my temples. "Fine." I grabbed the Motorola from the car's floorboard and requested an undercover unit to surveil Oswald Little's home until we got there.

By the time Colin and I had departed from Helen Montgomery's home just a mile or so away, Brooks and Dr. Goldberg and his forensic anthropology team had discovered a second thumb, arm bones, a few ribs, and a skull—all buried in Eugene Washington's garage.

And now a few researchers sifted dirt and concrete through large sieves as others laid out bones on a plastic sheet to re-create the skeleton. Colin stood over the huddle and snapped pictures on his phone.

The hole in the back of the skull was the size of a kumquat. Fractures spidered from that crater toward both ears. There was no obvious exit wound.

My pulse raced as Dr. Goldberg turned the skull this way and that. "It's definitely human."

"But then it can't be Oz Little," I said. "This person has hand bones—and *we* have Oz Little's hands. Can you tell from just looking how old this person is or how long he's been dead?"

"I can't say right now." Goldberg tilted the skull again, and this time an object dropped from somewhere inside of it into his hands. We peered closer at the metal flower-like object.

A fuse lit my brain. "It's the bullet. It looks like it stayed put all this time."

We took pictures of the smashed projectile before we bagged it for ballistics.

"And we'll have them compare it to the guns we found in the house," I said, leaning against what I thought was a solid, standing pile of push brooms, rusted spades, and rakes.

The whole pile toppled over, creating a chain reaction of falling piles, boxes, and a paint can filled with . . . not paint. After the ruckus died and the twentieth person came in to ask, "What happened?"; after every cat and roach had scattered three cities over; after I said "Sorry" for the thirtieth time, I crept over to that paint can that had spilled something not paint.

Cash—about sixty dollars in fives and tens, a tarnished gold crucifix, and a Louisiana driver's license. The name beside the picture of the black man's picture was RICHARD TRUDEAU.

My face numbed—Charity had mentioned that Richard Trudeau had inherited . . .

"What did you find?" Colin asked.

"I think the bones may belong to this man." I stepped away to let Colin and the other photographer document my accidental discovery. "He's from Louisiana. Didn't Judith say something about the hoard getting worse after Hurricane Katrina?"

"You think this Richard Trudeau was an evacuee?" Colin asked.

I shrugged. "I do know that he inherited Marcus Sandford's house."

"But how could he, if he's dead?"

"But who knows that he's dead?" I asked. "Who knows if those are his bones out there? A lot of people, including him, scattered all around the country after the hurricane."

"What the hell happened here?" Goldberg whispered.

"The envelope I found with the initials," I said. "There was an R.T., remember?"

Colin nodded. "I'll get Pepe to run this guy through Missing Persons."

"Yeah." I could barely hear over my pounding heart. "Maybe Ike knew that Washington was dangerous. He knew and had to—"

"Kill the monster?" Colin asked.

Electricity crackled across my skin. Solving this case—getting a confession, finding even more victims—would be a fuck you to O'Shea, to the captain, and to Lieutenant Rodriguez.

"You were right, Lou," Colin said. "On that first day, you called it. I know a whole buncha dicks who would've just said, 'Hell, he's old.' No digging, no autopsy . . ." He shrugged. "And I was one of them."

I pushed past the blue tarp and entered the dusty air. Over to my left and right, plots of land had been gridded with little yellow flags and yellow tape. *Another body.* In the backyard, another taped-off piece of land and more flags. *Another body.* A man and his GPR buggy rolled over a strip of land beneath the den's bathroom window.

Four possible bodies, a pair of dismembered hands, human remains in the fridge, human remains in his stomach . . .

Eugene Washington was a serial killer.

The three sisters stood at the white picket fence. Arms outstretched, their faces were lifted toward heaven as they prayed. News cameras and neighbors recorded their prayers and the latest adventures of the LAPD. The sun had dipped behind the trees, leaving us with a less Popsicle, more dragon-scale sky. Even with the roar of generators and the thwack of shovels against packed earth, even with the buzz and chatter of the forensics team, I could still hear the rustling of leaves from the magnolias and the lazy swishes of tall, tall palms that had found a wind wave to ride.

Dust, like mist, wrapped the house and glistened like pulverized diamonds in the glare of the bright lights. Someone's bones—that's what we were breathing. That's what was settling on our clothes, in our hair. Bones and rotting bodies and asbestos and lead from crumbling, chipped walls and pipes. My own death would come a little quicker because of 8711 Victoria Avenue.

Brooks took my arm and guided me toward Washington's rusted Le Baron. Dust covered the lenses of his glasses, and he plucked them off. "How are you today?" he asked.

My eyebrows scrunched. "That's nice of you to inquire."

"We're friends."

"We are?"

"I'm angry with you because . . ." He placed his hands on his hips, then turned to look at the scene behind us. "You almost died, Lou. Then you came back so quickly after being broken."

"And that's pissing you off?"

"Yes, it is. Why so soon? None of this madness is going away. You say it all the time. Roll the boulder up the hill all for it to roll down the other side." He clasped my hand and squeezed. "If you haven't noticed, we're all getting older. We're not college kids or even Taggert's age anymore."

I nodded and tears burned the back of my throat.

"We all have to figure out what's our 'more,'" Brooks said. "We cannot give the county of Los Angeles so much of us that there's nothing left once we retire."

"So what's *your* more, Spencer?" I whispered.

He blushed, then studied the leaves of the big magnolia. "Traveling. Asking Syeeda out. It's not a mystery that I carry a torch for that woman. And now that Adam's totally out of the picture . . . I think my parents would like that, too." He shrugged, then searched my face for clues.

"Go for it," I said, smiling. "You'd make her happy."

We hugged.

"Shall we return to the Hoard of Horrors?" he asked.

"Let's."

Still: what *was* my more?

And on Monday, after an appointment with Dr. Popov for blood pressure medication, and after a shampoo, relaxer, and trim from Herschelle, I planned to uncover that great mystery. After tromping through roaches and dead cats, after finding dismembered hands and a man that ate other men and knowing that somewhere else in this city, an equally fucked-up scenario existed and would forever exist . . . After all of that, I needed to know, had to know, my "more."

43

Eleanor Roosevelt said, "Do one thing every day that scares you."

And at seven thirty on Saturday evening, I had done one and seventy things that had scared me. I now stood in a strip mall parking lot down the hill from Oswald Little's Ladera Heights home.

The sun had left us, and now the sky sparkled with airplane landing lights and helicopter landing lights, with a star or three dotted in between. Cars heading eastbound on Slauson Avenue slowed as they passed us. There were no swirling lights or sirens, but we didn't need much to stand out in a mall lot known for the nasty Mandarin takeout joint.

Colin checked his Beretta.

Pepe and Luke talked about the World Series.

I checked my Glock, then knocked on the ballistics vest that protected my torso.

Serving warrants in the middle of the day always made my heart pump harder—gun battles and babymommas wielding knives to protect babydaddies hiding in the closet. But we were dropping by the Little home on a Saturday night. People were always bonkers on Saturday nights, and I hoped that Oswald Little and Ike Underwood were like logy, morning-time houseflies.

I brought the Motorola radio to my mouth and asked, "What's happening now?"

MacKenzie, the undercover cop now watching the Little house, responded. "Ike hasn't left the house. The truck's been parked in the driveway since I got here a little before five thirty."

"Any visitors?" I asked.

"Nobody in, nobody out."

"But we're not arresting him?" Pepe asked. "Even with his fingerprints on the dish?"

"Haven't completed an arrest warrant," Colin said.

"And we're still trying to understand the circumstances of his prints being on that dish," I said. "I'm hoping that he confesses to—"

"Killing a cannibal serial killer?" Luke snickered. "I'd cop to that. Get maybe a month in one of them private country-club prisons. Learn some Japanese and have them women who like jailbirds sending me tit pics and money. Sign me up."

"But what if it all goes left?" Pepe asked.

I shook my head. "If he shows his ass, then we'll hand it to him. With *mucho gusto*."

We were cops. The LAPD. Our motto: Handing People Their Asses Since 1850.

As Colin sped us up the hill, he said, "I hope Oz doesn't collect cats, trash, and human body parts like our buddy Gene."

I smirked. "You're such an optimist, talking about Oz Little as though he's alive enough to hoard *anything*."

Evening fog softened the glow of Garth Avenue's amber streetlights, erasing edges and making the world seem soft, creamy, and safe. Lamps and television lights flickered behind closed drapes. Some sprinklers *tcheted-tchetched-tchetched*, making lawns sparkle silver.

Ike Underwood's Ford truck sat in the driveway alongside Oz Little's Jaguar.

We strode up the flagstone walkway with our guns stowed but our fingers dusting the polymer butts for good luck. On the first level, golden light glowed between the slats of the shutters. Lights also burned in an upstairs bedroom. A UPS box, along with catalogs too big for the door's mail slot, sat on the front porch.

Pepe headed left, and Luke headed right to cover both sides of the house.

"Ike's expecting us, right?" Colin asked.

"Yep." I rang the doorbell.

No answer.

"And the UC said . . . ?" Colin asked.

"Mac said that no one's left the house." I banged on the door, then shouted, "Ike, it's Sergeant Norton, LAPD." I held my breath and closed my eyes, listening for footsteps, for a small dog barking, for a door creaking open or shut.

Other than the rush of blood through my veins and anxiety clicking up and down my spine like toppling dominoes, there was nothing to hear.

I twisted the doorknob.

Unlocked.

I glanced at Colin. "Uh oh."

He frowned. "Not good."

Gun now in hand, I pushed open the door.

The security system—a woman's pleasant voice—announced, "Front door."

Piles of mail sat in the stuffy foyer. Boxes of every size—from Amazon to Walmart—climbed the wall.

"LAPD," I shouted. "Ike, it's Sergeant Norton. Is everything okay?"

Our shoes squeaked against the dusty blond hardwood floor. The great room was littered with men's clothing, empty Budweiser beer bottles, and two days' worth of newspapers. It was not a hoard, just poor housekeeping. On the fireplace mantel, several framed pictures lay facedown.

I set two of those pictures upright—Oswald Little wore a black suit and a white mason's smock. In the second, Oswald Little stood behind a white Carnival Cruise Lines life ring.

Colin tiptoed past the dining room and into the kitchen.

My eyes landed on pizza boxes, more beer bottles, used and crumpled paper towels.

No Ike.

No Oz.

A few empty grocery bags sat near the filled kitchen trashcan. I glimpsed strips of paper. Coupons for orange juice and laundry detergent. A receipt from a recent trip to the supermarket for toothpaste, Budweiser, coconut flour, brown sugar, canned peaches, coconut extract, and fresh peaches.

"Hey, Lou." Pepe nodded to an open kitchen cabinet, then pointed to the white casserole dishes rimmed in blue cornflowers. "Just like the dish we took from Washington's house."

Colin cleared his throat, then said, "I've found . . . something." Dread coated those three words.

"What?" I looked at him over my shoulder and my stomach clenched.

Over near the patio door, Ike Underwood sat slumped in a suede armchair. He was staring at me, except that he wasn't really *staring* at me. A blood-fleshy hole the size of a kumquat, surrounded by the imprint of a gun muzzle, had penetrated his right temple. And in his right hand? A .44 Magnum revolver.

44

Ike Underwood's skin was the color of desert sand. But it was still. Too still. There were no popping veins in his temples. No throbbing vein in the middle of his forehead. That's because Ike Underwood had no pulse. Understandable—his brain had been scrambled by the bullet now lodged in the blood-flecked arm rest.

"Didn't see *this* coming," Colin said. "He didn't seem like the type."

My focus drifted from the gun to the entry and exit wounds in Ike's temples.

"Unless," Colin continued, "he knew he was going to jail."

I called for Zucca and the coroner on my radio.

Pepe and Luke returned to the living room.

"We checked every nook and cranny," Luke said. "No one else is here."

"Isn't Little supposed to be in Belize?" Pepe asked.

"This is his house, though," Colin said. "Does it *look* like he lives here?"

Pepe and Luke blinked at us.

"In other words," I said, "are there, like, balms or other prosthetic devices sitting around? Those sock things amputees wear to prevent chafing? Do some detecting, for Pete's sake, Peter."

Pepe grimaced. "Got it, Sarge." Then, he and Luke retreated back up the stairs.

"They're becoming lazier now that Pepe wants out," Colin whispered to me. "Shouldn't have to hold their hands on an investigation, you know?"

I turned back to Ike and studied the blood spatter on his blue jeans and sweatshirt and the flecks of bone and brain on the face of his wristwatch. "His watch."

Colin stared at his watch. "It's a Timex. So?"

"*So*, in the police business, this is what we call a *clue*."

Colin considered the watch again, then shrugged again.

"It's on his right arm," I said.

Colin said, "Uh huh."

"Which wrist is your watch on?"

He smirked, and lifted his left arm.

"And you write with your . . . ?"

"Right hand."

I lifted my left arm. "Me, too. Shouldn't have to hold your hand, Detective."

Colin's smirk faded. He whirled around to consider that watch on Ike's right wrist, and then at that gun in Ike's right hand.

"And look at the sleeves of his sweatshirt." I aimed my tiny flashlight at the right sleeve, at the unspoiled cuff. "He's holding the gun, right? *Pow.* Blows his brains out but . . ."

"Where's the blood?' Colin asked, peering closer.

"I'm not saying it's impossible, and maybe there are microscopic drops of blood I can't see . . ."

"Right," Colin said, nodding.

"But the watch. It's telling me that he's left-handed and so the gun—"

"Should be in his left hand and not his right," Colin completed.

I arched an eyebrow. "I could be wrong but . . ." I winced. "That would be like Harriet Tubman running that train off the track."

There was no sign that Oswald Little still lived in the house. Upstairs, the messy bedroom testified to an active living. The bowl on the nightstand contained two ravioli with still-wet red sauce. The remote control to the darkened TV set sat atop the rumpled blue comforter, and a sports store catalog sat on one of the pillows.

Suits too small for Ike Underwood hung in the master bedroom's closet, though. And in the adjacent bathroom, the bottles of cologne and hair tonics on the counter were covered in thick greasy dust. But the box of EpiPens prescribed last week to Eugene Washington? So new the box reflected the counter's light.

"He took the pens and let his friend suffocate?" Colin asked.

I nodded. "After fixing him a deadly dessert. Wonder how long Ike stood there and watched him die."

Back in the foyer, I found mail addressed to Oswald Little. Electric and water bills, a mortgage statement . . . "Not one envelope says 'Isaac Underwood,'" I whispered.

As soon as I said those words, I glimpsed a piece of white notebook paper and a dirty tan envelope, torn in half, left in a wicker wastebasket. The envelope bore the green sticker for certified mail. It had been addressed to Isaac Underwood and sent by Eugene Washington.

"Damn," I muttered.

Colin heard me curse and wandered away from the kitchen. "What's up?"

I pointed to the envelope, then waited as Colin took pictures. Latex gloves on, I plucked the envelope and letter from the trash. "Sent August twenty-fifth," I said. "And Ike signed for it the next day."

Colin put the letter together and read the handwritten note. "Ike, you are an old friend. My oldest living friend. I did everything needed. I have tried to be patience with you and to understand but that is no possible. The more money is necessary. And I am not being unreasonable just $1,000 more each month. He can afford. You can afford it. If not, then I will tell the police everything and ask for emunity. Remember I was there at the very beginning. And I did what you asked. I WILL TELL IT ALL. You knew what I needed and he knew what I needed when we came back. You took advantage of my weakness and what I needed. You fed me and I ate. Sincerely, Gene Washington."

Colin and I stared at each other, barely breathing even with open mouths.

"Ike had to kill him," I said. "Whatever they were up to—"

"Blackmail, not because he was a people-eating psychopath. Sending a certified extortion letter—that's a first for me."

"Why were they paying him?" I reread the letter. "*Everything you needed.* What—?" Numbness prickled across all of my face. Images of those hands, that skeleton, the hoard . . . "I think . . . Eugene Washington killed people for a living. The war and then . . ."

Colin considered me, then laughed. "You mean like a hit man?"

I nodded. "And he worked for Ike and some other guy."

Colin's smile faltered some as the theory took shape. "He says, 'He can afford it.' Who is 'he'?"

I shrugged. "Oswald Little?"

Luke and Pepe joined us in the foyer. "We don't see nothin' that tells us a man with no hands lives here," Luke said.

Pepe said, "No disability mods—no gel inserts, sleeves, cleaners. There's nothing here."

A moment later, Colin and I left the house for the driveway.

The older couple in the Mediterranean across the street huddled on their front porch. She wore a scarf over her hair. He held a phone to his ear. In the distance, sirens wailed, en route to Garth Avenue. The whole block would soon creep out from their houses, faces twisted, eyes narrowed, and for the under-forty crowd, camera phones lifted.

Ike Underwood's truck was unlocked—the cold cabin smelled of turpentine and spilled beer. In the glove compartment, I found the registration card in Ike's name. A sleek black Coach wallet sat atop the truck's yellowed owner's manual. The name on the Social Security card and debit card said "Oswald Little." The driver's license showed Ike's smiling face but the name there said, "Oswald Little," with the Garth Avenue address. The date near the signature: February 2012. Ike Underwood had been living as Oswald Little for three years.

Stomach churning, I backed out of the cabin and showed Colin the license.

"So Oz is dead, then," Colin said.

I nodded, then exhaled loud and long. "He disappeared in 2010 after retirement, then Ike popped up as him in 2012."

"So where is Oz? Where is he . . . buried?"

I shrugged, then muttered, "Damn."

"The house has a security system," Pepe reported. "But it wasn't set off."

"The panel's activity history?" I asked.

"The back door was opened at four o'clock. The front door was opened and closed at four forty-two p.m. The back door was opened and closed at five thirty-three. The front door was opened at nine forty-seven p.m."

"That last time was us," Colin said.

"The back door," I said.

"Ike could've opened it earlier," Pepe said. "Let in some air at four o'clock. Had enough air and closed it at five thirty."

"Or," I said, "someone could've come in at four, waited for him, killed him, left the body at half past five."

Ninety minutes later, Zucca and his team clanked into the house with lights and metal cases. Patrol cops had finished taping off the house.

I led Zucca to Ike Underwood's resting place in the armchair.

"Hey," Zucca said, "I know this guy. He was in charge of the cleanup at the hoarded house. Wow. He killed himself?" He squinted. "Gun's in the wrong hand."

"Uh huh," I said. "And there's no visible blood spatter on the hand he supposedly shot himself with."

"So I'm testing for GSR and prints," Zucca said, nodding.

"That big ass gun? Gunshot residue should be all over his hands— but I doubt that. And looks like the bullet came out here . . ." I pointed to the exit wound in Ike's left temple. "And lodged right there." The bullet's ass stuck out from the arm of the chair. "So check trajectory, too, please. And check where the shot started: flush at his temple, or elevated, like someone was standing over him?"

MacKenzie found me staring at shoe prints near the staircase. "No one came through the front door, Lou." The bearded undercover cop sounded panicked, and his pulse thrummed in his temples.

"You're positive?" I asked.

He waggled the small video camera in his hand. "I was even tapin', just to be extra cautious. Cuz I know how you get."

"Mind if I look later?"

"Sure—I'll upload it to the server. But no one came. No one left."

But someone *had* come to pay Ike Underwood a visit.

"How did he or she get in, then?" Colin asked.

"I think . . ." I crept over to the patio door and turned the edge of the brass handle. Unlocked. The door opened, and the security system announced, "Back door."

"He came through there," Colin said.

"Zucca," I shouted over my shoulder, "be sure to dust both inside and outside handles."

"Lou, don't move," Colin warned.

I froze. "What?"

He pointed to the hardwood floor. "Shoe print."

A lightly muddy tread had been left on the ground.

"Zucca," I shouted again, "we got something down here, too."

Out in the backyard, the cool, thick air kissed my face. People in the city below, blurry now behind the fog, would soon be asleep. Lights glowed for the club hoppers and first dates, late diners and all-night gamers. Back at Oswald Little's house, the pool hadn't been cleaned in months. Leaves and trash floated atop the slimy-green, murky water. The grass, though, had been cut, and water from the sprinklers beaded on the blades of grass. A low wrought-iron fence lined the property—at just two feet tall, it was more show than security. Beyond that fence, the hill dropped to the backyards of houses on the downslope.

Mini-Maglite out, I aimed the beam of light at the ground: two sets of shoe-print impressions made in the grass and mud led to and away from the Little house. "He came this way," I said to Colin.

We followed a barely-there trench down the hill. The muddy prints picked up again, leading us to a two-story Cape Cod with a well-kept, mosaic-tiled pool and outdoor teak furniture. The security light popped on, and the glare seared my eyes. I blinked away as spots swirled before me. Colin, too, squinted, and once we recovered our vision, we crept on the house's side to the front porch. A Honda Accord and a Toyota Highlander were parked in the driveway. The muddy footsteps ended at the front door.

"Ready?" Colin asked.

I took a deep breath and exhaled. "Yep."

He rang the doorbell.

I held my breath as my heartbeat raced in my chest.

The door opened.

"Detectives!" Sonia Elliott said, breathless. "How can I help you?"

45

I t's late. Almost midnight."

Sonia Elliott didn't want to invite Colin and me into her house. She stood there on the threshold, eyes glazed and hands clutching the neck of her flamingo-pink silk pajama top. Finally, she blinked and good manners found her once again. "I'm sorry," she said. "Please . . ."

She opened the door wider and stepped aside. Led us through the small foyer and into the living room. Jabbered about the long day, the noise up the hill, and the surprise of finding us standing on her porch.

The living room's Thomas Kinkade painting of the cottage by the creek clashed with the black-and-white photograph of gospel singer Mahalia Jackson, the one with her eyes turned to heaven and her mouth open in mid-hallelujah. The air smelled of cologne. Mossy. Warm. Like a countryside after rain. A crystal glass on the coffee table held amber-colored liquid. Was Sonia a whiskey drinker?

"To be honest," I said, "we're surprised to be here, too."

"Thanks for being so . . ." Colin paused to find a word. *"Accommo-dating."*

The church secretary blinked her heavily mascaraed eyes, then touched her rouged cheek. "What do you need?" She touched her eyebrow, and then her fingers disappeared into her short silver hair.

"Someone climbed over your gate today," I said, "and hiked up the hill, then came back here. Do you know who that could've been?"

"That's a strange question," she said, hand back on her eyebrow. "And really: it could've been anybody. You know people are crazy nowadays."

"So that's a no?" Colin asked.

"I didn't climb up no hill," she said, trying to laugh. "So that's a no."

A pair of men's glasses—preppy Ralph Lauren eyewear—sat next to the glass of whiskey. "Maybe your husband?"

"I'm not married. Came close a few times, but never found the right man." She shrugged. "Sometimes, the Lord says, 'wait,' and even now, that's what I'm gonna do."

No one spoke. Outside, the police helicopter circled the neighborhood and sounded like it was buzzing right above us. Somewhere in the house, Teddy Pendergrass asked me to close the door so that he could give me his all.

"Maybe your son took a trip up the hill?" I asked.

Sonia Elliott pursed her lips, then shook her head. "I guess women nowadays have children without husbands, but I'm not one of them."

"You told me a few days ago that you lived near Eugene Washington," I said. "This is nowhere near his neighborhood."

"I . . . I was . . . mistaken," she whispered.

"But you *do* live down the hill from Oz Little," I said. "Maybe that's who you meant?"

Her mouth popped open, then closed, then opened again, without one word being uttered.

"And you were *where* on Monday night?" Colin asked.

"I . . . I . . ." She jammed her lips together. Tears shimmered in her eyes.

I pointed to the west. "Ike's up there, up that hill, and he told us so much. So you should probably—"

"Can you protect me?" she whispered. "Protect *us*? I didn't . . . He made me bake it and . . . I love him. It's wrong, I know." She dipped her head, and whispered, "This all got crazy, out of control. He promised just one more, one more . . . Lord forgive me, forgive me."

My eyebrows scrunched. *Who did she love? Who was "us"?*

"*You* baked the peach cobbler?" Colin asked.

Sonia Elliott nodded, then whispered, "They said it would be more peaceful doing it that way. They were gonna kill him anyway. Gene was an awful man. A scary man, always has been. And it was just coconut. How can somebody . . . ? It was just coconut." Wide-eyed, she shook her head. "I didn't know he would suffer so."

Something thumped above us.

We froze.

Sonia Elliott's eyes bugged.

"Who's here?" I asked.

She stared at me for a long time before dropping her gaze to the carpet.

Somewhere, a clock ticked . . . Ticked . . . Ticked. Somewhere, Teddy Pendergrass crooned.

"Would you mind if we looked around?" Colin asked.

Her hand clenched her neck. The vein there pounded like a jack-hammer.

I opened my binder and scribbled a note. Then, I showed her what I wrote.

If you are being held against your will, swipe your nose.

She whispered, "I'll tell you everything in the morning." Then, louder, she said, "I'd rather you leave. I'm expecting guests, and I have to pre-pare for services tomorrow."

I scribbled another note. *He's in the bedroom. Swipe your nose if yes.*

Her trembling hand brushed across her nose.

I touched her arm, then directed her to the front door.

"Thank you." Fat tears tumbled down her cheeks, and she clicked down the short foyer.

Colin called for backup as he followed Sonia Elliott to the front door.

I pulled my Glock from its holster and kept my eyes on the staircase. Beads of sweat pebbled in my hair and stung the wound on my scalp.

I took the first step . . .

Third step.

Seventh . . .

Teddy Pendergrass . . . louder . . . *come on over to my place* . . .

My hands clenched so tight around the gun, I couldn't tell it from me.

Eighth step . . .

Colin, blue eyes hard, knuckles white, now stood two steps beneath me . . .

Come on and go with me . . .

The landing was just three steps away. Could've been the Swiss Alps.

That cologne—mossy, wet, countryside . . . He was near.

I reached the landing. Pressed back against the wall, but my racing pulse kept me from being flush against the flat surface. All of me tingled—I had my killer. He was just a few yards away from me.

I nodded to Colin.

Colin winked at me.

I took a deep breath and rounded the corner.

The murderer stood in the middle of the hallway wearing boxers and a gray T-shirt. There were tears in his eyes—and a .44 pointed at his head.

Sunday, September 6

46

M r. Tate," I said, my voice tight, my outstretched arms tighter, and my hands the tightest as they clenched the Glock. "I need you to put down the gun."

The ceiling felt low, and the dark wood panels on the walls made the hallway look and feel narrower than it was. There was a "click" in a bedroom, and Teddy Pendergrass stopped singing.

Bishop Solomon Tate flinched, but the muzzle of the silver .44 Mag remained snug against his right temple.

Colin stood a few feet behind me with his Beretta aimed like mine at the minister's torso.

"Why are you doing this, sir?" I asked.

Solomon Tate offered us a sad smile. "Because thirty minutes from now, the world will find out. And Sonia—she loves me, but she's a good woman and she'll tell it all. She was there with me at the beginning and stuck beside me even after I chose someone else.

"Dot, she was . . . losing her mind. Predicting crazy things after she lost our son. And I just couldn't . . . manage her sickness, calling herself a prophet—"

"Dot? You mean Dorothea? The one with the hankie?" *The witch?*

He nodded. "I loved her, but I had to—"

"Banish her?" I asked, my skin ice cold.

Bishop Tate closed his eyes. "And Sonia was there for me after the divorce and . . . She was pure—and did all that I asked even if . . . I'm done. The world will learn that I helped to create that . . . *monster.* That I knew what he was so long ago, that I used him to . . . I'm done. What's left?"

"Your family," I said, softer now. "Your kids. Your church. That's what's left."

He surveyed the ceiling. "The foolish man built his house upon the sand. And since the beginning, I built mine atop flesh and blood."

His words made me shudder, and my grip loosened.

He chuckled. "How do you think I got all this? Ike and Gene were ruthless, but they only did what I wanted them to. All I wanted was to help people. To just . . . I'm done."

"We'll work it out," Colin said. "We'll talk with the DA. Just lower your weapon, sir."

Bishop Tate flexed his fingers but didn't acquiesce. "How much is a life worth? The policies we took out on members were a quarter of a million each. But that's insurance. How much are they worth, in prison terms, Sergeant? Twenty-five each? Thirty? For me, I estimate two hundred years." He chuckled, then said, "What deal could the DA possibly offer me when I've already made a deal with the devil?"

Downstairs, the front door opened.

"Lou?" Pepe shouted.

"Up here," I shouted back, "but stay there. We're here with Bishop Tate." To the minister, I said, "I'm very good friends with—"

"No." He jammed the muzzle against his temple. The vein in the middle of his forehead bulged and banged.

My gut clenched. "Did you kill Ike Underwood?"

The minister's eyes widened. "We were in Vietnam together. I told you that, didn't I? He did everything I ever asked of him. I didn't kill . . ." A tear slipped down his cheek. "Even now, I can't stop lying. It's become second nature to me." He took a deep breath, then nodded. "Yes, I did. I killed Ike Underwood. He'd always wanted everything Oz had. Oz didn't have much of a family, but he had wealth. We needed money to build, and we knew that no one would notice him gone, that no one would notice that the real man no longer breathed. And we were right. For a long time, we were right."

"And where is Oz now?"

He swallowed, then said, "The crawl space beneath the house on Corning Avenue. Ike and Gene buried him when they did work on the house before selling it."

The house on Corning Avenue—now occupied by Hermie and her stuffed pooch.

"Someone called me pretending to be Oz," I said. "Was that you?"

He sighed, nodded.

"And Eugene Washington?" I asked. "Did you ask Sonia Elliott to bake the . . . ?"

"Yes. No. Yes. I . . . Ike and I . . . Gene was there, too, in the war. He came out . . . changed. We watched him in Vietnam eat . . . dead Vietcong . . . out of revenge, anger. We thought he'd stop once we came home but . . . We had all changed but Gene . . . We thought it was for the best. He was an abomination. He had lost control. I didn't know he was keeping hands and . . . Some, I didn't even know about, he just did that on his own, like the kid who joined the congregation after Hurricane Katrina."

My mouth was dry, and my hands loose around the gun. "Was Oz the first person you all . . . ?"

The minister shook his head. "He was just the first . . . *friend*. The others—they just . . . *had*. And so, we *took*. And Gene. He kept demanding that we pay him more and it had to end. He needed to be stopped. We didn't think anyone would care that an old man in a house like that . . ." Awed, he shook his head.

"Put your gun down, sir," Colin said. "Please."

The man shook his head. "I'm not leaving here alive. Either I'm gonna do it or you're gonna do it. I am still a servant of God and I still believe I'm here to alleviate suffering and I don't want you to suffer so just let me—" His finger flexed.

Boom. The shot echoed through the hallway.

Bishop Tate cried out in pain. Blood spurted from his shoulder as he crumpled to the ground.

My finger hadn't moved.

I looked back at Colin, and at his finger still pressed against the trigger.

47

H *e'll live.*

That's what I told the mistress as I handcuffed her in the driveway of her home.

He'll live.

That's what I told the wife after she'd sped from their home higher up the hill.

Charity Tate, dressed in sweats and a Blessed Mission baseball cap, stared at Sonia Elliott in the back of the patrol car.

"Did you know?" I asked.

"About their affair?" She turned to me with bloodshot eyes. "I had no idea. Why would he . . . ? With *her?*"

My cheeks burned. "I don't mean . . . I meant the murders? Did you know?"

Her eyes narrowed. "What? I don't . . . understand. You said, just now, that Sol's alive. Who else is dead?"

I stared at her—there was confusion in those Sophia Loren eyes. She didn't know. I touched her shoulder. "We have a lot to talk about."

Agitated, she bit her lip. "I can't right now. The neighbors have the kids, and we have an early start in the morning. The first Sunday service begins at . . ." She lifted her cell phone. "I need to let Elder Alexander know that Sol can't preach tomorrow and—"

"Charity," I said.

Phone to her ear, she gave me the one-minute finger. "Good evening, Elder. It's Charity—" She smiled as she listened. "Yes, I know it's late. Listen, the bishop's in the hospital." She smiled. "No, he's okay. Someone shot him . . . Yes . . . I'm going over there now. But for tomorrow . . ."

I sighed, then wandered over to Colin at the car. "She has no clue," I said. "Her entire world is soaked in blood. Her great dynasty built on a man's hands."

He tore his eyes from the first of hundreds of forms needed to be completed. "When will you yank her from Wonderland?"

I glanced at my wristwatch, then leaned against the car. "I'm not. Anyway, I'm gonna have to send you on a refresher course. Center mass, Detective. Center mass."

He shrugged. "I burped and the gun flipped back a little."

I said, "Ha. So the house over on Chariton. Dr. Goldberg's got some digging to do. Good luck with that."

He turned to face me. "I didn't squeal on you, Lou. About your pain. About anything."

"Who did?"

"Pepe. To show that he had the balls to be IAB. That's why Andreoff called, and that's why L.T. kept pulling my ear. *He* thought it was bullshit, too, but he had to go through the motions. He wants Pepe out because of all this."

Tears stung my eyes, but I clamped my lips together and breathed through my nose. "Hope he gets the job cuz he's nobody to me now."

Colin sighed, then crossed his arms. "How long is vacation?"

I dabbed my eyes with a knuckle. "Just a month."

"What are you gonna do?"

I shrugged. "Catch up on *Orange Is the New Black*. Learn how to surf. Buy a fern." I looked at my watch: two thirty-five. "It's Sunday now. I'm officially in Tahiti." My voice sounded wet and scratchy, but those feelings disappeared as I spotted Lieutenant Rodriguez's Crown Vic pulled past the tape. "You got this?" I asked my partner.

Colin also watched the Ford park and the big man climb out from behind the steering wheel. He sighed, then took a deeper breath before saying, "Yeah. I got it."

And I thought about the three prophetesses and their first greeting to Colin and me last Tuesday. *The detective and the chief join us today.* Had that been a prophecy? Had I, the detective, been training Colin, the future chief of the Los Angeles Police Department?

I pat Colin on the shoulder. "See you in thirty days." With a confused heart and a rigid spine, I left him there with his reports.

Pepe nodded at me as I passed.

I nodded back.

"Lou," he said. "Richard Trudeau's license, the one you found in Washington's garage? He's been missing since October 2005. That's, what, two months after Katrina?"

"Yep." I didn't stop in my step.

"We gonna talk about this?" Pepe called after me.

"Nope." I kept walking.

Lieutenant Rodriguez approached me. "It's for the best, Lou."

"Yes, sir."

"See you in thirty days."

"Yes, sir."

A female patrol officer drove me back the station. Neither of us talked. I sat with my eyes squeezed shut, seeing the glow of streetlights even with closed eyes. Back in the Porsche, my phone vibrated with a text message from Lena. *I know it's late but I've made my decision about Chauncey. Call me.*

But I didn't call. Instead, I sent a single text message: *What are you doing for the next thirty days?*

All around me, uniformed cops escorted bloody, surly men from the backseats of patrol cars to the cells deep within the building.

On my phone's screen, ellipses appeared. Then: *What do you have in mind?*

I bit my lip. New hair could wait. Dr. Popov could also wait—I had a feeling that nature's therapy would soon lower my blood pressure. I typed:

In the morning, chef's choice quiche. Then, how about a VIP suite at Mandalay Bay, courtesy of Victor Starr? Followed by surfing and Netflix and then . . . ?

Send.

Sam responded. *And then falling in love? I'm down. See you in thirty minutes.*

I threw the car into gear and cruised west on King Boulevard. *Thirty minutes. Thirty days.*

No cannibals. No hands.

Brooks had said none of the crazy would be going away soon. The buried bones of victims, freezers filled with ill-gotten gold, secrets, so many secrets. It would all be waiting for me. If not this case, then the next. Until then, though . . .

Thirty minutes. Thirty days.

That was enough time to start a new life. Enough time to find my more.

Right?